W9-BRI-309

SNOWFALL

MITCHELL SMITH

TOR®

A TOM DOHERTY ASSOCIATES BOOK
NEW YORK

TO MY FATHER,
DOCTOR MICHAEL SMITH

This is a work of fiction. All the characters and events portrayed in this book are either products of the author's imagination or are used fictitiously.

SNOWFALL

A Tor Book
Published by Tom Doherty Associates, LLC
175 Fifth Avenue
New York, NY 10010

www.tor.com

Tor® is a registered trademark of Tom Doherty Associates, LLC.

ISBN: 0-812-57933-X
Library of Congress Catalog Card Number: 2001054743

First edition: February 2002
First mass market edition: April 2003

Printed in the United States of America

0 9 8 7 6 5 4 3 2 1

From: ANCIENT ENTRIES—A Collection
*The truly remarkable succession of comets and
cometary fragments striking Jupiter's surface presents
us with all sorts of possibilities, ranging from a minor
enrichment of the giant's atmosphere with pre-organic
compounds, to—less likely—a negligible alteration in
its orbit, the effects of either of which might prove
interesting.*

ERIC DAVISOHN, PH.D.
The Amateur Astronomer
ISSUE 297, JULY 1998

*Collection's first copyist unknown.
First re-copyist unknown. Second re-copyist, Lil Dunn.
Third, Hiram Tolley. Fourth, Paul Fracelli.*
WARNING—Material never to be removed.
BOSTON TOWNSHIP PUBLIC LIBRARY

*Con esto, unos fragmentos de un diario, y un narrativo
con un poco de interés....*

HERNAN ALVARO DE CRUZ
Una vida en los archivos
PRENSA DE MERIDA—2663 A.D.
(REFIERASE A RAFAEL AGUIRREZ,
Los medicos ingenuos, #46610)

Ah, Warm Times, Warm Times!—"Oh, Paradise Lost," as the poet says. Before the Spoiled Orbit of Jupiter.

Today, we copied our Rand McNally again, the highway map of Colorado—where, I informed the children, we reside . . . up here in the mountains just below what we call "the Wall," the edge of the ice.

I wish to Our Lord we could get a topographical to copy. The men are always going on about it, how useful it would be. The highway map copy was fine for Warmtimes, hundreds of years ago. Not much use to us, alas, except for finding a few old-steel sites.

I've just finished reading our Aymond Chandler copybook again. We think we understand everything in these old books. We copy them, and read them with our Webster's, take our first names from them, and learn how to write and speak from them as if we lived in those times. But I think we misunderstand a great deal.—I don't believe this Aymond Chandler work could only concern breaking laws, and people talking and driving their machine-cars in the state of Map-California, which our Rand McNally shows to the west, against the Pacific sea.

There must be religious significance which we miss, and now will never know. This is likely true of our Chandler, even our Hunting on the Continent of Africa book the men love so much.

My face hurt today—old damaged nerve endings, just as Doctor Monroe said. How I miss that wonderful man. I'm uncertain, faced with illnesses and injuries he used to meet smiling, and I have little faith.

How could Mountain Jesus allow a baby girl to wander into dog-lines, and be so bitten and torn? My father used

to call me "Precious-as-Paper," and "Little Lark," after
"*Like the lark, which at the break of day ascending, sings
hymns at heaven's gate.*"

FROM THE JOURNAL OF DOCTOR CATANIA OLSEN

1

Sam Monroe was leading a two-day hunt. He had three Olsens and William Weber with him.

The five men, all senior hunters except William, were the left hand of a two-hand hunt of the last winter herd. Six other men, Olsen-Monroes and Richardsons, were playing right-hand, swinging wide to the west around the flank of Alvin Mountain to hunt the stragglers as the caribou trailed by. They had taken the dogs and sleds with them.

Sam Monroe was a big man, like all the men in his family, with heavy shoulders and a thick, muscled belly. His face was broad, deep-lined, and wind-beaten, burned the color of seasoned wood by more than forty-six years of sunlight glaring off snow. His hair, mustache, and beard were cropped short and grizzled gray.

Old for a Trapper, he was still strong and enduring, so breathed easily after their long climb up the glacier's col. Sam had never cared for slit-goggles, which, it seemed to him, made too narrow a world, so he left them in his parka pocket and squinted into the brightness of late-afternoon sunlight on the snow, surveying the great river of ice.

The Trappers called this glacier "The Old Man." It cut across their hunt country from north to south, paralleling the route of the great herds. Above the hunters, the glacier narrowed to only a mile or so as it shouldered its way between the two mountain peaks—Alvin, to the west; Mount Geary rising even higher to the east.

The river of ice was frozen in immense curtains, laceworks thousands of feet high, draped and festooned one upon the other as if a torrential mountain flood had suddenly been halted, stopped still in its race and rapids, and turned instantly to stone, perfectly white, glittering now in June sunlight.

Its stillness was deceptive. Among those enormous cataracts of ice were blue-black crevasses so deep that a large stone dropped into them soundlessly vanished, dwindled into darkness . . . and was gone, with no echo heard of its fall ending.

"They ran down the ridge." Sam Monroe pushed back his parka hood and stood leaning on his bow.

"More'll be along." Jim Olsen was a tall bony man with a thin, fierce face. He was eleven years younger than Sam, and preferred to lead the hunts he went on.

And the truth is, Sam thought, *the bastard is a good hunter.* He had a momentary vision of himself, older, his knees stiffened, trailing along behind the others while Jim Olsen led them. He imagined the men turning to look back down the trail at him trying to catch up . . . shaking their heads, saying to each other, "Why doesn't the old man stay home?"

"We're not going to wait up here, hoping they'll herd high. We'll go down for outrunners." Sam pulled up his parka hood. He was dressed, like the others, in dark-brown caribou hides cut and sewn into soft trousers, and a loose-fitting parka trimmed with wolf and lynx. His high moccasins were lined with fur and double-soled with elk leather, piss-tanned and boiled.

He led them over the east ridge at a trot. As they crossed it, the Wall loomed into view behind Mount Alvin's peak. Blue-white in the distance, the Wall ran across the mountain range west to east, horizon to horizon.

* * *

The Olsen-Monroes and other families of the Range had been told—by travelers stopping by to beg a hunt, and by Salesmen come to trade old-steel, southern paper, or copybooks for fur—that the ice-wall ran from the Atlantic Sea, thousands of map-miles to the east, all the way past the Range to the Pacific Sea, where people in water-boats hunted swimming seals.

The Wall was almost a mile high. The Trappers hunted along its base in the winter, sometimes, before the spring thaw. Then it became too dangerous. Clouds gathered along its rim, and storms crashed and thundered down the cliffs, so fools prayed to Weather to spare them, forgetting their copy-Bible.

In the three weeks of summer, great pieces of the Wall broke free and toppled from it, so the earth shook. Sometimes waterfalls poured down from the crest and foamed high surf in flooding lakes. These cataracts stopped toward the end of August, when all froze and became silent again.

Over the glacier ridge and down the flank of Mount Alvin, Sam led the hunters through late afternoon, never stopping to rest. After a while, the five Trappers left deep snow for thin snow, then thin snow for granite, and finally left that, and went down into the spruce and hemlock that forested the base of the mountain.

They made good time through these dark-green woods. Old snow and spruce needles crunched softly beneath their moccasin boots as they trotted along in single file. They carried yew longbows, each almost as long as its owner was tall, in their left hands. Thick hemlock branches plucked at the full quivers strapped to their backs, and caught at their arms and legs as they passed.

Even in deep green shade, the men could see the scattered tracks and occasional dung droppings that a small group of caribou had left when they split from the great herd to feed.

When he paused and bent to test it, the dung was still warm in Sam's fingers.

They trotted, almost silently, for another little while, then stopped. Standing still, the Trappers could hear through a rising breeze the very faint, soft, clicking sounds of moving caribou. The men silently braced and strung their heavy bows, then slid long arrows from their quivers. The arrows were perfectly made, strictly straight, and well polished. They were fletched with goose flight-feathers—edge-tinted in trade powder-paint with each Trapper's family colors—and tipped with broad hunting-heads filed from fine-hammered steel. Each arrow was banded in a hunter's personal pattern of narrow stripes, painted with evergreen sap and rock ochre.

Their bows ready, arrows nocked to strings of twisted thread-stripped tendon, the five men spread out and moved quietly down through the trees. The breeze was slightly stronger now as daylight dimmed, and they moved only when its slow chill gusts came through, so their sounds became the wind's sounds. At last they reached the border of a small clearing, deep in soft old snow and dotted with sprigs of seedling spruce.

The caribou were there. A branch-antlered buck, a younger buck in velvet, and a doe and her fawn were grazing along the clearing's other edge.

Sam stood watching the animals from a screen of hemlock. He saw a flicker of motion to his right, a distance along the clearing's edge. *Shit. It would be William, for sure. The boy is shaking that branch as if there were August blueberries on it!*

Sam decided not to wait. He stepped out from behind the brush as he drew his longbow, touched the arrow's feathers to his cheek, and released.

His bow pulled ninety Warm-time pounds, and the long arrow sprang from it humming. Across the clearing, the young buck had only time to come alert before the broadhead struck him, chopped into his chest, and knocked him down.

An instant later, Sam heard a bow-string twang behind him. *Jim Olsen*, he thought, and the arrow flashed across to take the older buck through the throat as the doe and her fawn leaped and landed running, crashing away through the evergreens.

The Trappers ran to the fallen bucks, drawing long double-edged knives from their belts. Sam and Jim, by custom, cut their own kills' throats, and touched their foreheads with bloody fingers. Then the bucks were strung up into branches by their heel tendons, and the men gathered round and butchered them. They tied off the bowels, drew out the guts, bellies, livers, spleens, gall, lungs, and hearts. . . . Then rumps, hams, ribs, and loins were butchered out and wrapped with the innards in the fresh hides, to make heavy bundles for carrying.

"William," Sam said, but smiling, since they'd taken so much good meat, "—when are you going to learn to be still in the woods?"

The Olsens nodded, and William said, "I was still." Younger than the other men, stocky, and with lighter-colored hair, William Weber ate so much that in the summer weeks he had fat on his body.

"Never still and never quiet," Jim Olsen said. "You fart loud enough to scare the herds away." The men laughed.

William, his face red, started to answer, and an arrow struck him in the back.

Very much as the caribou had, he gave a little jump and started to run. But Sam seized him as he staggered near, and dove with him into the evergreens as Jim and the other two Olsens jumped into cover beside them.

For a moment, they all crouched silent in the greenwood brush, arrows nocked to their bowstrings.

William groaned and tried to sit up, and the shaft stuck into the small of his back moved as if it were driving deeper into him. Jim leaned over to hold William still, and get a better look at the arrow. It was slender, painted black with pitch, and fletched with owl feathers.

"Tribesmen," Olsen said. "That's a Cree arrow."

"Why?" Tom Olsen spoke softly. He was young, not much older than William. "They've come down before, and they never hurt anybody!"

Now they have, Sam thought. *Pitch arrows, short wood-and-sinew bows. Soft puffs of fur around the string just below the bow-tips, to muffle the twang of the shot. And more than one of them out there, to take on five Trappers.*

Jim was staring at him, waiting for a decision.

"All right. Pick William up and let's get out of here."

The three Olsens—Jim, Tom, and a cousin named Chapman— took William's bow and quiver, then lifted him up and slid quickly back into the denser forest behind them. Sam stayed, down on one knee, his longbow held horizontal and half-drawn, watching for a Cree to show himself.

But nothing human stirred across the clearing, only small branches shifting in the breeze gusting down from the glacier ridge. The big blotches of caribou blood were freezing dark red in the snow beside the bundles of meat. . . . William had left smaller drops of his blood behind, still warm and bright in the failing light.

Sam looked along the clearing's opposite edge once more, then stepped quickly into the woods and trotted after the others. Now, William was leaving no blood trail, but the scuffling track of the men who carried him was easy to see, even in gathering darkness under the trees.

Carrying William, they would not be able to run from the Crees—or hide from them, either.

Jim had found as good a place as possible for cover in the forest, a space between two big fallen trees. Struck and split by lightning a few years before, they rested almost side by side in the snow. . . . Jim and the other two Olsens had laid William down between these logs and crouched beside him, waiting for Sam or the Crees, whoever caught up with them first.

Tom Olsen, watching the forest up-slope, saw Sam coming, waved him in, and kept watching.

Sam slid over the near snow-covered log and crouched low beside Jim. Behind them, William Weber lay still.

"See any?"

"No," Sam said. "But I guess they'll be along, unless they just wanted the meat."

"Which you don't think is so?"

"No, I don't think they just came by and wanted the meat. They were waiting for us to come down. I'd say there are maybe ten, maybe twelve of them, to start this killing trouble." Sam sighed, drew his long knife, and drove it into the log in front of him so the elk-horn grip was ready to hand.

"They won't rush us," Jim said.

"Not till night."

Olsen's bony face was taut with anger. "It was a Cree moved

a branch back there—and you mistook it for William being clumsy."

". . . Yes, I did."

"Your mistake—and likely to get us killed."

"When *you're* killed, Jim, you come complain about it." Sam crawled over to William. Someone had pulled the arrow out of him. He gripped William's arm, turned him over, and saw he was dead. His eyes were half-open, shadowed blue, and his tongue was hanging out of his mouth.

"Oh . . . Jesus."

The arrows came in then—one, then two more hissing close over their heads and flicking away into the woods. Sam and the Olsens bent their bows, looking for targets, but the spruce and hemlock stood so thick around them they saw only rough tree trunks through dark green boughs, and here and there a narrow beam of fading light on the snow of the forest floor.

It would soon be difficult to make out a man's shape. More difficult, if he was still. Sam and the Olsens knelt in silence, waiting for the next arrow. . . . It came from behind Sam, where Chapman Olsen was watching, and whacked into one of their guardian logs a foot from Jim's back.

Chapman returned the shot instantly, half rising to clear his bow-tip as he released. A man began to scream from that direction, then came running, staggering, out of the trees toward the Trappers' shallow fort. He wore his clan's sewn beast-suit of red fox fur and tail, and was masked in a false fox-head—its muzzle, of painted carved wood, studded with elks' teeth filed sharp.

The fox-man stumbled and whined. Chapman's shaft had taken him just under his left arm, and was sunk in fox fur to its feathers. The Cree called out in his language, gargling blood, and reeled first toward the Trappers, then away from them.

Sam rose to his knees behind the tree trunk and shot the Cree through the heart—the arrow snapping right through him—and the fox-man fell into the snow and pine needles, kicked, and died.

Then arrows came in like driven snow, sighing over the Trappers' low barricade, or cracking into the frozen logs, knocking loose little patches of ice and crumbled bark.

Sam and the Olsens kept low and husbanded their arrows. They didn't speak to each other, as if the fighting was making them too tired to talk.

Soon the sun sank past Mount Alvin. The mountain's shadow leaned over them and the light was almost gone.

The Olsens drew their knives as Sam had done, and stuck them in the snow or the logs in front of them, to be handy when the Crees came rushing with the dark.

When the tribesmen stopped shooting so much—saving arrows, or settling to wait—Sam leaned back for a moment to rest his cramped back. He stretched out his left leg to ease it, and an arrow flickered across his vision and nailed his leg to the log he hid behind.

The pain was very bad. It felt as if his leg was lying in a fire. Sam sat up and started to yank the arrow out. It had driven through his calf, caribou trousers and all, and pinned his leg firmly to the log. He gripped the arrow shaft to tear it out, and to hell with the barbs.

Then he saw Jim Olsen watching him. Jim made a face, as if to say, "Will you look at this old asshole? Can't even get his leg off an arrow."

Sweating, Sam took a deep breath and leaned forward to grip his leg at the knee and ankle, holding it as if it belonged to someone else. Then, with a sudden heave, he jerked his leg up along the arrow's shaft and off, over the feathers.

That hurt so fiercely that he fell back dizzy for a moment, sick to his stomach. And for the first time, as he lay under the curve of the log, taking deep breaths of icy spruce-smelling air so he wouldn't vomit, he was certain he and the Olsens were going to be killed.

We're not going to get out of this. My fault, for splitting the party and sending the other six men off around the mountain. If we had those six men with us, we'd be chasing these fucking Crees back up onto the ice.

His leg began to feel better now it was off the arrow. He thought for a moment about the tribesmen—Crees, or whatever the hell they were. Came trailing down after the caribou eleven or twelve years ago in little bunches, and didn't bother anyone. Called themselves Indians, Native Amers, though most were white. . . . They'd just hung around the caribou and took a few head, traded a little, and stayed out of the Trappers' way—until now.

Sam forced himself to sit up again, grunting at the pain, took off his bone-buckle belt and strapped it tight around his calf to stop the bleeding. He could feel blood in his moccasin, slippery around his toes. . . . When he got the belt fastened, he stuck his hands in his armpits to warm them for a moment, then got to his knees again behind the log, and picked up his bow.

All right. One of you bastards move just a little out there. That's all I ask of Mountain Jesus.

It was becoming night. The evergreens were clusters of black in deepening shadows. As the four men waited, listening hard because it was such uncertain seeing, another arrow came flirting, struck a low branch, deflected with a soft sneezing sound, and whirred away into darkness.

It was so quiet, Sam could hear one of the Olsens, probably Tom, whispering to himself, praying.

Sam found himself getting sleepy from the cold and the wound in his leg. The blood was frozen in the moccasin now; it felt like snow when he wiggled his toes. Looking out, it seemed to him the pattern of the forest had changed a little, a shadow had shifted in the darkness. There was one more—or one less—black tree trunk out there; he was sure of it. What he was seeing now, wasn't what he had been seeing.

He rose, bent his bow—the yew creaking in the cold—and shot at what was different.

A man yelped like a hurt dog, and what might have been a tree trunk rolled away, thrashing, then slowly settled . . . and after a while lay still.

When the Cree began shooting at them again, they shot carefully, aiming to skim just over the Trappers' fallen trees. Soon, Sam and the Olsens had to lie flat behind the logs, and couldn't raise up for even a quick shot back.

The moon was rising now, and the woods, which had been so dark, began to be lit here and there by slender beams of moonlight filtering through spruce boughs. The snowy forest floor glowed pale silver.

Jim reached out to touch Sam's foot, and whispered to him, "They're going to come in on us pretty soon."

Sam could see Olsen's teeth shine in the moonlight.

"—We should run out of here right now. Some of us would make it. . . ."

Jim looked at Sam expectantly, as if Sam was going to say, "Yes. Let's do that, and see how far I get with this hurt leg, how long it takes these Crees to catch me and cut my throat."

Sam didn't say it. He lay looking at Jim until Olsen turned away. *Son-of-a-bitch wants to get those skinny hands on Susan . . . wants to be head hunter, too.* Sam reached for his knife where it stuck up from the log, and worked the blade free. He was sorry he'd thought about Susan; that made the whole thing worse.

It had gotten colder; Sam had to put his fur mittens on. Tom Olsen tried to raise up, find a target—and one of the Crees put an arrow through the top of his right ear. Tom lay down fast, with his hand on the side of his head, and said, "You mother-fucker!" which was something no one said, because of Lord Jesus' mother. . . . Then the Trappers lay still, huddled with William's body between the fallen trees. They couldn't even look over the top of the logs, the moonlight now made them such fine targets.

They lay quiet, their long knives in their hands, and waited for the tribesmen to make up their minds.

Sam wondered if the Crees might just stay back and let them freeze to death. *It would be smart of them to make a fire back in the woods, then take turns watching while we freeze. I hope they're not that patient. I hope they come soon, so I can still move and kill one.*

He felt sorry even for Jim, now. And his leg was hurting so much he began to weep. The tears froze on his face. Snot ran out of his nose, and that froze, too. He wiped his nose with his parka sleeve, shifted his knife to his right hand, and took a better grip on it.

One of the tribesmen screamed in the forest. Then another man called out, yelled something. Suddenly, men were running through the trees.

The Trappers struggled up, long knives ready.

Goodbye, Susan. My little sweetheart....

Another Cree howled, and the tribesmen came rushing, their moon-shadows shuttling among the trees as they leaped and dodged past the Trappers and off through the forest, brushing aside thick branches, their moccasins thudding in the snow as they went.

Crouched gripping their knives, their mouths open in astonishment, Sam and the Olsens watched the Cree run past them and away.... Then, the tribesmen were gone, and the forest silent as if they'd never been.

"What happened?" Jim's bony face looked like a skull in the moonlight.

"I don't know." Sam tried to stand up straight. His leg was very bad. *I'm going to have to ask Jim Olsen to help me. That's what this has come to.*

"Why did they run away?" Tom still held his knife, ready to fight.

"What about William?" Jim said.

It seemed to Sam the Olsens were full of questions. "We take him."

"Take him?" Tom said. "Carry a dead man, when the Crees could come back on us? We're damn near dead, ourselves."

"We take William with us!" Sam took a step and stumbled. Couldn't help it.

A voice sounded from the forest. "Sam ... you're getting old."

I have been consulted on the potatoes. Notion apparently being that a physician should be able to heal a tub nearly frozen, so the buds were burned. My advice was to take a strap to Lucinda Sorbane, who is old enough to tend a fire.

Speaking of Sorbanes, Peter has coughed too long. Doctor Monroe was always worried about tuberculosis. Mountain Jesus and Weather help me, if that has come to the Range.

Treatment is rest. Rest and exposure to dry, cold air—the last no problem for us. In Warm-times, there was medicine for some strains of this so-tiny bacteria. Apparently not medicine for all strains. . . .

It occurs to me the copybooks do us few favors. They give us our language, our phrases, and old information—at the price of reminding us what we have lost.

The Salesmen also remind us of what we have lost, with their history tales, and lying travel tales of discovered Warm-time treasure, and monsters made in pregnant woman.

Peter Sorbane, that clever man, has been coughing too long. . . .

FROM THE JOURNAL OF DOCTOR CATANIA OLSEN

2

A tall man walked out of the trees into a shaft of moonlight, and stood leaning on a lance, looking at them. He had a longbow over his shoulder. A quiver and rawhide-web snowshoes were strapped to his back.

He wore hide trousers and boots and a thick fur parka of silver fox. The hood was up, shadowing his face.—Sam noted the silver fox. There was no mottle to the pelts; this man had come from the east.

"How do you know my name?"

The tall man threw back the hood of his parka. He had a short black beard down a lank-jawed face and a long straight nose above a flowing mustache. Deep-set eyes were shadowed in the moonlight.

"What, Sam," he said, "—no welcome for your little brother?"

". . . Jack?" Sam had to clear his throat. "Jack, you son-of-a-bitch!" He felt Jim Olsen stiffen beside him.

"Jack Monroe," Jim said.

"That's right," the tall man said. "And you'd be which Olsen? Jim?"

"Yes. Did you drive those tribesmen off?"

"I killed a couple. Guess they thought your right-hand party had come up on them."

"Well, then," Tom said, "Let's get out of here!"

Jack Monroe walked over and took Sam's arm to help him across the log. "You men bring that boy along. Looks like a Weber. William?"

Chapman Olsen started to say something, but Jim shook his head, and motioned to him to take William's legs.

The boy had frozen stiff and was hard to carry. When they were out of the forest at the edge of the mountain's valley, the Olsens put him down, and Jim sat on the corpse and pulled the head up until the body bent in the middle. Then, one man could carry it easily, and Tom picked it up and lugged it across his shoulder as the Trappers worked their way west through the valley's deep drifts.

Sam's leg gave him more and more trouble. *Shouldn't have left our snowshoes behind on the sleds, just because we were going to be hunting high. First mistake. . . .*

They traveled in a line, Chapman coming last, carrying William's bow, quiver, and knife as well as his own. Chapman looked back to the forest from time to time, to see if Cree might be chasing. Moonlight sparkled on the snowfields behind them, but no one followed from the forest.

Jack was half-lifting Sam along, and pacing fast. *Even stronger than he used to be—and he has his damn snow-webs.* Sam's leg didn't hurt anymore, but it weighed on him like a piece of frozen wood. He dragged it through the snow, leaning on his brother.

"You rendezvous at Hot Spring?"

"Same as always, Jack." Sam could hear the others laboring along behind them, kicking through the soft snow in moonlight. *. . . William lost—and all that good meat left behind. For certain, those Cree sons-of-bitches wouldn't have run too scared to pick that up.*

To the east, the moon—a sliced moon—was still high above Mount Geary's shoulder. Sam could see his breath and Jack's mingle before their faces in a small cloud of frost. When the moon set, it would be full dark, the darkness before dawn when only owls sailed silent above the snow. The Crees might follow, then.

It was going to be no pleasure to tell Helen Weber that her brother William was dead with an arrow in his back. She'd know who to blame, and she'd be right.

The leg no longer hurt, but after they stopped for a moment so Jim could take the boy's body from Tom, Sam had trouble getting back into his stride.

"Want me to carry you?"

Sam didn't have to look to see Jack smiling. "Kiss my ass," he said—a useful copybook phrase. It always reminded Sam that Warm-time people had been no different from people now. Only luckier. . . .

Jack moved fast, and Sam managed, and the Olsens kept behind them, silent. Once, Chapman started to run up to the front, take a turn breaking trail, but Jim stopped him and motioned him back.

Though nothing had been said, Sam knew what had happened behind him. He'd heard Chapman stomp off their trail, come up . . . then stop and step back into place.

Jim Olsen . . . The look on his face when he saw it was Jack come out of those woods. After six years thrown out, here comes my brother Jack Monroe back again, and saves our bacon. Something I've never had. Pig's bacon. Supposed to be salty and fat. Wild boar bacon's not the same. . . .

They reached Hot Spring at moonset. Jack left them without a word, and went up to see if Cree might be waiting. After a while, he came back. The Spring was all right.

They built a little damp-wood fire by the water, and huddled round it. The Spring flowed from under a rock shelf, and its hot water steamed and smoked in the night air. . . . The water here was no good to drink; it gave the trots. But it was wonderful to lie down in naked, so hot and soothing.

Sam, nursing his bad leg by the fire, wished he could do that— get out of his dirty furs and go and lie in the hot water. The water would ease him, take the cold from his leg, then take the pain. He imagined living the rest of his life in the Spring, swimming in steaming warm water though the years, even when winter blizzards came screaming off the Wall.

Jack had taken a stick of jerky from his parka, and sat cross-legged, chewing on it, looking into the fire. The three Olsens didn't say anything, though they glanced at him from time to time.

Sam sat with his bad leg stuck straight out. The wound was thawing in the fire's heat, and hurting more. *Look at those Olsens. Jim doesn't know whether to shit or go blind—another fine copybook saying. But only the Weather knows what the Olsens and Auerbachs are going to do about this. It was Auerbach Olsen that Jack killed, after all.*

Sam moved his leg away from the fire. It felt better frozen. *What a fight that was. Never saw a fight like that in my life. Old Auer was tough as a white bear, but not tough enough that morning by Butternut Creek.*

After a while, then a while longer, the stars faded over both mountains and the eastern sky began to turn blue. Jack Monroe and the Olsens had stayed awake, but Sam had gotten sleepy, and nodded, sitting back from the fire. He jerked awake once, when a branch cracked in the flames, then drifted off into a dream of remembering.

* * *

Jack Monroe was one of the best hunters on the Mountain Range. Not as good at trapping, true—he hadn't the patience for it. But he was a very good hunter, very strong, and a really fine bowman, probably the best archer in the six families.

The Monroes had been the second family on the Range. First the Richardsons had come, then the Monroes . . . and afterwards, Olsens, Sorbanes, Weber-Edwards, and the Auerbachs.

There had been, over the years, good and bad blood between the families, depending on marriages, hunting luck, where trap lines were placed, and whether the caribou herds came down early or late. Even so, they never fought, not family against family. They'd voted a law against that kind of fighting, and against duels. Later each family voted against any kind of killing, even *inside* the family. They felt this was proper as a rule of the Mountain Jesus, and sensible for people who needed every bow alive and healthy for trapping and the hunt.

When this law was broken—and it was, sometimes—the man who won the fight was sent away, and never came back to the mountains.

One had tried to come back, thirty-two years ago. A boy named

Michael Sorbane had killed a Richardson and run away. Two years later, this Sorbane had come back to the Range. . . . The Richardsons had wanted to kill him, and to prevent that, his own family had had to do it. His uncles had killed him with their lances.

That was the way the rule worked on murders and killing fights in the Mountain Range. And that was the way it had worked when Jack Monroe beat the brains out of Auerbach Olsen at Butternut Creek.

Sam had been there—and now dreamed it very clearly, so he saw that sunny afternoon again. In the July thaw, six years ago, a number of people had been at the creek, cleaning hides. The women scraped the skins as thoroughly as they could, then put them in the creek to soften and let the minnows clean away the tiny scraps their knives had missed.

Naomi Sorbane had been working there. She was Auerbach Olsen's second wife. His first, Sally Weber, had been killed by a black bear two years before.—Auerbach hadn't cared much for Sally Weber, but he loved Naomi. She was a skinny red-headed girl, what the men called a laughing fucker. She had liked to make love to many men, until she was married. Then Naomi had settled down and behaved very properly until Jack Monroe came after her. Jack was known on the Range for being a good lover, and Naomi started to have fun all over again.

Sam and Charlie Weber had been sitting under a tree, fletching arrows—anyway, Charlie Weber had been fletching. He was a wonder at it, stripping the long gray flight feathers, notching the arrow shaft, then fitting the feather vanes in with a line of hot glue dipped from a little trade-pot of boiling turpentine and caribou hoof.

Sam and Charlie Weber had been sitting there, talking, when Auerbach Olsen came walking up the other side of the creek. They saw him stop and say something to Naomi, who was bent over, working on a hide. Naomi said something back—and the next thing anyone knew, Auerbach was beating her, hitting Naomi with his bow-stave and kicking her, too, as if he wanted to kill her.

It happened so fast that nobody moved for a moment, then two women ran at Auerbach to make him stop. But he was a big man, and strong, and threw the women back.

Sam, Charlie, and another man, Allen Richardson, had all started across the creek when Jack came out of the tanning hut and saw what was happening to Naomi.

. . . Sam dreamed he saw Jack's face clearly, as it had been that sunny afternoon. Charlie and Allen Richardson had seen his face then, too, and stood still while Jack ran along the creek bank and went for Auerbach Olsen.

It was a terrible fight. Jack knocked Auerbach down and twisted the longbow away from him. But Auerbach drew his knife and got right up again. Sam was across the creek by then. He tried to come between them, and Auerbach cut him hard on the arm. After that, he and the other men stayed out of it. Two women took Naomi away; others kept the children back as Jack and Auerbach fought along the shallow side of the creek, Jack with the bow-stave, Auerbach with his double-edged knife.

He cut Jack right away, first on the hand, then low on his left leg. Auerbach was a big man, almost as tall as Jack, and heavier, but he was quick as a boy . . . at least at first.

Then Jack began to hit him with the bow. Ducking away from the knife, he stepped in and swung the bow-stave at Auerbach's legs, trying to break the big man's knees. He did this twice. Then Auerbach sliced down Jack's left side, but he was limping, and couldn't quite reach to kill him.

Both men stood back from each other for a moment, catching their breath. Jack's blood was spattered on the creek bank's pebbles.—Catania, who had just become the Doctor, called to them to stop fighting, but they paid no attention to her.

When they started again, Auerbach crouched low and went straight at Jack like a bull elk, to knock him down and under the knife. But instead of striking at his knees, Jack thrust his bow-stave into the big man's face, and the pointed tip struck him in the eye.

Auerbach's eye was knocked out of his head, and hung bleeding from a knotted red cord. He shouted at the pain, stumbled—and Jack raised the bow-stave high in both hands, then swung it down with all his might.

Everyone heard Auerbach's head break; it was a bad sound.

. . . Sam dreamed harness-bells were jingling as he and the others stood watching Auerbach Olsen die. Then he woke, and still heard the bells ringing softly on the cold morning air.

The sun had risen. The old snow on the meadow below Hot Spring had softened, then frozen again. The morning sun shone off the ice so brightly that Sam had to put on his slit-goggles to watch the sleds come in.

The right-hand hunters were trotting beside their three sleds. Each long sled was made of flexible lengths of spruce bound with fire-shrunk rawhide. The runners were railed with ribbons of thin beaten steel, and the sleds slid over the snow smoothly as sticks floated down an early August river.

There had been six men in the right-hand hunt, led by young Torrey Monroe—and there were six men still.

Sam got to his feet by the fire, leaned on his bow-stave to ease his leg, and watched them come in. Two sleds were loaded with meat. *Three bucks, at least. And all I brought back was a dead man.*

Torrey Monroe called and waved to them up at the Spring. Two of the men with him were Richardsons, Don and Tall-David. Nathan Sorbane was with him, and two Olsens: Bobby Olsen and Dummy, his son.

The six men were laughing as they braked the sleds, cursing the dogs to a stop. There were seven dogs to a team, lively dogs now, full of caribou guts. They were big solid animals, half wolf, savage, and very strong. Many had the round blue eyes and thick black-and-white coats of Sorbane breeding. Those were the best dogs in the mountains.

Torrey and his men climbed up to the Spring, still laughing. They came to the fire, and saw Jack Monroe sitting across from Jim and the other Olsens, saw William's body laid out on the snow by the smoking water. Then they were quiet.

Torrey Monroe was a tough young man, short and stocky, who usually had a smile on his face. There was no smile now.

"Hello, Sam." He nodded to Jim Olsen. "Jim. . . . What happened to William?" He said nothing to Jack Monroe.

"Tribesmen," Sam said. "Looked like Crees to us."

"Crees kill a Trapper?" Torrey said. "Why would they do that?—They didn't come after us?"

"We saw five of them," Nathan Sorbane was staring at William's body. "—All they did was *wave*!" Nathan looked ready to cry. He and Wanda had taken William and Helen to live with them when they were little kids.

"Where the hell were the rest of you?" Don Richardson was red in the face. He had a bad temper.

"Nothing we could do, Don." Sam wanted to sit down, get off his leg. "They were waiting in the spruce lead off the mountain. William was hit, first thing."

"You men," Nathan said, "—you take a kid out, and let a bunch of fucking people from Jesus knows where just kill him?"

"There were ten or twelve of them, Nat."

Torrey gestured to Jack Monroe. "And what about him, Sam? What's he doing back here?"

"He saved our butts, Torrey," Chapman Olsen said.

Jack Monroe stood, stretched the stiffness out of his muscles, then picked up his lance and started down to the sleds. He walked past Torrey and the others without saying a word.

"You see that parka, Daddy? That silver fox?" Dummy Olsen stood staring after Jack with his mouth open.

"Yes, son," Bobby Olsen said. "We see it."

The copy-Webster word for Dummy was 'retarded,' but 'dummy' was in there too, under *vulgarism*, so people called him that, and he didn't mind. . . . The Olsens and Monroes were like the Richardsons—if a word wasn't in copy-Webster, they wouldn't say it. They never made up words, or talked with their hands the way the Auerbachs did sometimes.

"Well, now," Torrey said, watching Jack walk away, "—this has turned into a shit day. To lose William, *and* have a killer come back after six years gone."

"Your family," Jim Olsen said.

"Let's get moving." Sam tried his leg and found he could use it, though the knee wouldn't bend. "People at home need to know about this trouble with the Crees."

"Right," Torrey said. He and Nathan picked up William's body, and they all went down to the sleds, Sam limping, leaning on his bow-stave. . . . Jack Monroe was waiting by the lead dog of the first sled—and after Sam climbed aboard that one, and William's body was lashed to the second sled, Jack reached out as though he had the right, poked the lead dog with the butt of his lance, and called, "*Musout!*"

That dog—known as Three-balls because he was always after the bitches—belonged to Torrey Monroe. Usually, he wouldn't run for anyone else, but the lance-butt persuaded him not to argue, and he led the team out with a lunge.

The runners hadn't set on the glare ice, so as the dogs pulled out—buckled pair behind pair, not drawing in a spread like tribesmen's dogs—the sleds glided away free and easy in a jingle of harness bells.

Except for Sam, and dead William, all the men stayed on their feet, running alongside the skimming sleds. Jack had started them so fast that Bobby Olsen had to sprint to catch up. Bobby grabbed the lead sled's curved grips, steadied the dogs, and leaned forward to talk to Sam, who was sitting back against the woven rawhide rest, wrapped against the cold in the sled's bearskin.

"Going to be trouble with your brother coming back, Sam. Doesn't matter how good he did against those Crees."

Sam looked up at Bobby's narrow face, reddened by the cold wind as he rode the back of the sled, hauling left or right to shift its weight, keep it running straight behind the team.

"Maybe. We'll see what happens."

"Something bad, Sam, is what'll happen."

Sam settled back in the furs. The sore leg had become something separate from him—or almost separate—so he was able to consider other things, even when the sled bounced a little, and hurt it.... *If Bobby thinks so about Jack, then for sure the others will. Bobby's gentle—most Trappers would have set a dumb child out into the snow to sleep. Or would have had the Doctor do it for them. Poor Catania.... But it hadn't turned out badly. Dummy was stupid, and a clumsy archer, but set him a simple task and he'd work till it was done, and no resting.*

The sun was well up, now, and the plains of snow blazed with reflected light. Sam dug under a fold of fur to his parka pocket for his goggles. He didn't like them, but truth was that after a while a man could see almost as much through those narrow slits as without them, though no one knew why.... He fitted them on, tied their rawhide string behind his head, and watched Jack—out in front and to the left of Three-balls—running over the sparkling surface of the snow.

Good glare crust, but even so will you look at that man run! Runs like a lobo wolf, head down, those long legs just working away. Looks like he's never going to stop. The copybooks say, "I was never so glad to see somebody." That's in copybooks quite often. And it's true I was damn glad to see my brother—and not just for his chasing those Cree away, either. I was glad to see him, killer or not, and gone the last six years, Jesus knows where.

Sam closed his eyes behind the goggles and crossed himself. *Thank you though, whichever, for bringing my brother back. Forgive him for what he did to Auerbach Olsen, though that fight was fair—and see to it we don't have to kill him to uphold the law.*

Sam bit the inside of his cheek until it bled. It was a secret thing he did when he wanted special attention paid to a prayer. Then he settled back and watched Jack run.

As the sun rose into mid-morning, the sleds swept on, tracking behind the galloping dogs in a music of harness bells. They circled west around Alvin's foothills, running the flat open tundra snow-fields that lay between the mountains and the distant great ever-green forest said to be far to the south, in Map–New Mexico. That used to be mountain and desert country, they'd been told by Salesmen—but now, and for hundreds of years, deep forest, and poor hunting.

The sun had begun to warm the Wall. The ice cliffs were mut-tering across the mountain range as falls and avalanches carved their towering faces. Those sounds would continue until evening and the setting sun left the Wall frozen and still again.

. . . An hour before midday, their dogs yelping greetings to those kenneled in dog-lines, the Trappers reached their home. Long Ledge. The Richardsons, Olsens, and Monroes had lived there from the first years they'd come to the Range, five long life-times ago. . . . Later, the Sorbanes, then the Weber-Edwards and Auerbachs had come.

A long, winding creek-bed curved through stands of spruce and some sheltered birches, along a narrow field backed by a high granite cliff. Called the Gully, it was filled with a stretch of ice until mid-July, then ran with water until September. A long ledge ran across the face of the cliff, halfway up, and weather had notched shallow caves into the stone there. Only a narrow path wound up the rock to the ledge caves, and above them the cliff rose sheer to its wooded rim.

The first families had started by living in those caves, high above the creek's valley. But after a while they had come down, made small round houses of elk hide and spruce-pole along the Gully's bank and then lived more like people in the copybooks, when those people were 'camping out.'

The Sorbanes had come, and the Weber-Edwards, and built houses. But when the Auerbachs came to the Range, they climbed up to the ledge to live, and still had their homes in the caves there. Only Auerbachs—some of them not even taught to read—would have chosen to stay in a place so cold and wet, with only a steep and narrow stone path down to the Gully. One of every three of their babies died, but they kept to the cliff just the same.

The made-houses along the Gully bank were small, with narrow fire-places in corner chimneys built of stone chinked with clay mud. The entrances were low, to keep heat in, and there was a saying on the Range: 'A great hunter still stoops to come into his house,' referring to the foolishness of too much hunting-pride—and to the mastery of women in their homes, as well.

There were many of these small houses below the cliff—and hide huts also, for storing fire-wood, smoked meat, bud potatoes, spring onions, and fresh meat for winter freezing.

. . . Now, at almost noon, the hunting parties returned to their home, and found it untouched by the Cree.

Young children were playing along the frozen creek-bed, and several older girls were bent, feeding the slow fires that warmed stones beneath rows of dirt-filled tubs of potatoes and onion sprouts. The hooped hide covers had been taken off the long plank tubs, for daylight sun.

The children heard the harness bells and ran to welcome the sleds as they glided over Eight-log Bridge. Some Trappers and their wives gathered to see what luck the hunters had had. Philip Richardson, the oldest man on the Range at seventy-one—an extraordinary age for a Trapper—set his willow-basket work down and came over.

When the sleds were parked beneath leafless birches, the hunters unhitched the dogs and stood silent as the Trappers came to them . . . then saw dead William on the second sled.

Where there'd been talk and greetings, silence fell even among the children—except for William's sister, Helen, who bent over him and tugged at his buckskins as if to wake him up. She called to wake him, then began to scream and cry until the Doctor, Catania Olsen, pushed through the crowd to her, and touched William to be certain he was gone.

"Arrow wound," she said. "How?"

"Cree," Sam said.

Then the Trappers murmured among themselves, and a woman said, "Oh, Jesus . . . oh, Jesus in the Mountains."

"Cree?" a man, a Sorbane, said. "Those tribesmen have been coming down for years—come down hunting."

"Only a few," another Trapper said. "And they always asked permission!"

"Carry him to Michael's house," Doctor Olsen said, and put her arms around Helen to comfort her.

Catania Olsen was a tall big-boned young woman with gray eyes and light brown hair she kept in one long braid. She had a scar on her face that made her ugly. . . . When she was a child, she had wandered into the dog-lines and they had dragged her down and torn at her. Part of her cheek, on the right side, had been ripped open, and though Doctor Monroe—who was the families' doctor then—had done his best, and sewn her up with a small steel needle and Salesmen's thread, she was left with that savage scar. It pulled the right corner of her mouth up slightly, as if she were beginning to smile.

No man would marry a face like that, so Catania was apprenticed to the Doctor, to become a Doctor herself.

She'd done well at it, and was liked, so even men who weren't her Sunday patients would do what they could to make her happy on holidays, and their wives said nothing against it.

. . . Catania started to lead William's sister away—and saw Jack Monroe sitting on a sled, looking at her. Her ruined face went white as Helen's. She stood staring until he smiled, got up, and walked away down the creek toward his brother's house.

A big man with thick shoulders was cutting firewood at a smoke shed as Jack walked by. The man's dark-brown hair was cut short, and his face had been shaved clean with a knife. Blue dots were tattooed across his cheek-bones, four on one side, four on the other. He rested the ax and watched Jack go by, his eyes a bear's eyes, small, brown, and interested.

At the sleds, Sam's wife, Susan, called to Catania to come back and look at his wounded leg. Susan was slight, and beautiful. She was carrying a child in an almost eight-month belly, and was pale and anxious about Sam and the mention of tribesmen, so Catania soothed her and sent her home to make a warm bed ready. Then the Doctor bent over Sam, sliced open his trouser-leg, and examined the wound.

Around her, people talked about the Crees coming down . . . and the return of an exile who had beaten the brains out of Auerbach Olsen many years ago, by Butternut Creek.

. . . Jack Monroe is back. My heart hurt when I saw him.

William Weber is dead. Arrow driven through lumbar process, abdominal aorta pierced. CD: internal bleeding and shock.

Sam Monroe is injured. Arrow wound transfixing gastro-soleus tricep. Fibula nicked—no fracture. Prognosis positive.

. . . When the men first came to me, on Christmas, when I was seventeen—three years before Old Doc died—they came all together to enjoy themselves. Well, to be fair, they came for my sake. But Jack didn't come with them. All during the night, while we were drinking potato-vodka and they took their gentle turns with me, I waited for Jack Monroe.

He came to me alone, in the early evening, three days later. And the first thing I did was cry. I got tears and snot all over his shoulder. He kissed my eyes. He kissed my scar. When he went away in the morning, he carried my heart in his hands, and I never got it back.

FROM THE JOURNAL OF DOCTOR CATANIA OLSEN

3

That night, Sam Monroe lay at ease on bear-skin robes before his home hearth. The pegged rawhide bed had been dragged close to a spruce-knot fire seething and cracking in the corner fireplace.

Susan had a stew-pot on—chunks of caribou steak, bunches of sprouted onions, and last year's potatoes simmering in a Salesman-kettle. They'd eaten the last of the elk.

Sam lay watching his wife as she worked, slight, pretty, big-bellied with their child—their first child—she bent to tend the food in ruddy firelight, her long black hair loose, and falling forward to shield her face.

My little one. . . . Scared to death on our wedding night. Truth is, I was too old for her . . . am too old. God knows what she thought I was going to do to her. Susan absently tucked her hair back behind her ear, so her face was silhouetted by the flames. . . . *Look at that little ear. A field mouse's ear. Truth is, I didn't do anything to her for two nights—three nights. She was so small, so pretty I was scared to do it.*

His leg felt better; Catania had cleaned the wound, poured vodka in it, and wrapped it in boiled cloth, the woven plant-stuff—linen—the Salesmen brought, and sold very dear.

Jack came stooping through the entrance, back from the privy. He went over to Susan's strapped-hide chest, took out the leather vodka jug, and came to sit on the bed beside Sam.

"How's the leg?" He pulled the stopper and tilted the jug up for several swallows, his adam's apple moving under the short black beard.

"Leg's feeling pretty good." Sam leaned over and took the jug.

"Not too much, Sam," Susan said. ". . . Dinner is going to take forever. These potatoes are frostbitten. Martha says her girls always watch the tub-fires, but they don't."

Sam took a short drink and handed the jug back to Jack. "Now, you tell me how the hell you happened to come on us, yesterday."

His brother sat looking at him for a moment before he answered. Sam was struck, not for the first time, how like a sled-dog's eyes Jack's were—the same bright cold light-blue gaze.

"I didn't 'happen to,' Sam. I followed you people around for two days."

"Like hell."

"No surprise those tribesmen jumped you. You were careless travelers." Jack took another drink, wiped his mouth with his hand.

Sam reached for the jug, but Jack held onto it.

"—I picked you up at Keep-on, saw the other bunch go off, and followed you the rest of the way 'round the mountain. Thought I'd save some trouble and talk to you alone at the Spring—but you never came out of the spruce, so I went up to see." Jack smiled. "You and those Olsens. . . . What's that copy-book thing? 'Babes in the woods'?" He shook his head.

"I know that was my fault," Sam said.

"Oh, you have fewer faults than most," Jack said. "You were always a good brother to me." He sat staring into the fire for a while. "—What is a Boxcar-man doing on the Range?"

"What?"

"A Boxcar-man, Sam." Jack touched his cheekbones. "The one with the shaved face and tattoos."

"Newton," Susan said. "His name's Newton."

"I saw those Middle Kingdom people come up-river, sailing ice-boats," Jack said. "*Big* boats. Your Newton is an eight-dot man; likely important among them."

"He came to the Range three years ago," Susan said. "He married Lucy Edwards, and stayed."

"We knew where he came from," Sam said. "He causes no trouble."

Jack said nothing to that, only sat beside Sam and looked into the fire.

. . . Later, Catania came visiting, and brought a jug and her willow-wood harp—a trade-instrument.

"Dinner's going to be late," Susan said. It was more comfortable talking about dinner . . . talking about anything but the Cree, and dead William Weber. She felt her baby heavy within her, and still, as if it were listening for news of more trouble.

"Don't need to feed me." Catania sat cross-legged on the floor furs and began to tune her harp.

"Well, I will feed you," Susan said, and stirred the stew, "—but the potatoes aren't cooking."

"Then leave them be," Catania said, "—and come and sing."

She and Susan sang 'Alvin Mountain,' 'The Fisher-cat Hunt', and 'Sentimental Journey,' a very old copybook song. The four of them drank vodka and sang old songs together. Sam had a fine voice, deep and true, but Jack could hardly carry a tune. He sang out harsh and loud, but what he sang was always off—though it sounded fine to him, so he said "What?!" when the others made fun.

Since Jack was a boy, singing had been the one body-thing he'd had no talent for.

Watching her husband as they sang, watching Catania, Susan saw how dear they both found that single weakness in him.

. . . After a while, they stopped singing and sat on piled furs watching the fire, while Catania played softly on her harp. Susan wanted to ask Jack where he'd been the past six years, but felt that would be rude. She remembered Jack from when she was a young girl, and thought he looked bigger—and when they weren't singing, grim.

She went to the fire to stir the stew. "I think the potatoes are getting done at last."

Sam was dozing when someone whistled outside the entrance. Torrey Monroe pushed the door-hides apart and ducked in. "Sorry to bother you."

Sam sat up. "Trouble?"

"No. But I think we better bring in our traps before those tribesmen steal the whole line. We can't afford to lose trade-steel traps. Other families are out getting theirs."

"All right." Sam eased his leg a little, saw it was bending better at the knee. "Why don't you go at daylight, pick 'em up. Take Jack with you."

Torrey glanced at Jack. "I guess that's all right."

Jack looked at him and said nothing.

"We go at first light," Torrey said, stooped, and went out.

"Trying to get rid of me, Sam?"

"Damn right, Jack. Damn right I am. I won't have—I just think we have enough trouble with the Crees. And speaking of those damned people, what got into them? That's what I'd like to know. Murdering a man. . . ."

Catania laid her harp down. "They've come south lots of times, in little bands, and never hurt anybody. We've traded hatchets and snare-wire to them for white furs. . . . They didn't want copybooks."

"Tribesmen think copybooks are unlucky," Jack said, "—part of Warm-times' going away. They say book-people live in the past, instead of dealing with the present."

"But there was no trouble with them," Susan said. "They were friendly—and they looked like us, except for their furs."

"Most tribesmen are white-bloods, now," Jack said, and tilted up the leather bottle for another drink. "Ojibway told me the whites went to the tribes when the ice came—went to be taught how to stay alive. So now, most are white-bloods. Red-bloods still run things, though—war chiefs . . . medicine people."

"Sounds like you know them," Sam said. His leg was stiff, but better. There was an ache, but it felt like a good ache.

"I know the Ojibway. Doubt the Cree are much different."

"Potatoes are done as they're going to be." Susan dipped out a wooden bowl of stew and brought it to Jack, along with a carved spoon. "Is that where you've been—with the Tribes?"

"Honey. . . ."

"It's all right, Sam.—This smells wonderful." Jack took a spoonful, blew to cool it. "I was with the Ojibway for a while, in Map-Michigan."

"Mountain Jesus," Sam said. "That's a thousand miles away!"

"Eat," Susan said, and handed him a bowl of stew.

"More," Catania said. "More than a thousand map-miles." She took a bowl of stew from Susan. "Too much," she said. "You gave me too much."

"I went to them," Jack said, "—and they let me stay a while." He ate some stew.

"A while?" Catania said.

"Three years and a little. . . ."

Sam swallowed a spoonful of stew. "Three years up on that ice?" Susan never put enough onions in stew, but he hadn't been able to tell her, she was so proud of her cooking.

"Good hunting up there, Sam. There are valleys, canyons cut back into the ice, right down to tundra. Some of them go back twenty, thirty Warm-time miles. You can hunt caribou, moose, white bear. . . ."

"But if the hunting is good up there," Susan said, "—then why would they want to come to our mountains?"

"Pushed." Jack ate a spoonful of stew. "This is good. I've missed our food."

"Pushed?"

"That's right. The Abenaki and New Englanders moved the Mohawks out, so the Mohawks had to move the Ojibway out, drive them west." Jack stopped talking to have another spoonful of stew. ". . . And I suppose now the Ojibway have driven the Cree. That's why these tribesmen are down here. No choice."

Sam set his dinner-bowl aside. "If all that's true, Jack, then these people are coming here to stay."

"Yes."

"And you're sure that's what's happened?"

"Pretty sure, Sam." Jack finished his stew, handed the bowl to Susan. "I was in Map-Michigan when the Mohawks came."

"And your host people lost?" Sam said.

"Yes . . . we lost. New Englanders came into it. They're ene-mies of everyone—want all the tribesmen out—but they were helping the Mohawks, then." Jack picked up Catania's vodka bot-tle, took a drink. "The Ojibway said those Boston people can make things with their minds . . . make monsters out of babies while they're growing in their mothers' bellies, change them in there."

Catania stopped eating. "But I thought those were just Salesmen stories—monsters and wicked people flying through the air."

"An Ojibway I knew—Raymond Grace—told me he saw a man flying through the air when they were fighting one night by Empty Creek." Jack stoppered the vodka and put it down. "—Said he saw a blue-robe from Boston sitting in clouds of blowing snow just over the trees, waving on a war-band of Great Lake Mohawks."

Jack was quiet for a while . . . seemed to be remembering. Catania finished her stew, stood, and handed her bowl to Susan. The hearth fire ticked, thumped as a piece of wood burned through.

Then Jack said, "A few days later, old Eleanor John told us that while we were gone fighting, a Boston person flew down on the village like a blue bird, like Rain-bird, and stood resting while the Mohawks killed the women and children. . . . If old Eleanor hadn't been out for firewood, they would have killed her, too."

"People you knew?" Susan asked that, then wished she hadn't.

". . . Yes," Jack said.

Silence in Sam's house, except for the fire's soft snap and rustle.

"Jack, I don't believe there is really such bad and un-scientific wisdom," Catania said. "Cruel flying . . . and, you say, monsters?"

"Ghost-Owl Ojibways said one of their bands was fighting Mohicans four years back. Said they were fighting on lake ice, and a thing the Boston people had made inside a woman—mixed with a wolverine's coming, then cut out of her—said that Made-thing came over the ice. And when it did, the Ojibway ran."

"But Jack, you didn't see it."

"No."

"I can tell you," Sam said, "—we've seen no such creature in the mountains."

"And hope you don't, Sam," Jack said. "These Crees are enough bad luck."

He sat silent after that, and no one asked him any more questions.

Catania, watching Jack in firelight, saw what he would look like when he was old. Saw that even now, though he was years younger than Sam, slight touches of gray were feathered above his ears.... Those tribesmen-tales of bad people flying, of wolverine-persons. Tales told to explain away defeats, slaughtered women and children. What woman, what child had Jack known, to fall so sadly silent, remembering?

"Honey," Sam said, seeing Susan quiet, frightened by the talk, "—that stew was so good. You never put in too many onions. It's always just right."

"Potatoes took forever," Susan said, but was pleased.

"It was very good," Jack said. "It brought the Range back to me."

Everyone sat quiet for a while, the only sound the dying fire's soft ruffling.... It occurred to Catania that small fires had filled many silences over the centuries.

Jack stood and stretched, his hands touching the hide roof. Then he reached for his bow and quiver, and slung them over his shoulder. "Goodnight. And thanks, Susan. My brother's a lucky man." He picked up Catania's vodka jug, touched her on the shoulder, and she stood with her harp to follow him outside.

After they left, Susan said, "He brought bad news."

"Nothing to worry you, Little Mouse. Come here and lie with me."

She did, and Sam lay back on the bed, hugging her gently. His leg felt fine, only aching, and he touched Susan's breasts ... then started to tug her pants down a little, despite her belly, but she stopped him. Soon she was asleep in his arms.

Sam lay awake for a while, looking into the fire. *I'm getting stupid as Dummy Olsen. Poor William dead, and Jack's back—which can't be allowed. Yet here I lie, a happy man, full of stew and vodka, and Susan with me. Happy as the Warm-time hunters must have been, when they went out camping with heat-stoves and liquors.*

The one foolish thing back then, was hunting with powder guns. Old Eric Sorbane's great-grandfather had known a man who'd seen a gun, long ago. Old Eric said the man told his great-grandfather that it threw a little metal piece—a copybook 'bullet' for sure—a far distance, and that piece hit hard when it hit. But it made so much noise it scared the other game away. And a handful of the Warm-time powder had cost thirty-one prime wolf or lynx pelts, when a Salesman had that so-old powder to sell. Also, that the gun didn't always do bang and throw the metal, but often made only a pissing sound.

Susan's weight was on his sore leg. Sam shifted her gently, so she murmured but didn't wake.

. . . Of course, it was possible a powder-gun was good for hunting in Warm-times. But not now, not for the Range. Those hunters should have seen Jack use a bow, or Torrey. Or me, for that matter. We could have shown them some real hunting.

Sam began to doze. He woke, kissed Susan while she slept . . . then fell asleep himself.

* * *

Just before dawn, Torrey Monroe was at the Gully's far-side bank, hitching his team to a light sled. Torrey's sled was narrower than most, with a fine frame steamed and formed of sapling members. Its steel runners were polished with creek-bed sand. . . . He'd harnessed the team, all but Three-balls. Three-balls gave him trouble, but Torrey booted him quiet and hitched him up.

When he finished, Torrey saw Jack Monroe standing behind the sled, watching him. Jack was carrying his bow, quiver, an extra quiver, and a *parfleche* of pemmican on a strap. He had a rolled bear-skin under his arm.

Torrey didn't like people coming up on him quietly, and didn't care for a killer's company in any case.

"People guarding all night?" Jack set his bear-skin on the sled, and gestured to the ledge. Two Auerbachs were standing up there, just visible as the sky lightened to the east. They had their bows on their backs, and carried slender lances.

"That's right . . . and Richardsons out scouting. Most of the rest of them getting their traps in." Torrey coiled the kennel line and lashed it to the sled.

"So, say forty men still home here?"

"Maybe more. Why?"

Jack didn't answer . . . went to the back of the sled, took the grips, and rocked the runners free.

"You ready?" he said.

"Yes, I'm ready—and I'll be driving my sled."

"All right," Jack said, stepped away from the back of the sled, and started running. He didn't speed up from a stand, to a walk, to a trot. First he was standing—then he was running. And Three-balls, seeing him go past, lunged after him, so Torrey had to scramble to get to the grips as the team hauled the sled away past potato tubs and store-huts.

Torrey rode the sled for a moment, then stepped down to run, hauling the grips a little left to miss a patch of thaw. Then they were out into the open, onto the plains of snow, and the harness bells rang like made music through the dark morning air.

. . . By noon, they'd eaten some jerky, and were resting cross-legged on hides high in the ridge of forested hills south of Mount Geary. The Olsen-Monroe traps had been set along these slopes for three years—after Jack's time. Before that, their two-families' line had been set west of Butternut Creek. Good country for lynx, marten, and fisher-cat. Not much for wolf.

"What are you getting up here?"

"Lately, mink," Torrey said, thinking that Sam had sent Jack up here to keep some Auerbach from killing him. "Mink and tree-marten. Three wolverines so far this season. White bears come through sometimes, break the traps. But not this year."

"Tigers?"

"No snow-tigers now. But Tod Sorbane said he saw one near the melt lakes last year." Torrey had been a little boy when Web Monroe killed one of the first tigers seen in the mountains—and died doing it. Snow-tigers trailing over the ice from Map-Russia, Doctor Monroe had said.

"So they come around. . . ."

"Well, one took two dogs five years ago. Bunch of Edwards killed that one. Hide traded for three very fine bucksaw blades, an ax, five pounds of steel rod, and two metal-files, also very fine."

"That's a high price," Jack said.

"Yes, it was." Torrey thought he and this exile had had enough conversation, so he stood and went to kick up the dogs. "Let's get onto those traps."

They both rode the sled as it raced down the ridge's reverse slope. The dogs, at a dead run, were barely able to keep out front.

Jack laughed with pleasure as they flew down, the dogs yelping before them, the bitter wind of their passage whistling in their ears. Torrey, sitting up front, looked back when Jack laughed. *What is in this man's head? The families will decide to kill him, Sam or no Sam, if the Crees don't kill us first. And here he is, laughing like a vodka drunk. . . .*

At the bottom of the ridge, they found the first set. It was empty. The fine trade-trap lay sprung and uncovered, its steel jaws snapped shut on nothing.

"Shit." Torrey bent to tug the trap's light chain and stake out of the snow. "—Damn jays."

Jack stooped to look. "Fox sprung it."

"Sure, after the birds scratched the cover-snow off it, showed the steel."

"If you have bird trouble, use little spruce branches for cover."

"Don't tell me my business." Torrey threw the trap and chain onto the sled, then called to Three-balls to follow. He led the team past a dense stand of evergreens and across an open meadow to another line of trees.

There was a wolf in the next trap. They heard it snarling at their noise and scent before they left the dogs and pushed their way through sapling hemlock. It was a big male with a silver-frosted pelt. The wolf stared at them with yellow eyes, and trembled, heavy muzzle wrinkled back from its fangs. Its left hind leg was chewed almost through at the first joint. Only a twist of wet red fur and white tendon still held the wolf to the trap.

Torrey went back to the sled for the hardwood club to kill the wolf with, so as not to ruin the pelt with a lance. . . . The wolf kept his eyes on him, then tried to rush, dragging the trap's anchor chain and snapping at the air as Torrey stayed out of reach. Each time he tried to step in, the wolf lunged to meet him, foaming with rage.

Then Jack, gone round behind, called softly, "It's time to go."

The wolf turned toward him—and Torrey swung the club, cracked its skull, and crossed himself as the animal died.

The next two traps were empty, robbed and fouled by a wolverine. But farther down the line, they found a red fox, then a mink, then two marten. Fair-enough trapping for so late in the season. . . . By late afternoon, the sled was stacked with frozen hides, traps, and chains. They had seen no tribesmen.

Swinging back west over the ridge, they coursed down through old snow into scattered spruce and dwarf birch, and ran along a frozen creek. The dogs were tired, and it was getting colder as the sun sank. West of Mount Geary, the Wall was silent as its ice-cliffs chilled with approaching evening.

The round shadows of the hills slowly flooded the creek bed as they traveled along, shading them from the orange glare of sunset off the fields of snow. Torrey, running ahead of the dogs, breaking trail, slowed, then stopped. He shoved his slit-goggles up on his forehead to be certain he'd seen an elk standing in the birch saplings more than a hundred long paces away. The elk was there, an antlered bachelor buck—and safe at that distance.

He heard the harness-bells sound softly to a stop behind him, and knew Jack had seen the elk too. The animal was alert, standing staring right at them. Torrey slowly eased his bow off his back, braced, and strung it. He nocked an arrow to the string . . . and started off to the left through the snow, one slow shuffling step at a time, to circle wide for at least a possible flank shot if the elk started and happened to run close enough past him.

After four slow steps, he saw there wasn't time—the elk was already shifting in place, high stepping and ready to run.

He stood to watch it go. More than a hundred-fifty Warm-time pounds of good meat set to run away, the best eating there was, except for grouse. He pressed his bent knee to his bow-stave to unstring it—and jumped a little in surprise at the ringing thump of a bow-shot just behind him.

Torrey stood, eyes wide as a fool's, and watched a tiny ghost of goose-feathers flick away through evening air in a high, swift, looping arc—then whisk out of sight past a slender birch just as the buck, reacting to the sound of the shot, leaped into the saplings to meet it.

He heard the buck grunt—and the crackle of frozen small branches as it ran through the trees. . . . Then the sound of thrashing in the brush as it fell.

Torrey began to run, and Jack ran up alongside him, the long-bow on his back again. He was pacing along, not grinning at Torrey at having made such a shot. It was the finest bow-shot Torrey had ever seen. Not only because of the distance—more than a hundred paces—but because Jack had planned it so well, judging just where the buck, hearing the bow, would leap to meet the arrow. *Men who want to kill this one for coming back, had better catch him asleep.*

They found the elk lying tangled in frozen branches fallen in an ice-storm. The long arrow had taken him behind the left shoulder. The buck was still alive but dreaming, its eyes already glazed.

Jack went to him, murmuring softly as if to an injured sled dog, "It's time to go. . . ." He stepped over a long branch behind the buck, bent to cut its throat, then touched a fingertip of blood to his forehead.

They camped at nightfall farther down the creek-bed, camping low to keep their fire out of sight. It would be only a morning's run to home.

Torrey unharnessed the dogs, staked them out, and fed them an armload of elk guts—Three-balls fighting to keep it all, as usual. The guts were freezing as the dogs snarled over them. It sounded as though they were chewing bones.

Jack had dug some twigs and old branches from under the snow, broken them, and stacked them into a small cone. He took a handful of powdered birch-bark from his pouch, tucked it into the branches, and struck sparks into it with flint and steel. He blew gently into those, and the fire budded . . . then blossomed as bright red far-southern flowers were said to do.

Jack sat cross-legged on his bear-skin, and watched the flames.

Torrey cut two thick wide loin-steaks from the butchered elk, then slit the gall bladder and spinkled some of that on the meat. He took two branches Jack hadn't used for the fire, sharpened the ends, and stuck them up in the snow to lean by the flames. Then he draped a steak over each, went to get a rolled caribou hide from the sled, and sat across the fire from Jack.

The white fat edging the meat slowly began to broil and sputter, and a faint drift of smoke carried the smell of steak cooking. The sun had set, and the night came down as Jack and Torrey sat watching the fat begin to char, the meat turn a rich brown, running juices.

Torrey leaned forward, speared each steak with his knife, and turned its other side to the fire. "That was the best shot I ever saw."

"Luck."

"No, it wasn't."

. . . When the meat was done, each man pulled up a cooking stick—the steak still hanging from it—and began to eat, holding the scorched stick with one hand, biting into the meat, then slicing the mouthful free with a casual pass of their knives.

After a few mouthfuls, Torrey got up and went to the sled, dug into his possibles-sack, and came back with a small rough chunk of salt. He and Jack scraped some of it onto their steaks, then Torrey put the salt away. That piece was almost big enough for strangers to kill each other for. Salesmen said it was an old saying: Kill a stranger for salt, a friend for steel, a brother for paper.

Salesmen claimed that some of them, traveling alone with salt to sell, had been murdered down in Map-Arizona—which was very bad, since no Salesman would go that way again, except with others, and for triple prices.

. . . They finished the steaks, and Jack thrust his knife into the snow to clean the meat juice off the blade—then picked up his bow, and got up to go into the woods to shit. . . . Afterward, he took a wide circle around the camp, then climbed a nearby hilltop and looked out over the country. It was cold for so late in the winter. His breath froze in a glittering cloud, then showered slowly down, a little snowfall.

The moon was rising, its light glowing on the hilltops falling away to the east. Looking north between Mount Alvin and Mount Geary, Jack could just see the thin bright moonlit line of the Wall. He heard an owl call below the hill, and turned to listen. When it called again, he cupped his hand to his mouth and hooted back the same single mournful note. The owl replied, a little uncertain, and Jack called to it again—a cooing sound, low and gentle. Then he stood still, leaning on his bow-stave.

For a little while, nothing happened. Then Jack saw a fleeting shadow come racing over the moon-bright snow. He searched the night sky between the shadow and the moon, and found the horned owl flying silent through the air, a swift, soft blur of rounded wings. At the same moment, the owl, nearly overhead, saw Jack—and in a quick tumble of feathers turned in the starry sky and flew away faster than he'd come.

Jack went back down to the fire, smiling.

"Was that you fooling around up there?"

"Yes. That's a lonely owl . . ."

"I couldn't tell which was which," Torrey said. "—Sounded like a pair of lonely owls to me."

Jack laughed, went to the sled for the *parfleche* of pemmican, and came to sit on his bear-skin by the fire. They ate slices of pemmican with poor-metal mugs of evergreen tea—snow-water and spruce needles Torrey heated over the fire in a little metal trade-pot. Susan had made the pemmican with cloudberries, dried partridge breast ground fine, and trade-honey—all boiled with goose fat, then packed in a small roll of cured hide. Sam and poor dead William had decoyed the geese into nets at the melt-lakes beneath the Wall. It was a sweet pemmican, and they ate almost half of it.

Torrey leaned forward to blow the failing flames a breath. "We've seen no Crees up on the trapline."

"No. Wouldn't waste their time coming to look for just two men. They'll be moving in a bunch from now on, hunting for the most of us they can find."

"And why the hell would they do that?" Torrey tossed a handful of twigs into the fire. "Why look for a fight that's going to get some of them killed?"

"Well . . . because it's worth it to them."

"*What's* worth it to them?"

"This range," Jack said, and sat looking into the fire.

Torrey didn't want to ask more questions with answers like that, but after a long silence, he couldn't help asking one more. "I suppose you saw strange things, six years gone."

"Yes."

"Well . . . what was the *strangest* thing?"

Jack said nothing for a little while, apparently considering. Then he said, "Chicago City."

"You're telling me a story," Torrey said. "—Or maybe just a lie." He put his hand on his knife in case this killer-come-back took offense.

But Jack smiled. "It's east in Old Illinois. There's a big snow-field on the ice, far as you can see, and a frozen lake beside it. Three days travel to cross that lake, and very rough ice.—Buck-skin boots on the dogs, or they'll cripple."

"But you can see Chicago City?"

"There are twenty, maybe twenty-five big square houses with rows of square window-doors. 'Buildings,' like in copybooks. And it's just the tops of these, sticking up out of the snow higher than Long-Ledge cliff. . . . There's a very big black one, sticks up even higher than the others. Men on top of that one look like chicka-dees in the top of a tall tree."

Torrey was sitting with his mouth open, like a child listening to the book of Walk-on-the-Moon.

"—The Ojibway go into those houses for steel; they climb in through the window-doors. Did when I was with them, anyway." Jack drank some tea. "They find good knife-makings, broadhead makings, down inside those houses—those buildings. And they climb to the roofs; I saw some of them up there on the black one, waving their arms. They said that one went down under the ice forever; there were square holes inside that you could drop a rock into, and never hear it land."

"Damn...." Torrey shook his head. "So everything is true. The copybooks are *true*."

"Seems they are."

"And you're not lying?"

"I'm not lying."

Torrey sat staring into the dying fire for a while. Then he looked up at Jack with a sad smile. "I'd say the people who used to live in a place like that, they wouldn't think much of us, would they? Running around after caribou, and trapping things." He took the trade-pot off the coals. "I guess we've come a long way down."

"I suppose we have."

Torrey poured himself a little more evergreen tea, and sipped until it was gone. Then he stood, shook the snow from his caribou hide, wrapped himself in it, and lay down.

Jack sat a while, watching the last coals burning...then smothered the fire with snow, and lay down in his bear-skin to sleep.

"God bless," Torrey said.

"God bless."

...That night, Jack dreamed of Neesilak and their boy. He dreamed the baby was learning to walk, staggering back and forth between them, his black eyes wide with surprise at this thing he was doing. And Jack and Neesi looked at each other over the little boy, and laughed.

The dream was so good that it remembered Neesi even better than Jack did. He had forgotten how the fine strands of her long black hair, a true red-blood's hair, would sometimes blow across her mouth when she laughed, so she had to spit them out with little *puh-puh* sounds.

Something woke him: the owl, calling over the hill.

He lay quiet and closed his eyes, hoping the dream would come back, but it didn't. Instead, he dreamed an old dream of his, one he knew very well. He knew it was a dream, even *in* the dream.

It was the snow-tiger killing his father.

Jack stood high on the hillside beside Sam, and they looked down the steep slope as the tiger, huge and bright-striped, with a ruff of white around its throat, came bounding over the frozen stream-bed toward their father.

In the dream, Jack thought what he'd thought when it happened. *I'm going to see my father die.*

He saw, far down the slope, Web Monroe draw and shoot, draw and shoot. Jack knew each arrow struck the tiger, but didn't look to see. He only watched his father; to see as much of him as he could. . . . Web Monroe dropped his bow, took his lance from where he'd propped it in the snow, and leveled it at the tiger as it came.

Even from the hill, Jack could see his father's face clearly: it looked stern and impatient, as if he'd had to wait too long for the tiger. Then, all striped in black and gold, the beast leaped upon the lance and man like a living fire.

Jack had no dreams after that. Or if he had, he'd forgotten them by morning.

Drunk all day. Perhaps with happiness; perhaps not. I'm afraid of the Crees. They are men, and they are here, not just foolish tales of mind-magic and monsters more than a thousand Warm-time miles away.

Drank vodka, played the harp from our best copybook of songs. Is middle C really the note of a well-strung bow? I believe a Warm-time pitch pipe would be worth all we have.

Ruined one panel of a copy because I was drunk. Martha will be very angry. Ink no help—spruce tar and trade-graphite. It stinks. Copy was of copybook Buck-the-Dog Calls Wild. Read to pieces.

Lanced a boil—usual good job. Hot pack for drainage, etc. Fundamentally, I am a boil doctor. I am comfortable with boils, vodka or not.

Jack's still out on the mountain.

FROM THE JOURNAL OF DOCTOR CATANIA OLSEN

4

Late in the morning, with a ringing shake of harness bells, Three-balls led his tired team across Eight-log Bridge into Long Ledge. Torrey Monroe was at the sled's handles. Jack trotted alongside the load of blood-stiff furs, frozen meat, and jingling traps and chains.

A patrol of Trappers, Richardsons and Webers, had met them a distance out and passed them through, with some hard looks at Jack Monroe. The patrol had already taken a Cree scout, a white-blood, blond and green-eyed. They'd caught him at dawn, tied him to a tree, and put their knives to him for information—and for William Weber's murder.

When Jack and Torrey went by, the tribesman was drifting and dreaming at the tree, singing his death song. He was naked and bright with blood. There was blood in the snow all around him.

Ned and Alice Richardson led that patrol. They were older people—almost forty—and remembered Jack very well. Ned had given him a hard look, but Alice a soft one; she had taught him loving matters when he was a boy, before she married Ned.

Phil Weber, cleaning his knife from the Cree, had given Jack only a nod. Phil was a good fisherman. When he and Jack were boys, they'd gone for spotted trout and char in the melt waters churning along the foot of the Wall.

. . . Coming into Long Ledge, Torrey drove the team past potato-tubs and smoke racks to the dog-lines. Home was full of busy people. Trappers were in from their hunting, from picking up their traps. Now, at their houses, they were packing sleds with supplies, polishing runners, mending harness, and sharpening lance-tips, arrow-heads, and knives.

Others gathered in groups, leaning on their lance-staffs and talking. All the men were armed. Most of the young women were armed as well, and the older boys.

Little girls were going from sled to sled, taking the clusters of bells from dog harnesses and putting them in small soft leather bags for safe-keeping. Silence over the snow, seemed the rule for war.

People called to Torrey as he went by. No one called to Jack. They glanced at him, then looked away, except for the children, who stared.

At dog-lines, Jack and Torrey unloaded the sled, staked the dogs out, set melt-water down in big wooden bowls, and fed them. Then, shouldering the elk meat, the skins, and traps, they walked down the Gully's bank to Sam's house . . . left the goods beside the door, stooped, and went inside.

The house was crowded with men talking and drinking vodka. They turned to look as Jack and Torrey came in. There were women, too—Catania Olsen, and Joan Richardson, Martha Sorbane, and Susan Monroe. Martha stared at Jack in an unfriendly way. She was related to Auerbachs.

Sam was sitting by the cold fireplace with his leg up on a stool. The room was hot, packed with so many people that no fire was needed. He waved Jack and Torrey over, and they wove through the crowd; the Trappers there were all elected people—lead hunters, most of them, or craftsmen—the important people from each family.

"Listen," Sam spoke quietly to Jack. "I talked with Ned Richardson and Peter Auerbach and some others last night. Two things are agreed: you stay a few days while this Cree thing is settled. No family man will kill you, those few days.—But then you go, and never come to the Range again."

Jack said nothing. He sat cross-legged by Sam's stool, and Susan brought him and Torrey slices of cold venison and little leather cups of vodka.

". . . It was the best I could do, Jack."

Jack drank some vodka, reached up and patted Sam's hand.

"Damn you," Sam said. "Well, maybe we could pay the Auerbachs. And if the Monroes begged forgiveness. . . ."

"I'm not begging forgiveness," Torrey said, and cut another piece of venison. "I'm not the one killed a Trapper."

Jack finished his vodka. "So, you're going to fight these Crees?"

"Hell, yes," Sam said. "What else is there to do?"

"Run."

Two Sorbanes, nearby, heard Jack say that, and one of them, Rodney Sorbane, spoke up. "Did you say we should run out of here?"

"That's right."

"Personally, I have nothing against you," Rod Sorbane said, though he looked angry just the same. "But when a man says something stupid at a time like this, I wonder why he says it. Is he a coward . . . or what is he?" Sam and Torrey, who were sitting to either side of Jack, shifted away in case there was trouble. But Jack just chewed a bite of venison and swallowed it before he spoke.

"I'd guess the scouts are saying these tribesmen came down with their women and kids."

"Yes. So what?"

"And how many fighting men?"

". . . A few hundred."

"At least four to five hundred," said a man standing in the back. It was the tattooed Boxcar-man, Newton.

"All right," Jack said, and he set his venison aside and stood up. "We have several hundred Cree come down from the ice with their families. Several hundred—and I'd say likely more. And they have attacked our people, which they never did before. No tribesman brings his children to a fight, unless he has no choice. These people have no choice."

"You're saying they're driven down?" Tattooed Newton had a slurred accent, a sort of slow speaking.

"Yes."

"And by who?"

"Likely Piegan or Ottawas. Maybe Ojibways."

"Ojibways live way east, up there."

"Not any more," Jack said. "They were pushed west, themselves. Mohawks pushed them out, because New England was pushing the Mohawks."

"And how would you know that?" Jim Olsen said. He was sitting with all the other Olsens, except Catania.

"Because I was there."

The Trappers sat silent, and if anyone thought Jack Monroe was lying, no one said so. They sat considering how far away that was. More than a thousand map-miles east, and onto the ice.

"What difference does it make?" said Joan Richardson. She was a tall handsome woman with long red hair. "I don't care why those people are coming down off the Wall. We need to fight them, regardless!"

"Maybe more than four, five hundred warriors," Jack said. "What do we have? One hundred and sixty, maybe one hundred and seventy fighters?"

"Nearly two hundred, if you arm boys over twelve years old," Catania Olsen said. "—And the stronger women without little children."

"Two to one against us," Jack said.

"At least," said Tattooed Newton.

"Then we'll just kill them all!" Joan Richardson was pale as paper. "What's the matter with you men? There are little children outside this house. Who is going to guard them against those Cree?—Men with no balls?"

Newton laughed, and Joan turned on him. "You come outside," she said, and put her hand on her knife. "You come outside, Spotted-face, and laugh at me!"

"Joan," Sam said, "—we don't have time for this."

But Joan kept her hand on her knife. Tattooed Newton was smiling, watching her.

"This is my house, Joan," Sam said. "Behave yourself or get out."

Joan took her hand from her knife, but slowly. She seemed to dislike Tattooed Newton, and argued with him always—though some of the older women doubted the disliking.

"Monroe," Rod Sorbane said to Jack, "I'd like to hear you say it—that we can't beat a pack of no-book savages. I'd like to hear you say that."

"What I'm saying is: win or lose, it will cost you too many people killed! I'm saying you will have more people killed than this range is worth."

"Sounds like coward's talk to me," Rod Sorbane said.

"Mountain Jesus. . . ." Tall-David Richardson was sitting with his wife. "There's nothing south but tundra prairie . . . and south of that, only forest forever. If we run, where would we run to?"

"We would run to wherever there are no five-hundred Crees," Jack said, and he walked through the crowd, and went outside.

People were quiet after he was gone, then the tattooed man said, "He made sense."

"Are you saying 'run,' Newton?" Martha Weber had never liked Tattooed Newton—a stranger, a roamer come from nowhere onto the Range three years ago. He had stayed and worked and kept quiet until Lucy Edwards, who had no sense at all, fell in love with him, married him, and made him by marriage a Weber-Edwards and a Trapper. "—You saying 'run'?"

Newton considered, then in his soft slurring way, said, "Fight first. Kill some, see how it goes. If it goes well, stay. If it goes badly—run."

And after another long while of talk and arguing and several near fights—the women particularly fierce—it was decided so.

* * *

Once the meeting was over, Rod Sorbane stood outside for a while talking with his cousin, Perry, then walked up the Gully to his father's house and went round back to the privy.

He was standing in the narrow stone coop, pissing in the tanning bowl, when Jack Monroe came in behind him, struck Rod on the back of the head with his fist and knocked him to his knees. Then Monroe took him by the neck and drove his face down into the piss bowl.—And quickly as he'd done it, Jack let Rod Sorbane go, and walked out of the privy without a word.

Rod, his face wet, the collar of his fine caribou parka soaked and stinking, started to leap after Jack, enraged.—But he had what copybooks called 'second thoughts.' He thought Jack Monroe would surely kill him. So he wiped his face and stayed in the privy while his parka dried a little, so ashamed that he wept.

...When the meeting people had left Sam's house—Joan Richardson and Jim Olsen the last to go, reluctant, unsatisfied—Susan and Catania unwrapped the bandage on Sam's leg, and Catania squeezed the arrow wound gently, until a little pus ran out. Then she bent, smelled the pus, and pressed the wound again, so Sam winced at the pain. When no more pus came out, Catania washed the wound with vodka, and bandaged it with cloth hot and steaming from Susan's trade-kettle.

"It's good enough to fight on," Sam said.

"It will do for standing with a bow," Catania said. "—Not for fighting with knife or lance."

"...All right."

Susan sat on the bed, held her swollen belly, and said, "Sam ... oh, Sam."

"Little Mouse," Sam said, and hugged her. "—Nothing is going to happen to me. I'm too old and ugly to die."

"You are not," Susan said. "You are not. ..."

Catania took her medicine pack, and left. She walked down the field along the Gully's bank and heard troubled voices as she passed the houses. Women's voices, high and thready with uncertainty. Men's lower, attempting comfort. Catania felt the gifts of medicine, the accomplishments of it, shrinking as she walked— as if, merciless, Lady Weather leaned over the Range, bringing a storm that had no treatment, no preventitive.

...In the evening, the third relief of scouts went out from Long Ledge and swept in widening spirals through snowy woods and fields, then the rises and foothills of the mountains. A left-hand party led by Michael Auerbach found a Trapper named Bert

Weber-Edwards—who had been with the second relief of scouts—shot with arrows and scalped. The left-hand tracked two Crees from that place, caught them near High Hill, and cut their throats.

With the scouts out, and evening light faded to full dark, every man fit to fight—and thirty-three of the strongest women—left Long Ledge. Except for Catania, Joan Richardson, and Lucy Edwards, who were nearly thirty, the women were all young. Some had lost babies; some had no children yet; and others loved to hunt and wanted to fight the tribesmen. Joan Richardson's boy, Del, went with them, though he was only fourteen, and perhaps too young.

The Trapper army numbered one hundred and ninety-three. With only Sam Monroe riding, they ran beside thirty gliding sleds and muzzled dogs, silent as owls flying over the bone-white snow. Only the stars were out, so no shadows ran before.

Behind them, they left the older women, and those with babies, or pregnant. They left the children, and sick, and the few elderly.—These all climbed the cliff's steep and narrow track up to the long ledge with the valuables of their households—copybooks, tools, salt, and furs. All the women carried lances. Most slung bows as well, and double quivers fat with arrows, while others carried babies on their backs. . . . The young boys and girls led the little children.

When these people had filed up the path to the ledge, and stored their goods in the shallow caves where Auerbachs lived, there was no one left below. The Gully's houses were all empty and dark. . . . They posted sentries at the ledge. The moon had risen then, and the lance-heads shone in its light.

* * *

The second relief of scouts had found nearly three-hundred Cree camped along the Hollow, where Butternut Creek came down from the hills and out into the snowfields and stands of birch. The second relief had found them; the third's left-hand had confirmed they were settled for the night. All these tribesmen were warriors. No women, no children were with them.

The Trappers raced toward the hills, a long cold run, and now by moonlight. The sled runners hissed over a glittering sand of snow as they ran.

Michael Auerbach was waiting where the birches began. His parka was stiff and black with blood. He waved the sleds down to slow sliding, the trappers to an easy trot, and led them away through the trees. Past bare birches—and north, distant between Mount Alvin and Mount Geary—the Trappers could see the Wall shining, sparkling in moonlight, a great band of jewelry let down from heaven to mark the limit of the Range.

Sam Monroe had gotten off his sled to trot with the others, limping badly, but keeping up. Catania stayed beside him, and took his arm when he stumbled.

The Trappers filtered through the trees, and the moon threw their black shadows before them, shuttling and shifting as they came on.

At the edge of the Hollow, a Cree guard—who had been sitting against an icy birch—stood up stiffly and wrapped his marten robe closer around him. It was a robe of thirty-six skins, beautifully tanned and sewn. The tribesman, a young blue-eyed white-blood, not much more than a boy, yawned and stood leaning on the tree. Two fires still glowed along the creek bed. The others were dark, men asleep around their ashes.

There was a sudden sharp whacking sound as a long arrow hit the young man's head, went through and nailed it to the birch's trunk. He sagged, fastened and dying.

Now, the frozen woods around him were alive with running men and women. A tall girl paused to lance the boy as she went by, and the Trappers rushed out and struck the Cree camp.

There were almost three-hundred warriors there, wrapped sleeping in their furs. They slept—since they were not blessed and costumed for battle—only as men and not as spirit animals of their clans.

The tribesmen were all awake before the Trappers reached them, but 'awake' is not up and out of the robes and ready for battle. Forty or fifty men lying near the woods were lanced before they could fight.

Then the bitter air was full of arrows. The light, owl-feathered Indian shafts flicked almost silent. The Trapper longbows sent their arrows humming.

The Trappers had come in three columns—one straight into the camp, one up along the creek bed, and one through the woods to the tribesmen's flank. Caught between, the Crees were slowly driven together, so they fought at last crowded in a bunch. Their numbers made a massed target of moonlit men cursing, shouting challenges, and singing their death songs as the blizzard of Trapper arrows—each bound to strike a man—came whistling in.

Even then, so many and so brave, the tribesmen might have done better, but those men lost tangled in their furs at the fight's beginning could not be made up, and their names, called out as the Cree fell, did not bring them by magic back to battle.

Still, it was savage fighting. The Trapper columns had charged in deep, and some were too close for bow and arrow. Here and there, they and the tribesmen came together with knives, lances, and hatchets.—The frightened died when they flinched or tried to turn away. The brave stabbed and slashed through their enemies to turn and charge again.

Sam stayed out of it, afraid he would stumble, and some Trapper die to save him. He limped here and there, and shot the Crees he could mark for certain in such swift shouting confusion. He saw Catania fighting with her knife, saw tall Joan Richardson, her red hair floating black in moonlight, kill a man with her lance. That man died in dumb-show, his cry lost in the shouts and screams of others . . . dull sounds of savage blows, and the bright chime of steel on steel.

A little later Sam saw his brother for a moment in the sudden moon-shadows of the battle. Jack was wading through the fighting as if it were a winter storm, and no tribesman stood long against him.

. . . In this last of the battle, Ned Richardson was killed, and Alice, too, as she stood over his body. Toby Edwards, Gale Sorbane, Ted Monroe, and many others died.

Sam heard the Cree singing their death songs together. Beautiful singing, though they still fought hard. A war leader stood in front of them, shouting in book-English for one of the Trappers to come against him. He was a tough-looking old man—a true red-blood—wearing a bear-claw necklace, with a broken feather in his hair.

Some of the Trappers, angry at the friends they'd lost, drew their bows to shoot him down, but Torrey Monroe waved them back. He took a running jump at the old man, struggled in a glitter of knives . . . tripped him, then stabbed him to death. When they saw that, the Crees rushed at Torrey, and the Trappers had to shoot fast to save him. Jack Monroe and Tattooed Newton ran in then, and together killed two more tribesmen, one after the other.

Torrey walked from the fight laughing as if he was drunk. The little finger of his left hand had been cut off, but he seemed not to mind it.

The few Cree left threw down their weapons, and refused more hopeless fighting. It seemed they thought it undignified. They stood staring at the Trappers with contempt, and turned to slap their buttocks at them, laughing among themselves.

Each stood still then to keep his honor, and sang his song until his throat was cut.

. . . After the battle, some of the Trappers were sick, and walked into the woods to vomit. Catania went to work on the wounded men and women, binding and bandaging, giving them trade-drugs, flower-juice drugs of various sorts, and water and honey—except for people wounded in the belly. Those, if their guts were torn, she rolled gently onto their sides, prayed for them, then thrust a mercy-needle up into the base of their brains.

Trappers walking among the tribesmen dead didn't approve when Tattooed Newton butchered one of the Crees, and cut a piece of celebration meat. Though, after a moment, he threw the meat down and walked away.

The Trappers let it pass, but it seemed to them that Newton had picked up bad habits, where he came from.

Big fight. Forty-three men and nine women killed. Twenty-seven seriously injured.

We won.

Lost Ned and Alice. Morgan Weber and Phil Weber. Three Sorbane brothers. . . . Tom Monroe, and many others. The Auerbachs and Richardsons have lost the most.

Brady Auerbach has a compound spiral fracture of the right femur. I don't know what to do with it.

FROM THE JOURNAL OF DOCTOR CATANIA OLSEN

5

The dawn came soon after the fighting was over, as if it had been frightened to come before.

By its light, the Trappers saw the Hollow—smelling like a privy—was puddled with freezing blood. They counted the Cree dead, so many scattered, so many more in heaps where they'd stood together at the last. And the Trappers saw their own. Fifty-two dead in the fighting; eight more given peace by Catania, or sure soon to die.

Sixty dead; another nineteen badly injured.

That left one-hundred and fourteen fit to fight.

Sam was sitting on a dead tribesman, resting his leg while he and Jack talked, their breath smoking in frosty morning light. . . . Torrey Monroe joined them; he looked sick. Catania had put a fire-heated Cree knife blade to the stub of his lost little finger, and the pain—the first he'd felt since the fight began—had been surprising. "Well," he said, "—what do you think?"

"I think we lost too many," Jack said. "And we'll lose too many more, fighting this way."

Jim Olsen came over. He had dried blood down the right side of his head, where one of the Cree had hit him with a hatchet. "And what other way is there, Monroe?"

"To hunt them," Jack said. "—Not fight battles with them." His parka's sleeves were sliced, his forearms cut where knives had reached him.

"But we have women and children," Sam said. "We have homes. We're not free to scatter and hunt these tribesmen, wear them down in a year or two—"

"Might not work, anyway," Jack said. "There are a lot of them."

"Less than there were," Jim Olsen said. "Good many less."

"Less of us, too." The stub of Torrey's finger hurt as if the hot steel was still smoking against it. He was sure it hadn't hurt at all until Catania did that. *Doctors.*

Jim Olsen gave Jack a hard look. "You've brought us wonderful luck," he said, turned and walked away.

The Trappers put their wounded in the sleds, then prayed for their dead and raised them into the birches, tying them to branches there. It was not what should be done, not visiting time on High Hill, but it was the best for now.

Bobby and Dummy Olsen sat by a fresh-made fire, fixing recovered arrows that had been damaged striking bone. They straightened the long shafts across their knees, rolling and bending them . . . then dampened the bloody fletching with snow and spit, combing out the flight feathers with their fingers. They checked that each broadhead or pile-point was still firmly set, and put each restored arrow in a bundle with its fellows: Richardsons fletching edged blue; Olsen-Monroes, yellow; Weber-Edwards, green; Sorbanes, red; and Auerbachs, black.

Nathan Sorbane and Don Richardson walked over to Sam, Jim Olsen following them, and Don said, "We think it's important to keep after them, but there are men worried about leaving their families too long." Don Richardson was a hard man, but now he had no brother, and tears had frozen on his cheeks.

"Then let's swing back home," Sam said. "But swing wide, north to Hot Spring, so we can strike them if we find them on the way."

"That would make sense," Jack said. His hands were black with freezing blood, his and other men's. "—Make sense if we knew how many there are. But together, we can hold Long Ledge no matter what, so I say get home right now, do our patrolling from there."

"Who said you have a say?" Jim Olsen said.

"That's enough." Sam got off his dead tribesman and stood with a grunt of pain. "We can send a strong scout to the Ridge to check the east country. If they see trouble they can't handle, they can run south to us, cut our trail at the Spring. . . . At least we'll have a better idea what we're up against."

"All right," Don Richardson said. "But the doctor wants the wounded sent home—wants to go with them."

"Send them home," Nathan Sorbane said. "But keep Catania. If we fight again, we'll need her."

"Sam," Jack said, "—listen to me. We should get back to the Ledge *now*. Don't waste time circling up to the Spring."

"Why don't you go back with the wounded, Monroe?" Nathan Sorbane was pale as paper. Since the fight, he'd had a bad pain in his chest, where a Cree must have struck him. "We don't need you."

"Nathan," Don Richardson said. "Michael Auerbach's dead."

"I didn't know that. I thought he was—I thought I just saw him."

"He's dead—arrow through his throat. So you'll have to take the scout out to the Ridge. Strong scout, thirty or forty people. You can catch up to us past the Spring, the long way home."

When this scouting party was called for, many Trappers were too tired from fighting, or had had enough fighting for a while. Others, who were stronger or still angry, gathered to go north to the glacier ridge with Nathan Sorbane.

Jack, Tattooed Newton, and Torrey Monroe came—and Lucy Edwards, Newton's wife. Jim Olsen also, with Tom, Chapman, Bobby, and Dummy. There were several Auerbachs, Joan Richardson, and her boy, Del.—Catania came also, complaining about leaving the wounded.

Almost thirty other men and women gathered with them by the sleds. They were all weary, some had been hurt, but it seemed to them there was no resting yet.

Torrey's sore finger-stub gave him trouble harnessing his team. Three-balls had found a dead Cree's arm, wanted to take it with him, and had to be kicked to good conduct.

While the dogs were being harnessed, Nathan Sorbane walked the line to be certain none were too tired to haul, and no Trapper too badly hurt to run. . . . Then he went back to the lead, and whistled them out. The Hollow's snow, streaked and crusted with frozen blood, stuck and peeled where the sled runners passed, as the strong scout of eight sleds slid away in morning light.

Sam stood leaning on his bow-stave and watched the sleds track north. . . . Jack didn't look back.

* * *

Just after noon, Nathan slowed them in fields bordering a stand of hemlock. He was an older man, and though very strong, couldn't catch his breath for the pain in his chest. The Trappers and their teams were all weary, the dogs drooling through silencing muzzles as they hauled along.

Nathan called a halt, and the Trappers stood in bright sunlight blazing off the snow, while Jack Monroe and Chapman Olsen worked out to the left and right for any trail or trace.

The others stood watching them, resting from so long a run from dawn to the fat of the day. They had found no sign of the Cree. A wolf-pack—the lead bitch, a big male, and two bachelors—had followed the sleds for a while, trotting two bow-shots back in bright sunshine, then had veered away into evergreens.

Jack, searching far out on the field, paused to look again, then started back. But Chapman, down at the wood's edge, was kneeling, and did not get up.

When they reached him, the Trappers saw he knelt in a confusion of sled ruts and moccasin tracks. Hundreds of snow-marks led along the forest, going east.

Nathan pulled off a mitten, bent, and picked up a dog turd. "Frozen." He washed his hand in snow.

Jack came over to them, paced through the trackway. "Two . . . three hundred," he said. "Anyone see a man's moccasins here?"

Chapman Olsen shook his head. "No men."

"Then we have their women and children," Joan Richardson said. "We can run them down."

Torrey looked at the tracks. "Kill them?"

"What else?" Joan said, and plucked her bow-string so it sang.

"Question is," Jack looked back to the west, "—where are the rest of their fighting men?"

"Running out." Harold Auerbach was seventeen. "Running out, if there's any left."

"Running up our asses is more like it," Jack said. "I've known other tribesmen to do this. They send their woman and kids in a big circle, away from the fighting. They go, turn in a few days, and swing back."

"These won't be coming back," Joan Richardson said. "Let their men fuck trees from now on, to get babies."

Chapman, who was tall and thin, drew up one leg and leaned on his lance to rest. "Didn't these women care we might search them out—and no warriors with them?"

"I'd say those men in the Hollow were their back-trail guard," Jack said. "If they were still alive, they'd be coming up behind us now."

"I doubt that," Nathan Sorbane said. "Near three-hundred men to spare for a back-trail guard? I don't believe that for a minute."

"Depends how many they have, all told," Jack said. "We need to forget about these people"—He kicked at the moccasin tracks. "—And get home."

"You don't order this scout," Joan Richardson said. "Nathan, do we go after them?"

"Yes," Nathan Sorbane said.

The Trappers went on, following the trail the Cree women and children had made. The snow grew softer with sunshine, so they had to stop and strap snowshoes on. They ran, shuffling fast as they could with those, until some of the women and boys grew sick with tiredness, staggered, and dropped into the snow.

Nathan would let no one ride a sled and burden the tired dogs. When Trappers fell, others lifted them and helped them along. One of the Webers, a handsome boy named Pat, went down and was helped up. But a little farther on, he sat down in the snow again, and wouldn't get up and run.

Jack Monroe came back, knelt and spoke to him—but when the boy just sat and shook his head, Jack hit him in the face and broke his nose. Pat fell back in the snow . . . and when he got up, bloody to his chin, Jack had already gone back to running by Torrey's sled. . . . Pat, no longer handsome, blood freezing to icicles down his face, drew his knife, and ran after the sleds.

When he caught up, Jack paid no attention to the boy, didn't look at him—just kept running, running alongside Torrey's sled. . . . Then Pat sheathed his knife, ran beside Jack, and kept up all the rest of the day with blood frozen on his face.

Nathan halted them in spruces when the evening light was gone. The Cree women had camped there before them; they had made twelve fires, and left a baby's bone rattle behind.

The Trappers fed their dogs frozen caribou guts, and left them to lie in harness. Then they ate handfuls of snow with pemmican, wrapped themselves in fur robes unpacked from the sleds, and lay down in the snow to sleep.

Torrey Monroe stood first south-side guard. He drifted through the spruce, and knelt for a while to stick the stump of his little finger into the snow to cool it.

. . . At moonrise, Lucy Edwards came to relieve Torrey. And while she stood still in spruce branches—listening, watching moon-shadows—her husband, Tattooed Newton, came quietly to join her. Lucy was a slight woman. Her husband was large. They stood together, silent, in a bower of green branches.

At the deepest dark before the dawn, Jack Monroe went from sleeper to sleeper and woke them. But when he touched Nathan Sorbane, Nathan didn't wake. He had died in the night—of a mistake in his heart, Catania said, when she examined him.

The Trappers buried Nathan in snow; there was no time for tree-tying. Bobby and Dummy Olsen prayed the Fear-no-evil for him—then Jack Monroe led them out at a run, following the frozen trail the Cree women had left behind them.

Late in the morning, the tracks led them up a steep climb to the glacier's ridge. The Trappers had left the sleds back on the level to rest the dogs, though Joan Richardson argued they'd need them to chase.

"First, let's see," Jack had said. "—Let's see what we're chasing."

Joan, eager as a hunting dog, was first to the ridge crest and stood looking out over the great glacial valley, her long red hair blowing in the wind from the Wall. . . . She called no cry of chase.

Jack and Torrey came up to her.

As he looked, Torrey put his hand up to shade his eyes. "Jesus in the Mountains!"

The snowfields below them fell away to the wide ice-river, the Old Man, that ran past Mount Alvin and on to the south-east. Huge crevasses broke the glacier here and there, and the ice shone like a trade-mirror in places where summer melt had frozen.

The Cree women and children were five long bowshots below the ridge, a winding rank of buckskin brown against the brilliance of the snow. Burdened with packs, humpbacked with slung babies, their dogs—fan harnessed—hauling sled loads at an easy trot, the Cree were moving along in no great hurry. Perhaps two hundred of them—perhaps more than two hundred.

They were crossing the glacier, moving to meet a distant band coming south. Those more women and children, since no adult forked figures could be seen, but only the tiny silhouettes of robes and buckskin skirts.

There were seven to eight hundred Cree in that great band.

"We can still go down and kill some," Joan said. "We can drive them like caribou."

Tattooed Newton had come up with the others, and was standing watching the tribespeople. "But they're not caribou, and there's a good thousand all together. We're forty-odd. If we go down there, those women will be doing the killing—not us."

"This many women come down," Jim Olsen said, looking out across the valley, "—this many women, means that many men."

"We need to get home," Jack said.

Joan Richardson set her lance's butt into the snow. "We're supposed to meet our people at Hot Spring."

"*Home!*" And Jack was off, back down the ridge at a run.

Joan called out, "You are not the leader here!" But Jack was gone down the slope, and the others after him.

. . . It was a long haul past the base of Mount Alvin, some men and women staggering with fatigue, so now a few had to ride the sleds for a while behind laboring dogs, before getting off to run again.

They ran through the afternoon as if to pass their long shadows and leave them behind. Some dogs failed, had to be taken out of harness and put on the sleds. And even those Trappers who had always treated their teams harshly, standing no nonsense, now called to them like lovers, crooned their names to urge them on as the sun lowered west to nearly touch the mountain peaks.

. . . They heard the battle before they saw it.

As they raced south across the wooded slope above Long Ledge cliff, a sound like many people singing badly came through the sunset air, filtering like a wind through spruce and hemlock.

Most of them had never heard a sound like it. They and their dogs cocked their heads to listen as they ran.

But Jack and Tattooed Newton, running, glanced at each other—and Newton shouted, "Battle! . . . *Battle!*"

The Trappers whipped their dogs and ran like madmen beside bounding sleds, reaching to snatch bow-cases and extra quivers from the loads. They raced through the woods kicking clouds of snow, leaping over buried boulders and icy scree, until at last they broke from the trees, coursed along the rim of Long Ledge's granite cliff . . . and could see.

Sunset light shone richly across the snowfield beneath Long Ledge, heated the colors of hide sheds and rows of houses along the Gully far below—and warmed as well the rich and various colors of the Cree warriors' furs.

Tribesmen held the Gully and home. The Cree were costumed, pelted, and masked as their clan totems, so it seemed that huge minks, wolves, bears, and foxes ran among burning houses, while strong bands of giant wolverines guarded Eight-log Bridge. . . . In the wide white tundra meadows out across the Gully, hundreds of warriors were killing the men of the Six Families.

"Our people came home too late," Newton said. The tattooed dots on his face stood out like best-ink on best-paper. "Cree got here before them."

The scout Trappers stood high on the cliff's rim, and stared out at dying fathers and brothers and sons. Their loved ones were only distant tangled knots of gray-furred figures, standing in swirling floods of masked and costumed tribesmen.

The Cree had crimsoned their hands and animal masks for the fight, so the last of the Trapper army seemed to the watchers to be drowning in blood rapids. And the faint uneven roar of shouting was like the sound of such a summer river.

"Let's go! *Let's go!*" Del Richardson, only a boy, and other young Trappers tossed their lances and began to run along the cliff's edge toward the long forested slope down to the Gully.

"Hold them!" Jack shouted, and the older men and women lunged to grip the young ones, and wouldn't let them go. When Del fought against her, Joan Richardson struck her son with the butt of her lance, knocking him down. The other young people were tripped, wrestled, and held, so none got free to go and die.

Torrey cried out "Oh, no—oh, no!" He was staring down the sheer cliff face at the ledge that ran across it. The narrow path that led steeply from the ledge to the field and Gully below was lined with people descending. The women and children were going to join their men.

The scout Trappers leaned over the cliff's granite rim, yelling for the women to turn back. But the wind from the fields below, that had carried the sounds of battle to them, now blew their voices back into their mouths. A few of the distant figures beneath turned white faces up, but then went on along the path.

The men with wives and daughters there raved and howled in anguish, screamed out the women's names and the names of their children . . . threw rocks and pieces of ice down to get their attention. Again, some of the women looked up, and children pointed to the top of the cliff. But the women must have thought the little yelling figures, outlined in the glare of the setting sun, to be only more Cree, and turned away to file down the narrow path to Home and the field of battle.

The struggle there was almost done. Only small whirlpools in the tide of tribesmen could be seen on the meadow snows. Only disturbances here and there on wooded rises showed where men were fighting.

Below the cliff and its long ledge, Crees had seen the women coming down to fight rather than hold fortress the little while they could. . . . These bands of warriors, the totem wolverines who had been guarding Eight-log Bridge, turned and ran to meet them.

High on the cliff, Trappers wept as they watched the women reach the Gully field and file out in a long battle line. The women, some with babies on their backs, held their bows ready to draw. On each woman's left, her oldest child stood with a lance to guard her while she shot. Younger children stood to her right, holding high the quivers of arrows.

One of the women was singing a copybook song. The Trappers heard a little of it on the wind.

Then the Crees came on, more and more of them running in from the meadows and across the bridge. There was a soft booming sound, and a hiss as the first flight of the women's arrows flew.

Jack lay in the ice at the cliff edge and looked down. A few figures still wandered on the long ledge below . . . then went into the Auerbach caves.

"Ropes!" he called, and was up and running to the nearest sled, snatched the coil of leather dog-line, shook it out, whipped an end of the braided leather around his waist, and knotted it tight.

Myles Weber saw what he intended, seized a coil of line from another sled, and reached to take the end of the first rope to knot the lengths together. Chapman Olsen brought a third length and tied it on.

Catania called, "Jack—" but he was gone over the rim so fast that the Trappers had barely time to get their grips on the braided line, dig moccasin-boots into ice and snow to hold him.

There were nine men on the rope holding Jack's weight . . . paying out line. These were lucky men; they had something to do, rather than stand at the cliff's edge and watch the women and children dying far below. They were lucky men—but still, they heard.

Jack swung for yards back and forth through freezing air along the cliff's granite face. He fended off the rock with hands and feet as he struck it. The men above were lowering him fast—in a few seconds he was only seventy or eighty feet above the long ledge. His hands were bleeding from warding off the stone. The dog-line was thin and very strong; it cut into him as he went down, and twisted so he spun, swinging, striking the cliff. He saw gray rock and snowy meadows whirling in his sight with the shouts and screams of distant battle. The spinning made him sick, and he swallowed vomit as he went.

The rope paid out, and out, and dropped him to the ledge with a jolt that knocked him to his knees.

Then Jack was up, his knife in his hand in case Cree had passed the women on the path. But the long gallery was empty, cave entrances covered by hide curtains.

The battle noise was worse. Below, women were screaming like snared rabbits. Jack looked down just once, and saw at the bottom of the path a semicircle of women still standing before the cliff face, children gathered behind them. The women seemed like tiny jointed dolls drawing toy bows, thrusting with slender lances at the warriors battering against them.

Jack looked down that once—then ran along the ledge shouting, "Come out! *Come out to me!*" The rope snubbed suddenly, yanked him to a stop. The men above must have seen it; they slacked him more line so he could run farther, calling past cave mouths.

An old woman he knew looked out from an entrance. A Weber . . . what was her name? She stared at him, and he called to her. *"Where are the others?"*

She shook her head and pointed to the fields below. A tall blond woman came out to stand beside her. The woman was pregnant, her belly bulging under her buckskin shirt.

Another old woman, and Susan Monroe, walked out on the ledge. Susan looked at Jack as if she didn't know him. Her face was white as a Christmas mask, her belly swollen as the blond woman's.

Jack heard shouting, and steel on steel sounding behind him down the ledge path. A woman called out, and was silenced. The Cree were coming up.

An old man, and the blind girl, Sarah Richardson, came out of the cave and stood with the others. They held knives.

When Jack stepped toward them, the rope tugging at his waist, they backed away as if he'd come to kill them, even after he sheathed his blade. He reached out and caught Susan by the wrist. When he touched her, she seemed to know him at once, and said, "Sam's dead."

Jack picked her up, cradling her swollen belly against him, and ran back down the ledge, the braided rope whipping above him. He threw back his head, whistled a shrill hunting whistle—and the leather line snapped taut and bit into him like an animal. He was yanked up off his feet, then dropped a little.

The blond woman came awkwardly running, hugging her belly. She said nothing, but reached up to grip his shirt as the rope bit into him again and he was rising off the stone. He had Susan in the crook of his left arm, and lifted the blond woman with his right. Lifted her up and held her to him.

Someone was screaming down on the path. There was the sound of moccasins, running. The line seemed to be cutting Jack in half as it raised him . . . raised him so he swung slowly up into the air, then higher.

He felt the surges of effort through the line as the men above heaved and heaved again. The rope permitted no breathing. He couldn't fend off the cliff rocks as he swung and struck. The women were being hurt.

Something silent flicked up through the air just past Jack's head. He heard it whack against the stone higher. Then another—and a shout. The Cree were on the ledge, shooting. An arrow came up and touched his shoulder before it rang on the rock and struck a spark he saw.

There was a hissing by his head, and Jack strained his neck to look up. Small figures high above were leaning over, bending their bows, shooting down as the Cree shot up. First two and three, then a flight of Trapper arrows hummed down and passed him like sleet. They hummed . . . then hissed as they went by. Jack could see only their quickness, the disturbed air.

He no longer knew that he was rising, barely knew he held the women to him with arms hardly his. The rope was what he knew. And a blizzard of arrows—silent ones coming up, sounding ones coming down—so he and the women were in a shroud of speeding steel and feathers.

Jack looked down and saw Cree on the ledge, shooting. Saw three lying dead, bristled with arrows.

The blond woman jolted against him, and sighed. Jack saw an arrow's owl fletching risen from her back.

Susan began to slip. He felt her start to slip down, begged his left arm to hold her tighter, and prayed to Mountain Jesus to help him, which he hadn't done for many years. Men were calling. He wasn't sure from where. He looked down, and saw the blond woman's eyes were white, turned up into her head. She was dead.

He tried to let her go, but his right arm was cramped, reluctant. Slowly, slowly it straightened, so she fell away looking beautiful, turning in the air.

Jack brought that arm across to Susan, and was able to hold her tight.

When the Trappers hauled them up over the cliff edge, they had to pull them apart, wrestling to get Susan free. Jack couldn't get his breath; the rope had cut his breath out of him. Catania saw that, pushed him down in the snow and knelt shoving and pounding at his chest and belly to drive air in and out so he could catch a short breath . . . then a longer one.

The Trappers had picked Susan up and put her on a sled, wrapped in furs, when Del Richardson called *"Cree!"* and pointed down the cliff rim's wooded slope. Distant men in animal masks were coming up through the scattered hemlocks. One or two were running closer.

The Trappers jumped to the sleds, shouted their resting dogs up, and whipped the teams to a run—sliding in swift hissing circles, undecided which way to go.

"Where?" Jim Olsen called, "—Where?"

"South," Jack said, up and staggering to stand at the grips of Torrey's sled. He took a breath to call it out. *"South!"*

Big battle. We lost. All men dead but a few. All women dead but a few. All children dead. Only forty-three of us alive.

Mountain Jesus—how have we deserved this?

An arrow came after us in the strangest way, when we were running free and the Cree far behind. It flew as if to say farewell, and struck Penny Weber in the throat. . . . That laughing girl strangled as I wrestled with her on Torrey's bounding sled. I went mad with people dying, and struggled with her, trying to suck the blood from her mouth so she could gain a breath.

What doctor is a doctor, who cannot make a gift of one more breath?

Our copybooks are gone. Our Bible, and three hundred and fifty-one others, all gone except for the medical books and journal in my pack. And how can we perfectly remember the passages of our books? We will half-remember, quote almost—tell the stories, but less and less correctly as the seasons pass, so we become slowly less civilized, forget the Warm-time world, and settle to savages.

Before it is forgotten, here is a poem blessing darkness over light, that might have been written for us. I only remember it now, because I put it to harp music.

> On deathbed couch, all those who sigh
> As shadow comes, would, if wiser, cry
> "Alas" for all the blossoms so bright,
> But fated not ever to colour the night.
> For daylight won, means nightshade lost,
> And sunny blooms do darker petals cost.
> Yet every gaudy day must end, and soon
> All will shine in silver under the moon.

So play thy praises, you morning birds,
Of apricot suns and breezy apple days,
And leave to our poets' painting words,
The evening's fine dusk and cool array.
As the owl has a richer note than any lark,
So may our dying be but rising up, at dark.

This poem was called 'An Ode to Evening.' It was written by Sir Thomas Terhune, who lived from 1627 Warmtime, to a date I cannot recall . . . as I cannot recall the copiers' names. Soon, all names, all passages will be forgotten. As we will be forgotten.

FROM THE JOURNAL OF DOCTOR CATANIA OLSEN

6

They ran south with Penny Weber dead on Torrey's sled. Some tribesman, come to the fight too late, had seen them passing and tried a lofting shot.

Jack rode the back of that sled for a while, until he could take deep breaths. Then he stepped off, and soon was running at the front, leading even Torrey and Jim Olsen. He ran as if he had as much to run to, as away from.

The Trappers and their dogs fled through the night at first in clear starlight. When a late-winter storm came following from the mountains, its shrouding fine snow hardly slowed them, since it was the memory of their dead they ran from, as well as the Crees.

Behind them—when they finally staggered to rest, and rest the dogs—they could hear the Wall growling under the storm. Through the long last of the night, they heard great ice-towers falling away, so the air trembled like a beaten drum-head.

. . . In clear morning, they shook snow off a dwarf evergreen that stood alone in the prairie by a little frozen creek, then chopped it down and made a fire.

"South?" Torrey said, as if they hadn't already been going south. He was standing by the fire with his mittened hands held out to it.

No one answered him, since there was no other way to go where there would not be Cree, soon enough.

They stood by the fire, and chewed jerky as if there had been no battle, no loss. As if they were only traveling on a hunting trip, and had nothing so new or important to consider that talk was necessary.

Joan Richardson, Lucy Edwards, and Catania took Penny Weber down to the creek, stomped on the ice to crack it . . . then took off Penny's clothes, put her in the water, and washed her clean of blood and the shit that had come out when she died.

They cleaned her, and let her rest there for a while. . . . When they took Penny out, the water froze and glazed on her in the wind, and she could stand up straight in the deep snow, armored in ice. Then they brought more water up from the creek in the dogs' leather water-buckets, and poured that over the body until it shone, sheathed and glittering in the morning sunshine. So, though she would not stand her winter watch on High Hill—as Trappers always had before their families took them for burial—her eyes were open, looking north to the mountains.

Catania whispered, in Penny's ear, a message to take to the others. Then she said the Lord's Prayer aloud.

When she was finished, Jack said, "Time to go," kicked the dogs up, and ran them out at an easy trot as the Trappers fell in beside their sleds. No one else said anything—as if, it seemed to Catania, what was not spoken of, could not be.

* * *

On the Gully field at Long Ledge, the night's storm over, a hundred bonfires roared. The tribesmen were burning the Trapper dead. It was a great celebration—the sending of any revengeful spirits up to the sun to be calmed and given other hunting country.

In wolf robes and bear robes, in fox masks and masks of wolverines, the Cree danced the hopping dance that other tribes made fun of. They ate the Trappers' food—meat, onions, and potatoes—while they waited for scouts to bring their women and children back to them from the glacier.

It was no light matter to seize new country. No light matter to have to name these new everythings—mountains and creeks and springs and caves—name each thing, and be certain the names were lucky.

Seven war chiefs had gathered around the smallest fire to begin naming. This fire was a cleansing fire, and burned copybooks only. This being done not from notions of prideful ignorance, since none of the chiefs were fools, but rather to insure that the tribe dealt with what was real and present, instead of matters only recalled or imagined, however interesting, useful, or amusing they might once have been.

There was an old saying: 'Proof of the pudding'—though there was some question what a pudding had been. But 'proof of the pudding'; these copybook people had lost their lives and their home. And the Cree had taken both.

The youngest chief—Richard Much—was the fiercest chief, and he was demanding a judgment while he stirred the fire with a stick. A shaman's son, Buddy Chewapa, only one-quarter red-blood, had performed a bad act, so bad it might rot the tribe's winning. He had killed a blind girl, simply because she'd fought and cut him with a knife—and so might have ruined the sight of things-to-come for everyone.

Buddy Chewapa's father was an important shaman, though he sent no curses, so the other chiefs might have let that go.—Not Richard Much. He had once asked Buddy's father to send curses to his brother-in-law, and Buddy's father had refused. Richard Much took any refusal as spit in his face, and never forgot it.

"He must be sent." Much poked the fire up to snarling. Leaves of paper curled and crisped and sailed up into the air in the smoke. "Look at this. There's a ton of this ancient crap."

"She cut him. Maybe she was asking to be killed." Bill Chase had been an important man once, but Chief Chase was getting old.

"You saying *you'll* read the future for us, Billy? Now that this has happened? Blind girl murdered?"

"I didn't say that."

"Damn right you didn't. And nobody else is going to, either." Much bent close to stir the fire like a man teasing a tough dog, daring it to snap. "Buddy Chewapa has to get our looking-luck back. A few of those people ran—so let him go after them, and bring us their ears, and forgiveness."

The other chiefs were older men, and more reasonable. But they were tired from the fighting, had lost friends . . . and three of them were frightened of Richard Much.

* * *

At the second halt, at noon, the Trappers' dogs lay down in snow to sleep and couldn't be roused.

Men and women, still silent, wrapped themselves in furs and lay down beside their teams. Only Jack and Tattooed Newton stayed awake to back-trail a while, to be sure of no close pursuit. . . . When they returned, in late afternoon, they woke Torrey and Ben Weber to watch, then lay down to sleep—Newton with his wife, Lucy, Jack with Catania.

When Jack woke, it was night, and snowing white feathers by moonlight. He lay still, listening to Catania breathe beside him.

He'd been dreaming of the blond woman he'd let fall at Long Ledge cliff. In the dream, she fell and fell . . . but still stayed near him, just below, then slowly reached out and touched his foot. Jack lay warm in furs, the snowfall stroking his face, and wondered if he'd been right to let the woman go, even though dead. It was a question, duty to the dead. His ribs still ached from the rope.

He raised a little on his elbow, and saw the sleeping dogs and Trappers mounded by snow, white under moonlight, and still. Susan lay under snow and furs on Torrey's sled, and a man with a lance was standing beyond. . . . One of the Auerbachs, watching.

In soft late-winter snowfall, the Trappers slept as still as the dead. Some would be dreaming, Jack thought, dreaming of their wives and children, their lovers and friends. These dreamers would have the worst awakenings.

Catania murmured, and Jack threw back his furs and stood up. It was a failing snow, and wouldn't hinder them. He walked out to the Auerbach on guard.

"I'll stand for you," Jack said. "You go back and get them up. We need to be travelling."

"There's no fucking hurry now," Bailey Auerbach said. The snow was caked silver in his eyebrows and beard. "People need the sleep."

"They can sleep later," Jack said. "Go get them up, but quietly."

Bailey stood looking at him. He was yellow-haired, a big, heavy-boned man, like most Auerbachs. He was thinking whether to do what Jack told him to.

"Go on," Jack said. "Do it."

Bailey considered, then nodded and lumbered away. The snowfall was so light, now it was barely a fall. By dawn, it would be clear and colder for fast traveling. Fast traveling for them . . . fast traveling for others.

Though told to be quiet, some Trappers woke weeping, calling out. A girl sobbed as she remembered. Many wandered the camp like children, clutching fur robes, seeking comfort.

A man named George Edwards sat with his head in his hands, and wouldn't stand up. His wife and three children had been killed at Long Ledge. Although Torrey Monroe and others grew impatient with him, since everyone had lost those they loved, George paid no attention.

"Put him on a sled," Tattooed Newton said, and other Edwards picked George up as if he was wounded, and put him on Ben Richardson's sled.

When Jack came back to the camp, he said, "We move," and most of those who had the strength to argue with him, chose not to.

But Catania argued. She ran up beside Jack as he led out Torrey's yawning dogs. "Why push them so? They're very tired."

Jack turned and gave her a look she'd never seen from him, impatient, and cold. She thought at first he wouldn't answer, but he did. "For two reasons. To sweat out sadness—and to stay ahead of the Crees."

Catania considered the medicine of sweat, and saw its value. "I see. But the tribesmen aren't coming after us."

"Maybe not, unless a thinking-ahead chief finds a reason to send after us, kill us all."

"But why?" Catania saw that Jack's ribs still troubled him. He was not running as smoothly; there was the slightest hitch to his stride.

Jack clicked his tongue at Three-balls, who kept turning in harness to bite a slacking bitch behind him. "Why? So his grandchildren can sleep at Long Ledge, and not dream our grandchildren are coming back." Running, he reached down and took Three-balls by the scruff of his neck. "Don't you turn again," Jack said. "—You understand?"

Three-balls looked grim, but kept hauling and didn't turn again.

Catania asked no more questions. She kept up with Jack for awhile, helping break trail for the runners behind them, then dropped back to be with Susan. Susan, riding Torrey's sled, had said nothing to anyone since Jack had brought her up the cliff. And said nothing when Catania trotted alongside, worried about the baby, only a few weeks to due.

They ran the night out—moving swiftly, but stumbling often, they were so weary. They ran the night out, and into the day, farther south than even hunting scouts had traveled. There was game; they saw elk herding into a shallow draw off to the east. A herd worth following, if they'd had the wish and days to do it—and a home to bring the meat to.

But they hunted no elk, chased no foxes for the fun of it, had no traps to set along the rare creek beds. The dogs hauled, and the Trappers ran stiff as celebration stilters . . . until they had to walk awhile before they ran again. The snow prairie lay almost flat as far as they could see, and empty now but for the shadows of hawks' wings once, as two swung over.

At evening, they cold-camped again, ate crust-ice and the last of their battle jerky, and sat silent on fur robes in the snow. George Edwards had ridden Ben Richardson's sled all day, and hadn't answered his sister, Lucy, when she'd gone to speak to him. But now, as night came on, he got up from the sled and went to Ben Richardson and apologized for adding load when Ben's team had been so tired. Then George took his lance and went out on watch.

Jack woke them before dawn—and then some men and women said no to going, wanting rest and rest for their dogs. They argued, but Jack didn't answer them. He went and whistled out Torrey's team, then ran away beside the dogs and never looked back.

"Mountain Jesus damn that son-of-a-bitch," Jim Olsen said, and was slow to roll his furs and follow—as many others were slow to follow, but followed just the same.

The day after, with many wearied to sickness, they saw the line of forest green stretching across the horizon.

I have no medicine for sorrow.

FROM THE JOURNAL OF DOCTOR CATANIA OLSEN

7

Buddy Chewapa's arms hurt, and hurt worse the harder he gripped the handles at the back of his father's sled. The prairie snow was smooth going. Fast going. And cut arms were a small thing when such good luck had followed bad luck.

One quarter red-blood, and born into the brown-bear clan— Buddy had cut his arms like a woman to express his surprise to everyone, his shock at such an occurrence, in no way his fault. The girl on the ledge had seemed to see him. She had struck at him with the long double-edged knife all the snow-devils carried. He had ducked away, and when she struck again, had killed her with his hatchet.

It was true he'd noticed she moved oddly the second strike— stabbed where he wasn't. He'd noticed that, but his right arm and hatchet hadn't understood it in time.

But after he killed her, he knew. And Paul and Edwin-Jim had seen it. They'd stood staring at him with their hands over their mouths, while others along the ledge were shooting up at the rising devil. "Uh-oh. . . ." That was all Paul Kisses-the-Girls had to say. "Uh-ohhh. . . ."

"She wasn't blind!" At once, Buddy knew it was the worst thing he could have said. How many times had his father told him? "Nothing is true and complete, until it is spoken of."

Then he'd cut his arms and sung about his bad luck, and also mentioned the Windigo as having come to cause it. But none of that helped, and he expected the chiefs would blind him as justice for bringing down such bad fortune.

Who would have supposed that such an error, such lousy luck, would have turned out so well by the chiefs' kindness—and left him a war-leader of more than fifty men following to finish the last snow-devils? The youngest war-leader since Sam Shevlin.

So, running behind his father's sled—"Take it," his father had said, "and live to bring it back."—running with seven sleds and fifty-two men, it seemed to Buddy that sore arms were a small price to pay.

* * *

The Trappers halted just short of the treeline, reluctant to leave the prairie's spacious light for such greenwood, dark even in the day.

It was no sole stand of trees. There was no end to this forest visible east or west. The crowded ranks of fir and hemlock seemed, with only the slightest dips or rises, to roll on south forever.

"If we go in there," Bailey Auerbach said, "—we'll never come out."

No one else said that was so. But no one said it wasn't.

Tattooed Newton went up to Torrey's sled. "How's the finger?"

"Probably doing poorly without me," Torrey said. "What do you think of these woods?"

"Sooner we're in, sooner we're out."

"If there is an out," Torrey said. "And I've got some hungry dogs, here."

Joan Richardson heard him, and came over. "We all have hungry dogs. We should be hunting now, not still running away from nobody."

Jack had been standing looking at the forest. He walked back to them, and said, "We need to be getting on."

"What about going east for a while," Newton said, "—travel alongside those trees, but stay in the open?"

"No." Jack didn't appear to intend to say more, but the three of them stood looking at him, unsatisfied. "We need to go in now and learn its ways, not be driven in and scattered if some Cree have come after us."

"Come after us?" Torrey looked angry at Jack for saying such a thing. "They won! They killed all our people! What makes you think they'd bother coming after us?"

"Because I would," Jack said, and walked away toward the forest line.

"I'd like to know," Torrey said, "—who made Monroe lead dog out here. I sure as shit didn't mark a vote for him."

"No," Newton said, "—but I say okay," using that handy Warm-time word. "I say follow along. He makes good sense."

"Speak for yourself," Joan said to him. "You don't speak for me."

Newton smiled at her.—Likely, Torrey thought, the only smile from any of them for some time. But Newton had often smiled, or laughed, since he'd come to the Range. Seemed to be easily amused.

. . . Jack walked into the forest as if it were a wind-storm, bending into the foliage, using his bow-stave to ward off the thick, damp-needled branches. His buckskins were soon soaked, then freezing. Many of the trees—firs—were the biggest he'd seen; four men couldn't have circled the trunks with their arms. Some of the trees were even bigger than that, and more than a bow-shot tall. Where those trees stood, the forest opened into aisles.

Still, there was no seeing any distance in these woods. *Fighting here . . . who stays silent longest, wins.* It was a thought so sad—more fighting, more Trappers dead—that it stopped Jack's walking, and he stood for a while as if sick. It seemed to him that coming from war, he'd brought war with him back to the Range.

He heard the Trappers following, managing their teams and long sleds over pine-needled snow between the tree-trunks. The going was just good enough for sleds lightly loaded with extra arrow-quivers, furs, and possibles-sacks. Only Susan Monroe was riding.

Jack heard the dogs panting as the teams moved past him. Dogs and Trappers equally weary, and hungry.

He let them all go by, watching to see they were together and no one left wandering behind—then trotted back the way they'd come. Back through the trees to more trees, and through those . . . and through more, until almost by surprise he was out of the

forest and into the open again, where the sun, sinking to afternoon, shone gold on white along the prairie's snow.

Jack stood and watched for a while, seeing nothing to the north
but distance. He saw nothing in the true world, but saw clearly
in his mind a swift black line of men and dogs sliding south over
the snow. He saw them so clearly he could almost count them,
almost find their faces where they'd thrown parka hoods back in
the warmth of hard traveling.

So sharp was this imagining that he took off a fur mitten, bent,
and put the palm of his bare hand on the crusted surface of the
snow, to feel the faint vibration of men coming on.

The ice was still against his hand, but in his mind the men
drew nearer.

Jack watched a while longer, then turned and trotted back into
the forest, following runner tracks and paw prints as he went.

It was still light, but darkening when he caught up to the Trappers quietly as he could—and was satisfied when Jennifer Weber's
lance point came from a tree's shadow to meet him. She tilted
the lance's blade away, and looked a question.

"No one yet," Jack said, went on to stop at Ben Richardson's
sled to see how Susan did . . . then trotted ahead to travel with
Newton at the lead. Susan had looked up at him, but said nothing.

They traveled through the evening, and then until dark, when
men's and women's faces were pale patches moving amid the
trees, the teams' gray fur like a creek barely seen, slowly flowing
through the forest.

At a clearing roofed high by great trees' foliage, Newton said,
"Good a place as any." Jack agreed, and didn't argue against fires.
They needed fires to take the place of food, for warming.

Kicking through the dark, they found fallen branches and broke
them, stripped old bark for punk, and scraped three fire pits into
pine-needled snow. They sparked with flint and steel, and huddled
round with their dogs—gaunt men and women looking into the
flames as if they might see there all that had been lost.

They made the fires, but never replenished them . . . and when the fires died, the Trappers slept. They slept as still as the dead, with the great pillars of trees, black in filtering moonlight, standing close around them like huge sentinels of a silent army.

* * *

In the morning, Lucy Edwards found her brother, George, lying dead in his furs beside the Weber sled. He had lain on his long knife so the blade slid into his heart.

Tired Trappers came and spit on him, and only Catania and Dummy Olsen would touch the body to drag it to a tree and hang it up by the neck. Then the Trappers broke camp, and left the sinner swinging.

. . . They ran on south. It was hard traveling for people used to open country. Deeper and deeper into the greenwood, wrestling the long sleds, kicking snarling, starving dogs around and past endless great tree-trunks, and through thick damp strands and twining hedges of holly, greenbrier, green lace, and hemlock. The snow lay thin on the ground, but the air was cache-cold, heavy, and wet. Their furs grew soaked, dripped, and weighed them down.

The afternoon of the next day, faint sunlight sifting through the trees, Joan Richardson and her son, Del, were scouting forward, seeking the easiest way and looking for small forest birds to bring down with blunted arrows. Joan had just struggled around the trunk of a giant fir, shoving a smaller evergreen's foliage aside, when she heard a sudden loud rattling snort.—Standing a few feet away in a narrow clearing, staring at her, was a huge wild bull, shaggy, and spotted black and white. It was the biggest animal she'd ever seen.

The bull lowered its massive head, snorted again, and hooked its black horns to the left. They were each long as a man's arm, and curved sharply to the tip. The beast's round dark eyes were on her, and green slime swung from its muzzle.

Joan had never seen anything like it; it was large as two white bears together. It looked too big to kill with anything.

She heard Del coming up behind her, stopped him with a hiss—and that was all it took, just that little sound. The great bull pawed the snow once, and charged.

Joan Richardson was a fierce woman, so Del was startled to see his mother come running back around the giant tree-trunk quick as a frightened squirrel. He thought it might be Cree—then the bull came grunting past him at a gallop, brushed him with its shoulder, and knocked him away into the greenery.

As he struggled up, he saw the huge animal lunge out of sight around the great tree—and his mother come flying out the other side, still holding her lance and running like a deer.

The bull circled after her, bawling with rage, hooking a sheet of bark from the fir as it came. Del felt the ground shaking under his feet when he stood to drive his lance into the animal's belly as it charged past him. The bright steel struck into a moving wall of spotted black and white, and the lance was wrenched out of Del's hands, spraining his right wrist badly.

Joan ducked around the tree-trunk again, and the bull hesitated, bawling. Del reached over his shoulder to pull his bow free, but his wrist hurt so much he dropped it. He drew his knife with his left hand, and waited for the bull to charge.

His mother, running from around the tree, saw him standing there with only his knife. She screamed "Del!" whipped her lance level, ran at the roaring bull's shifting haunches, and struck with all her strength.

* * *

Ben Weber, and Bobby and Dummy Olsen, were breaking trail—kicking their way through, bending green branches down and stomping to snap them—when Dummy touched Bobby on the shoulder and stood with his head tilted, cupping his left ear, listening. They were all quiet for a moment. Then, as Ben opened his mouth to say something, they heard distant shouting—a woman—and a terrible roar, like a tiger's, but deeper.

Ben was gray-haired, but a quick thinker. He jerked his thumb in the direction of the noise—and took off running the other way, back to get help. Bobby Olsen unslung his lance and ran toward the roaring, and Dummy drew his knife and ran after him.

When Bobby burst through the brush, he saw the great bull whirling round and round in a little clearing of trampled greenery. He thought at first the animal must be trampling Joan and Del to death—then he saw Joan standing white-faced in among hemlock branches across the clearing. She was shooting arrows into the bull as it spun, roaring, then dashed back and forth in short, furious charges. When it turned toward her, Joan faded back into the hemlock boughs. When it turned away, she came out and shot it again.

Bobby saw Del come running out from the left, yelling to make the bull turn from his mother.

Bobby knew what the bull was. A salt salesman named Mayhew had shown him a copybook of animals, drawn down south. This animal was a wild-cattle bull, but big. Too big to try with a lance, though he saw the Richardsons had done that. There was a length of lance shaft sticking out of the thing's haunch.

Bobby stepped back a little and took the bow from his shoulder. He pulled a shaft from his quiver, nocked and drew it to his ear, and shot the bull through the throat. It bawled, heaved sidways toward him, and charged, staring with great bulging eyes, hooking and tossing its head.

Del ran up beside the bull and struck it in the flank with his knife. The animal bucked and turned aside, and as it looked over its shoulder, Bobby shot it in the throat again. It shook its head, spraying a mist of blood. Joan's bow thumped across the clearing—and the bull suddenly kicked, slipped, and fell to its knees with a thud, goring and butting at the snow. Bobby shot it behind the ear. The animal groaned and toppled over on its side, kicking and pissing . . . and died.

* * *

That night, for the first time since Long Ledge, a few of the Trappers laughed—and most of the others were able to sit back against the sleds, talking and resting at ease as they watched the huge sides of beef roasting over thick fir branches in clouds of sparks.

The dogs, fed on guts and innards, lay growling and gulping under the trees.

None of the Trappers had ever tasted beef. It was copybook meat—and Lucy Edwards and Louise Sorbane were doing their best, cooking it. They'd hung the meat high on thick whittled stakes, away from the sputtering fir sap, and caught the running fat in wooden stew-bowls to pour down the roasting meat again. They complained of the firewood, but there was only evergreen to be had.

When Lucy finally called the meat done, the Trappers came crowding. There'd been nothing to eat since the fighting but the last of the jerky, some little woods birds, and one rabbit boiled with spruce needles in a soup. . . . They hesitated on getting their shares—such thick slabs sizzling, smoking on wide wood-chunk platters, seemed too much, too lucky. They tasted, then began to eat like wolves, a few weeping at the pleasure of it.

The beef-steaks and ribs were the sweetest game, aside from deep-winter partridge, any of them had eaten—except for Tattooed Newton, who had eaten beef, and other meats, before.

Jack and Catania sat with Susan by Torrey's sled, stripping hot fat from beef-ribs with their fingers, then licking their fingers clean. Susan ate, but didn't talk.

"Oh, my," Catania said. "Sam would have loved this so. . . ."

Susan stopped eating, and bowed her head.

"—Beef. It would have been such a pleasure for him."

Jack looked at Catania. "Talk about something else," he said.

Catania smiled at Susan. "Sam always loved camp meat—even better than your good cooking, sweetheart."

Susan threw down her beef-rib, and started to cry. She hugged herself and rocked back and forth, weeping and gasping for breath.

Jack leaned over and hit Catania in the face with his open hand.

Then he stood up and walked away. People who'd been watching, turned aside and ate their food.

The blow had knocked Catania over, and she sat up and wiped her nose—it was bleeding. She'd held on to her piece of meat, and began to pick the snow and pine needles off it. Susan still wept beside her, and Catania whispered in her ear, "Now, little sweetheart; isn't that better? Isn't it nice to cry? Oh, poor Sam. We all miss him so. . . . But you don't want his baby to be sour, do you, all sad and full of sorrow?"

She picked up Susan's beef-rib, cleaned it, and handed it to her. "Now, blow your nose and chew this good meat as Sam would have had you chew it. Swallow this good meat as he would have had you swallow it for your baby's strength—and don't insult your husband's memory anymore."

That night, Catania was asleep when Jack came in from back-trailing and lay down beside her. He turned her to him, and kissed her face where he'd hit her. He'd hit where she wasn't scarred. "How stupid I was," Jack said, "—to interfere with your doctor business. Forgive me." And held her until she slept again.

* * *

The trappers went south five days more, eating fire-dried beef. The forever forest made them nervous. The trees stood too close, allowed no brightness and distant seeing, and their green perfume grew heavy to breathe.

"These damn woods go on too long!" Chapman Olsen was back-scouting with Tattooed Newton.

"Keep your voice down, Chappie."

"All right. But what do you think?"

Newton looked at him with a show-nothing face. "I like it."

That morning, Bailey Auerbach and Ellis Sorbane found a spring—and not too soon, the water-skins had been flat for a day and night. The spring was small, a narrow puddle beneath the trees; it took a long time to fill the skins.

Soon, the snow became shallow and spotty, mixed with ever-green twigs and needles. The dogs hated hauling over it, the sleds always sliding off line. South, as it slowly grew warmer, the sleds would have to be re-built to travvies, and some of their load—furs, arrows, possibles, leather buckets, trade-pots, bowls, and camp kettles—back-packed for carrying.

Vines grew here and there, twisting up different trees—leaf los-ers like birches, and a tree whose foliage looked torn and eaten. . . . It was sometimes almost warm as three-week summer on the Range.

The evening of the sixth day, they finished the last of the dried beef, drank spring water—dark, and tasting of tree bark and leaf-mold—and some women began to sing at the fires. This was the first singing since Long Ledge.

Though it seemed to Jack the singing was necessary, he sent two Auerbachs, Bailey and Philip, to add to the night guard. Then he went out again himself, for a while. It was one of the reasons people did what he said—his doing more than he told others to do. That . . . and some were afraid of him.

The singing evening became the best since the roasted bull. Even those Trappers still silent, smiled occasionally. . . . Belle Ol-sen, Louise Sorbane, and Sally Auerbach sang together, and Ca-tania made harp sounds to accompany them. The women sang 'Trick or Treat,' which had clapping in it, and 'Pokey Style,' and 'Smoke Gets in Your Eyes,' which was true enough at the green-wood fires, and made people laugh.

Then the women called for a man's song, and Lucy Edwards made her husband get up. People clapped and called "Sing . . . sing!" and waited to see what Newton's song would be, since he'd been a stranger from somewhere else.

Tattooed Newton stood up in yellow firelight, big and bulky, his dark hair cut short. He stood still, didn't shift restlessly as Trappers often did when considering this or that.

Then he cleared his throat, and began to sing a song about teeth. The words made little sense, but the tune was pretty and full of notes that ran up and down like birdsong. While he sang,

Newton danced, shuffling backward, then forward. He drew his knife and juggled with it, flipping it spinning in the air over his head, then danced under to catch it by the handle without looking.

It was nice, and different from Trapper dancing. Trappers usually leaped around to harps and drumbeats, swung each other in circles, jumped fires, and did somersaults. This was a neater kind of dancing.

When he finished, everyone clapped—and Newton sang another song and danced while he sang it. This was a song with the words *Choo-choo* in it, and the dance was a strange leaning dance. He would lean one way, doing little steps, then lean the other way, and make puffing sounds. . . . After a while, he sang faster and louder, his eyes tight shut. He sang "Chatta-choo-choo. . . ." even when the women stopped humming with him, and Catania stopped clicking sticks to his rhythm. He sang as if he were dreaming, and it began to make people nervous.

Lucy went over to him, and put her hand on his shoulder. Newton stopped singing right away, opened his eyes and looked down at her—a bad look, as if he didn't know her. Then he smiled, shook his head, went with her and sat down.

Dummy got up after that, and danced his animal dances. No one else did those, except children. The children used to do those dances. . . .

The Trappers could call out the name of any animal, and Dummy would dance it perfectly. Nodding around a fire on all fours, his hands and feet turned in, his butt wagging from side to side, he was more a bear than a bear was. And when he danced an owl, goggling, swiveling his head, and preening under his arms, he was every owl they'd seen, perched right there. . . . Dummy was wonderful at that, and at singing fucking songs. When he sang one of those, everyone laughed so loud that Jack came back to camp to see what was happening.

It was a good evening. And for the first time since they'd left the Range, the Trappers asked Catania for the "Now-I-lay-me-down," and she prayed it after the fires were out.

We are in the dark woods.

Continuing spruce tea—good for all.

Women are coming to me with dreams. They dream of their dead fathers more frequently than others. What does that mean?

The men are ashamed of losing the war. They will need new women, new families now, or there will be trouble— in spite of my Sundays.

No one has come to me for Sunday-fucking, anyway. Their lost ones still speak to them.

The men and women, the little children who were killed, will begin in time to fade from my memory . . . as will our lost copybooks, though now I imagine each lying open before me. And I will forget the sea-ship Pequod's crew, the harpooners' wonderful names.

FROM THE JOURNAL OF DOCTOR CATANIA OLSEN

8

The next morning, Torrey Monroe found a naked girl singing in the forest.

On scout, moving more cautiously since Joan Richardson met the bull, he had just ducked under thick hemlock branches when there was a high, vibrating sound, like a note on a bone flute. Torrey stopped moving, stopped breathing, to listen.

His heart was pounding. He was startled to be so afraid, and supposed the fight with the Crees still troubled him. Taking a deep breath, he held it to listen carefully. The sound was like a child singing. Torrey took a two-handed grip on his lance, and went on through the hemlock branches.

Ahead, hanging vines twisted up into the trees, tangling into a thick blanket of greenery. He eased his lance-head through, carefully working a passage-way. Beyond, sunlight struck down through the firs into the biggest clearing he'd seen in the forest. The light glowed over a wide snow-spotted slope where a little creek ran through into curtains of vines beyond.

A girl was washing in the creek, not seeming to mind its chill water, bordered with ice. She was singing what sounded like a children's song, high-pitched and simple. Torrey couldn't understand the words.

She was naked, except for a necklace of small gold nuggets strung on loops of leather cord, and was plump as a baby. She raised water in her cupped hands, splashed it under her arms and down her breasts, then bent to scoop more water up so her buttocks rounded with the motion.

The girl's hair, gleaming light brown, was loose to her shoulders. Her skin was white as best-paper, and painted in broad stripes of green that ran across her back and belly, circled her legs in patterns the cold water did not wash away.

There was no one else in the clearing.

Torrey watched as she stepped up the creek bank, took a woven brown cloth from a tree branch, and dried her feet. She put on soft leather shoes, then stood in the snow to dry her body, singing her odd melody. The high walls of the clearing, draped with vines in thick folds and falls, made a huge vaulted room, all green and sunlit gold.

The girl dried herself—gently at her breasts and privates—and that began to give Torrey a hard . . . until such prettiness reminded him of Charlotte Edwards. Charlotte had been a loving friend to him, and he had seen her walking the ledge path to fight the Crees. Seen her among the others, and shouted down to her . . . but she hadn't heard him.

Torrey looked through the hemlock branches once more, then stepped carefully back, and left quietly the way he'd come.

. . . He found Jack Monroe heaving at a stuck sled. The dogs had pulled off-angle, wedging the sled sideways between tree-trunks. Jack listened to what Torrey had to say as they worked together.

When the sled was free, Jack turned and whistled twice—a jay's harsh call—and the Trappers, strung out along the trail, came to them quietly.

* * *

Jack, Torrey, Ben Weber, and Catania knelt together in hemlocks, and looked out through the trees' foliage and a curtain of vine into the clearing. It seeming so bright with sunlight after their days in dark woods. They'd left the other Trappers waiting back by the sleds, their bows strung, arrows nocked.

The girl still stood naked in chill air by the little creek—only she hummed her song, now, instead of singing it. Jack and the others knelt silent, watching as she stooped to pick up a carved-wood comb from a bundle of folded cloth.

The men watched the girl comb out her hair, her heavy breasts swaying with the motion of her arm. As they watched, Catania watched them, and listened to the green girl's humming.

Torrey leaned over and murmured in Jack's ear. "Well, are we going to talk to her, or go on by?"

Jack didn't turn his head. "Why is she alone?"

"Why not?" Ben Weber whispered. "What does she have to be afraid of, in all this forest shit?"

"Maybe us," Jack said.

Catania stood and went quietly back into the forest. Jack supposed she might be angry with him for watching the girl so long, a girl who seemed to be a gift for any harsh passerby.

But in a few moments, they heard Catania begin to sing at a distance among the trees. She was singing the song the girl had sung, singing the melody . . . mimicking the odd words. "*Mazy doze . . . dozy dose. . . .*"

The girl in the clearing started in surprise. She dropped her comb and cowered, hands over her mouth, staring into the greenwood where Catania sang. "*An liddel lams be ivy. . . .*"

Jack and the others saw the vine curtain shake as Catania pulled a tangle aside and walked into the clearing. She was naked, except for her moccasin-boots. She'd taken off her buckskin shirt, her breastband, and hide trousers, and left her weapons in the woods.

The painted girl stared at Catania and scuttled backward on all fours, her breasts jiggling, her mouth an "O" of fear.

Catania held up open hands. "Now, little lady," she said, "—don't be frightened."

The girl moaned, frightened perhaps by the ugly scar down Catania's cheek, the hunting scars and fresh battle scars on her body.

"Now listen to me—do you speak book-English?" Catania smiled. "I won't hurt you. I have friends with me, and they won't hurt you either. . . . Aren't you cold without your clothes on? I am."

The painted girl seemed about to scream, and stared at Catania as if she held a drawn bow.

"Oh, for the Weather's sake!" Catania kept smiling, trying to be patient. . . . Then slowly stopped smiling. She had noticed something. While the girl crouched staring at her, red round mouth open, shoulders trembling so those ridiculous breasts shook like deer-foot jelly . . . all that while, her bright brown eyes were watching Catania as calmly, as coldly as a wolverine's. Not frightened. Not frightened at all.

Then it was Catania who began to be afraid. The clearing seemed too sunny, too thick with southern air. She stood thinking what she should say to this little pretender with her fear-filled face and wolverine eyes. Bits of gold hung shining between the girl's breasts.

Catania walked over to the green girl, bent, gripped her by the arm, and hauled her to her feet. "You fat little bitch," she said, "—I'm afraid, and you're not. So what's your secret?"

Someone laughed, high over their heads. "Wise woman!" said a voice from the air.

All around the clearing, the tangled vines and foliage began to shake, the green draperies swaying in sudden folds. Catania looked up to see men coming down from the trees.

Jack and the others had gotten to their feet when Catania went to the girl, Jack holding a branch aside with his left hand, balancing his lance in his right.

When the laughing voice came from high in the trees, he'd turned and shoved Ben Weber hard. "Run! Get back to the others!"

Jack counted a hundred men—more than a hundred—sliding, scrambling down vines into the clearing, foliage falling away so woven netting showed beneath. The men were stocky, light-haired, and pale where skin showed below the sleeves and hems of short green robes of woven cloth. The hair was shaved from their faces, and they were painted with broad bands of green. Gold bracelets gleamed on their arms.

Some had axes strapped to their backs, others short, T-shaped bows—cross-bows, like Salesmen carried when they traveled.

Torrey, standing just behind, took his bow from his shoulder, but Jack said, "Stand still," then bent to lay his lance on the ground, set his bow and quiver beside it.

Out in the clearing, Catania stood naked in the midst of men, while more slid down the vines and jumped to land light as lynxes.

"*Such* a wise woman. . . ." It was the voice of the one who'd laughed.

Catania looked up. High above, a short fat woman in a green woven robe was clambering down through vine-laced branches. Catania saw her soft shoes and plump white calves under the robe as she came lower. . . . When she was still higher than Catania's head, gripping only a cord of vine, the fat woman opened her hand and fell. Four men caught her.

Catania hoped that Jack was gone, so these people couldn't find him. She hoped he was gone and safe . . . but wished he was with her, just the same.

"What's your name?—Cata? Catan?" The fat woman walked over and reached up to run her finger along the scar down Catania's cheek. She looked like the painted girl, the same pale skin and short round body, except she had only one bright brown eye—the left. Her right eyelid dimpled into an empty socket. The woman's hair was graying light-brown, and braided into one thick intricate rope that hung down her back.

She stroked the scar on Catania's cheek with soft plump hands . . . traced it again. "Name?"

"Catania." Catania stood still.

"Ah. And is that your man, the big one over there in the hemlocks?" The woman's voice was low and pleasant, but difficult to understand because she slurred her words, and said some differently.

She kept touching Catania's face until Catania put her hand up, took hold of the woman's fat wrist, and pushed it away.

"Jack?" the woman said, smiling while she rubbed her wrist where Catania had gripped it. "Isn't 'Jack' his name?"

"Yes." Catania thought these people must have been watching the Trappers for days, and come close, to know their names. She saw the men turn to look, and Jack came out of the evergreens armed only with his sheathed knife. He walked across the clearing to Catania and the one-eyed woman, paid no attention to the men.

The one-eyed woman watched Jack come, then stepped in his

way and put her palm against the buckskin at his chest. The painted men stood still and watched.

"He stands like a tree, doesn't he?" she said, and looked over her shoulder at Catania. Her eye was bright as a bird's.

"Now," she said to Jack, "—I'll tell you what to do, Hunter." She patted him. "Go back to your people and tell them to stay just where they are. We won't hurt them."

"As you say, Little Mother." Jack smiled at Catania, turned and walked away past the painted men into the woods, and was gone.

The one-eyed woman looked after him. "Not a fool," she said, and seemed displeased, though Jack had obeyed her. She beckoned to a man with many gold bracelets on his arms—he'd been standing by the creek, talking with the singing girl.

This man came to her, and the fat woman whispered in his ear. He nodded, waved four . . . five men to him, and they trotted across the clearing, the way Jack had gone.

Torrey stepped from the woods in front of them. His bow was drawn to the broadhead. "What's your hurry?" he said—a copybook phrase, and useful.

The man with gold bracelets pulled back his crossbow's string with one hand, and cocked it on a notch of steel. He was a strong man to be able to do that.

"Carlson!" The one-eyed woman called across the clearing. "No fighting!" She looked back at Catania. "You tell that Ninefingers to let them by. They won't hurt tall Jack; they just watch that your people don't go to Gardens."

"Torrey. . . . Let them go."

"In a while." Torrey held his bow bent, the arrow's fletching hard by his ear.

Some of the painted men shifted a little.

"Stand still," Torrey said, and they did. . . . Soon after, he eased his bow and lowered it. "Try to catch him now," he said.

The man wearing many gold bracelets gave Torrey a bad look, then he and his men ducked into the evergreens and were gone.

"Torrey," Catania said, "—go back to the others."

"No," the one-eyed woman said. "We'll keep foolish Nine-fingers with us." Some of her painted men went to stand by Torrey, but didn't touch him.

The naked girl picked up a folded green robe from the ground, shook it out, and wrapped herself in it. Then she came to the one-eyed woman and kissed her on the cheek. The woman took the girl in her arms, and hugged her till she grunted like a puppy.

"This is my daughter, May," the woman said to Catania. "—We wondered if you snow-hunters would harm a pretty girl bathing naked, with gold at her throat. We wondered if you were foolish."

"Not that foolish," Catania said.

When the woman smiled, her empty eye-socket opened a little, and Catania saw a winking edge of wet red. "My name is Mary," the woman said, stroking her daughter's hair. "You hunters don't hunt girls? Or care for gold?"

"We don't hunt girls, or care for gold."

"Not yet," Mary One-eye said, and laughed. "I'll tell you what, Catania Scar-face. You go and put on your clothes. Then you and the Nine-finger fool will come with me to Gardens."

* * *

Jack Monroe ran through the forest as fast as he could. He bit his lip in rage as he ran, and blood dripped into his beard. *To have watched for who might follow—and not for who might wait. A bad mistake, his mistake and no one else's.*

He stopped running for a moment, and stood without breathing, leaning on his bow-stave. He felt, as he'd felt many times before, something like a hand gripping gently at the back of his neck . . . and knew that painted men were coming behind him now, quiet as a breeze among the firs and hemlocks. *Better than I am, in the woods. Coming, but not chasing.*

Jack started running again, as fast as he could—leaping the

fallen timbers that crossed his way, running though branches whipping at his face. He felt he'd held the Trappers as he'd held the blond woman at Long Ledge cliff—and let them also fall.

As he ran, he heard a partridge drumming in the woods.

* * *

Catania and Torrey followed Mary One-eye and her daughter a long way, out of deep forest to woods where more sunlight shone on even shallower snow. No painted men walked with them, though Catania saw shadows in the trees.

The painted men had left Torrey his weapons, and brought Catania her lance, knife, bow, and quiver from the greenwood— so she and Torrey walked armed, and Mary appeared not to mind. It seemed to Catania these people didn't intend to kill them. Or if they did, not now.

They walked through the sunnier forest, then along the edge of a steep valley . . . and down a path that led to another path. Then down that, into a many-house place—that must be a town—with a wide fast creek, almost a small river, running through it.

It was the first town Catania had ever seen, and wasn't what she'd thought it would be—nothing like the drawings in copy-books, so she supposed error had crept in where copy-drawing was concerned. Here, there were no hard streets, or buildings made of baked brick or stone. This was a tree-house town of wooden staircases spiraling up great red-barks—the tallest trees she'd ever seen. The staircases climbed more than a bow-shot high, and vine bridges hung from tree to tree, swaying as green-painted people crossed them. Children in green woven cloth were running up there, shouting, playing. . . .

Torrey stared. "Mountain *Jesus* . . ." There were very small steep-roof wooden houses everywhere up in the air, houses carved elaborately as memory-sticks, and fastened to tree-trunks or out on thick high branches.

Catania grew dizzy looking up. Stove smoke drifted through the trees.

In one way, this town was like copybook towns. People moved all over it, thick as herding caribou.—There was no place Catania could look without seeing them. It was frightening to be amid such a crowd of strangers, some of whom might be bad. . . . She wondered how anyone could sleep in the midst of so many people, and supposed they must keep night watch against themselves, have guards to guard them from each other.

"Nine hundred," Torrey said. "I count at least nine hundred the herd."

And since Torrey was a chief hunter, Catania supposed he was right . . . and these, only the ones they saw.

Catania was afraid Mary One-eye would take them climbing up in the trees, but the fat woman stayed on the ground, walking steep and narrow paths where people painted in stripes stood aside to watch them pass. To Catania, all these looked alike. It was hard to see how even their families picked them out. Each person short and pale, fair-haired, with both men and women wearing robes, dark green or brown. All seemed like brothers and sisters. . . . Twice, little girls reached out to stroke Catania's furs as she passed.

Five or six men, bigger than the others, stood along the way in green robes, with gold bracelets on their arms. These carried axes, had crossbows on their backs, and bowed as Mary One-eye passed.

Catania had read of bowing, but had never seen a man do it, and found it strange. She saw, as they walked past one of these men, that his forearms were webbed with thin white scars from fighting. His pale eyes, as he looked at her, were a fighting man's—wary, observant, and cruel.

Like Jack's, she thought, and was sorry she'd thought it.

Torrey put his hands over his ears as they walked, and Catania realized the town was noisy with talking and other sounds. She'd been looking so hard, she hadn't been listening. There was talking along the path, and talking and shouting up in the trees, as if these people had never had to be quiet, and under it all was a constant rattling noise like elk bucks made, fighting in season— and from farther down the valley, a low growling that never ceased.

Catania started to cover her ears as Torrey had, but thought that might be an offense to the painted-people, so didn't do it. She wished more Trappers had come with them, and would have been happy to see even Jim Olsen scowling, leaning on his lance.

There were those noises . . . and there were smells. The town smelled of strange cooking, and too many people in a place.

As they walked a low part of the path, Torrey took his left hand from his ear and pointed up a slope. Catania looked, and saw wide sheets of light-brown cloth and brightly colored cloth hanging from high tree-branches. Under those trees were big wooden boxes with parts that moved and shook back and forth. A woman was sitting before each box, with a boy standing beside her, pushing parts of the box from side to side. . . . Catania thought those parts were called shuttles, though she couldn't re-call where she'd read it.

"What are those things?" Torrey said, and May, Mary's daughter, grinned and looked back at him.

"I think," Catania said, "that they're weaving trade-cloth. I don't remember what the machines are called that the shuttle goes through. . . . Booms."

"*Looms*," Mary's daughter said, and laughed at her.

"Thank you," Catania said, surprised such a pretty girl had not been taught manners.

Mary One-eye struck her daughter backhand across the face, a very quick blow that sounded *smack*. Mary had done it while walking, and kept walking, so Catania saw that manners were still being taught to May.

The girl followed her mother with tears in her eyes, and didn't grin or laugh anymore.

Now, they saw potato-tubs along the spotty snow on the val-ley's slope, all set out in the sunniest patches. These were like the Trappers' warming tubs, and were set over slow-coal beds.

There were sheds beside the tubs, and several little animals with horns staked out to graze. Goats, Catania thought, like the white goats on the Range, but smaller and close-coated. . . . Past the tethered goats, there were pole racks with plucked birds hanging in smoke over hardwood fires.

"Smell that smoke?" Torrey said. "That's not birch, and not alder either. . . ."

"Oak," Mary One-eye said, and led them past a group of painted people to a level place where green things grew in many long rows in starting boxes. There were more things growing than ever grew on the Range. Many painted people were tending them, putting bulbs or cuttings in big baskets caned in black-and-white crosshatching.

Catania recognized onions, but not much else. There were ranks of other things that looked like people's brains sticking out of the dirt, and round green things the same size, and feathery green fronds sticking up. The whole field was full of plants. . . . The deep growling noise was louder here.

"Garden," she said to Torrey. They were walking down a path between all the growing things. The town, Catania supposed, had been named in the garden's honor.

"That's right," he said, "—that's what it is. I see onions and I see cabbages from copybooks. But what are those brain things?"

"Cauliflowers," May said, but didn't laugh at him. "And the others are carrots."

"Cauliflowers. . . ." Catania had read of them, and was disappointed. She had supposed they were colored blossoms that were also good to eat—and had imagined Warm-time people sitting in food restaurants, telling jokes and drinking Seven-Up and eating an arrangement of flowers.

. . . Mary One-eye led them along the creek a little farther, and Catania saw four big sawed-plank houses down the valley— houses much too big to be for people—that had been built beside a wooden bridge over a steep waterfall. That was where the growling noise was coming from—the noise, and a smell like hoof-glue, but stronger.

"Aren't those what were called buildings?" she said. May didn't answer, probably afraid of laughing again at such ignorance.

"Yes," Mary One-eye said. "We make our paper there."

". . . You make paper?"

"I don't believe that," Torrey said.

May turned to Torrey, and said, "Yes. We make paper."

"But what is that noise?" Catania said, and supposed she must be a barbarian, as far as these town people were concerned.

"We have a water mill to grind the pulp," Mary One-eye said, "—and the rest is our business." She turned and walked up a steep path to the left. As they climbed, five goats came trotting down past them. A painted little girl followed, with a stick.

"I haven't seen a dog," Torrey said to Catania. "I don't think these people keep them."

At the top of the path, Mary stepped to the left at the trunk of a great red-bark, and was gone. Then her daughter ducked after her, and Catania and Torrey stood looking down into a deep hole under the roots of the tree. The hole had been carved to resemble a woman's genitals.

"I'm not going down there," Torrey said. "—And don't you go, either."

"I think we have to," Catania said. Mary's hand and arm appeared at the bottom of the hole. "*Catania*," she called, and beckoned her down.

"I'll wait up here," Torrey said.

Catania set her lance against the tree-trunk, handed Torrey her bow and quiver, then climbed down.

"Yell if there's trouble." Torrey leaned over to watch her. "Then I'll come down."

Turning sideways to slip through the entrance, Catania looked up, and saw Torrey's anxious face in a shield of sunlight.

We have come to a wonderful Garden town, and many
Garden people, painted green.

A clever woman named Mary rules them, and is deciding what to do with us.—How strange to feel myself a
child again, and at the mercy of others. Mary plays the
mother, but a mother with a knife.

I want to feel more kicking by the baby in Susan's
belly.

FROM THE JOURNAL OF DOCTOR CATANIA OLSEN

9

It was the prettiest living-place Catania had ever seen. She bent beneath a low ceiling, and stared.

The small, round room was like a fox's den, like snow caves children dug in play, or hunters dug in deep drifts when blizzards caught them in the mountains. It was burrowed under the root arches of the great red-bark, and floored and roofed with polished planks of yellow pine—laid first one way, then the other, like the pattern of a fine basket.

Mary One-eye and her daughter were sitting on cloth bags—*cushions*—to one side of a baked clay fireplace. There was a clay pipe leading from the hearth up through the tree's roots, then, Catania supposed, out into the air. A small fire snapped hot and rolling in the stove, its light glowing off many little trees and blossoms hammered out of gold and hanging from the ceiling, so there was brightness everywhere. . . . There were scatters of the thick, soft cushions, each with sewn decorations of little forest birds—shown only perched, never flying, with all their true colors accomplished in dyed thread.

"Sit," Mary said, and kicked a cushion to Catania. Two jays were sewn on it in blue. Their eyes were black beads.

Catania sat cross-legged . . . and saw the room's low walls were covered with coarse white cloth, painted along its upper edge with leaves and evergreen branches. The evergreens stayed the same, but the leaves slowly changed their colors around the room, to show the shift of seasons. There was an art-painting under the cloth's leaf border.

"This is a beautiful house."

"Thank you," Mary One-eye said, and began braiding her daughter's hair.

It struck Catania that these were pattern people—their caned baskets and rows of neat vegetables, their woven cloth, paper making . . . their way with designs of polished wood in this pretty room under a tree. They were pattern people as the Trappers were hunting people, and they were ruled by a woman who weaved what nets they needed.

The art-painting beneath the wall-cloth's border of leaves and branches told a story that circled the room.—A huge tree was shown, tilting back as if it was falling. Further along, a bright yellow woman was painted being born out of its torn-up roots. She was naked, the yellow umbilical cord still curling back from her belly into the tree. The woman was smiling.

Slowly turning her head to follow, Catania saw that a green man was being born between the yellow woman's legs. Only his foot was still tucked inside her. He was painted crying, his mouth stretched wide—and out of it a little kid goat was struggling free. The goat was red; its button horns were blue. Its slender tongue was sticking out, and a large yellow egg stood balanced on it.

Catania turned to see the yellow egg shown cracking, with a partridge's head thrusting out. The bird's beak was open, and there was a rectangle wedged into it at the circling painting's end. . . . A starved blue-gray dog was running in the rectangle.

"Do you know that painting-story?" Mary One-eye completed one casual braid, and started on the other.

"I don't know the story—but it's about changes that are only changes, never becoming a difference."

"Or becoming only a *slight* difference," Mary said.

". . . I don't know what the running dog means."

"Few do," Mary said. "Are you hungry?"

"Yes, I am—and Torrey would be, too."

"You like that sturdy Nine-fingers, don't you?" Mary said. Catania thought she was being asked that—then saw Mary was talking to her daughter. "Giving him little looks. . . ."

"I don't know him, and there's no reason for me to like him," May said. "He's just a snow-person like all the others."

"Liar," Mary said. She finished the second braid, and gave May a push. "Get up and make us some food."

"I'm not a liar," May stood up at the hearth; she didn't have to bend under the low ceiling. "—Anyway, he smells of dogs." She took a brown-skinned smoked duck down from a hanging hook, then potatoes and some sort of other vegetable, white and pale blue, out of baskets along the wall.

Mary One-eye smiled at Catania. "Isn't she going to like your foolish Nine-fingers?"

"Probably so," Catania said, and smiled back, supposing Mary was making woman-fun as a courtesy to put a stranger at ease. "—And now we've mentioned it, she won't be able to stop thinking how little she'd care for that handsome, strong young man. And how foolish you and I were, to have said such a stupid thing."

"Yes," Mary said. "And she'll visit him from time to time, to be reminded just how wrong we were."

"That isn't even funny," May said. She was slicing vegetables on a wood shelf beside the hearth.

"Then she'll dream," Mary said. "And wake wet between her legs."

"And one day," Catania said, "—she'll go to him and say, 'I don't like you, and I want you to leave me *alone*!' "

Mary One-eye laughed. "And how long, after that—the first baby?"

"Still a full year," Catania said. "If she's strong."

"A bare nine months," said Mary, and leaned sideways on her cushion to reach up and spank May on the butt.

May said, "Oh, that's *so* humorous," using a fine Warm-time word.

Mary and Catania laughed, and Catania knew then that the Garden people would probably not kill the Trappers soon, and perhaps not at all. Mary One-eye had no need to pretend pleasance.

May put the pieces of potato and odd blue-white vegetable into a trade-pot, and poured water over them from a clay jug. Then, she hung the pot on a little swivel arm of iron and pushed that into the clay stove, over the fire.

Mary was sitting with her good eye shut, as if she were dozing.

Catania, glad not to be looked at for a while, thought the swiveled cooking arm was a clever idea, a civilization-notion that saved women burns. . . . It struck her, after watching May prepare food, that Warm-times must have been wonderful times for women, with everything made gentle, to save them injury. That was clear in every copybook. Almost always, the women's sorrows were love-sorrows or loneliness-sorrows. Only in the very oldest copybooks did women's children die more often than they lived.

This little house, so comfortable and in a town, might almost be a Warm-time house, though without the detective police or Clinic Mayo. And the town almost like ancient Detroit, but making paper instead of four-wheel traveling Chevies. . . .

Mary opened her good eye. "How old are you, Catania?" Her 'are' sounded like 'urrr.'

"Twenty-eight years old."

"You can call me Mary."

"Twenty-eight, Mary."

"You look older.—It's a hard life, isn't it, up in the mountains?"

"No. Not the life."

Mary sat looking at her, round face pale even in firelight. A stripe of green paint shone across her forehead. "So. Who has set you running from your homes? I see you and your people still running, even when you're standing still. Some of your people were crying at night . . . and you left a sad man hanging in a tree."

Catania said nothing.

"Have tribesmen set you running?"

". . . Yes. There was a battle."

"Ah. Blackfoot?"

"Cree."

"Cree. . . . And you are all that's left, Catania? Forty-one now, since the sad man was left hanging in the tree?"

"Yes."

"Cree.—Not Kipchak people from the west? You've seen no horse-riders with odd eyes?"

"No. None of those."

"And have you seen things that were not men—but not animals either?"

"No," Catania said, and smiled. "No story monsters. Only the Cree."

Mary turned to look up at May. "Are you making onions?"

"Mother, I'm not making onions. We have potatoes and turnips. I'm not making onions."

"I've read about turnips," Catania said.

"Reading about them," Mary said, "—is better than eating them."

"I'm *not* making onions."

Mary made a face. "I was going to have a boy," she said to Catania. "But I wished him to a her in my belly—and see my reward."

"I have no children," Catania said.

"Then you lost none to the Cree."

"Only dear friends."

"And were these tribesmen satisfied with killing your friends, and taking your home—or are they following?"

"I think they were satisfied."

Mary One-eye scratched her round belly. "And who thinks they weren't satisfied?"

"Just . . . Jack Monroe thinks they might follow."

"Oh, I see. Just your Jack." Mary turned to her daughter. "May, sweetness. . . ."

"Mother, if you want onions, you come cook them."

Mary sighed. "You spoiled bitch. . . ." She said nothing more for a while, only sat on her cushion, watching Catania. Catania looked back, but politely, and also watched May slice the smoked duck and set portions aside. . . . Mary One-eye had an easy way, but she was not easy, and Catania reminded herself to be careful, and not pretend she could match Mary in silences.

"Your paper. . . . Did the paper the Salesmen brought us come up from Gardens?"

"No, no." Mary shook her head. "They bargain with us for best-laid, and take that south. Do you know a Salesman named Bruce Nolan?"

"No. The trade-people who came to us were Mathew Dittmeir

and Ed Ward. Those were the ones who brought us paper and steel-bricks every year. Ed Ward's father used to come—but he was killed by someone, traveling, when I was a little girl."

"I don't know any of those people, Catania, but I do know you were never traded fine paper. Whoever it was, traded you rough reams—and we don't even make that, paper with no cloth in it at all."

"Cloth? I thought paper was made from trees, made from wood ground up in a mulch."

"How we make paper, is our secret. But any paper is better if Mexican puff-cloth—cottie—is in it." Mary turned on her cushion. "May, aren't those turnips done?"

"Almost."

"Did you cut them small? If you didn't cut them small, they'll take forever."

"I did."

"Little pieces?"

"Little pieces."

Mary sighed, and she and Catania sat silent again.

* * *

Torrey had stood by the tree, holding his lance, until he grew tired of standing. Then he leaned against the rough bark. It was the fat of the day, and people painted with stripes of green came up and down the path—stepping around him with a look, as if he was a chancy dog off his lead. They stared down their noses at him, even those who were shorter.

He would have been more comfortable with a Trapper beside him. Even an Auerbach for company would be better than standing here alone guarding this den, this entrance hole. He would have to go down with his knife if there was trouble. . . . leave the lance. Leaning against the tree, he could hear soft voices. He'd heard the women laughing—Catania laughing—and that seemed a good sign. A sign of no more trouble, at least not right now.

He wasn't ready . . . the Trappers weren't ready for more trouble. They were heart-weary.

Jack Monroe, Torrey supposed, was always ready for trouble. And Tattooed Newton. Newton would be good company standing at the tree with Garden people going past, and staring. Newton would stare right back; he thought everyone was funny.

Torrey scratched a shoulder-blade against the tree's rough bark. . . . While in the forest and running south, it had been easier to think of other things than what had happened, and who was dead. But now, unless these Garden people came to kill them, there was nothing else to think about. Though what had happened still felt too strange to be possible, so considering it was like trying to grip something too slippery to hold.

It seemed to Torrey that all the dead people—and the Range as it was—must still be somewhere, and not gone entirely. But it was difficult to imagine even Mountain Jesus' hands as being large enough to hold them. . . . Could even the Weather's son hold Mount Alvin and Mount Geary, and all the country between them? Could a sensible man believe that? And the fur animals, the caribou herds—could all that be held in cupped hands?

Torrey thought not, which made the sadness permanent. . . .

Though he was on watch, he was startled when the Garden girl, the singing-girl, popped up out of the tree-root hole like a marmot. One moment she wasn't there—then she was.

She held a wooden plate of sliced bird-meat and pieces of potato, and something else white. She handed the plate to Torrey with an angry face, as if he'd said something bad to her—then popped back down into the hole exactly like a Mount Alvin marmot when an eagle came over.

She'd been dressed, but he remembered her naked. Even angry, she had eyes dark and rich as a fisher-cat's fur.

Torrey squatted with his back against the tree to eat. The meat was smoked duck with something odd in the flavor. He ate it all, then licked the grease from his fingers.

As he ate the potatoes, a thin old man with his left hand missing walked up and sat down on a big stone across the path. There was a green stripe painted across his mouth. He and Torrey stared at each other for a time, and the old man scratched the stump of his wrist, as if it itched him.

Then, suddenly as before, the singing girl came up out of the hole again. "Daddy," she said to the one-handed man, "—Mother's busy and I'm busy. You go make your own dinner."

Then she looked at Torrey as if she were surprised he was still there—unpleasantly surprised. "What happened to your finger?"

"I bit it off to make a whistle," Torrey said, and she snorted and went back inside.

And here we are, Torrey thought. *Old man with a hand gone. And me with a finger gone. Two stumpies.* He handed his plate over to the old man, and watched him eat the white things that weren't potatoes.

"Your daughter has bad manners," Torrey said. The old man said nothing.

* * *

"Do you fart?" Mary One-eye asked it with her mouth full of smoked duck. "—I mean when you're with other people."

"Not deliberately," Catania said. The duck was delicious. It had been smoked with an herb that tasted green and salty. The turnips were not delicious.

"We do, sometimes," Mary said, "—when we're visiting. To be friendly."

"I understand. . . ." Catania didn't know if she was supposed to fart, to be polite.

"And you're the . . . shaman for your hunters?"

"Doctor," Catania said. "I'm a scientific physician—as scientific as I can be."

"Is that so?" May had given Mary a lot of food; her plate had been piled with it. Now there was less. She was a busy eater.

"We're not fools," Catania said. "We're book people—we had more than three-hundred copybooks!"

"Ah. . . ."

"Those are gone—but I have my medical books with me. And they're very scientific."

"I see," Mary said, and picked up a duck leg to chew. She seemed uninterested.

"I suppose we could let your people copy my medical books. . . ."

"Oh, we have our own." Much attention given to the duck leg. Big chewing.

"And I have a dentist's book—for teeth," Catania said. Mary's brown eye turned black. "Mark Inskip, DDS, *Basics of Modern Dentistry*. Tufts University Press. It's got drawings copied in it, and it's very, very old."

"Well," Mary put the gnawed duck-bone down, "—we might take a look at that, though as I said, we have several medicine books of our own."

"Also, I have *The Missionary's Medical Primer* by Walter daSilva, MD. And *General and Special Surgery* by Cheryl Miller, MD, and Roger Tosukawa, MD. These also have many drawings copied in them."

Mary One-eye sighed and ate a piece of turnip. "You bad girl, Catania—you know I want the dentist book, and the others, too. How did you know how much I wanted them?"

Catania thought of lying, then decided not. "When I told you about the dentist book, the pupil of your eye grew larger. That happens whenever anyone is very interested—when a man first sees a girl, or game . . . or a woman sees a baby."

Mary put her face in her hands. "I should have known that. How could I not have known it, not even noticed such a useful thing?"

"A Salesman told me, years ago, after we traded. I traded a lynx pelt, a wolf's, and seven fine martens' for an iron pot that had three little legs so it could sit in a camp fire. A spider, he called it. Then he told me all Salesmen watch eye-pupils when they trade, and that I could have gotten *two* pots."

Mary turned on her cushion. "You hear that, May?"

"Yes." May was standing at the hearth, licking her plate clean.

"What does it teach you?"

"To watch the center of peoples' eyes—and remember that we don't know everything." May put the plate away.

Mary made a face of surprise at Catania, at such a sensible answer. "But still too stupid, too selfish to be a Lady," she said, then put her plate down on the floor. "And what do you want, to let us copy those three books?"

"Some time to rest here," Catania said. "And food—then more food when we leave."

" 'Some time' could mean anything," Mary said. "And 'food' could mean any amount of it."

"Two Warm-time weeks, then, and food enough so none of us stays hungry. Then food enough to travel, with none of us hungry, for another Warm-time week."

"A lot of food," Mary said.

"Food is eaten and gone," Catania said. "Knowledge rests forever."

"You've given me a lesson of eye-pupils, Catania Scar-face—but I don't need lessons on the worth of things from you, or from anyone."

"I apologize."

Mary shifted on her cushion, raised her left haunch slightly, and farted. "And your people will accept this, and want no more? Your men will accept it?"

"I'm sure they will."

"Your Jack will accept it?"

". . . Yes."

"Very well," Mary said. She spat in her palm as Salesmen did, and reached to strike Catania's outstretched hand. "It's a sealed bargain."

"It's a sealed bargain."

Mary stood up, easily for one so fat, and stretched. "Some of my people thought it would be better to kill you all. But that would have cost us fighting men."

"Well," Catania said, "—you could poison us. Isn't there foxglove in your woods? Aren't there bad mushrooms? I was told there were poison mushrooms, death-angels, in the forest."

Mary looked down at her. "I like you, Catania. Your people are lucky to have such a wise woman. . . . Very wise to open yourself like an interesting copybook, so I will not want to kill you and yours, even if I find a reason for it."

Catania put her plate on the floor and said nothing.

"You see this, May?" Mary One-eye said. "Our woman from the mountains, our wise Scar-face, even knows when to be silent."

Catania still said nothing.

"Now, you go," Mary said. "Carlson will take you and Nine-fingers back. Go, and be certain *our* bargain is your people's bargain."

Catania was starting to climb from the house, noticing that the entrance roots were trained into narrow steps leading up, when Mary called after her. "And for poisoning with death-angel mushrooms, physician—what warning? What remedy?"

Catania stepped back down. "Doctor daSilva's Primer says no bad taste, and so no warning. Treatment is only vomiting—vomiting soon." Then she turned and climbed up into cool air and sunshine.

* * *

"We're not children," Jim Olsen said. "You don't decide for us, Catania." His face was drawn; faint fire shadows ran from his eye-sockets to his mouth. The Trappers had gathered in deep shade at the freshest fire, some standing, others on sleds set around it.

"Garden Mary decides for us, while we're here," Catania said. "Carlson says he'll show us where she wants us to camp."

"And if we just keep going?" Martha Sorbane said, "—and have nothing to do with these people?"

"The bull-beef is gone; we have no food. And we're tired; we need some days of rest, and eating." Catania thought of adding that their sorrow needed a resting time as well, but decided not to. "It doesn't harm us that they copy my three books."

"We found bull-beef once," Joan Richardson said. "We can find it again, or take what we want from these people. I think they would give us food, rather than fight."

"They don't have many fighting men," Torrey said. "I think only about two, maybe three hundred."

Tattooed Newton was lying on a sled with his head in Lucy's lap. "Whichever," he said, "—more than enough to clean our clock." Certainly a Warm-time phrase, though none of the others had read it.

Jack had stood leaning on his lance, listening. "Catania says they've been watching us for days. Did any of us know it? . . . They're better than we are in the woods."

"So you say," said Bailey Auerbach.

"Do we have them?" Jack said. "Or do they have us?" And he walked away.—That was a thing that annoyed many of the Trappers. Jack Monroe would say something, then walk away as if all was settled. And who then could chase whining after him to disagree?

A stone's toss from the fire, Garden Carlson sat cross-legged in his green robe on gathered hemlock branches, rubbing grease into the wood of his crossbow with a little piece of bird fat. His gold bracelets caught a shaft of sunlight as he worked.

"I've made a bargain," Catania said, "—and it makes sense. These are dangerous people to disturb. So we rest two Warm-time weeks, then go."

"I'm tired of Cree people and green people," Dummy said. "I want to go home."

There was a silence. Then Bobby Olsen said, "We're going on a long hunt, Dummy. That's what we're doing."

"I want to go home and see Lala," Dummy said. That was his name for his sister, Lorraine. "And I want my puppy."

No one said anything to that. . . . Then Myles Weber, who'd been sitting by the fire, stood up. "Let's follow that fucking gold-bracelets over there, and camp where they say. I'm sick of talking about it."

And as if he'd heard from so far away, Garden Carlson got up, slung his crossbow, and stood waiting for them.

Mary One-eye likes me, but is afraid of Jack, so she may have him killed if I'm not careful. She and her Garden people would be happier if Jack and Newton weren't with us. Some of our other men, too. They aren't as civilized as people who listen to a Lady. . . . Well, Newton may be civilized, but not in the Garden way.

I've felt hard kicks from Susan's baby—a great relief for me. Susan seemed not to care. Her mourning can't be good for the little one; it will be born sad.

Mary took me up the valley to a long house propped on tree-stumps. It's their copy-house. Only women copy, and they sit on a fine shining wooden floor. There were stacks of wonderful paper, and southern steel nibs for their pens, not goose-quills. They are making two copies of each of my medicine books, tracing the drawings through the thinnest paper I've ever seen.

Mary let me watch the work, but perhaps, once we finish our talking, she intends to keep her secrets by feeding me death-angels. It would suit her sense of humor, after my mentioning them.

Sense of humor . . . sense of humor. What wonderful phrases jump out of copybooks, gifts from Warm-times.

FROM THE JOURNAL OF DOCTOR CATANIA OLSEN

10

Buddy Chewapa had signaled a rest, and stood to catch his breath from running. . . . He could have killed Edwin-Jim days ago, but he hadn't. They'd been friends since they were little boys, and Edwin would have been too great a loss. How many friends to the bone did a man make? Very few.

Still, he could have killed him, because the sinful man found hanging in the tree had cost them four days sitting and praying, waiting for a sign to go past that unlucky place and track down the last snow-devils left alive.

Edwin-Jim had found the bad thing—had smelled it stinking, and of course knew why it had been hung up to rot. He might have come and said, "Dead deer." Or "Dead Trapper dog."

Instead, he'd made a fuss, and men had gone to see. It was a twice-killed man up in a tree. Bad luck and no shit. One of the snow-devils hanging by his neck for anyone to see, with his suicide knife left stuck in his heart to pin his ghost to him, so it couldn't get away.

Edwin-Jim had come and told; the men had gone to see. Then all of them camped on the trail and wouldn't move until good luck came along. . . . Buddy had thought of ordering them to go on, then decided not to try that and fail. Better to wait.

And there they'd sat for four days—talk talk talk—with the Trappers' trail so plain a child could have read it. A losers' trail with runner ruts left plain, dog shit unburied, and, the day before, a length of woven leather line dropped and left behind them.

The snow-devils were running from bad luck and dying, but bad luck and dying were chasing right behind them—or had been, until the hanging man.

Then, Buddy had understood why chiefs were so bad-tempered. It was because most men were fools, and had to be kicked in the ass or pulled by the nose to get anywhere. Realizing that, he'd taken care to have a dream of okay last night. He woke shouting that a white bear had appeared to him as he slept and walked away south through the forest, looking over its shoulder to be certain he was following.

This dream, when he told it—all false and a lie—had gotten the men up and back on the snow-devils' trail. Now, Buddy knew why chiefs were bad tempered—and not to be trusted for truth.

But he had the men moving again, and was leading them fast. They would chase the battle-losers the rest of this day, and perhaps catch them the day after next.

* * *

The Trappers had been taken by Gold-bracelet men far down the creek valley to camp along the stream. They'd driven their dogs over pecky snow to the paper-making buildings, where white water fell down steep rocks under ragged crusts of ice. Then they'd been led across a log bridge and on down the valley to a slope wooded lightly with pine saplings.—They'd gone like tired children, as they were told.

"Stay in your camp," one of the Garden fighting men said, and set three other Gold-bracelets to watch them.

The dogs were fed from wooden buckets of mash the Garden people brought, then were staked in lines, and the sleds checked for cracked frames or nicked runners. The John trench was dug high on the valley's slope, away from the creek. . . . The Trappers settled in, ate from the baskets of vegetables and smoked birds brought to them—then, in evening dark, rolled into their furs and slept.

It was restless sleeping, still sick with bad dreams, so some sounded like sleeping dogs, whimpering as they hunted the dead through their lost mountains.

. . . In the morning, a Gold-bracelets walked into the camp as if it was his, and took Catania away with him to visit Mary One-eye.

"You eat eggs?" Mary said, when Catania climbed down into her house. Mary was alone, cooking in a trade-pan at the hearth.

"Yes. From ducks . . . geese, when the birds fly in and stay."

Mary stirred yellow eggs in her pan. "We keep crows in cages. This is crow eggs and onion and cheese from our goats."

"It smells very good," Catania said, though it smelled odd, likely from the cheese.

"You are the worst liar." Mary lifted the pan away from the fire. "What haven't you had?"

"Cheese."

"Never?"

"Never. But I've read about it many times."

"Sit down . . . sit down." Mary bent her head to smell the eggs. "Wonderful. There is no civilization without cheese."

"I'm sure it's going to be very good."

Mary held the pan back over the fire. "Tell me, tall person: don't you people lie?"

"Of course we lie."

"About what?"

"About hunting . . . and about love."

"That's all?" Mary left the pan over the fire a little longer, then took it away. "We're ready to eat."

"What else is there to lie about?"

Mary stared at her, then used a big carved spoon to serve the eggs onto two wooden plates. "Eat every bit of this. It's good for you." She gave Catania a smaller spoon to eat with, then came and sat on a cushion beside her.

". . . Well?"

"They're . . . they're very good. Salty."

"That's the cheese. Never put salt in cooking eggs, Catania; it makes them tough. Well, is it good?"

"It is good, very good. I taste the cheese; it makes my mouth feel funny."

"You don't have to finish it—I'll let you not finish it just this one time."

"No . . . no, it's good."

"Sure? If you don't want it, don't eat it. My husband will eat it."

"No, I do want it. It's salty, like char eggs, but it's good."

"All right. Did you have southern pepper?"

"On the Range? No, we couldn't afford pepper. It's like to-bacco, it's so expensive."

"Well, there's pepper in those eggs."

"Pepper in here?" Catania took a considering bite.

"The tiny black things are pepper." Mary was eating fast.

"That's what's harsh?"

"That's it."

"This is what the chefs did with Warm-time food, isn't it? Complicated things all made together."

"Chefs did that, Catania, yes—and cooks did simpler."

"Well, this is very good."

"I suppose I am a chef," Mary said. She finished her eggs, and sat back on her cushion with a sigh.

Catania hurried to eat the last bites. She liked the taste of pepper better than the taste of cheese.

"Give me your plate." Mary stood, took them to the hearth, and licked them clean. "I'm going to show you how we make paper. . . . Well, I'll show you *some* of how we make paper."

"I'd like to see it," Catania said. "The eggs were very good—and now I can say I've eaten cheese from goats' milk."

Mary looked at her. "Yes, you can," she said.

. . . When they went down the valley toward the growling noise, Catania first walked beside Mary, but the fat woman put out her arm and gently pushed her back a step, so then Catania went a little behind.

As they passed Garden people, the men and women stopped whatever they were doing, and bowed. Showing respect to Mary, it seemed to Catania—or perhaps they were afraid of her.

They walked down paths along the creek to the big houses—the buildings—just past the bridge across the water. The growling noise was loud enough there to make the ground tremble a little. Catania had a sudden imagining of a great bear chained inside one of the buildings, and that Mary was leading her there to be killed and eaten by it.

It was such a well-pictured thought that Catania sniffed the air for a bear's rank scent, but smelled only a strong glue-pot odor.

As they came to the first building, which was as high as three men standing on each other's shoulders, Catania saw it was very old. All three buildings looked old. They were made of wide fir planks adzed roughly even, then pegged together as a Range smokehouse was built, though they were so much bigger. But old, and slowly rotting over the waterfall's foaming current.

Their roofs were covered with dark narrow boards overlapping, that might be copybook 'shingles,'—could very well be shingles—and along the edge of the roofs were large figures carved to look like vegetables, with peoples' heads growing from them. All these heads had their mouths-open, as if they were singing. The carvings were very fine, though the wood was splitting from age and weather.

The building smelled of glue and spoiling wood. Mary pushed at planks; they squawked and swung aside and she walked into the building. . . . *I am walking through a door*, Catania said to herself, following, and was surprised how much sense a door made if you had no thick hides to hang. She stepped onto a trembling plank floor and into the sound of deep growling, and water rushing underneath.

It was dark inside the building; there was only a small fire burning in a stone pit. The Garden people being cautious of fire, apparently, in such an old wooden place.

Catania saw something very big moving in fire-lit darkness. She ducked away, drawing her knife.

"No, no," Mary said, laughing—and Catania saw, after a moment, it was a great shadowed boulder of rough granite-stone, turning and turning in the wall of the building.

"It's a wheel!" And it was a wheel right out of copybook drawings, but gigantic, and turning with a big age-blackened log through its middle to hold it up. And as the stone wheel turned, it ground and ground at another big log—a new white log with its bark gone—that lay slanted down a shelf of thick timber, so its end rested against the turning stone that chewed at it, slowly eating it up. That eating made the growling that shook the building.

There was a pit beneath the turning stone . . . and the wheel was spitting out shreds and chips and crumbs of wood down into it, everything it chewed from the end of the white log.

"That's first-pulp!" Mary had to shout over the wheel's growling. "It goes into the pit, and we take it out and grind it under a smaller wheel in the next building. Grind it finer—that's second-pulp. Then we soak it in hot water!"

The sound was hurting Catania's ears. She started to cover them with her hands, found she was still holding her knife, and sheathed it. . . . She watched, saw what was happening—and suddenly realized what must be causing it. *"The water falling down is making the wheel go around!"*

Mary nodded, smiling. . . . Garden people, all of them men, came out of the darkness and went under the wheel to the pit. They moved strangely, in a line, all stepping together—right foot, left foot—as if they were dancing. Some ducked side by side under the wheel, down into the pit, then began handing up wooden buckets filled with the shreds of log, the little bits and pieces and crumbs. Buckets of first-pulp.

Those waiting took the buckets and walked away all together in a line, high-stepping as if to music. Then the ones in the pit climbed out side by side, and danced away into darkness where the firelight didn't reach.

"Come look at the wooden wheels!" Mary beckoned Catania to follow her. She went close beside the great wheel, then down narrow wooden steps that shook and trembled.

The stair descended through the building's floor . . . and out into air and sunlight and misting water almost under the great wheel—the rough stone close enough to reach up to touch. The noise was very loud, and Catania put her hands over her ears, ducking low. It seemed to her there could be a bad accident if anyone was caught by the wheel. She imagined blood coming down into the pit, so that first-pulp became red pulp.

Here, huge square beams went this way and that way over the rushing water, supporting smooth round logs stuck through big wooden wheels beneath the turning stone. Each of these wheels was a different size and had pegs sticking out of its edge—pegs thicker than a man's leg. . . . Catania saw that the pegs of each wheel fitted into the pegs of the one below, so they all turned together, some faster, some slower.

She looked down through noise and water spray, and saw that the lowest wooden wheel was the biggest. It stood on its edge and stuck into the falls. The edge had wide wooden feet like a duck's all around it, and the wheel turned and turned in the foaming water so it made Catania dizzy to watch it.

"*Called 'gears'!*" Mary had to nearly shout, since all the wooden wheels screamed and groaned as if they were hurting as they turned.

Garden men had come down here, also, and were dancing their work as they did above. They carried little wooden buckets and dipped fat from them—fat from the goats, Catania supposed. They dipped the fat all together to the rumble and squeal of the wheel-gears, then poured it into where the wheels were turning.

Catania saw it was a remembered work-dance, not something they'd just decided to do.

"*Dancing.*"

Mary nodded. "*Duty-dancing. There is nothing more important than that.*"

"*This is wonderful. . . .*"

"*And from this building,*" Mary said, speaking loud, "*—to the next and second-pulp grinding. Then slurry-sticking onto woven cloth. And in the third building, rollers and our treatment.*"

"*Treatment . . . ?*"

"*Our secrets for finishing the paper, Catania. And no one else will ever know them. . . . Last is drying, cutting, stacking.*"

Catania tried to stop looking at the gear-wheels. Their turning was making her feel sick. Their screaming noises and the fast water running beneath were troubling her.

Mary saw it, and took her arm. "*Enough for today,*" she said. "*If you're good, and I decide to, I'll show you the second-pulp building. There, the dance is more intricate.*"

" '*Intricate*' . . . ?"

"*Complicated,*" Mary said, and led the way back up the steps and through the building's floor. There, it was a little quieter, with only the stone's harsh grinding. "Really, Catania, you people must have copied a dictionary."

"We had a Webster's . . . but we don't use all the words."

Garden people were still duty-dancing at the pit. Catania saw their lips moving. They were singing, or praying.

Mary went to the plank door, pulled it open, and they walked outside. It was a great relief to Catania to leave such noisy civilization, leave the worst of the growling and wheel-screaming behind her, and breathe cold air that didn't smell of wet chewed wood.

"Thank you, Mary," she said, and meant thanks for showing first-pulp, and thanks for coming away from it. "—I see why wheels are wonderful; they do so much. They used to move Warm-time Chevies from one map-state to another, and now they move the strength of water from one wheel to another."

"Yes," Mary said, and led the way up the path. "Our pulper is called a mill. It's four-lives old."

"Aren't you afraid of fire with buildings made of such old wood?"

"We're very careful," Mary said, "—and we have a Put-out-fire dance that everyone knows how to do."

"If something did happen," Catania said, "I suppose you could build it again."

Mary looked back at Catania, surprised. "Our mill was built by a long-ago Lady with the Rules of Engineering," she said, "—and that's why it's a treasure to care for."

* * *

"They are not as civilized as we thought."

Catania lay beside Jack just after fucking. She drew her fur aside to be cooled from sweating, and lay watching the stars.

"And why not?"

"Jack—they couldn't build their making-paper mill again! At least, not build it properly. They don't know how. They tend it like children doing what they've always done—they tend it dancing. And they sing . . . or they pray; I don't know which."

Jack raised up on an elbow beside her, and looked out over the camp, its dying fires . . . sleeping Trappers. Catania saw he was watching for Tall-David Richardson, standing guard down by the creek. There would be one or two Gold-bracelets along the creek as well.

"—I think they're afraid we'll hurt the mill."

"There he is," Jack said, meaning Tall-David, and he lay back down. "We won't hurt the mill. . . ."

"But it's so sad," Catania said.

"What, Trade-honey?" Jack said, and turned to kiss her.

"Don't you see, Jack? It means the Garden people are sliding down. It means we're all still sliding down, not coming back up to Warm-time ways."

"Didn't you know that?" Jack settled into his furs. "I thought you knew that. When I was in Map-Missouri, the people there talked about a man who tried to make black gun-powder lifetimes ago. But it only hissed and made smoke. When he kept trying, it finally made one of the old bangs and killed him. After that, everybody felt it was too uncertain to try in cold country—and bad luck, besides."

"It's just so sad! We're not stupid, Jack. Garden Mary's not stupid. Why are we all still sliding down?"

"Don't know. . . . Nobody has that many copybooks, really—and very few How-To-Do's. Mostly bad-people stories, and complaining stories, and love stories." He blew a puff of frosty breath up in the air, apparently to watch it silver in starlight.

Jack did odd boyish things at times, occasions that caught at Catania's heart as if he were her son and lover both. There was something boyish in his fierceness, too—but supported by a fighting man's cunning, and his terrible strength and quickness. . . . His contradictions, she supposed, held her to him, his sometime kindness out of coldness. *Contradictions.* Was there no word Warm-times didn't have?

Jack blew another breath, and they both lay watching it haze and glitter and slowly drift away. "Warm-time people had the weather to try things, and not starve if those things went wrong. The world hadn't been bad to them yet, made their hopes so cold. . . ." He sighed, turned away from her, and soon slept.

Catania lay awake remembering the Garden people dancing their work. Duty-dancing at a first-pulp mill they could never build again. It was very sad, and frightening. It was a future-look at a bad future. A future, she supposed, that men like Jack and Tattooed Newton would manage well in. . . . A future bad for women, unless—like Mary One-eye—they became frightening.

* * *

Jack spit tobacco juice onto fragile snow. Just coming this far south, brought the summer nearer already, though the nights still froze things hard.

He'd chewed tobacco twice before, in Map-Michigan. It had been traded up a very long way, from south of south in the Empire, then up to Middle Kingdom, then a long way north to Map-Michigan. Not much of it had cost a sled of furs, though the Garden people seemed to have enough for easy sharing.— Joan Richardson had been given a bite, and swallowed it, not knowing better. Which made Trappers laugh, who hadn't laughed for a while.

The Garden people were rich. Jack had known men in Map-Missouri who would have come to this creek valley in numbers to take every valuable thing they wished. Take the pale fat girls as well. . . .

Carlson Gold-bracelets—brown-eyed, his nose smashed flat in some old fight—sat cross-legged opposite Jack, chewing, spitting, and keeping up a conversation as they played. Carlson had won two games through the afternoon, but was losing now. He was a thoughtful checker player. Too thoughtful; he didn't care to take chances. . . . On the ice in Map-Michigan, the Ojibway had gambled for teeth or finger-joints, if they had no furs or dogs or daughters to spare.—Though none with fierce wives had dared gamble their girls. Better go home to the hides with teeth pried out than owing their sweet Moon-Shadow-Cynthia or Our-Dark-Doris to a warrior likely mostly white-blood, and lacking courtesy.

Carlson Gold-bracelets had won two true stories to be told, and now was playing the third game for an oath to fight beside and never against, a much more serious matter.

Jack let Carlson crown, certain he'd be so pleased he'd move that piece immediately and without care. Carlson did—and was jumped three times. It was the turn of the game, and Carlson said, "Now, I meant by 'beside and not against,' that unless the Lady orders it, I will not fight you."

"I understand," Jack said, and jumped another piece while Carlson was considering his honor.

They were playing on a caribou robe by the cooking fire in the Trappers' camp. Each morning, the Garden people brought them food—potatoes, cauliflower, the unpleasant turnips, and smoked birds strung on twisted plant-stem cords. Enough food, but never more than enough. The dogs got a mash of turnips and bird guts.

The first morning, Mary One-eye's daughter, May, and another Garden girl had come for Catania's books and taken them away to be copied. They'd taken Catania away as well, most mornings afterward, to visit with Mary in her house under the tree.

"This was a good bargain," Tattooed Newton had said to Jack. "We have women crying and men still silent. They need rest, time to swallow sadness and shit it out."

"A good bargain," Jack had said, "—if the Green-paints keep it." As so far they had.

But Catania slept badly under the furs with him. She turned and turned and muttered in her sleep, so Jack knew the Garden Lady frightened her. She was afraid of what Mary One-eye might decide to do—afraid, and always being sent for. . . . Sent for to-day, she'd said, to spend the night under Mary's tree.

Jack gave Carlson Gold-bracelets a piece to jump—and in consequence, jumped two more of his. The Garden people lived too soft a life to play good checkers.

Carlson seemed upset, face wrinkled as a worried dog's. "You win the game."

"Listen," Jack said, "—you're a fighting man and a man of honor, so I know you'll keep your wager-word as best you can, and never fight against me if there's any other way." And saying so, he saw the obligation weigh a little heavier on Carlson Gold-bracelets. The Garden people lived too soft a life.

Torrey came over, said "Hello, Carlson," and sat beside them. "Listen, Jack, we need to run the dogs a little. They're rested and they're fighting, and we're getting dogs hurt."

"You decide what to do," Jack said. "Or ask Jim Olsen." Jack had learned from watching the Ojibway war chiefs, the red-bloods, not to waste commands on slight matters where any foolish or troublesome person might feel free to disagree.

"Well . . . I think we need to ask Garden Mary."

"You don't trouble the Lady for that," Carlson said. "You have no need to see her. I can tell you to go and run your dogs. But don't run so far that it's rudeness, and being bad guests."

"All right." Torrey stood up. "We'll go out one team at a time. No sled, just two people holding harness. Run them, and come back in."

"You can do that," Carlson said. "Don't do more, because we're still copying your books, and you have another week to rest here and be fed."

"A bargain is a bargain—with us as with you," Torrey said to him, and walked away.

"I meant no criticism." Carlson Gold-bracelets set the checkers out on the board again. The checkerboard was decorated with painted hardwood leaves that turned seasonal colors around its edges. In the middle of the board, a thin blue-gray dog was painted running.

"Don't you find the crossbow slow?" Jack said.

"Slow but sure," said Carlson, using one of the best of Warmtime's phrases. "You set this game's wager."

"On this game," Jack said, "—I wager for true friendship between us." And saw that Carlson could find no way to politely decline.

* * *

It had been a hard run for the Cree through the last of the day, and tiring. Meant to be tiring, since Paul Kisses-the-Girls had come with Edwin-Jim during a rest, and told Buddy that the warriors were getting weary of being in deep forest, where nothing could be seen that wasn't close.

"They wouldn't whine like women, if I wasn't so young," Buddy had said. "If Chief Much was here, they wouldn't say a word."

"Right," Paul said.

"—But because they're mostly older, they think they know everything, and I know nothing."

"Completely right, Buddy." Edwin-Jim had nodded as if he had good sense. "They complain like women with the monthly bloods."

"What are we going to do?" Paul had looked worried, so Buddy knew the men had spoken seriously to him.

"I'm going to run their asses off," Buddy'd said. "And that'll do two things—it'll make these old so-called warriors too tired to trouble me, and it will get us to the snow-devils sooner."

"Smart," Edwin-Jim had said. "—Smart." He was a friend, but he was such a fool it was disturbing to have him agree.

. . . Still, it seemed to have worked. The hard-running day was done, and the men had gone into their furs at dark with no complaints from any of them.

Buddy slept until almost dawn. Then, waking from a dream, he lay in his furs in the last of branch-broken moonlight. He'd dreamed of his mother, and the lake camp. The dream hadn't made sense, but it had left recalling behind it, so he lay remembering and remembering. . . .

Uncle Paul had been in the dream. He'd played father to Buddy when he was little, while Buddy's real father, Charlie Chewapa, had been away trying to learn magical secrets—changing belly babies and so forth—from New Englanders. Which he hadn't.

"I'm a deaf man to deep magic." That's what Charlie had said to his friends when he came back after several years to practice ordinary spirit-sending. He blamed Buddy's mother, Charmian, because she was all white-blood, and had taken some of his power, fucking. So sometimes he beat her up.

But Charlie Chewapa was fair to Buddy, though he didn't love him. He never hit him, even with his hand.

And though not deeply magical, Buddy's father did have a good self-spirit for healing. He bought expensive dried plants and flowers from off the ice, and spit their juice into sick children's mouths and eyes and ears—and sometimes right up their asses—to make illness too sick to stay.

Buddy's father hadn't been in the dream. Uncle Paul had been, but he walked away and left Buddy and his mother fishing a borehole through the thick lake ice.

She'd caught a char, and pulled it up and cut it open to clean. "Buddy," she'd said, "—you're holding your line too tight. Just in your fingers . . . to feel the little nibbles."

Buddy remembered that part of the dream very well, and had wakened wishing it had been longer. . . . His mother had died when he was sixteen years old. He'd gone hunting with Edwin-Jim, Pete Elbow, and Chris LaPlace. They'd been gone a moon month down the mile-deep valleys where the ice had cracked and pulled a little apart. They'd killed four white bears and skinned them out.—It was a very good hunt. But when they got home, everyone Buddy waved to had turned and walked away. There was no one in his yard when he went there, and no kids or dogs around either.

He'd pushed through the hides and called hello to his mother, and there she was. She had the pops.

Only Charmian's eyes were showing. All the rest of her was covered with little red bubbles; her eyes looked out through bunches of them growing on her face. When she saw Buddy, she tried to get up from the bedding, and Buddy heard some of the bubbles break on her back when she moved. His mother opened her mouth when that happened, and made a sound like one of the little birds that flew over the ice in the warmer weeks.

His father had been gone, gone again for more than a year, this time far west, talking with the Blackfoot. No one else, no shaman, would come to their place, so Buddy stayed with his mother and cared for her. Sometimes she would shit a little brown water, and he cleaned that up, and he cooked soup for her with fish-heads and bones for strength. Buddy would put his mouth on his mother's and squirt in some soup, but she usually could not hold it down.

The little red bubbles broke, but new ones came up on her hot skin. After seven days, she got soft and full of holes, and smelled like spoiled meat. Then, she was dreaming all the time. Two days later, Charmian Chewapa died.

After that, Buddy was a boy with a bad temper, and was no longer friends with people there. He went out onto the lake edge, broke the thin ice, and slid his mother under. When he visited, five prayer-days later, she was floating by frozen reeds, looking up at him. She was fine, except that the tip of her nose was worn out from bumping on the underside of the ice. . . .

Buddy turned away from those memories, to hide from them in sleep. . . . When he woke at first light, a partridge was drumming in the woods.

I have been shown a first-pulp paper mill. I drew it as well as I could remember, folded the drawing and hid it in Jack's belt. He thought that was funny, since we can't build such a thing. But I hope we will meet people farther south who can. I do know this—the wheeling gears work; and what works, sensible people should be able to try until it's built again, and maybe better.

Mary took me up the valley to their copy-house. They've almost finished with my books, the drawings done very beautifully, but decorated with vegetables. I told Mary I thought any art was a bad idea on a page of scientific medicine, because of possible later confusions. She listened, but did not agree.

Jack says Mary's right eye is missing because, when she was younger, she broke it with her thumb while the Garden people watched, then pulled the juice and broken stuff and optic nerve out of the socket, and threw that away to show what she could bear—and would bear—for herself and for Gardens.

Jack said he once saw a Map-Missouri woman, much older than Mary, who had done the same thing. And what she said to do, her people did, or she had bad things done to them.

FROM THE JOURNAL OF DOCTOR CATANIA OLSEN

11

At dawn, Catania woke—and farted before she could prevent it.

Jack turned to her under the furs. "And what was that, little lynx?"

"Nothing."

"Nothing . . . ?" He held her with one hand, and began to tickle her with the other.

"*Don't!*" The tickling and struggle made her fart again—and they laughed, wrestling naked under snow-powdered furs.

"I'm going to wash." Catania threw back her wolf-skins, got up and went down to the creek, scattered snow icy under her bare feet. This sparse snow and the night-time cold, but no winter winds. Summer was coming—a longer, warmer summer here.

She'd intended to put a trade-kettle on the fire for hot water for washing. Jack's liquids and her liquids had dried at her groin.—But coldness had called as if it was something of the Range that she could keep, so she walked naked along the creek, then stepped down the bank and into swift black water.

Ice or stones under there bruised her feet, and her legs were numbed as she sank into shallow whirling rapids streaming away toward the waterfall and mill. Her legs, then her hips, then all of her grew numb to her neck. She was locked into water that first burned, then soothed the burn, then took all feeling away. It was like death—but a death she could climb out of, and up the slope to a fire.

It occurred to Catania, as she steadied herself against the current on slippery stones, that real death might be something similar—and all her lost friends with their lost children might be standing by fires on a higher bank, still trembling after their climb from death's dark river.

As a death, this seemed not bad at all. She knew she swam, but felt no body in such running cold. Little flakes and chips of ice came floating swiftly by her, and Catania reached out to catch them with stiff slow-folding fingers—caught one, and chewed on it like a child.

She ducked her head under—and that was a shock. The cold renewed itself, slapped her face so it stung. When she lifted her head to take a breath, Catania felt water freezing in her hair.

It was a puzzle, she thought, that discomfort sometimes felt better than ease—the world saying, "Wake up! *Wake up!*" and driving life into a person like a weapon, or a strong man's dick.

But soon the stream began to hurt her more, so a slow, thudding ache coincided with the beating of her heart. Catania could trace cold flowing into her bones—could name each bone as it came in. Death clearing its throat, taking a first slow easy breath to begin its song.

She tried to stand up . . . lost her balance on mossy stone, then regained it and stood up out of the water into air that felt so warm she shivered with the pleasure of it.

All those others died at Long Ledge. They're dead—but I'm not. She thought that, and was ashamed.

Catania climbed the bank and trotted through snow to their fire, toes and nipples stinging. Dancing in place on caribou-hide bedding, she picked up a wolf-fur to dry herself.

Jack was already gone, and most of the Trapper men gone with him for a morning's hunting, trying for another wild bull or a forest deer. They didn't like depending on Gardens for food, and liked it less since the Garden people had been almost rude the last two or three days, offended in some way—perhaps by Mary's having shown Catania the first-pulping. Perhaps simply tired of visiting strangers.

Mary hadn't asked Catania to come see her again. Garden Carlson hadn't come to play checkers.

Catania finished drying herself, and laid the fur out by the fire's bed. She dressed in her buckskins, then sat to wrap her footcloths and pull on moccasin-boots. . . . A last light flurry of snow came down through pale sunshine, lay on the backs of her hands for a moment, then melted.

A few women had gone hunting with the men, but most had stayed in camp. They bustled by their fires, heating washing water in trade-kettles, shaking out furs, neatening sled loads, sewing, combing out their hair. They did these household chores for comfort, since they had no houses, had no families anymore. Some had taken the gentler sled dogs off their lines, and hugged and spoke to them as if the dogs were children, or Warm-time pets.

Catania walked across the camp to Torrey's sled. Susan lay on it, bundled in furs, her small face pale amid the pelts' harsh deep grays.

"Are you feeling well this morning?" Catania put her hand on Susan's forehead, and felt proper warmth . . . faint damp.

Susan didn't answer. She lay beautiful and remote as a queen in a copybook, her black hair swept back in gleaming wings behind her ears. Lucy Edwards had been tending her, and Catania supposed she must have combed Susan's hair so beautifully and fastened it at the back with a long bone pin.

Catania knelt at the sled. "Listen, little dear one; all this sadness is spoiling good health—for you and for Sam's baby."

Susan looked at her, but said nothing.

"—Maybe I've been treating you too gently, Susan. Maybe I should dump you out of that sled . . . give you camp-work to do so you won't be feeling so sorry for yourself. You are not the only person who has lost somebody. There are women here who have lost everyone—and have no baby coming to comfort them."

"Catania," Susan said, "—Sam is alive. He's alive and hurt and lying under a hemlock tree, waiting for us to come back and help him."

". . . No," Catania said. "That's not true."

"Yes, it is. I dream it every night. If it wasn't true, Catania, I wouldn't dream it every night. He's so badly hurt, and been lying there so long . . . he's getting sicker and sicker!" Susan began to cry. "He looks like an old man, a little sick old man lying under the tree, hiding there. And he's so ashamed to have me look at him. He's dirtied himself because he's hurt so badly . . . and he's *ashamed*."

"Susan. . . ." Catania reached under Susan's soft heavy hair, gripped the nape of her slender neck, and shook her slightly, as if she were a distracted puppy. "Susan, listen to me. These are lying dreams. Sadness dreams.—Sam is dead. He died with the others out in Long Ledge fields."

"He's hurt so badly," Susan said. "His side . . . his right side is black with old blood. We need to go back. Sam would never have left us, Catania, if we were hurt and alone. I have to go back. Jack has to go and help him!"

Catania suddenly saw Jack believing this dream might be true, saw him leaving to go back to the mountains, and the Cree, to try to save his brother. She put her hand over Susan's mouth. "Don't say that! Don't say these things to Jack, or I'll kill you!" Then, Catania took her hand away. "I . . . I didn't mean that I'd kill you. But Susan, you stay quiet, and let me talk to people about these dreams. I promise I'll talk to them. And if we decide Sam needs our help, then we'll all go north . . . and we'll make him well, and bring him back to you."

"Soon," Susan said. "*Soon.*"

"Yes," Catania said. "Soon." She kissed Susan on the cheek, then stood and walked away through the camp, searching for someone to talk to.

Tattooed Newton hadn't gone with the hunters. She saw him standing down on the creek bank, looking at the flowing water.—Catania had never felt comfortable with Newton. Hadn't known him long enough . . . hadn't grown up with him. A good hunter, though not the best—and a wonderful fighting man, likely strong as Jack, if not quite so quick. . . . And he was strange, not really a Trapper though Lucy Edwards loved him, and they were married.

Even before Lucy, though, Newton had never come to Catania on Sundays after service. Perhaps he thought that kindness fucking was a funny thing to do, as he thought so many things were funny. He had come to the Range as if fleeing something—something that must have been dreadful, a tale-monster, if Tattooed Newton ran from it.

Catania walked down to the creek, wanting a man—not some sorrowful woman—to talk to about Susan.

Newton noticed her coming, and raised a hand in greeting.

"Newton . . ." she said.

He turned his crop-haired head, his broad clean-shaven face, and looked at her with small brown eyes that rarely blinked.

"Newton, Susan is not getting better."

No answer. He stood looking at her.

"—She dreams about Sam. That he's alive and hurt under a hemlock tree."

"He's dead." Newton looked up as a flight of ducks came in over the trees, whirring and wheeling, looking for still water to settle into.

"She's sure not. Newton, did your people—your other people—did they have a medicine for such sadness?"

The ducks, disappointed by this quick-running creek, sailed off with swift wingbeats.

"My 'other people,'" Newton said, "—would ask for an order come down the river from some petty lord, or magistrate, or two-dot clerk at Island. And when the order came, they would break Susan's neck, cut the baby out, and set it sucking on some slave milker 'til Market." He smiled an odd smile. "A practical people."

"I see. . . ."

They both stood for a while, watching the water. It seemed Newton wouldn't say any more, but he did. "Susan thinks she died when Sam Monroe died. She's only staying in her body until the baby comes."

It sounded like a truth Catania should have known, a truth that Mary One-eye would have known at once. A truth Catania also would have known if she'd been more interested in her patient and less interested in herself, and Jack, and happiness.

"But will the baby bring her back?"

Newton smiled. "Possibly, if it's a charming baby."

Catania couldn't recall the Warm-time word 'charming' ever being used in conversation before.

* * *

Late in the afternoon, through a Gardens grown quieter than usual, Catania walked to Mary's house, summoned by a Gold-bracelets.

When she climbed down the root entrance and went in, she saw that only May was there, making something out of goat-hair yarn with two straight little clicking sticks.

May looked up, but said nothing. She kept clicking the sticks, and Catania saw she was doing a sort of weaving in her lap. "Is that the old crocheting?"

"Knitting," May said, and said nothing else.

Catania sat and was quiet, too. It was embarrassing to be always asking questions of these people, who were only almost civilized. It was tiresome having to do that, while being careful not to ask such a wrong question that Mary might kill her and all the Trappers, so the question wouldn't be asked again.

We're orphans, Catania thought—*worse than orphans, because we have no parents and no families either. We are lost people.* It was a thought sad enough to make her cry. Instead, it made her angry.

She and May sat quiet, except for the clicking knitting-sticks. It was a sound that grew annoying.

A long while later, a Gold-bracelet man Catania didn't know came down into the house with his ax in his hand. He gave Catania such a bad look that she stood up and backed away. She thought she might be able to kill him with her knife—the house was small, cramped for swinging an ax.

Mary came down behind him, pushed him aside, and said, "Your Cree have come following you, Catania. And who is to blame for that?—You and your people." She put her finger to her cheek and pulled the skin down to make something like Catania's scar. " 'Just Jack,' " she said, imitating Catania's voice very well. " 'Just Jack thinks they may follow. . . .' "

"How many?"

"Fifty-two, and a foolish boy who leads them."

"How far?" Catania said.

"Those who've been watching, say only one morning away, now. It will cost me peoples' lives to kill them, and we *must* kill them or they will go back and bring more south to take what we have."

Mary's daughter put her knitting down, and said, "And how will you pay us for that, you tall ugly?" May's face looked like an angry dog's. Her teeth were showing.

The Gold-bracelets swung his ax slowly back and forth—and Catania heard bird calls outside Mary's house. It sounded as if birds of every different kind had begun to sing . . . then more and more of them.

Catania's heart was beating so fast it took some breath away. "We'll fight them for you, Mary. It will be the last of our battles, not the first of yours."

"Even so," Mary said, "—even so, you will pay me if I lose a single man."

"Pay what?"

"What I fucking choose," said Mary One-eye, and made a motion with her hand that folded air three times.

. . . On her way to tell the Trappers, Catania had to stop to vomit a little by the path. Her fear, and the unfairness that Mountain Jesus had allowed in sending the Cree, made her sick. And she was sick at Jack's having known the tribesmen would follow . . . having known it so well that he might have been the bad luck that called the Cree down.

She trotted along the lower path that ran by the creek. Garden people hurried past her the other way, the women with small children in their arms. Catania looked up and saw people gathered high on the swinging bridges . . . high in the little wooden houses in the trees. The women up there were making bird sounds, whistling birdcalls that rang louder and louder, until together they made only a great shrill noise. Several Gold-bracelets ran down the path with crossbows in their hands. One turned a little to hit her hard with his elbow as he passed.

Catania began to run; the tumult of whistled birdcalls seemed to drive her. At the paper-mill bridge, she saw lance-heads shining in sunset light. The Trappers, armed, were coming from their camp across the creek. They had two sleds and two teams with them. The other dogs were barking in the lines, concerned at being left behind.

As she ran to them, Catania saw that Jack was leading, looking calm . . . content. Seeing that, she understood he was only at ease, only fully himself in fighting. That seemed to her the saddest thing of all.

"The Cree," he said.

"Yes. Fifty-two . . . fifty-three of them." Catania wiped a little vomit off her buckskin shirt. "A young man—a boy—is leading." She saw that only Susan had been left in camp.

"And Mary's people?"

"They'll kill any Cree we don't, but they blame us for bringing the tribesmen down."

"Oh, thank you, Lord Jesus," Rod Sorbane said, and there were tears of happiness in his eyes. "—Oh, thank you!"

And other Trappers called out, "Thank you, dear Lord!" So happy, now they were rested, to have a chance to face the men who had killed their loved ones.

Catania was surprised, then not surprised, and found she now felt better herself. She'd thought only of the unluckiness—not of the luck.

"How close?" Newton said.

"They're tomorrow-morning away. The Garden people have followed them in the forest."

"Then we go to meet these warriors," Torrey said, and seemed as happy as if it was to be a wedding, in the woods.

* * *

In early evening, Buddy called a halt, but allowed only one fire of dry fallen branches, so little smoke would rise to drift among the trees.

The warriors gathered as close to the fire as they could, and held hands in groups of clansmen. The eagerness they'd had when they started, the willingness to run deep into strange forest to avenge the deaths of friends and recover future-looking luck, had turned to thoughtfulness . . . concern that now, more friends might be lost.

Despite Buddy's dream of the white bear leading them, the men felt uncertain, disliking such close woods. It also seemed to many that the snow-devils' luck, so disastrously bad in holding a range the Cree must have . . . that this luck was bound to turn if the Trappers had any magic at all. And they must have some magic, or they wouldn't be men and women, but only animals.

"They have luck," Buddy said to Philipe Cruizan, one of the oldest warriors, when Philipe mentioned this at the fire. "They have luck, but it's *mauvaise fortune*, weak luck and bad luck, while ours is strong. I feel it humming in my chest."

"Please The Weather," Cruizan said, "—that you're right."

To make themselves less uneasy, since a spirit chase allowed no totem masks or furs, the men began to paint. Dipping in the color pot, they coated their hands bright red . . . then pressed them to their faces, so palm prints and prints of fingers showed scarlet in the firelight across their eyelids, noses, and mouths. When they were painted, they felt better, felt lucky enough to dance the circles-within-circles—but only to soft humming, without drums.

* * *

As the Trappers went along the creek through Gardens town, the shrill birdcall chorus slowly quieted, so they left silence behind them.

As they climbed the valley path, a spruce cone fell in front of Catania. She looked up and saw Mary One-eye standing high above, on a swaying bridge of woven vine-rope. Naked in the cold, her fat round body striped in coils of green, she stared down at Catania as if they'd never met.

At the head of the valley, Carlson Gold-bracelets appeared from the skirt branches of a hemlock, and walked along with Jack. "Our wager's proved," he said, "—of fighting together."

"Yes. But this is *our* battle, first."

"Yours if you win it," Carlson said. "We will be as a weapons belt, buckled loose in the forest around you as you go." He walked away, stepped into the woods in an odd sidling fashion, and was gone.

Jim Olsen and Newton had come up. "Back-trail our trail?" Newton said to Jack.

"Simplest is best." Jim Olsen said, and said nothing more to start an argument.

"Yes," Jack said, "—back-trail, then wait for them to come. And knife-cut spruces for plant sap to rub on ourselves, so their dogs won't smell us if they bring them up."

"Only knife-cuts," Catania said. "Don't ring the bark and kill them. Be careful not to kill any of Gardens' trees."

Torrey and Tom Olsen led out, scouting at a trot through scattered woods . . . then on into deeper forest, back the way they'd come almost a Warm-time week before. After a long while running, they reached the Trappers' last camp, and waited for the others. They had seen no Garden men at all.

"Here?" Myles Weber looked impatient, happy to be getting ready to fight.

"No," Jack said. "This smells sour from our old fires' ashes. I noticed it—and they'll notice it. We'll back-trail a little more, set fresh fires for them to smell as they come on. I want a small open space. We'll show them we've camped there—and just left. They'll find fresh sled tracks, dog-shit . . . and an old knife-sheath thrown away."

. . . Near dark, backtracking, they found a small clearing in heavy brush, with greater trees beyond. Jack looked around, and said, "Yes."

"How could it be better?" Newton said, and called softly, "Start fires, and feed the dogs. We need them shitting."

"We wait here for them?" Jennifer Weber stepped in place as if she had to pee.

"In a way," Jack said. "We stay in the clearing only long enough to make a camp to draw them in." He made a gathering motion. "The tribesmen will be tired of close forest. They'll want to come into the clearing, to be together with no trees touching." Jack spread his arms wide, to show how much the Cree would want openness. "They'll come with first light, and it will seem that we've just left. They'll see the sled-tracks, hear our dogs going south—and they'll think they have us. They'll gather here, then run us down."

"How do you know what they'll do?" Pete Richardson said.

Jack smiled. "Tribesmen have little patience, and Mary One-eye said their leader was young, a boy. *More* impatience.... They'll come in all together—and we'll be in the evergreens, with this clearing held in our hands." Jack cupped both hands together, to show how. "—A still hunt, left hand and right. And a few of us back on the path . . . to hold it, and keep them grouped here under the arrows."

"It will work," Tall-David said, and most of the others listening agreed.

"Martha," Jack said, "—just before first light, you and Myles drive the dogs back the way we came. And not quietly."

"I won't do that," Martha Sorbane said.

"I won't either," Myles Weber said. "I intend to fight."

"I'll tell you my 'why' once," Jack said. Darkness had come down, so he seemed a gray-furred ghost of Jack Monroe. "—I'll tell you once, but not again. I'd be very sorry to have to kill you, so that other people will do what I tell them to."

Neither Martha nor Myles said anything.

"—Martha, you're old. Myles, you're old and small. You both are better used drawing the Cree to follow." Then Jack walked away into the dark, calling for four small fires.

Joan Richardson and her son, Del, came over. Del carried a spruce torch—and by its light, Martha looked at Catania and said, "Your lover is a bitch's son, and bad luck."

"No, this is good luck," Joan said, spinning her lance shaft across her fingers. "These Crees are a gift from Mountain Jesus." And Del agreed.

* * *

One of the best arguments for ancestor-spirits, when shamans and big talkers discussed the matter, was the sudden refreshment of weary men, of runners particularly.

Who but a caring ancestor of the same blood and spirit would enter a tired runner and give him, as a gift, fresh strength?

"Thank you, Five-Bear-Claws," Buddy said, and leaped a fallen tree to keep on running, with the thud and rustle of his men coming behind him. It was odd that he'd called on his mother's grandfather, who'd been all white-blood and supposedly not to be trusted, but that was the spirit that must have come to visit.

There was smoke in the trees. Paul Kisses-the-Girls, scouting, had found the snow-devils just gone from their camp.

While the spirit was still in him, Buddy thanked Five-Bear-Claws for the end of this chase. Another day or two might have been another day or two too long. Some of the older men had already gone deaf, and didn't hear when he spoke to them.

Buddy glanced over his shoulder as he ran, and saw that the warriors had their hatchets out. Gray dawn light shone on bright steel.

There was a little clear space just ahead. Buddy ducked and ran through it fast, in case the Trappers had left a bowman behind. But no one shot at him. The little space opened into a bigger clearing, shadowed from sunrise by trees at its edges.

The campfire ashes still smoked. The mealy snow was rutted by sled runners. The place smelled of snow-devils and their dogs.

Buddy ran dodging from side to side, being careful of a back-trail guard. But the Trappers had been too frightened to leave one.

He stopped running as his men came in. When they gathered, Buddy said, *"Shut up!"* softly as he could and be heard. He listened. Dogs were yelping . . . south.

"Hear that?" he said. His men nodded.

It was a question whether to send back to the Maynard brothers to bring up the teams and sleds. But this forest snow was now so poor and shallow, it seemed unnecessary. Sleds would only slow them.

Edwin-Jim was jogging in place, watching him. Some men were catching their breath, others jumping up and down, all bad feelings forgotten now they were so close.

Buddy called, "We run them down!"—tossed his hatchet whirling in the air, and caught it as it fell.

The men shouted—happy with their leader, now—and followed him down the Trappers' sign, running fast so as not to be run over.

The clearing narrowed, south, to a close-treed track streaked with yellow sunrise shining through high foliage. Buddy led down the snow-devils' path. He thought, *I will be a chief* . . . and how that would have pleased his mother.

He still had his spirit breath, dodged past big tree-trunks at a run—and saw a tall red-haired woman step into the path before him. A Trapper, with a lance. Another woman, face scarred like a warrior's, stepped out beside her.

Edwin-Jim yelled with joy. "This is their back-trail guard!" He ran up beside Buddy so they came to the women together. Edwin-Jim was laughing like a fool.

The women's lances leveled, steel heads shining. Buddy swung his hatchet, struck the red-hair's lance aside and ran on into her to knock her down and put the hatchet in her head.

As he hit her, the woman grunted and went to her knees. Buddy was struggling with this red-haired woman, who was quick and almost strong as a man, when he heard Edwin-Jim make an odd noise, and saw him come staggering past with a loop of rope, blue and shining, hanging out of his long buckskin shirt.

Buddy, wrestling with the strong red-hair as if they were making hard love, saw it was Edwin-Jim's guts come out. The scarred woman had cut his belly open.

Using all his strength while gripping her knife-hand's wrist, Buddy could barely hold the red-hair woman down. He raised his hatchet to chop the witch before she could twist her knife-hand free—and someone lifted him up off her and away. He thought it was Paul Kisses-the-Girls or another warrior; he could hear shouting and fighting behind him.

He turned to tell Paul to let him go—but saw it was a tall Trapper with a short black beard. The man looked thoughtful, not hurried. Catching Buddy's swinging hatchet by the handle as if they'd both intended that, he reached across and did something with a knife.

There was a terrible burning, as if Buddy's throat had caught fire; he was afraid to reach up to touch it. He walked a few steps away and no one bothered him. He could hear the fighting back on the path. He could hear the warriors very clearly, trying to force a way through, make room for the others crowding behind them.

He could hear, but he couldn't breathe, and trying made terrible noises. He leaned against a tree, felt sick and sat down.

Still hearing war cries, Buddy saw only the backs of six or seven snow-devils fighting to hold the narrow way against his men. Most of the warriors were still in the clearing, shouting. Then there was twanging music, and a great whisper. The men in the clearing began to scream.

Buddy felt something pouring into him, running inside him like slow water. He looked down and saw he was soaked with red all down his front. Going home like this, his buckskins ruined, it would be difficult to face his mother, who had scraped them so white, worked them so soft. . . .

Great battle in the woods.

We won—killed fifty-one Cree in an ambush (a perfect Warm-time word). We lost Max Auerbach, Tatum Sorbane, and Evelyn Weber killed, and have nine wounded. The Garden people hunted the two Cree dog-holders, caught them, and burned them on their sleds.

We kept the best of the tribesmen's dogs. I'm sorry to say it, but the Garden people intend to eat the others. We are keeping this sadness from Dummy.

Now our people are happier—and so am I. Lance medicine, arrow medicine, and knife medicine has cured us of much sorrow.

I know, by our pleasure, how far we are from being civilized.

FROM THE JOURNAL OF DOCTOR CATANIA OLSEN

12

Garden Mary, having lost none of her people, came smiling to the Trappers' camp in the evening. She crossed the creek bridge, then walked up along the bank with May and eleven other plump girls dancing and singing around her. They were singing a very old Warm-time song, 'Dancing in the Dark,' though their melody sounded odd.

Musicians came behind them, playing flutes and deep-bellied drums. And there were other Garden people following with skewered goat meat and birds to roast, a pot of trade-honey, and a small keg of vodka. Four men came last, carrying someone sitting up in their arms.

Mary One-eye walked into the camp, calling out that she'd brought celebration girls, celebration food—and the Garden's doctor, to help tend the injured.

This doctor, a withered elderly woman in a green robe, was the person carried by the four men. They put her down on a stool at the nearest Trapper fire, and set a small leather chest in the snow beside her. . . . Catania had never seen this woman before. Her wrinkled skin was painted with green leaves. She had no feet; the stumps of her ankles were sheathed in beaten gold.

Mary came to Catania and put an arm around her waist. "Now," she said, "—you will see how scientifically medical we are. And all learned *before* your three fine books."

"Her feet. . . ."

With a one-armed hug—a strong fat-woman's hug—Mary stood on tiptoes to whisper into Catania's ear. "Wouldn't it have been foolish for my Lady-aunt to allow knowledge to walk away?"

When Mary let go, calling for pepper for the goat meat, Catania went to the doctor and bowed as the Garden people bowed, in respect for her age. She couldn't bow to the old woman's skill until it was shown.

"Welcome, colleague," Catania said, since that had been the doctor-to-doctor greeting in a copybook, *The Mag—Magpie's?—Obsession*, by Douglas. A wonderful book of secret kindnesses and successful surgery for blindness, unfortunately not given in detail.

It seemed to please the old woman. "Dorothy is my name," she said. "Fat Mary mentioned hatchet wounds." Her slurring Garden voice seemed to have withered with her.

"Hatchet wounds and knife cuts. And some penetrating injuries by arrows—four, one with the head resting in bone, the tibia."

"Ouch," the old woman said.

"Yes . . . ouch."

"And you've done what?"

"In the open wounds, bleeding vessels pressed to clot, or burned shut. Some cuts cleaned and sewed. Hatchet wounds cleaned and left open to rest for two days before sewing."

" 'Cleaned.' " Doctor Dorothy shifted on her stool. "Anyone can say 'cleaned.' "

"I clean with poured boiled water, then vodka."

"That's all? No little friends from the forest? No green helpers? No dust from correct fungi?"

"No. I believe that simplest is best."

The old woman smiled her first smile. "Doctor," she said, "—all simple people believe simplest is best."

Because the woman had no feet, and was so old, Catania kept her temper.

"I'll look at your arrowhead stuck in bone," the Garden doctor said. "Bring him to me."

"Her."

"Bring her to me. We'll deal with that, first. Catania is your name?"

"Yes."

"Catania, when you use vodka in a deep wound, it leaves a little slime—you know the word?"

"Yes, I do."

"Well, it leaves a little slime of tissue-meat killed. And that can make a comfortable bed for the too-tiny-to-see-but-actual bacteria coming later to visit.—Are you angry?"

"No. Go on, say what you were saying. I know about the too-tinies."

"I'm saying that in deep wounds that have bled, unless made with rusty metal, better a clean cloth cord left in for draining, than your rinse of vodka."

Catania said nothing.

"You are angry," the old woman said. "But there are two reasons you shouldn't be. First, a doctor's deaf pride kills her patients. And second, I could be your grandmother . . . and grandmothers know more than granddaughters."

Catania was surprised to feel tears coming into her eyes, then realized it was sorrow for the elderly Trappers left behind to die, sadness refreshed by this old woman. "Forgive my rudeness," she said, bowed again to Garden's doctor, and motioned to have Jennifer Weber carried over.

Jennifer had made no sound, and made none now, though the sharp steel was in her bone.

"A brave girl," Doctor Dorothy said, when Jennifer was laid on a caribou hide before her. The old woman leaned forward, bracing herself on the golden stumps of her ankles. She examined the wound in Jennifer's leg by firelight. Midway along the shin, a black stub of arrow-shaft stuck out of crusted red swelling.

"Pooh," the doctor said. "Girl, you'll be dancing in a Warm-time month. Dancing in summer." The old woman leaned sideways to open the lid of her leather chest, took out a wooden bottle, and poured green liquid over her hands. "Vodka and forest friends," she said to Catania.

Then she rummaged in the chest again, brought out a small tool made of two slender steel pieces fastened together almost at their ends, so they swiveled and closed like trade-scissors, but with little teeth in their jaws. The doctor poured green liquid on this tool, looked at Catania, and said "Pliers."

Catania was astonished. She'd imagined pliers were much bigger, and had been used to bend thick metal wire and turn large screw-bolts and so forth. But that was reading and imagining. This was seeing.

A number of Trappers had come to watch, and stood in a circle around them.

Doctor Dorothy leaned over Jennifer again, and said, "What's your name?"

Jennifer said, "Jennifer," but very softly. She looked sick. The pain was making her sick.

"Speak up!" The old woman bent to hear.

"*Jennifer....*"

"That's better," the doctor said. And she whipped the pliers down and hit the girl with them, hit her hard on the nose—then quickly leaned the other way, reached down with the pliers click-clicking, caught the arrow stub and yanked and twisted. The arrow made a snapping sound and came out with a blurt of blood.

"What happened?" Jennifer lay with her hands to her face. "She *hit* me!" Jennifer began to cry. "And my leg—"

"It's all over, Sweet bush-berry, all over." The doctor bent and crooned at Jennifer as if she loved her. "Your pretty nose isn't broken, and you were very brave."

The old woman looked up at Lucy Edwards, who was watching, and said, "Take her away from me. Take her to be with her friends, let the wound bleed, and give her one drink of vodka and no more."

When Trappers had carried Jennifer away, Catania bowed to Doctor Dorothy. "Thank you for a lesson," she said. "Doctor Monroe never thought of doing that—and I have never thought of it."

"It's a mind trick," the old woman said. "A distraction by a small pain from a large one. Useful only for a moment, like most of what we can do for hurting until dreaming gas is found again, or the morphing—some damned butterfly, I suppose." She leaned over to put her pliers back into the leather chest. "Catania...."

"Yes, Grandmother?"

The old woman smiled. "What is stuck in bone must be gotten

out quickly. Fumbling with it this way and that only causes more harm, more chance of rotting."

"I see. . . ."

"And with this injury, once it's bled awhile, I *would* use vodka. Pour it in, then rinse it out quickly with boiled water. Then bandage lightly with boiled cloth."

"That's what I do."

"The bone was split. She will probably lose her leg. Have you done that medicine?"

"Twice. I've taken off a boy's leg and a man's arm. Both were spoiling. The little boy died while I did it. His heart stopped beating."

"Yes," the old woman said, and she looked very tired. "Well, don't wait too long if you smell the leg going. Take it at the knee—good flap."

"I will."

"And a drain!"

"Yes."

"May be all right, of course. She's young, and we got the arrowhead out soon. But most of the time, when I've tried to help a bad bone that is touched by the air, I've done more harm than good."

"Doctor Monroe told me, 'Better a leg than a life.' "

"Sad," Doctor Dorothy said, "—but true." A perfect use of the Warm-time phrase.

"We are strong people. Perhaps Jennifer will keep her leg."

"Hope and despair are both dangers to doctors," the old woman said, and crossed her legs to be comfortable. The gold sheathing her stumps glowed in the firelight. "Now, show me a hatchet wound. Veins are easy to deal with; white-string tendons are not."

At other fires, the Trappers had begun to dance to the Garden peoples' drums and flutes. Garden girls were dancing with the Trapper men, some with their robes pulled down so their breasts showed and shook as they stepped.

Catania, going to bring Mark Richardson over to the Garden

doctor—he had a hatchet-cut deep across his left shoulder—passed Mary One-eye watching the dancers, smiling and striking the palms of her hands together in time with the music.

"You don't mind your girls dancing with our men?"

"No," Mary said, and raised her voice against the drums. "It's fucking I'm looking for. New seed, hybrids, cuttings and starts for Gardens. We've been growing too few men, too many girls—and all too much the same." She turned to the dancers and sang a song without words to the Garden music, her plump hands pattering a swift uneven rhythm.

Helping Mark along—"I heal fast," he said, walking hunched with the pain of the wound—helping him along, Catania thought that Mary's wish for new-crop babies was likely the reason she'd let the Trappers stay. And might let them stay a little longer.

Through the evening and into the night, it became an eating party, then a drinking party, then a fucking party. Mary's daughter, May, danced with all the Trapper men but Torrey. She never looked at him.

Mary One-eye smiled at everyone, and drank as if she were young, but touched no man. Only Dummy Olsen tried to touch her, and she turned him away gently.

Late at night, Tall-David Richardson came to Catania, drunk, and asked for kindness fucking, though it wasn't Sunday. A Garden girl had danced with him but said 'no' to lying down, afraid of having a too-tall child and being laughed at.

Tall-David asked, but Jack came over and said, "Go away." And Tall-David went, unsatisfied.

A little later, while Catania and Mary One-eye were sitting, watching Rod Sorbane jump-dance over a fire, Mary said, "Do you now hold yourself only for him?" And had no need to name.

"I try to."

"Poor Catania," Mary said. "Tomorrow, I will let you see our library."

* * *

In the morning, men and women came to Catania whining like children over their headaches and bad bellies. The Garden vodka was a different vodka than they were used to; it had green stuffs in it. Some women thought they'd been poisoned because, when they shook their heads, they could feel things moving inside and hurting. These women were upset, and asked for medicines she didn't have.

Catania—who felt sick herself, and supposed it was a bad smoked bird that troubled her—was very patient, listening, nodding. But Big Millie Auerbach had come twice, each time claiming she saw double of everything and was very ill, sicker than anyone else—the others being only fools who couldn't hold the potatoes' spirit.

The first two times, Catania listened carefully, even moved her finger back and forth in front of Millie's face to see that her eyes followed together and the pupils were the same size.

The third time Big Millie came, Catania led her down to the creek edge, still lacy with ice, saying it was to pick a watercress sprig for pain. She told Millie to stand on the bank with her eyes closed—then pushed her in.

Big Millie was cured by that. So were the others, just by seeing the cure. Catania's stomach also felt better after she'd run across the camp and into the forest, while Millie chased her with a heavy piece of firewood.

It would have been a longer run—the Auerbachs were violent people—but Catania managed a sort of conversation with Big Millie while running, ducking, and dodging behind trees. She asked her if she didn't feel better, and claimed that the water-cure had been medical, not a joke at all, and the others ignorant for laughing.

Millie, who wasn't clever, finally began to believe that might be so. And after a last, half-hearted chase through frozen brambles, she threw the firewood down and went away muttering.

Still, since some Trappers kept teasing Millie, so she stayed sullen, Catania decided to go to Mary One-eye's house, remembering her promise of the library.

"I'm going to Mary's," she said to Jack. He was sitting cross-legged on a hide, playing pick-up sticks with Torrey. Jack's big hands and long fingers moved delicately over the stack of thin little peeled and polished twigs.

"You shifted one," Torrey said.

"Not yet." Jack looked up at Catania. "Be careful going to Mary One-eye's house so often." He paused, thinking. "What she wants, won't be what we want."

"Jack, I know I have to be careful."

"Going to see her is not being careful, Catania." He opened his hand, showed it empty to her, then slowly closed it. "Each time, she will try to take a piece of yourself from you. That's what chiefs do."

"And if I stay in camp today, I'll have more trouble with Big Millie, unless you so-strong men protect me."

Jack and Torrey both laughed, and said they couldn't go against Millie. They said they were afraid of her.

As Catania walked away, Torrey said, "You moved that stick."

"No, I didn't," Jack said, and tried very slowly, very carefully to slide a little twig free of the heap without disturbing any other. "But now, I did."

"My turn. You can watch how the game should be played." And it was true that Torrey, though he had short fingers—and now only nine of them—had a light touch with pick-up sticks. He began to slide a stick from the bottom, which was a trick he had that had won him wagers. Jack, pretending to look close, blew a quick silent breath at the heap, and a twig moved a little.

"Did you—what did you do?"

"Nothing," Jack said, but kept his face too still when he said it.

"My game," Torrey said, and sat back. "This is a game I have won right now!"

"I didn't do anything!"

"I have won this game," Torrey said—and turned as five Trappers walked toward their fire.

Jim and Chapman Olsen, Bailey Auerbach, and Joan Richardson with her son, Del, came up. They were carrying their lances.

"We're going back north," Bailey Auerbach said. He said it, but Jim Olsen looked it.

"Why?" Jack said.

"Because. . . ." Bailey said.

"Because we don't like these woods," Jim Olsen said. "And because we belong in the mountains, and don't want to go south into other country."

Torrey stood up, but Jack stayed sitting.

"And because we're tired of you telling us what to do," Joan Richardson said. "We are free people."

"If you go north," Jack said, gathering the pick-up sticks, "—the Cree will hunt you and kill you."

"We just gave them a lesson down here," Chapman said. "They'll leave us alone, now."

Jack stacked the polished twigs in his grip, then dropped them into a heap for a new game. He studied the pile . . . then lightly, carefully picked one off the top. "Your turn," he said. Torrey knelt, studied, then lifted another twig away.

Jack looked up at Chapman. "*Because* of our forest lesson, they will hunt you harder. They'll kill you all, so their dead can rest down here."

"We'll go west, then, before we go north," Chapman said. "The Cree don't own all the mountains."

"No," Torrey said. "The Blackfoot own those others, west."

"It's bitter," Jack said, "—to be whipped out of our country." He stood up. "I know, because I've been driven out of country three times, now. But there's no longer a place for Trappers on the Range."

"You say," Joan Richardson said.

"Yes," Jack said, "—I do. And the Cree say. And the Blackfoot in the western mountains say. And all our dead people say."

Jim Olsen shifted his hand on his lance. "And *I* say we're going back north. We'll find a place where no tribesmen live."

"Not only us," Joan Richardson said. "Susan is talking about going back with the baby, and Tall-David wants to go, and some others."

Jack reached behind him, where his lance leaned against a sapling pine, and picked it up. "No," he said. "Susan and my brother's baby stay here and go south. Most of us stay here and go south. You five can go back north—but no one else, without killing."

"You're telling us what to do!" Joan Richardson made an animal's face.

"Not telling you five," Jack said. "But telling the others, yes."

"If you want to go," Torrey said to them, "—then go alone."

"If only five go," Jim Olsen said, "—then the Cree *will* hunt and kill us. You know that. And five people are not enough to make new families in the mountains."

"Too bad," Jack said.

Del Richardson drew his knife, and Tattooed Newton said, "Go where?" from just behind him. Newton had come over from his fire. He had a Garden ax in his hands.

"Go or stay," Jack said to them. "Fight now, or not, but no one goes with you."

"I don't think they want to fight," Newton said. "I think Jim's too careful for it."

Jim Olsen gave Newton a bad look.

"Oh, dear," Newton said. "I've upset him."

"If you want trouble," Joan said to Newton, "—you can have it with me."

But Newton only smiled at her, which seemed to make Joan angrier, so her knuckles grew white on her lance-shaft.

After a little while of silence, Jim Olsen said, "There will come a time."

"I hope not," said Jack. "There are too few of us already."

"Still one too many," Jim Olsen said, and said nothing more. Del Richardson sheathed his knife as they turned and walked away.

"Might have done better to kill him." Newton seemed to think the argument was funny. "Why do you want all these hanging on your tit, anyway?"

"I don't know," Jack said, and he and Torrey sat down again to play.

Newton smiled and shook his head. " ' . . . that reason knows not,' " he said. Certainly a copybook phrase, or part of one. He tossed the Garden ax spinning into the air, and caught it coming down.

* * *

Catania, across the creek bridge, walked along the low path past raised beds and warming-tubs, then climbed the high path to Mary One-eye's house.

She called at the entrance tree, then climbed down the root steps and stooped inside. Mary was sitting on a soft blue cushion, staring into her fire. There was something cooking there in a trade-kettle. It smelled like bird and onions.

An old man was sleeping by the hearth. His left hand was gone.

Mary smiled at Catania, and said, "I hear you were just chased by the angry Millie."

"Yes. It was because of a joke."

"Come sit by me, tall Scar-face," Mary said, and leaned to tug another cushion beside her. "Doctors, and any women who know what others don't, should never joke. Otherwise, they may be joked *at*, and that spoils power."

"I don't need power," Catania said.

Mary turned from looking into the fire. "I don't care what you need for *you* and you shouldn't care what you need for *yourself*. Power is necessary for growing fear and respect—as great trees grow—so your people do as you order, and are saved from ignorance, foolishness—"

"Yes, I understand."

Mary looked very unfriendly. "Don't tell me you understand, until I have finished telling you."

"I didn't mean to be rude."

"I don't care what you meant to be."

Catania was quiet.

"There," Mary said, and smiled at her. "That's how I first knew you could be a truly wise woman, even though you'd been nothing but a healing-whore for simple people. I knew, when you knew to be silent."

Catania sat and looked into the fire, and Mary put an arm around her and hugged her. "There," she said. "There. . . . Are you angry with me?"

"I'm frightened of you."

"No need to be," Mary said, then reached across and touched Catania's left breast through her buckskin shirt. She squeezed and weighed it in her hand, but not like a lover. "You'll bleed in a day or two."

"Yes."

Mary took her hand away. "At the beginning of winter, I had a pain in my heart that made me fall down. Since then, I have had two bad pains, but I haven't fallen down. Old Dorothy Gold-ankles said my heart was choking."

"Let me look," Catania said, and leaned to stare at Mary's lips. Where there had been a frightened Catania a moment ago, there was now a doctor.

"What are you looking at?"

"To see if your blood is running red enough. What did Doctor Dorothy say to do?"

"Catania, she said to eat little meals and lose some of myself, and not to worry. What do you say?"

"The same. And go for long easy walks every day. Also, don't climb in the trees."

Mary smiled. "The day I have not been in a green sister, I'm better dead."

"Then let the men carry you up."

"They carry old Runaway Dorothy. I am not carried, Catania, unless I've made a victory harvest. . . . The reason I tell you this is that my daughter, May, is clever, but not yet wise. Another of our girls, Ruth, might do, but she's selfish. She's in your camp, fucking—she'll go when your people go." Mary leaned forward to look into the kettle. "Bird-meat boiled gets tough."

"If you don't want the girls to come to us—"

"I told you I do; we need new sap running. We have too many girls. Seven or eight could leave, and leave us stronger."

"Gardens seems strong enough to me as it is."

Mary smiled. "You're a liar—or a fool, which I doubt. If your Tall Jack had come down with two-hundred fighters instead of forty, would he have been courteous to me, and bowed his head and called me 'Mother'?"

". . . Possibly not."

" 'Possibly not.' " Mary had imitated Catania very well. "Sweet Ugly, listen to me. Wise women weave the ways that hold all people safer, costing only hands or feet or eyes. And have to, because our cold world is full of Tall Jacks—though yours is certainly a wolf of wolves." Mary reached over to stick a testing finger quickly into the stew, then tasted the tip. "Too hot. I know you love him; every creature here, every bird and sister tree knows you care for Tall Jack—and they know that he is past any caring but small-caring and kindness for you. You and he have come together too late."

"Not so."

Mary said nothing, only sat on her cushion and looked at Catania. She sat silent until Catania said again, "Not so." And still Mary sat silent.

Catania, after a while, wished to say something instead of 'Not so,' but couldn't.

Mary leaned over and stroked her hair. "I know," she said. Then she turned to look into her kettle. "This fucking thing is starting to boil." She reached to pick up a large wooden spoon, and used that to swing the kettle a little out of the fire.

"My daughter is *supposed* to be the cook, here."

"I can go get her," Catania started to stand, "—send her to you."

"No," Mary said. ". . . I need a better daughter, Catania, to be the Lady of Gardens when my heart chokes itself. I need a wise daughter, deserving obedience. I need a daughter who will break her right eye, pull it out, and offer it to the people, so they will know she is a serious person who will watch over them with the eye she spared." Mary smiled. "Don't look so frightened. I would never hold you here, unless you were strong enough to be held."

Mary threw the wooden spoon whirling, hitting the old man in the head. He woke with a grunt and start.

"Get up," Mary said, "—and take this doctor to the library." She smiled at Catania. "Didn't you come to go to the library?"

"Yes."

"Think," Mary said. "Think of why else you came, why you come and come again to see me, though it frightens you. There are two people in every person, Catania, and what one of them wants is secret. So go, think of what your second person wants— and how much must be given, to get it."

The old man led Catania up out of Mary's house into sunlight and spring air. The weather was warming, day by day. Catania felt a burden and a freedom both, being out of Mary's house, and supposed the woman had taken a piece of her to keep, as Jack had said she would.

The one-handed man went before her along the high path through Gardens. And as they went, Garden people gave Catania friendly glances. Once, beneath a swinging bridge, three little girls slid giggling down a vine rope—one, two, three—and trotted alongside, plucking at Catania's buckskins and reaching up to touch her knife's bone handle.

She stroked them like puppies as they hurried beside her. Then they were gone, popped down out of sight into a deep-root house like mountain marmots.

The one-handed man stopped by a narrow vine ladder, tied and knotted together, that swung up and up into a fir tree so large that eight men could not have joined hands around its trunk.

"If you can't climb," the one-handed man said, "I will have men carry you up." He had a green stripe painted across his mouth.

"I can climb," Catania said. "Will you tell me your name?"

"Paul Bongiorno," he said. "Climb to the bridge at the top, not the lower one, and tell the guard that Mary allows your visit."

"Thank you, Paul."

"Don't look down," Paul Bongiorno said.

. . . But Catania did look down. She looked down as she reached the first bridge. The bridge was long, hanging between distant thick branches, and it swung slightly in a breeze. Catania had grown uneasy watching it as she climbed up . . . and up. So she looked down.

There had been much deeper gulfs in the mountains—even Long Ledge had been higher than this from the base of its cliff— but here, she was climbing on something that moved under her moccasin-boots, that gave and creaked and swayed this way and that so nothing was certain except the rough gray-brown wall of bark behind it.

Looking down, she saw everything tiny, too far away, and became dizzy from the distance there was to fall. The vine-ladder leaned away from the fir's trunk; it leaned back so she had to grip the cross-cords, the *rungs*, very hard to keep from leaning farther and farther back, until she was hanging with nothing but air beneath her.

Catania was sorry she'd passed the first bridge. She could have rested there, and if it swung in the wind, so what? *So what.* . . . Wonderful phrase. She couldn't remember where she'd read it.

She thought Garden people must be staring up at her, squinting in the sunlight to see her so high against the trunk of the tree. They would be looking and wondering what might be wrong, why a grown woman was clinging and not climbing, where little children went all day.

Catania looked up instead of down, and very high above her, as high above her as the ground was down below, she saw a man watching. Gold glinted on his arm.

A doctor cannot show herself a fool, or no one will trust her. Catania got her left foot up onto the next cross-cord—rung—and then her right. But that made her lean back and out even more. *Everyone is watching this fool....*

She couldn't understand what the problem was. She'd climbed this high—now what was the difficulty? Perhaps the vine-ladder's lines had loosened, come undone in places....

The ladder began to shake, and that frightened Catania so she couldn't pretend any longer *not* to be frightened. Something must be broken.

The shaking grew worse. She tightened her grip—and thought if she fell past the swinging bridge she might reach out and catch something there to save herself.

"Your hands." A pleasant slurring Garden voice.

Catania looked up, and saw that the Gold-bracelets, this one leaner than most Garden people, had come down to her. "... What?"

"Your hands hold you close to the ladder; your feet climb." He swung around and came down beside her like a red squirrel. She could smell the pine-sap in the green stripes painted on him, and the comforting odor of a man's sweat.

He reached around the small of her back, and hauled her upright against the ladder's vines. When she had a closer grip, he slid down past her. She felt his hands on her ankles. "Left," he said, and lifted that foot to the next rung up. Then "Right," lifted that foot and set it in place. "Left ... right, left ... right ..." And Catania went up so easily, holding the ladder close to her, climbing properly, that the Gold-bracelets soon let her ankles go, swarmed up past her, and was gone.

She found him waiting at the top bridge. He had his ax in his hand.

"Why are you here?" he said, as if he hadn't seen her before.

"Mary said I could see the library." Across the bridge, there was a long house made of adzed planks. The planks were painted green and seemed to be sewn together with plant-cord twisted thick.

The Gold-bracelets considered it. "But she's not with you."

"No." The long house was supported by great branches. It lay across three of them as if it had fallen from the sky.

"If you've given me a lie, I'll throw you down the tree."

"I'm not lying."

"Then go across." He gestured at the bridge with his ax, and smiled. "You won't fall."

Catania walked over the bridge, careful to stay in the middle, on the short pieces of wood knotted across it for a footpath. The bridge swayed back and forth as she went, and Catania wished there were vines along the sides . . . anything to hold on to.

She reached a platform of planks. There was a starved blue-gray dog painted on them—painted running to the right. The house's roof came out over this platform to make a shelter. There was a wooden door like the one at the first-pulp mill, so she supposed this was a building, not just a house.

Here, standing on planks pegged together that hardly moved, she looked down for the second time, and saw, through the great tree's sweeps of green foliage, almost all of Gardens stretched beneath her, the fast creek foaming through it. It was more than a bow-shot to the ground.

The building's wooden door was shut, and Catania wondered how to deal with it. She saw a wooden latch with a cord, but supposed she first ought to warn the people inside that she was there.

On the Range, this had been done by whistling or calling at the hide, so she said, "I'm here."

No one came out to greet her, so she called louder. "I'm here!"

Catania heard someone laughing, and looked back. It was the Gold-bracelets at the other end of the bridge. Laughing, he imitated hitting the door with the knuckles of his hand.

Catania did that, though it hurt. Then did it again.

The latch moved. The door swung open, squeaking on metal fasteners. A little fat man, wearing a gold necklace over his green robe, stood there looking angry.

"You don't have to break it!" he said. And Catania realized he meant the wooden door. She had hit it too hard.

"I'm sorry."

He put his finger to his lips. "Speak quietly; this is a library. Why are you here?"

"Mary said I could come and see it."

"Well . . . all right." The little man seemed annoyed. "Come in and see it—but don't touch anything." He was very pale, fat as a baby, and the only Garden person Catania had seen who wore no green paint.

Catania followed him inside, onto a wood floor as polished and clean as the copyplace had been. But this room was bigger—it was wide, and as long as a knife could be thrown and be sure to stick.

There were wood benches down the middle, all as smooth and shining as the floor. Big square holes had been cut into the building's sides, so daylight came in. . . . Two Garden men were sitting on the benches with copybooks in their laps. They were reading to themselves in silence, instead of reading to other people—which seemed selfish to Catania.

The room was bright with sunshine, and smelled of paper. Copybooks were stacked flat along wide shelves up and down and along the building's sides between the square light-holes. *Windows.* Catania looked through one. *These are windows.*

All the copybooks were made as they'd been made on the Range—which must, Catania thought, be the civilized way. They lay in thick flat folios, the long pages bound together along their top edges. Those edges folded over twice, for strength. They were bound with smooth small cord sewn through and through, then tied off in a tasseled knot.

The little fat man stood watching her, likely in case she tried to touch something.

"My name is Doctor Catania Olsen. What's yours?"

"Peter," he said. "I'm called Necklace Peter."

"How many copybooks do you keep here?"

"We have six-hundred and forty-three." He pursed his lips. "The 'three' are your medicals. Now, we have them, too."

"Six-hundred and forty-three. . . . That's many more than we had."

"We have W. Farber, M. Chouteau, Robert Frost, L. Timmons, Raymond Chandler—"

"*Raymond* Chandler? Are you sure that's right. Not *Aymond*?"

"Aymond isn't a *name*. Never was."

"But Peter, we had a very old four-times-recopied. Author: Aymond Chandler."

"Then it was copied wrong four times. 'Aymond' is not a name! . . . We have him, and we have other ancient authors. We have William Carson; we have Hamilton Basso; we have Terrence Eastman; we have John O'Hara; we have Louise Chang; we have Max Niles; we have Arthur R. G. Solmssen and Michele Henridon. And we have many more than that."

"I would like to hold one."

Necklace Peter looked at her. "Your hands are dirty." Then he said, "Oh . . . all right," and walked back to the wooden door. There was a trade-pot on the floor in the corner; a white woven cloth was folded beside it. "Come here, and get those hands a little clean."

Catania went obediently to wash. It occurred to her that Necklace Peter had no neck, so his name sounded doubly apt. There was certainly no Warm-time word more perfect than 'apt.'

She sat on a bench away from the two silent readers, and Peter brought a copybook and laid it open across her lap.

"Ever read him? Apparently he was named for the cold, as it came down."

"No."

"Very, *very* old book."

"We didn't have him." Catania turned the pages, admiring the copying. It was a book of poems, beautifully done in perfect square little printing with rich black ink. Copied with steel-nib pens, no question. "But we had wonderful things, and also very old."

"What?—Be careful turning the pages."

"I know how to handle a copybook."

"Well . . . just be careful." Necklace Peter sat beside her on the bench and watched her hands. It made Catania nervous.

"We had the Websters, of course, and the Bible-book, and we had *Beach Red*—"

"About?"

"Fighting with loud powder-guns in very warm weather."

"Not interesting," the little man said. "Did you have Paul Dirac? It would be about the Physics."

"No."

"Did you have a book on the nearly-thinkers—the little machines that were clever?"

"The computes. No, but many mentions."

"Did you have an encyclopedia?"

Catania laughed. "If we had had one of those, even the tribesmen would have come and served us like our dogs, though they don't care for copybooks. Do you have one?"

"No," Necklace Peter said. "But someone has one somewhere. . . ."

"We had *Or the White Whale*."

"Oh, I doubt it, not the whole book."

"Yes, we did. We had the whole book from walking down to the salty sea until the ship sinks in it. It made pages two hands thick."

". . . The ship *sinks*?"

"Yes." Sitting so close to Necklace Peter, Catania could smell him. He smelled like a baked potato. "—It sinks, and Rachel comes looking for her lost children."

Peter was quiet for a time, seemed to be thinking of the *Pequod* sinking. "And that whole book is gone now?"

"Gone," Catania said, and the small word seemed too heavy to hold, referred to too great a loss. "—My friends, and the children, and all our copybooks." The sunshine and quiet in the library, the beautiful printing and smell of paper seemed to press down upon Catania. She began to weep.

"Gone," the little man said, and looked very sad.

The two other Garden men glanced up from their silent reading, and Catania turned her head aside so no tears would fall to stain '*Stopping by Woods on a Snowy Evening.*'

I have been to Gardens' library. It is high in a tree, and they have six-hundred and forty-three copybooks, now including my medicals. Words, and the smell of ink and paper, made me cry.

Necklace (Neckless) Peter has loaned us two copybooks— one we used to have, and the men so much enjoyed. The other has this passage in it, a passage the little man thought I'd like. And I do like it, but sadly.

> ... the times we come among strangers, to be
> astonished by their differences from those we loved;
> the change of line, colors various, the different air
> that from room to room proclaims our oddness here,
> far from what we knew.
>> Are future's flowers the same to see, or songs we
>> sing with these new people the notes we heard
>> before? I think not. Even children's voices sound
>> here in slightly different tune than those of the little
>> ones who chanted through our house before the
>> change. . . .

This was from The Wine of Days, *by Megan Reilly. Megan Reilly is many hundreds of years gone—I'm not sure if Megan was a man's name, or a woman's. But a Reilly long dead still murmurs in my ear. Could even Mountain Jesus do a greater thing?*

FROM THE JOURNAL OF DOCTOR CATANIA OLSEN

13

North, on the range that had been Trapper Range and now was not, five chiefs walked along the cliff's ledge in evening, scuffing a light spring snow, to call on Richard Much and mention what he already knew—that the boy and fifty-two warriors he'd sent south would never return.

This was known because almost three Warm-time weeks had passed without word, because Charlie Chewapa had dreamed his son was dead, and because others had dreamed their fathers, husbands, or sons were dead.

No one had had a good-news dream. The women were cutting their arms.

Richard Much came out of his cave house, and listened to the chiefs. He thought a while, then said, "Important people make important mistakes—and learn important lessons from them."

Then he went back into his house, and left the chiefs standing with no invitation to supper.

* * *

For days, the Trappers had lain at ease, eating, sleeping, tending their wounds and their dogs. The men had fucked some of the Garden girls who came to the camp.—The best of these girls were Cross-eye Jane, Francine Kemp, Nuncie Lewis, and Ruth Bissel. Ruth Bissel, very short and wide, was tough for a Garden girl, and had hit Rod Sorbane with a rock after a misunderstanding.

Mary's daughter, May, had come too, but made love with no one. Torrey seemed to dislike her, and walked away every time she came.

The Garden people smiled at the Trappers, now, smiled at Catania when she passed them on her way to climb to the library. Mary had been nice, and said she could go when she wished. The

Gold-bracelets guarding the library, who'd helped her on the ladder, was called Frank Catlin. He seemed always glad to see her.

This was the best time for the Trappers since the Cree came down—the best time Catania had had with Jack. She noticed more and more small things about him; she looked for little oddnesses recurring, was pleased when she found them, and held them to her as . . . charming. Newton's fine word.

Catania knelt at the creek and looked at her reflection in the water every morning, as if her scar might have gone away, peeled out of her face by Mountain Jesus as she slept. If, as she knelt there, she covered her face's right side with her hand, then the left side seemed pretty. So, when she was with Jack, Catania began to take care that the left side of her face was turned to him. . . . One evening, when she had done that, sitting by the fire, he had stood and come around to sit on her scarred side, then leaned over to kiss where the dog had bitten her.

There was no question that he cared for her, but he never said so. And she thought, from certain silences, he must have lost someone dear to him in that distant war on the ice, in Map-Michigan.

Still, these first after-battle days were the best days since the Crees came to the Range.

On the fourth best-days evening, when Catania, Lucy, and Martha Monroe were cooking a goat stew, there was a quarrel between Micah Olsen and Tall-David Richardson over a Garden girl. Jack watched them but didn't interfere.

Jim Olsen came between them and made Micah sheath his knife.

It occurred to Catania, tasting the stew, then putting more Gardens pepper into the kettle, that days so easy might be bad for men tuned to trouble. So, after they'd eaten, and with Mary One-eye come to visit with Carlson Gold-bracelets and the little librarian, Catania sat cross-legged by the fire to read from the copybook Necklace Peter had lent them. It was one they'd had a copy of on the Range, *Hunting on the Continent of Africa*.

The men loved this book. She read them a favorite passage:

C. stopped the Dodge and stood up to glass the ridge. He stood with his elbows braced on the top of the windscreen and looked through the glasses a long time. 'There's our old gentleman,' he said, finally. 'Making for the thorn at a rate of knots.'

I looked, but without the glasses there was nothing to see but sun-scorched grass and scrub brush, and the hills rising up beyond, miles away. The hills were golden brown as hemp rope, and they trembled when you looked at them through the heated air.

'We'll just drive over a little closer,' C. said. And we did that, and he drove over every bush and pit and warthog burrow until he finally said, 'Righty-oh!' and put on the brakes. Driving was the only thing C. did without thinking about it.

Then he climbed out his side, and I climbed out my side, and the boys jumped off the back with the rifles.

'Walk from here,' C. said. 'We'll take the rifles now, and just go and have a dekko in that thorn.'

C.'s getting so very British was the only way you had of telling that something just the least bit, just the slightest bit sticky might be coming up. Another way of telling was that the boys, who were both Wakamba and therefore absolutely brave, handed us our big guns very nicely, and then got back up into the truck.

'Now I'll just be over here to your left and a few steps back,' C. said, and we started to walk the long way up the slope of a wide low ridge, where the thorn grew like a rolling straw-colored sea cresting along a beach. My Red Setter boots made soft crumbling noises in the sun-dried soil.

It was a hot afternoon for such a long walk. There was plenty of time to consider how pleasant camp would be about now, with old Ali filling the canvas bathtub and grinning his sweet cannibal grin full of lovely filed teeth.

Cold francolin, and of course the first bottle of Tuskers with that. Yes, all that would be very pleasant, about now.

After a long time walking, C. said, 'Look there.' We were deep into the thorn, and he was pointing off to the right, to a kisi bush standing a little isolated from the others.

'Where?' I said, and then I saw it. It was a long shadow of darker brown, lying under the bush in the narrow shade. This long shadow had a tail that was curling gently this way and that.

'I see him,' I said. And as if he had been waiting for some acknowledgement, the old simba grunted and heaved himself up, coughed to clear his throat, and came at us in one wonderful leap that became a driving bounding run, straight at us and terribly fast.

He was kicking up puffs of brown dust behind him as he came, and making a soft chuff-chuffing sound, like the little mine trains that climb the grades of the Sierra in the north of Spain, but he was coming faster than such trains run.

I smacked him with the left barrel at just under fifty yards and the .460 solid took him a little low and the old man switched ends and spun over like a car in a crash. Then he rolled to his feet and came on again, still making that gentle chuffing noise and coming very close now, so the noble lion eyes were like amber fog lights shining through the dust.

I took what time I could, and the right-barrel's bullet hit him just under the chin, killed him and dropped him flat. He was very close, then, and I could see the amber eyes slowly shut as if I and my busy-ness and intrusion and noise making had bored him beyond bearing, and he'd decided to go to sleep and to hell with me.

Dead, he was smaller, just slightly, as all the dead ones are, and his hide was scarred along a shoulder where some *younger male had ripped him, driving him out of the pride to be alone. He looked very heraldic, very peaceful now, with the bright bitter smell of cordite drifting over him like memorial incense.*

'That second, was a pretty shot,' C. said. He didn't mention the first.

The Trappers all whistled with pleasure when Catania finished. She had read it so quickly and quietly it all made sense. Even not knowing what a francolin was, or a Dodge, exactly—some sort of traveling machine—a person seemed to know what those things were while she was reading, as if everything was understood. The Trappers whistled, and Mary and the two Garden men clapped their hands together to make spanking noises.

The reading had struck Jack Monroe sharply, which surprised him. He had heard nothing from *Hunting on the Continent of Africa* for more than six years—had heard nothing read from any copybook, since the Map-Missouri men didn't read books, and the Ojibway considered them unhealthy.

Now he was remembering twice: the copybook hunt, and the Old Range and its men and women, before he was sent away. They had come to him—Sam and the others—as he'd listened. It made him uneasy, so he tried to think only of the hunting in the story.

The bow would be wrong for that lion. For that swift beast, a man would need friends and lances, same as for a snow tiger. Or one of the Warm-time guns the story hunter used.—And no reason, Catania would say, that people now couldn't find the way to make gun-shoot powder, couldn't find the way to make two-barrel guns. It was only people, after all, who'd done all those things, guns and Dodges, before becoming unlucky with Weather.

"No reason," Jack said aloud, smiling as he saw Catania cross the camp and kneel to speak to Susan Monroe. Then she came back past the fire and spoke to Martha Sorbane.

Mary One-eye, and several other women, stood and went to

Susan. The Trapper men and Garden men stayed where they were.

Susan lay on a hide behind Torrey's sled, buckskin trousers unlaced and stained dark at the crotch. Her eyes were squeezed shut, and she was holding a leather strap so hard her knuckles were white.

Catania opened her medical pack and took out a leather bottle of vodka. She rinsed and scrubbed her hands, then dried them on a piece of white boiled cloth.

Lucy Edwards knelt and took off Susan's moccasins, then gently tugged her trousers down and off, so Catania's hands would stay clean.

Cooing and comforting while she did, Catania slid her hand to the girl's vulva, then eased her fingers in to feel the cervix. Its little mouth was pouting open.

She put both hands on Susan's belly, and waited. In a while a contraction came, pulsing.

"Wonderful, Trade-honey," Catania said. "Sam's baby is coming tonight."

"Do you want our doctor?" Garden Mary was standing watching.

"I don't think so," Catania said. "This baby wants to come out."

Mary One-eye sat on Torrey's sled, and the other women settled on hides to wait. Joan Richardson brought branches and a burning brand to make a fire. . . . The men had drifted away.

The evening was so warm—warm as a summer week on the Range—that Susan needed no cover. She lay naked on the hide, except for her deerskin shirt, her knees up and spread wide. Lay with her eyes closed, the shadows of Joan's fire moving on her skin.

By full nightfall, baby-giving had seized her.

Catania had washed and rinsed her hands again, and tested the girl's warmth and wetness. Susan was panting like a dog lying in harness after a long run. Her dark eyes were open wide.

"Do you want some water, Sweetness?"

Susan nodded, solemn as a child, preoccupied—dreaming awake of what was happening to her.

After Catania gave her a sip of water, the girl cried out, startled by a sudden stinging pain. It frightened her more than the deep, slow, rolling cramps. She felt that something had torn inside her.

When Catania smiled down, it made Susan angry. Who was Catania, who had to stick a peeled hazel twig up her so she wouldn't have babies from being any man's Sunday doctor—who was she to be grinning as if she knew what this was like?

The sudden sharp pain came again, and Catania saw Susan frown so severely she became ugly, her face flushed dark and straining. She groaned a long groan that ended in a gasp, and her knees rose higher. "Oh . . . Mountain *Jesus*!"

Dummy Olsen sat up against a pine tree. Susan had wakened him, calling out. He stretched, yawned, then stood up and walked over to see what was happening.

When Susan saw him, she screamed, "Get away! Get *away*!" And put her hands down to cover herself.

Dummy looked at her, astonished, with his mouth fallen open. He began to cry, and Joan got up, turned him away, and walked back into camp with him.

"Oh, I'm sorry," Susan said. ". . . I'm sorry." And she heaved into another spasm, grunting and grinding her teeth.

After a while, Catania saw the top of the baby's head bulging slowly out at Susan's groin, stretching the circle red.

"Push again."

But Susan shook her head. "No," she said. "No."

Mary One-eye elbowed Catania aside and stared into Susan's face. "*Finish your work*," she said.

Susan gasped and took a breath. She took another breath, screamed through gritted teeth . . . and the baby's head came out of her.

"It's coming!" Catania knelt with her hands ready. "The baby's coming!"

A contraction shook Susan and rippled through the muscles of her belly. She threw her head back and shouted. Blood flicked across Catania's arms as the baby's shoulders shoved free . . . and it spurted out, wet red, into her hands.

* * *

Susan woke before dawn with the baby at her breast. She had forgotten whether it was a boy, so she looked—and then remembered she'd called him Sam, after his father.

She thought he seemed like Sam, already—sturdy, restless, and strong. Catania and Sally Auerbach were sitting beside the sled, and they said so too.

They could hear Trappers singing at fires across the camp, singing softly so as not to disturb the baby. It seemed to Susan this child was a promise of luck for them, and new beginning.

"Is he perfect?" she said to Catania, just to be sure, though all the women had said he was perfect.

"Better than perfect," Catania said. "Big Sam would be very proud of you."

"Big-Sam then . . . and Small-Sam now," Susan said, and went to sleep.

Sally said she'd watch them, so Catania walked through the camp looking for Tattooed Newton, to thank him for having said such a lucky thing by the stream, about a charming baby coming to save Susan.

She found him with Jack and some other men in a long clearing farther down the creek. They were drinking vodka in celebration of the new Sam. The moon was up, and its light shone with the star-lights of the Dog, the Bear, and the Belt.

Here, in this open field, the men had almost a hunter's distance. They were night-shooting at pale split-pine stakes—shooting, it seemed to Catania, for the joy of feeling the longbows jump in their hands, hearing bowstrings hum, and seeing the swift stitching of arrows' flight through shadow.

The pine stakes were missed as often as struck. Del Richardson,

Pat Weber, Harold Auerbach, and other young men shouted and chased though darkness, wrestling and tripping, looking for the misses. Arrow fletching tufted the field like small pale flowers in moonlight.

Catania watched the men a while, concerned someone might be hurt with so much drunken shooting and running here and there in darkness. She watched a while, then went away and left them without the weight of woman-care or a woman's words, so they might play like boys a little longer.

. . . In the morning, barefoot in dark green robes, their long hair braided in coils on their heads, Garden women came past the Trapper camp. They carried cloth bags with them for picking little forest friends, and sang as they walked along the creek, their robes swaying. They were singing a song about the Marrying Mister Snow.

Some little children had come, and ran everywhere among the sleds and fires. The Trappers laughed and caught them, played with them roughly, rolling the children over like puppies, picking them up and squeezing them till they squeaked.

Then their mothers called, the children scurried to follow . . . and the Trappers looked after them, standing sad with empty hands.

The morning grew warmer, so the shallow snow thinned and crumbled. No new snow had fallen in the night, though the fringe ice lingered along the creek's edge. The forest's sky was a darker blue than the mountain skies had been, and high clouds like tufts of ermine sailed and sailed across it on a southern wind.

Jack woke Catania, who'd been up most of the night sitting by Susan and the baby. She yawned and stretched, then got up and put on her moccasin-boots and buckskins to follow him through the camp to the dog-lines. Torrey was there, his shirt off, picking spring ticks from Three-ball's ears. Garden May, the top of her robe folded down and tucked into a green sash, was kneeling, helping him, and slapping Three-balls on the muzzle when he tried to bite her.

It was the first time Garden May and Torrey had been seen together. It appeared they'd gotten tired of disliking.

"This weather's getting too warm," Torrey said. "If Warm-times were much warmer than this, I wouldn't have liked Warm-times."

Three-balls growled, showing his fangs, and Torrey and Garden May both hit him on the head with their fists, thump-thump, so he blinked and grumbled.

"We're going into Gardens," Jack said, "—to find a present for Small-Sam. I can trade my boot knife, if they don't want a pelt."

"They'll want the knife," Garden May said, as if the Garden people weren't her people anymore. "Let me see it."

Jack slid the knife from his moccasin-boot, and Garden May took it and weighed it in her hand. The blade was heavy, sharpened along both edges, and more than a man's hand long. The handle was the blade's wide flat tang, wrapped in steel wire.

"It's fifty-fold iron strip and steel," Jack said. "That's Mohawk work."

"How'd you get it?" Torrey said.

"Without honor. A man came at me who was too old to be fighting. If there'd been a way, I would have sent the knife to his son and said I was sorry. But those days were gone."

Garden May gave the knife back. "One of the Bracelets will give you a fine baby's present for it."

Torrey stood up from Three-balls, said, "This weather will bring more ticks," and pulled on his shirt to go into Gardens.

Garden May went with them, her naked breasts striped with green paint. . . . Catania, as they walked along, imagined Jack on sun-glare ice in a terrible fight with a gray-haired tribesman—a true red-blood with a worn, dark, deep-lined face, black eyes, and eagle feathers at his throat.

They walked into Gardens through sunshine that made the Trappers squint. People were friendly toward them, bowed little bows to Garden May, and she bowed back.

The valley was full of sunlight come down between tall trees, brightening the green and patches of snow. A light haze drifted in the air; faint layers of dust and pollen shifting like woodsmoke with earth-smell and goat-smell and potato-smell.

The Trappers heard loom shuttles clacking on the slope where the weavers worked, and Catania said, "Perhaps a woven-cloth thing." She stepped ahead to lead them along the high path past Mary's house . . . then out onto the field where the cloth was made.

This was where the clicking and clacking sounds had come from, from eight big looms spaced across the clearing. There was a woman sitting tending each one, with a boy sliding the shuttle back and forth for her through the web of becoming-cloth.

By each loom, on platforms set above the gound, other women sat cutting cloth with hook-blade knives, then folding, and sewing along edges.

Above the slope from the looms, were wider platforms with long wood tubs of dye, each full of bright red juice, or bright yellow juice, or blue, or green. Men were tending these, soaking woven cloth, stretching it, then wringing it around peeled wood posts.—These men were splashed with the colors of their cloth. They were singing some soft song, but Catania saw that they worked as men, not dancing their tasks as those in the first-pulp paper mill.

A tall dead pine to the right, its bark stripped away, was draped with a huge cloth dyed bright yellow and blue. The cloth hung wide from the tree's crown, flowing over its branches in rich folds to gather in furling color at its trunk.

"Last drying," Garden May said. "We hang them up with a rope and pulley."

"We had little trade-pulleys," Catania said. "But we didn't have blocks and tackles. We read about them, but we didn't have them."

The colors in the cloth were wonderful—so rich that the blue and yellow stripes seemed to tremble and shift places in the sunshine.

"Blanket-pelt," Jack said. "A little woven goat-cloth blanket."

"Perfect for the baby!" Catania did a little dance. "So fine for him in this warming weather, instead of fur."

"The correct thing," Garden May said. "And blankets for babies are made here. But what is a lucky color for him?"

"We have no lucky color," Catania said. "We have lucky words and numbers. . . ."

"Green and yellow are Gardens' lucky colors."

"He was born at Gardens," Jack said, "—and should have their luck." He went up to the first loom, Catania and the others behind him, and raised his voice above the clacking. "I have a knife to trade for a blanket."

The woman looked up at him, then back to continue her work. She pointed with her little finger at the loom to her left. "Her husband fights," she said.

The Trappers went over to that loom, where a younger woman was working. She glanced up at them, but didn't seem friendly. There was a brown birthmark along her jaw.

"I have my short-blade knife," Jack said, "—to trade for a blanket."

The woman stopped stepping on her loom's toes, and looked up at him. "A blanket for you?"

"No," Jack said. "For our new baby. His name is Small-Sam."

Then the birthmark-woman seemed more friendly. "Let me see the knife."

Jack drew it from his moccasin-boot and handed it to her.

"This is not a short-blade knife," the woman said.

"Shorter than my other one." He unsheathed the long knife at his belt to show to her.

The woman turned the boot-knife in her hands. "Has this done anything unlucky?"

"One unlucky thing," Jack said, "—how I got it. But I used that bad luck up. Now, it's a clean knife, and I could give it to Mountain Jesus or the Rain-bird, and not be concerned."

The birthmark-woman plucked a thread from her weaving,

touched the knife's edge to it, and the thread parted. "My husband is a fighting man," she said, "—a Gold Two-bands. This is something he would like."

"Tell him it's Mohawk work," Jack said, "—balanced to turn once in a campfire throw, turn three times to catch a man running away."

"What colors do you want your blanket?"

"Green and yellow," Catania said.

"We have a bargain." The birthmark-woman reached out and slapped Jack's hand with a hand that sounded hard as his, from looming. Then she got up and went away, and the Trappers and Garden May sat on their heels in the sunshine, to wait for Small-Sam's blanket.

They saw the birthmark-woman talking with other Garden women at a folding-and-cutting-and-sewing platform higher on the slope. . . . The boy who'd been making her loom's shuttle go back and forth stood on the loom's framework and rested. He stuck his tongue out at Garden May, and wiggled it.

She got up and walked toward him, and the boy laughed and ran up to where the men were dying the woven cloth. Garden May made a finger sign after him.

"He's my daddy's sister's son, Charles," May said when she came back. "He's so bad, I like him."

The Trappers and Garden May waited, and Jack took out a piece of tobacco—the third piece he'd won playing checkers with Carlson Gold-bracelets. He used his big knife to cut it into smaller pieces, and they chewed and spat while they waited.

After a while, then a while longer, the birthmark-woman came over to them, carrying folded cloth.

"Here," she said. She shook out the folds—and a small and very beautiful blanket came down. It was striped yellow as a bird's-egg yolk, and green as hemlock branches, and was sewn along its edges with red thread. A little flower of the same red thread had been stitched into each corner of the blanket.

"Is the bargain accomplished?" the woman said.

"It's a fine blanket," Garden May said, when the Trappers said nothing.

Catania reached out and touched it. There were tears in her eyes. "It's beautiful as the baby," she said.

Jack drew his long knife and held it out to the birthmark-woman. "Give your man this knife, also," he said. "It's old-steel work, and has never failed me."

But the woman smiled, shook her head, and wouldn't take the long knife. "The bargain is accomplished," she said, folded the blanket, and handed it to Catania.

Torrey touched it with a finger. "It's soft."

Very happy with the baby's blanket, and Garden May happy for their happiness, they walked back along the high path to Mary One-eye's house and called down to her, but no one was there.

They went on to the creek's fast water, and along the bank, going two by two, Torrey and Garden May in front. Catania saw those two were walking as together people, not just people who fucked. She wondered what a wise woman would see, watching her and Jack walking side by side. She wondered that, then imagined the blanket was a blanket for their own baby, and they were always-together people.

Crossing the creek bridge, they walked up the slope to the Trapper camp. . . . Just past the first fire, Tattooed Newton stepped out from a stand of three small pines. He was armed, and there was blood on his face.

"We have trouble, Jack," he said.

Trouble.

14

"The Olsens and Bailey came for me." Tattooed Newton said. "I killed Jim—at least, his guts are out. And Chapman and I were fighting, but I had to quit."

"Why was that?" Jack said. He walked over to his fire in no hurry, picked up his lance, bow, and quiver. "Why quit fighting?"

"Joan and Del came. She has Lucy."

Catania took great care to put the baby's blanket down on a hide, to keep it safe; then she picked up her bow and quiver. She felt no fear or surprise at the trouble, only weariness.

Torrey had run to his fire and come back armed. Garden May came with him, carrying an ax.

"They're up past the pines," Newton said. His forehead was cut; blood was running down his face. "Chapman, Bailey, Joan, and Del. Micah and Tall-David are up there too."

"Let me talk to them," Catania said, but Jack was already walking away up the slope. He went eagerly, as if to people waiting with a gift for him. Newton and Torrey followed.

"No one can hurt my Nine-fingers," Garden May said, as she and Catania trotted to catch up.

They went past pines, and Catania saw other Trappers, twenty or more, standing downslope by the creek. They were armed, and watching, but weren't coming up the campground.

Jack led into another small stand of trees, then stopped to look and listen. Through the foliage, Catania saw Newton's face beside her, streaked with blood. His dark eyes looked darker.

"You sure Jim Olsen's dead?" Jack said.

"I stuck him, first thing," Newton said. "He was quick, but he's dead or dying.—I'll tell you who's friendly up there. Myles Weber is up in a tree; he shot Bailey in the leg. They'll leave him alone for a while."

Jack stood amid the pines' green branches, thinking, as though what was happening was only interesting. "All right," he said. "We'll go up there now. I don't want them settling in."

"We kill them?" Torrey said.

"No," Jack said, and led them up through a scattered grove of small evergreens.

The others were waiting past those trees, across a narrow field. There were much bigger trees standing behind them like a wall. It was where the forest started again, south of Gardens.

Nearby, on puddled snow, a Trapper lay on his side with a double handful of shining red and blue guts out in a heap. Catania saw it was Jim Olsen. His dead face was white as bone. Beyond, Chapman Olsen and Micah Olsen stood together, armed. Tall-David Richardson and Del Richardson were to their left.

Joan Richardson stood beside her son, with Lucy Edwards kneeling before her. Lucy's hands were tied behind her back. Joan held a knife to Lucy's throat; there was a fine line of blood under the blade.

"Be still, Newton," Jack said, though Newton hadn't moved.

Behind Joan, Bailey Auerbach was sitting against a tree-trunk. There was blood on his right leg.

Jack walked out across the field as if there were no trouble, using his lance as a staff. His bow was across his back, unstrung.

Newton and Torrey followed him, Torrey to his left, Newton to his right. Catania strung her bow and set a broadhead arrow to the string. Then she and Garden May went out into the field.

Catania was frightened, now. She had trouble catching her breath.

"Hello, Jack," Joan Richardson said. "Some Trappers aren't doing what you say, anymore." She smiled down at Lucy, moved the knife-blade slightly.

Catania heard Newton make a soft humming sound.

"Look up to the left," Torrey said. They looked—and high in a tall tree, a buckskin shirt, stuck on the end of a bow-stave, was waved through green branches. "Old Weber. They can't shift that way, or he'll kill a couple of them."

"Jim's dead," Chapman said, and took a long step to the right, away from Micah, for room to draw his bow. He had an arrow nocked.

"Do," Catania called to him, "—and I'll kill you." She had turned to her left, drawn and leveled her bow, aiming at him from a rock-throw away, just past Jack. The arrow's fletching rested at her cheek.

There was movement where Tall-David Richardson stood, and Catania supposed he was ready to kill her if she shot, and perhaps before. But she kept looking down her arrow shaft at Chapman Olsen's bow-stave, held half raised, his lean belly, and wrinkled brown buckskin shirt. A string of red beads had been sewn down one side of the shirt. She saw the darker edge of his belt below, its yellow horn buckle . . . and noticed Chapman wasn't breathing now; his belly wasn't moving in and out.

Then she stopped paying attention to those things. Time had slowed to dull, measured thumps, hard to hear, perhaps her heart beating.

Now Catania could see a small grease stain on Chapman's shirt, a little to the left for a perfect killing shot, but still a fair mark. She put everything out of her eyes but that small spot, and it seemed to grow slowly big as a man's fist . . . then big as an open hand. It was an easy mark.

Someone said something too softly for her to understand. Catania felt her draw-shoulder begin to ache, and reminded herself to loose the shot if she heard Tall-David's bowstring twang, since she might miss once she was hit. She listened for that, and the soft grunt a person gave when they threw a lance or knife.

"One of you kill that bitch," Chapman said. Catania heard that, saw his belly moving as he said it. Her bright impatient arrow-head followed that slightest movement.

A woman said something near her. Not Garden May.

A man called, "Don't. *Don't!*"

Catania relaxed her right hand only a little, to begin to release the arrow.

The same woman said something more, and Catania glanced that way. Susan Monroe had come up the slope, and walked into the field between them. She looked pale, and was unsteady on her feet. She held the baby in her arms.

"Don't!" Torrey called out. "No trouble. No fighting near the baby!"

"The Weather damn you, Susan," Joan Richardson said. "Get out of the way."

Catania looked back to her aim. Then she heard Jack say, "What if Susan *hadn't* come with the baby, and we fought? Then there would be another two or three Trappers dead or crippled. Soon, being so few, we would be beggars wherever we go. And what would Ned Richardson have said to that? What would Sam Monroe, Nathan Sorbane, and Peter Auerbach have said? What would all our dead people say to Trappers fighting Trappers?"

"That's just talk," Del Richardson said.

"It's good sense, Del," Torrey said. "Jack's trying not to kill you!"

"He tells us what to *do*!" Joan made an animal's face, and moved her knife on Lucy's throat. A thread of blood ran down.

"Joan . . . *Joan*," Susan said. "We're not in our mountains, anymore. We're running and we're with strangers here and we'll be with strange people all the time until we find a new place. We *need* to be told what to do, just for a while."

"*You* need," Joan Richardson said. "I don't need."

"Who pays for my brother?" Chapman lowered his bow.

"Your brother fought—and lost his fight," Newton said. "He was quick, but not strong enough."

"Catania," Jack said.

Catania heard him as she'd heard the others, as if from a distance.

"Catania, ease that bow."

Catania blinked, and eased her bow. She bit her lip when her draw-shoulder hurt losing the strain. The arrowhead twinkled in the sunshine as she lifted the arrow from the string, twirled it in her fingers, and slid it over her right shoulder and down into the quiver.

She saw Chapman Olsen looking at her. Now, it was hard to see the little grease stain on his shirt.

Jack strolled over to the Olsens as though nothing bad had

happened. He walked past them, past Tall-David and Del, and went over to Bailey Auerbach. Bailey was sitting with a band of cloth, soaked red, tied around his calf, where Myles Weber's arrow had gone through. "How's that leg, Bailey?" Jack said.

Bailey looked up at him, but didn't answer.

"Catania," Jack said, "—come look at this leg."

"She *better* look at it!" Myles called down from his tree-top. "I stuck my arrowheads in shit, Bailey. Your fucking leg is going to fall off!"

"You dogs," Joan Richardson said. She sheathed her knife, put her moccasin-boot in Lucy's back, and shoved her down on her face. Then she smiled at Newton. "You can come and get her, since you love her, since you want her so."

"These are things," Garden May said, "—that are never done in Gardens." But she didn't seem disturbed.

* * *

In the evening, just before sunset, Tattooed Newton put on his trousers, laced them, and left a private place in the pines to go into the camp for food. His forehead was sore where Catania had sewn in thread stitches.

He said hello to Myles and Helen Weber, and their boy, Pat, who were standing camp guard in case of more trouble . . . then came back to the private place with a smoked grouse and two cooked potatoes. He stood for a moment looking down at his wife.

Lucy lay naked on the fur robe, despite the chill of evening, her arms flung out, her long light-brown hair spread loose. The fur was wolf, dark gray and frosted gray, so she looked as if she were lying in evening mist. Lucy lay still, but her eyes were open, eyes nearly the color of the fur.

She was a slender woman, with wide hips and small soft breasts. Her face and arms were dark with weatherburn, but the rest of her body was white as goat's milk, turning golden now in sunset light.

A thin red-scabbed line ran across her throat—Joan Richardson's mark. The hair at her crotch was soaked and curly from fucking, and Newton could see a little pink fold of her, unfolded.

There was a lot to look at. He saw how complicated she was, and it struck him there was nothing and no one else just like her anywhere.

Newton set the food down on a hide, stood over her, then fell on top of her like a cut-down tree. The breath left Lucy in a grunt, and he lay on her, pawing at her arms, her small breasts, licking her throat where Joan had hurt her, licking in the light, sweated fur of her armpits. He licked and gently bit her as if he were going to devour her skin, then her fat, then her muscle and guts so he could see everything down to her white bones, with nothing left hidden from him.

"Oh, my cannibal," she said. He was tickling her, rubbing at her with his hairy chest. He was so big, so heavy that she couldn't push him away, so she began to hold him instead, gripping his shoulders and crooning to him, puffing for breath under his weight.

"My cannibal. . . ." It was her secret name for him. She never used it where anyone else could hear. The first time she had called him that in fun—having recalled from childhood a Salesman's tale of the Boxcars' supposed habits—he had turned, his face twisted like an angry bear's, and hit her, knocked her sliding across the floor of her father's house. Lucy had thought he was going to kill her then—but was only frightened that her father and brothers might come into the house and catch him.

After that one blow, Newton's face had changed, and he'd laughed and said, "Well, it seems that's too true a word to run from. . . ." Then he'd bent down, picked her up, and sat on the bed with her in his lap, pinching her nose to stop the bleeding. When she was feeling better, he had gone outside and cut the hand he'd hit her with, cut it deep across the back. The hand was no good to him that winter.

Lucy never asked Newton about his life in Middle Kingdom, where he'd come from. "Dot-men come from Big Ol' Missy," the

Salesman had said. "Boxcars run that river, eat people now and then. . . ."

Lucy never asked Newton about any of that. And she didn't mind that he would eat raw meat and sing odd songs, or that he was so big and looked strange with his short dark hair and dark bear's eyes. He had four blue dots tattooed on each cheekbone, and shaved all the hair off his face with his knife every two or three days, but she didn't care what anyone said about him.

. . . Newton groaned, lifted himself, and rolled off her. They lay holding hands for a while, then he got up, covered her with a fur against the evening cold, knelt and fed her pieces of potato and smoked grouse from his fingers, as though she were a little child.

After they ate, and the sun went down, they slept. Newton dreamed of his father, standing huge and smiling, reviewing the troops of the East-bank army. His father was wearing the Helmet of Joy. . . . Then he dreamed of a footrace, woke from that dream of running—and heard running as he woke.

Lucy woke to that sound as well, and they were up and out of the furs together. Then armed.

Many torches wavered from the forest at the top of the camp. Gold bracelets shone in their light. Nearly two-hundred Garden men with cocked crossbows stood along the edge of the wood. The only woman with them was Mary One-eye, standing at the middle of their line, naked but for green paint. The torches threw shifting shadows across the snowy ground.

Now, all the Trappers were up and armed. The Auerbachs ran along Fast Creek, to hold the bridge behind them.

Jack stepped up the slope, and called out to Mary One-eye. *"Not one of yours has been hurt in our troubles!"*

She walked down to meet him. The Gold-bracelets stayed where they were. "No," Mary said, "—and not one will be. If you kill yours today, you will kill ours tomorrow."

"Our trouble is over," Jack said, loud enough for everyone to hear.

"And our trouble with you, will not start," Mary said. "Your second Warm-time week ends tomorrow, but since you fought and we did not, we give you one day more, and food for that day . . . then food for traveling."

"We'll go," Jack said, "—and go easily."

"You will certainly go, easily or not." Mary started back to her men, then turned. "I don't say you're bad people. But you are too sad, and like an injured animal that bites its wound and whoever comes near it."

Then she walked away. She should have looked odd to the Trappers, and funny—a fat little lady, naked but for green paint, trudging barefoot up through the last of spring snow. She should have looked odd, but she didn't.

"It's ended well," Catania said to Jack as they lay down again. The Gold-bracelets and their torches were gone from the forest edge. "It's ended well, despite what Mary said. Only Jim was killed, but not by you, and you didn't kill the others."

Though Jack nodded, she saw his eyes in firelight, and felt he might have been more comfortable with killing.

"No," Catania said, as if he'd said otherwise. "You went the wise way. There are not enough of us left."

He turned to her then, and hugged her, and she felt the bitter strength he restrained, and with what difficulty.

. . . In the morning, before sunrise, Catania went back to the field on the edge of the forest with Martha Sorbane, Donna Weber, Wanda Sorbane, and Mercy Richardson. While those women prayed, Catania tucked Jim's guts, nearly frozen, back inside him, and sewed his middle up.

They all prayed over him for a while, recommending him to Mountain Jesus as a hunter, which was a good recommendation. Then they picked him up and carried him down to Fast Creek, the coldest water they had. They set him to soak and put on what ice he could, while other Trappers came to pray along the bank. Then all of them sang the ancient 'Rock of Ages.'

Though Jim could gather only the thinnest glittering coat, the

Olsen men took him out and went into the woods with him, to tie him up into a tree. A poor substitute for watching from High Hill.

When Jim was gone, all the Trappers who'd heard of the Garden blanket, those men and women who'd stayed away during the trouble, and even those who'd caused the trouble, came to see it folded around the baby. Only his little red face was uncovered, his dark eyes peering out at them from green and gold.

Seeing the baby in his wonderful blanket made good feelings out of bad feelings, so even Joan Richardson came and touched the weaving, to see how soft it was.

Catania went to the Auerbach fire, cleaned the arrow wound in Bailey's leg again, and bandaged it with fresh boiled cloth. He said nothing bad to her, and said nothing about old Myles Weber claiming to have put shit on his arrowheads.

None of the Trappers, except Martha Sorbane, had given Catania bad looks that morning. And only a few had given Jack and Newton bad looks. Still, the morning moved stiffly, as if it had been sick at sunrise and was still recovering. What-worse-might-have-happened drifted through the camp like wood smoke.

* * *

At midday, a small Garden girl named Paula came to camp, and found Catania playing scissors-paper-and-stone with Susan and Garden May. Jack sat watching them.

"Our Lady Mary wants you," Paula said to Catania. "What is that game?"

"Sit here and play," Catania said, getting up.

"Don't go to her," Jack said.

"Better that we know what Mary wants, than we don't."

"If you aren't back by evening," Jack said, "—we'll come for you."

. . . Catania was frightened, walking alone through Gardens, though no one threatened her or gave her bad looks, but was less frightened by the time she came to Mary One-eye's house. By then, she'd grown tired of being afraid.

"Have you come trembling?" Mary said, smiling at her from a cushion by the hearth. Only the one-handed old man, Paul Bongiorno, was with her. "There was no need for that. Do you want vodka?"

"No, thank you."

"Good," Mary said, and stood up. "I have two things to show you, Tall Scarface." She did a little dance to stretch from sitting. "You come with me, and I will make you a wiser woman than before. Perhaps wise enough. . . ."

Mary led up out of her house. Carlson Gold-bracelets was waiting on the path.

"Hello, Carlson," Catania said, to see if he was still friendly after the trouble in camp.

"Hello," he said. "Tell Jack I will not play checkers with him anymore."

"I told him not to," Mary said. "Your fierce Jack was clever to win honor from this fool."

"I still have some left," Carlson said.

"*Fool*," Mary One-eye said. "You may come with us to help me in the high places, but only for a little way."

Carlson Gold-bracelets bowed, and walked behind them as Mary climbed the high path higher. She took Catania past several under-tree houses with thin green-painted sticks standing in front of them . . . then out to the end of the cloth-weaving field, and up into the forest.

There, Mary stopped and leaned against a tree to breathe.

"Are you all right?"

"Catania—if I was 'all right,' I wouldn't be trying to make you a Lady. I would have the luck-time to find a competent girl and teach her. You know the word 'competent'?"

"We had a Webster's, and we used it."

"Yes. . . ." Mary kissed the tree she'd leaned on, and walked along the forest ridge, with Carlson now holding her left arm and helping her over tangles and deadfalls. Catania saw that though she could stroll very well, and dance, and even climb a net ladder into a tree, Mary had difficulty with more continuous effort. She took Mary's other arm and helped lift her when they climbed over huge fallen timbers of great trees, grown along the spine of the ridge.

Carlson and Catania helped Mary One-eye along until even the sounds of the looms, even the growl of the mill were gone, swallowed by the forest. They helped her over evergreen scrub and shallow snow, and got no thanks for it, only muttering and bad looks.

The ridge broke into wooded slopes and deep valleys. It was the highest ground Catania had seen in the forest, and they walked a long way through it. Mary needed support along these steep ways; Catania heard her panting like a puppy.

At a wall of cracked gray stone flaking away under ivy, Mary said, "You stay here." Carlson Gold-bracelets folded his arms and leaned against the rock's snow-powdered ivy-leaves to wait.

Mary One-eye led Catania along the wall for a little way, then down great shattered slabs of the wall, fallen, so they climbed deeper into a valley so narrow the sky was only a strip of blue above them.

Cold air had settled into this place like a slow river. It swirled around them as they traveled, Catania helping Mary over rotting logs and fallen stone.

"Here," Mary said.

The rock to their left had become a long shelf, with a great hollow beneath it that went back into darkness. Mary ducked into that as the Garden people ducked into their tree-root houses. When Catania went after her, Mary took her arm and held her still.

"Listen to me," she said. "Where we were walking was a Warm-time road. If you dig down, you find broken black pieces. No one—*no one*—has ever come here but Ladies who've given an eye. I make an exception for you, Catania."

"Thank you," Catania said.

"Don't thank me. It is not an honor. It's something else: it's a wisdom maker." She kept her grip on Catania's arm, pulling her deeper into the dark.

Catania thought she saw light far ahead. "What is that?"

"Take off your boots," Mary said, "—and shut your mouth. This is a quiet place."

Catania bent and took off her moccasin-boots and foot wraps. When she stood barefoot on icy uneven stone, she saw a distant shaft of light coming down through the rock's high ceiling ahead of them.

Mary walked on, and Catania followed. The stone ceiling had split along a narrow crack. Icicles hung in sheets along it, and these shone in soft uncertain sunlight filtering down.

To the left was a low wall, smooth, and mottled gray, with big pieces of dark ice along its top edge. Catania saw something painted on it. She went closer. It was a starved blue-gray dog, running.

She touched the stone beside the running dog—and her fingertip slipped in grease, then stuck, frozen to the rock as if it was a knife's frigid steel she'd touched, on the Range. She tried to pull her hand away—but was caught there, had to stoop and breathe on the place to warm it before she could tug her finger free.

"This wall isn't stone!"

"No," Mary said. "It isn't stone, and isn't a wall, either." She took Catania's arm and led her past the running dog. There were two narrow steps there, up into darkness.

"Go in," Mary said. "And be the first to see them with both eyes."

"What is it?"

"Go in."

"What *is* it?"

"Go in, and learn."

Catania climbed the first step, then stopped.

"Did you breed cowards," Mary said, "—on your Range?"

Catania closed her eyes, climbed the second narrow step . . . and took one step more. The air was still and very cold.

When she opened her eyes in gloomy light, she saw a round steel rail, a withered seat, and a big thin-spoked wheel. Then she turned—and shadowed rows of little people stared at her, smiling, their eyes bright as beads.

Catania shouted and fell. She saw her father running to her—a dog was tearing at her face, dragging her along the ground. The bite was so strong it didn't hurt, but she felt the pulling, and heard fangs scrape on her bones.

Her father reached her. She saw sunlight flash on his knife, and tasted her blood and dog blood together.

. . . Catania roused, and saw a folded little foot in a rotted shoe. She yelled and rolled away, scrambling to her feet in the narrow place. A withered lady was sitting with her head thrown back in dim light, laughing at something past Catania's shoulder. The little foot was hers.

Backing away, Catania hit the round rail with her hip. Now, she saw there were many people sitting in long rows down a narrow way. They were mottled gray and black, crumpled and shrunken as last year's spoiled potatoes—but dressed like children's dolls in scraps of woven cloth. . . . Most still had their eyes—dry, buried, shiny black buttons peeping from deep sockets—with fluffy hair and brows sifting over them. They had wrinkled little noses, with nostrils twisted tight.

One had an eyeless child on its lap. The child wore a dress, and was hugging something . . . a lump of fur with ears.

Catania stood still, and took a breath of air as thick and slow as freezing water. Staring into shadow, she recalled her vision of the dog's biting, and saw that these were people of remembrance, Warm-time people long dead in their big steel box with the running dog painted on its side.

"*Catania*," Mary called, standing down by the two steep steps. "Catania, come out now, or they will keep some of you."

"I'm coming," Catania said—but didn't move. She was hearing sounds . . . a faint continuing roar, like Gardens' waterfall, like distant water thundering from the Wall in a morning melt. She heard this sound very clearly, and it wove and wove until she thought she could see things through the dark ice of the box's long windows.—But not dark ice. Dark glass . . . *glass*. Through it, Catania began to see bright-colored things go by, rushing. . . .

She walked down the narrow way as if there were miles to go between these rows of people. Her bare feet slipped in cold grease as she went—and she supposed that Mary One-eye, and all the Garden Ladies in their times, had come and rubbed bird fat on the steel to save it from rusting.

Catania walked in close dimness to look at those who must have been Warm-time people—look at them as a doctor should. But she couldn't bring herself to touch them. She was not doctor enough for that.

She saw no sign of trauma, no bone-ends protruding from shriveled skin. None of their heads, frizzed with tufts of hair, had been broken. The leather of their throats had not been cut. . . . They might have starved to death, but it wasn't likely, not sitting so neatly in their rows.

No, they had frozen to death in a night. And rested in cold the centuries since—cold that must have come to seem warm to them, so they sat easy, dead, and smiling in shadow.

"Come *out!*" Mary was behind her, tugging at her arm, and Catania let herself be pulled back and back past the rows of people. She was helped down the two steps, then her bare feet felt stone beneath them.

"Look," Mary said. She led around to the blunt front of the big box, where letters—spotted and missing pieces—said, TURBO-BUS.

"It's a Warm-time traveling bus."

"Yes," Mary said, "—a traveling bus. There were black wheelings under it during the first five Ladies' lives, but they broke and rotted away."

"What does 'Turbo' mean?"

"I don't know. Peter Librarian says it means going around and around."

"Maybe it traveled around and around someplace," Catania said, and began to weep.

"There, now. . . ." Mary took Catania's arm and led her away from under the split stone ceiling and sheets of icicles, out to where she'd left her moccasin boots.

Catania couldn't stop crying. She tried to catch her breath.

"Now, you're wiser," Mary One-eye said, "—and see where Gardens gets its memories." She made Catania sit down on a stone, then knelt and rubbed her cold feet until they were warm again. "Better?" she said. "Better?"

"Yes," Catania said, and slowly stopped crying. She leaned away to blow her nose between her fingers.

"Peter Librarian," Mary said, "—and Librarians before him—believe the traveling bus was caught when early Cold-time snow came down a hillside all at once, and stopped their going. Covered them up, so they froze and died. Then, later, a summer melt made a sudden river that took them under the ledge."

"It's so *sad*."

"Yes," Mary said. "Sad, and happy." She wrapped Catania's foot cloths, then put the moccasin-boots on her as if she were a child. "Aren't you wiser, now?" she said.

"Yes," Catania said. "I learned that bright things pass by. . . ."

"Well learned, Tall Scar-face." Mary stood up. "And if you will only give an eye—just break it with your fingers and show it to the people—you may come and do as I did, and ride on the Running-dog bus for three days and three nights with no water and no blanket and no food. Then you will travel with the travelers, and become truly wise."

"I can't—"

"Don't say a thoughtless 'can't' to me, Catania!" An angry Mary. "—I know you better than you know yourself. You are wise already, and will become wiser. Then, what service will you do? Only spread your legs and dream of love with a man whose strength comes from death, and will go back to it?"

"Mary—"

"I'm offering you the gift of all of yourself. Don't refuse it."

Catania stood up from the stone. "Your people aren't my people."

"And yours are *not* a people, anymore. Their place is gone, and what they were has gone with it. They will be nothing until they have a new place, and have lived three lives there."

"Then the more reason," Catania said, "—not to leave them."

Mary stopped looking angry, and smiled. "Oh, see, see how clever you are, to have found such an answer? Clever enough, and strong enough to hold my people in your arms when I am gone."

"No."

"Clever," Mary said, "—and see how strong, to refuse me." She stood watching Catania, her head cocked like a bird's for better seeing. "I promised you two wisdoms. Would you like to see the second?"

"I don't know. . . ."

"Oh, but you do know! You would be eaten with curiosity, otherwise." Mary made an odd frowning face. "Look at me, then. *Look* at me. *Look . . . at me. . . .*" Mary's frown grew deeper, and she slowly crouched . . . then squatted as if she were shitting. She began to huddle in upon herself like an unborn baby, grunting her way tighter and tighter, until she was curled close in her green robe, and shut in upon herself. She groaned as if in great effort, and her face, bowed into crossed arms, was dark with blood.

Catania was afraid for Mary's heart, and said, "Don't do . . . what you're doing." But Mary One-eye didn't seem to hear her, only kept knotting herself into herself, making the sounds of strain.

"*Mary,*" Catania said . . . then stared. The fat woman, now a large green lump upon the stone, shifted and rocked from side to side. Then heaved . . . heaved, and lifted up.

Catania thought Mary must be standing—be starting to stand as she rose. But there was no part of her still on the stone. She lifted a little, then more and more until she hung in the air—no higher than Catania's waist, and no lower.

Mary, in the air, a great green-cloth ball with a dark and swollen face, began to slowly roll, making a snoring sound of great effort.

Catania shouted for help where no help could come. The shout echoed under the stone. She drew her knife, backing away, spitting like a cougar at dogs beneath its den. "Don't," she said. "*Don't!*" And turned and ran from under the rock shelf into sunlight.

Outside, she slapped her face to waken. "Foolish dream," she said aloud. "Foolish dream . . ." She tripped and stumbled over rocks and a rotting hemlock trunk, almost falling on her knife.

Then she realized she wasn't dreaming, sheathed her blade, and shouted back to the deep rock ledge. "You fat bitch!" She'd heard from Salesmen about hypnos-fooling, and now it had been done to her. "You one-eye thing, you fooled me *stupid!*"

Catania thought of going back to kill Mary One-eye for proving the truth of Jack's tale of nasty wisdom—the Boston flying wisdom that always brought badness with it. She was thinking of going back with her knife, when she heard a soft sound that grew louder.

Something moved in shadows under the rock ledge. It swayed a little from side to side. Then a hunched wad of green, with feet tucked in, sailed slowly out into the light and staggered through the air as high as Catania's head. It made a sound of snoring as it came.

If this is so, Catania thought, *then everything is dreaming.* And she ran from that wisdom, as much as from Flying-Mary.

* * *

Catania ran until she was sick with running, and stopped to lean against a tree trunk to catch her breath. Someone was calling, faint and far behind her. She thought it might be Mary One-eye, calling her name.

There was a Catania then, that ran on, ran away along the ridge through pine, hemlock, and fir, to where Carlson Gold-bracelets waited. . . . But the other Catania was tired of running, and when she'd caught her breath, turned to walk back the way she'd come.

She found Mary lying in sunlight by a fall of stones, not far from the gully. The little woman's robe was soaked with melting snow, and she was trembling. Her lips were blue-white, and when Catania put an ear to her chest to listen, she heard the heartbeat stumbling.

"I'll build a fire," she said, stroking Mary's forehead. "Then you'll be warm, and we'll go home together. Carlson Gold-bracelets will be worried about us."

Mary nodded and took a deep breath. "It must . . . it must have been a frightened Scar-face, to run so far away."

"Yes," Catania said. "A frightened Scar-face. Two new wisdoms, were one too many."

Mary smiled, then coughed a catch of a cough. It was the cough Catania had heard from old people, when their lips were so pale.

She broke dead sticks and stacked them, shaved fine flakes of wood from one, then struck her flint and steel to make a spark, and blew it into fire.

"Better," Mary said, as the warmth came to her. She was lying on Catania's caribou jacket, and her lips had become more red than blue. "Better. . . ."

"Will Carlson worry?"

"He will worry, and wait," Mary said, and lay silent, resting for a while. Then she turned on her side to watch the fire. "Listen . . . what I just did, my mother's sister learned to do from an old Dreaming-man who came to Gardens. My aunt was our Lady, then." Mary cleared her throat, and coughed a little. "The Dreaming-man had no sense, but he told stories that going-sitting-in-the-air was done in New England, and other things, too. He said a man there, named Asa Phipps, had learned to keep warm with his mind—learned it hundreds of years ago, when the cold first came down."

Mary closed her eyes, and Catania thought she was going to sleep.

But after a while, Mary opened her eyes and said, "This man had a gift in his mind to warm himself. And it seems that from *his* gift, the New Englanders discovered others' mind-gifts, and bred those who had them. . . . At least, that's what the old fool told us."

Mary reached out and pushed a twig deeper into the fire.

"I've heard of mind-done things," Catania said. "Jack said he'd heard of them—that one was seen in a storm . . . and monsters. But I didn't believe it. There is none of that in any copybook I've read."

"My sensible Sweet One," Mary said, "—copybooks don't hold all wisdom. Perhaps our age of ice has been a teacher, too. . . . And as to these mind-gifts, I don't know any other, but I learned from my mother's sister that what you do is push and push and *push* the ground away. And if you have the piece of jelly-meat in your head that allows it—and you push hard enough so it hurts—then the ground can be pushed away from beneath you, so fools think you are flying as birds fly."

"It's very frightening to see," Catania said. "It makes real things seem less real."

Mary took a deep breath. "I'm feeling better." She took more deep breaths. "My aunt couldn't go far or fast, traveling in the air, and neither can I. A little way only, and with great difficulty—though enough to remind my people of obedience. Walking is much easier."

Mary slowly sat up. "I could try to teach you that wisdom, Catania. Perhaps you have the piece in your head to do it."

"I would rather run behind our dogs."

"I know," Mary said. "It is startling—but still a poor wisdom compared with the Running-dog bus." Then she was quiet, staring into the fire, one-eyed, old, and weary.

"Are you comfortable? Are you hurting?"

"Yes—and no, Doctor." . . . As soon as she was able to stand, they walked back along the ridge in the afternoon, going slowly, though Mary seemed then as strong as ever. As they went, she took Catania's hand.

"Don't disappoint me," Mary One-eye said, and said nothing more until Carlson Gold-bracelets came to meet them, looking worried.

* * *

Catania found Jack, Torrey, and Pat Weber above the Trapper camp, testing sleds for frame cracks and loose lashings. Myles and Donna Weber were polishing the steel runners with shale stone.

The Richardsons and Olsens were checking sleds at their fire. Joan had one of the dogs on its back, scratching its belly while she examined pads and paws, the dog grunting, kicking with pleasure.

Catania stood by a pine watching them . . . watching them do their Trapper chores. Now, it seemed to her they were like strong children, not quite grown—even Jack—and knowing only those narrow things that comforted them.

Catania saw herself telling them about the Running-dog bus, and Mary-in-the-air. She saw herself telling—saw them as they heard—and, deciding to say nothing about the two wisdoms, hoped that decision would prove to be a third.

Mary One-eye had taught her too much—too much for her to stay in Gardens to *become* a Mary, using wisdoms like nasty flying to frighten people, and giving an eye so orders would be obeyed. How could such bad things come to good?

But still, those wisdoms had had their way, and she was not as much a Trapper as she had been.

I have been shown two wisdoms, and am those two things wiser, but less happy. If our joys, like children's, are the pleasures of ignorance—then how sad must be All-knowing God?

Jennifer Weber will keep her leg.

We leave Gardens tomorrow. We go south.

FROM THE JOURNAL OF DOCTOR CATANIA OLSEN

15

The camp stirred through the afternoon and evening with getting ready to go. The Trappers packed the sleds with furs, tools, and weapons, as well as the travel-food the Garden people brought. Two goats, a big billy and small brown milking nanny, were part of that food, kept alive so as not to lose their meat by spoiling in warming weather.

The weather was already spoiling the snow. They would have to drag-travvy soon.

When the food came, the Garden children came with it to play with the gentler dogs, and say goodbye to Trappers who'd been kind to them. Those men and women who had lost their own children, had made goodbye presents of carved little jointed dolls for the girls, small bows and blunted arrows for the boys. The Trapper women, particularly, held and stroked the children, and were reluctant to let them go.

Later, at full dark, Garden May came with five other Garden girls—Francine Kemp, Ruth Bissel, Cross-eye Jane, Nuncie Lewis, and Small-Paula, each carrying an ax and a big cloth sack of their possibles. It was surprising Small-Paula came, since she'd been in camp only one time before, but she said that Mary had sent her.

The Trappers, restless, slept then woke throughout the night. Catania tended Bailey Auerbach's arrow wound, then unbandaged Jennifer Weber's leg and smelled the injury, which didn't stink and was plugged with yellow. She bandaged it with fresh boiled cloth, and saw Jennifer settled in the Webers' sled to ride.

"Go easy with her," Catania said to Helen, and Helen said she needed no advice on sledding her dead sister's child.

The stars were washing away into gray, and Catania was standing by the Weber-Edwards' fire—tired, and eating some small smoked bird that still kept its little toasted feet—when Carlson Gold-bracelets came through the camp and said that Mary wished to see her.

"Don't go," Lucy said. "Let her come here to say goodbye."

Carlson gave Lucy a bad look.

"I'm happy to go see the Garden Lady," Catania said, so he would look better, and he did.

"Go where, Catania?" Jack said. He had come up behind her.

"Mary wants to see me."

"She's seen you many times. Now, we're leaving."

"Don't take advantage," Carlson Gold-bracelets said to Jack, and put his hand on his ax. "If I fight you, I will have no honor left."

"*No*," Catania said, and stood between them. "I'll go to her to say goodbye."

"A short visit," Jack said.

"A short visit."

* * *

Mary was sitting cross-legged on a red cushion by her hearth, combing her hair out with a trade-comb that looked to be made of silver. Her long hair was shaded light brown to gray, like a mink's pelt.

She looked up at Catania, and said, "I see you have decided wrongly."

"I am going."

"The weakness-choice."

Catania said nothing.

Mary gestured to a cushion. "Sit down," she said, and set her comb aside. "Silence will not do you now, Scar-face. And we have become friends and *that* will not do you now. Tell me, what if I take a hand from you—the hand you use to grip your bow? What sort of Trapper will you be, then?"

"A different sort of Trapper when I leave," Catania said, though her throat seemed to close while she spoke. "—As you have already made me a different sort of Trapper."

"And if I *take* the eye you're too weak to give?"

"I will have one eye left to find my way."

Mary sat watching her, interested as if Catania might change to someone different. "... And if I take your feet, as my aunt took Doctor Dorothy's feet to make her stay?"

"Then, I will go slowly."

Mary sat without speaking for a while. The fire ticked and muttered in the hearth. "What a waste," she said, and sighed. "What a waste of a Lady you are! It makes me very angry that you will surely learn a duty some day, but won't accept it now for Gardens." Mary showed her teeth and opened both eyes so her empty socket showed red. "—We make *paper* here! And you come from people living with animals and by animals and as animals, and make *nothing*!"

Mary rose from her cushion as if her heart was strong. "I could take both your eyes, Catania, so your tears would sting the hollows for many years."

"Then, I would travel blind."

Mary stood and looked at her. "Those answers," she said, "—those are the answers I would have given. They leave me more disappointed, more angry with you for running away. Don't answer so well, my Scar-face. Don't make me angrier."

"I'm sorry I cannot please you."

Mary began walking back and forth, in and out of the fire's shadows. "I thought," she said, "—I thought the Weather had brought me a true daughter. I thought you were a gift to Gardens."

"I would be, if I could."

"You liar. *Liar!*" Mary was weeping; tears had come from her eye and from where her other eye had been. "It's all for a *man*. A man already lost to you and everyone!"

"Not true. Not all for a man."

"Don't you tell me what is true and what is not."

Catania said nothing. She imagined the blue of the morning sky, and that she was out under it, riding a sled away.

Mary wiped her tears with her sleeve, and sat down on her cushion again. "And if I have Tall Jack's eyes taken, unless you stay?"

". . . Then Jack would lose his eyes, and I and other Trappers would lose our lives—and you would lose your paper-mill to burning."

"Ah. . . ." Mary blew her nose on the hem of her robe. "An answer even better than mine would have been. What a *waste*."

A man, a Gold-bracelets Catania didn't know, came down into the house.

"Dear Lady," he said to Mary, "—one of the Dog-men will fight us or come into your house. What is your wish?"

Mary smiled. "Surely this will be your Tall Jack, Catania. A last time, now, to think of your answer again."

"He wouldn't want me to give a different answer than I have already given."

"Let him come down," Mary said to the Gold-bracelets. "Then go, and leave us alone."

Catania had grown used to Mary's house, and had thought it large enough. But when Jack ducked in and stood stooped beneath the ceiling, the room became small as if by mind-magic, so he seemed to fill much of it.

"At least," Mary said, sitting on her cushion looking up at him, "—at least it *is* a man."

"I came to say thank you," Jack said to her, and Catania saw him look at the painting that made a story around the room. "—Thank you for Gardens' hospitality."

" 'Hospitality,' " Mary said. "No wonder we make no words better than Warm-time words. They made them all, and each just right." She got up off her cushion with a grunt. "Do you want vodka, Tall Jack?"

"No."

"Well, I am going to have vodka.—Catania?"

"No, thank you."

Mary went to her shelves, humming a soft song without words. She poured vodka into a leather cup, then searched for a time among her little wooden boxes for what forest-friends she wanted to flavor it. "But Jack, you came for my Scar-face, more than for thank-you's."

"I came for both, since we're leaving."

Catania saw Jack's shadow as the hearth-fire threw it moving against the painted wall.

Mary One-eye stirred her vodka with a fat finger. "Now, I asked your doctor to stay, and threatened to take a hand . . . take an eye . . . take her feet to keep her with us to become a Lady."

"Get up," Jack said to Catania. "We're leaving."

"I threatened," Mary took her finger from her cup, and dried it on her robe, "—but she gave strong answers of no." Mary smiled. "Then I mentioned taking *your* eyes, Tall Jack, but still our Catania gave strong answers, and said yours would be as strong."

Jack reached down, took Catania by the arm and lifted her to her feet.

"It makes me angry," Mary said, and she was no longer smiling, "—to see that strength of hers shown only to refuse service to my people."

Jack led Catania toward the tree-root stairs, but Mary stepped in their way. She stared up at them with her one eye. "And for what good reason? Why, for *you*."

"And other reasons," Catania said.

Jack said, "Stand aside."

"Listen to him bark. A tall two-legged dog-man, a savage dog-man with nothing left in him but a few more *bites*—" Mary threw her vodka up into Jack's face.

Then Jack was gone from Catania's side—and gripped Mary One-eye, grappled her to him like a lover, her hair twisted in his fist, her head forced back. The point of his belt knife rested, a bright decoration, beneath her only eye.

Mary seemed pleased. "Bite, dog!" she said, "—and my people will burn your Trappers on their sleds. And burn the new little baby with them."

"Don't," Catania said. "Jack, don't hurt her."

But it was the Fighting Jack, now, and only his shadow moved along the wall.

". . . What if I apologize?" Mary said, and she smiled under the knife. "Do you know that Warm-time word, Tall Jack? It's a very good one. . . ."

Slowly . . . slowly, he lifted his knife-blade away, loosened his grip on Mary's hair, and stepped back from her.

"We're going," Catania said.

Jack wiped his eyes with the back of his hand, and sheathed his knife.

"Go," Mary One-eye said. "Run until you have nothing left to run from . . . and nothing to run to." She went to the hearth, and tossed her vodka cup into the fire.

* * *

Through the morning, the Trappers cleaned their camp. They finished the last packing, drowned their fires with Fast Creek water, and filled in the John trench with fresh dirt and old snow. Then they combed over the slope to find anything left behind.

There were no visitors from Gardens, though it was a sunny morning, and warm enough to further soften the snow. None came to say goodbye to the Trappers, or to May and the five Garden girls going with them. No children came, or Gold-bracelets, and there was no farewell music or drums.

Jack chose the order of traveling: Torrey's sled first, then the Richardsons, then Weber-Edwards. The Olsens, Sorbanes, and Auerbachs coming after. Jennifer Weber and Bailey Auerbach were the only riders. Susan Monroe had made a wrap-poozy of the beautiful Gardens blanket to carry Small-Sam on her back.

Three-balls danced in his harness, whining, eager to run. When Jack came trotting up the slope, his lance balanced in his hand, Torrey called *"Musout!"* The team hauled as one dog, and the sled jerked, skidded, then slid away fast up and out of Gardens' small valley and into the trees.

Jack led them south—but turned a little as they traveled over thin snow and pine needles, wending between great evergreens to come to the smaller tree, a birch, where Jim Olsen rested bundled in the branches. Tree-resting was poor resting, compared to staying in ice, but it had become too warm for that.

The Trappers braked their teams, tied them off, and came to say goodbye, touching the resting-tree in turn, while Chapman and Micah wept. Catania recited the 'Now-I-Lay-Me-Down,' for Difficult-Jim Olsen. Then, done praying, they went to their teams to travel.

As the sleds began to pull away, Mary One-eye stepped out of hemlocks, and called, "*Catania. . . .*"

Some Trappers strung their bows and went into the woods, thinking there could be goodbye trouble, that some Gold-bracelets might have come with her. But Mary had come alone.

"Catania. . . ."

"Careful," Jack said, but Catania went to the hemlocks to meet her.

"My sweet Scar-face," Mary said, and hugged her as if there'd been no disagreement between them. "I thought you'd stop here to say goodbye to that foolish man.—As you can now say goodbye to this foolish, fat old woman." She stood on her tiptoes to kiss Catania's scarred cheek.

"Mary, I would have stayed . . . if I could have stayed."

"Oh, you were not ready for it yet." Mary smiled. "I'll have to live long enough to make another Lady.—Here," she took a folded page of paper from her robe's pocket. "A copy-present from Necklace Peter."

"Thank him for me," Catania said. "And Mary, walk every day, but try not to climb—"

"Yes, and eat less and so forth. I will obey you, Doctor, as you have *not* obeyed me." She took a breath. "I have come to ask your forgiveness."

"Forgive you for what?"

"For what it is that requires forgiveness, Catania. Say that you forgive me."

"I don't—"

"Say, 'Mary, I forgive you.' "

"I'll say it, but I have no reason to."

"*Say* it."

". . . I forgive you, Mary."

Mary One-eye sighed. "Thank you," she said. "Now, goodbye, Sweet Scar-face—your people are waiting."

"Goodbye," Catania said, hugged her, and walked back to the sleds.

"Remember, Catania," Mary called after her. "Remember that I am forgiven. . . ."

Necklace Peter sent me a present from the library—a copy-poem about weather, probably since I'd loved the R. Frost so much.

This is called 'Persephone.' It was written by J. Reed in an unknown year.

> Each time our blue earth turns around,
> Before it meets its moon for spring,
> My last year's love comes whistling down,
> And does his seasonal thing.
> He wraps me in rain like a treasure,
> Then lays me to sleep in the snow,
> Where I dream up my flowers for pleasure,
> Then die, so the sunlight will grow.

We have left Gardens, and are in the dark forest. I miss my second mother, Mary, but am glad to be gone. She asked too much.

FROM THE JOURNAL OF DOCTOR CATANIA OLSEN

16

Though Jack held them in, the Trappers kept the habit of running-from—driving their teams over the poor snow through brush and bramble and between great trees as if more Cree had come down and after them.

Only near each nightfall, when the dogs grew weary, did they slacken their pace.

It took a Warm-time week of forest running—south, then east—to ease them. As they eased, the winter eased and the forest began to thin, until, in their second week of traveling, they came into almost open country, with more and more hardwood. The snow here was leaving the ground to winter-kill and sparse spring grasses.

It was as warm, already, as the Range became in its short summer.

On the morning of the fifteenth day—when the last of the Garden food, except the nanny goat, was gone—Donna Weber and Wanda Sorbane, out scouting, killed a black-tail deer. Wanda shot it from a far rock-throw away, and struck it in the heart.

"That's good luck," the Trappers said, and thought their fortune was changing with the season.

"Good luck," Jack said, lying with his head in Catania's lap as she rinsed his eyes with boiled water. His eyes were still sore, still very red from the vodka-drink Mary had thrown into them—though, a few days ago, they'd seemed to be getting better.

"Good luck for now," Catania said, "—but trouble sooner or later. Chapman hasn't forgotten Jim lying with his belly open. Joan Richardson hasn't forgotten. Or Bailey. . . ."

"New country will keep them happy." Jack sat up, then stood. He never rested as long under her hand as Catania wished. Even so, these days were the best she'd known, a contentment so sweet she feared its loss each morning, when she woke.

"And what new country will we be able to keep?"

Jack reached down and gently pinched her nose. "I'm thinking of hills I've heard of, in Map-Arkansas. Good hills, hardwood trees, and five- . . . maybe six-week summers."

"I thought there were bad men near there, in Map-Missouri."

"The people I knew will be gone," Jack said. "They were short-lived men." And he went off to the cook-fire to slice some more venison.

. . . The next few days, the sun shone so that the last of the snow died under it and was gone. Then the sleds had to be unpacked, their rawhide lashings cut, so the bent-wood members could be taken down and fitted together differently to become drag-travvies.

The long runners were the difficult things—had to be paired, then bound with re-knotted rawhide to the frames for half their lengths, so only the ends of their steel edges dragged on the ground.

In travvy, the teams could pull almost as fast as on soft snow, but the dogs didn't like it, even though the country opened so they often ran on wiry winter grass, instead of working through woods. The travvies were unbalanced hauls, and the grass cut the dogs' pads.

"Where are we?" Torrey said. He and Jack were sitting by a small pit fire at sunrise, checking the dogs' feet. Three-balls had shoved and snarled to be first, and now lay between them on his back, grunting with pleasure. The Trappers had camped between two low rises, with no trees near, and dug pit fires to burn dry grass safely.

"I think we're in Map-Texas," Jack said. "This is south of where I've been before."

"And now we keep east?"

"Now we keep east."

"Booties back on?"

"No, the grass will wear them out. Their pads'll toughen."

"They better," Torrey said. "We can't have lame dogs."

Catania and Garden May came back from peeing, and sat down with them. "Is it a lame dog?" May said to Three-balls. Still on his back, he lolled his tongue for her; he liked Garden May.

"We don't get something today," Torrey said, "—we need to cook the nanny goat."

As if an open-country angel had heard him, Dummy Olsen waved from the top of the north rise and called—softly for Dummy—"*See 'em over there? See 'em over there?*"

Only a few Trappers got out of their bedding to see, since Dummy was not reliable. But Del Richardson ran up to look, and saw them too.

"Deer . . . deer!" They were little light-brown deer with white butts, grazing in a shifting herd a long way off over the winter-kill grass. They all seemed to be young spike bucks.

"I've heard of those." Jack came up the rise and looked out, squinting. "Don't think they're deer. . . ."

"Wild goats," Chapman Olsen said.

But Myles Weber said, "Not goats, either; look at those split horns."

"Goin' huntin'!" Dummy ran down the slope and the other Trappers followed him, hurrying for their bows and quivers and lances.

Jack had to tell no one what to do.

Susan, the baby, and Jennifer Weber stayed in camp with limping-Bailey Auerbach. Martha Sorbane, and Myles and Helen Weber stayed to guard them.

The others ran out into the country as the sun rose into a cloudy sky. Micah Olsen, Pat Weber, Rod Sorbane, and Wanda Sorbane ran north as fast as they could, to pass the herd . . . then turn to drive it in.

The others spread out across the grassland a lance-throw apart, and trotted away over ground that slowly rose . . . then slowly dipped—but never so high or low they lost sight of the animals.

"*Antelope* is what they are," Jack said to Ruth Bissel—Ruth, May, and all the Garden girls were eager on their first hunt, trotting along in line, bare breasts shaking.

"Antelope. . . ." Ruth passed it along. "Antelope."

The herd watched them, seeming curious as the Trappers came

through grass grown higher and higher, so they left long tracks that parted the stems like fingers reaching.

Jack looked for the drivers, for Micah and the others swinging north behind the animals, but couldn't see them.

"Slow," he said to Ruth Bissel, and she passed 'Slow' down the line. As the Trappers heard, each eased to a jog trot barely faster than walking, and crouched a little. The tall grass, killed by cold and streaked black, had died standing, so it rustled as they went by. Rustled in the morning wind, also. The wind—from the north and cold—was blowing into their faces.

It carried spring rain with it, instead of snow. Beyond the antelope herd, a dark haze swayed along the horizon. It billowed out like Garden cloth in a breeze, and the Trappers could see its long soft steps in the grass as it came.

The Trappers slowed and stopped to unstring their bows, coil the twisted sinews, and put them in their belt-pouches to save from wetting. Then they began to trot again, balancing their lances in their hands. The Garden girls, whose breasts were sore from running, held their left arms across to cradle them and went on, swinging their axes one-handed.

The antelope turned and turned under the rain, like char in the fall of a summer stream, as the storm came near and nearer— then struck the Trappers with darkness, and drenched them. Their line was staggered in wet wind and blowing grass. Small-Paula fell and got back up again, and bright lightning snapped so close they ducked like a team under the whip, the dead grass hissing and seething around them.

Out of darkness and stinging rain, an antelope came sailing flashing past. The Trappers could hear distant whistles and shouts on the wind as the drivers came running behind the storm. Antelope leaped through, bounding right and left, then away, gone down the wind like leaves. The steel of lance-heads shone in the rain along the Trapper line.

Two more antelope came running together, side by side, to pass by Newton, Lucy, and Nuncie Lewis. The Garden girl gripped her ax with both hands, threw it and almost hit one, so it jumped left—wet and shining from the rain—and the other jumped to join it. That was the antelope Newton killed. He rose from the grass and threw, and the antelope went down. As he jumped to cut its throat—batting the thrashing head's small pronged horns aside—Lucy ran to throw at the other, but threw short. The antelope were very fast.

Down the line, one came jumping from a squall of rain and lofted past Jack, its eyes wide.

Jack turned as it went by, his muscles loose and easy, saw the place he wanted—and his lance hummed away, streaked just over the animal's back, and vanished into rain and dark grasses.

He stood astonished at missing, then laughed, and trotted through the rain to find the lance.

. . . The rest of the day into afternoon—a day now clear, and warm enough that many took off their buckskin shirts—the Trappers dealt with meat.

They skinned, dressed, and butchered out three antelope—offering slices of raw liver to reluctant Garden girls, each slice sprinkled with gall—then rested roasts wrapped in belly fat amid the grass-fires' coals. Roasts, loins, and racks of ribs were hung on lances—butts driven into the dirt to hold them at a slant, long shafts bending with the weight—set close enough to the fires to cook, far enough to save the lance-heads' temper.

There were no wild onions to flavor, no hill thyme, no potatoes to roast alongside. It was meat alone—killed and cut and cooking, so the hot sweet smell settled in the camp with drifts of smoke, and fat ran spitting into the fires. Where the smoke rolled up thickest, at a big pit-fire with damp grass thrown into it, sliced bundles and thin shaved strips of meat hung on rawhide lines—stretched across the pit between two travvies to cook, dry, and cure for jerky, and for pemmican when bird-fat and berries were found.

The Trappers butchered and cooked, but delayed their eating for the pleasure of anticipation. They shouted and danced to Dummy's drumming, and young Del Richardson and Pat Weber wrestled, rolling through the camp as if the meat had already made them stronger.

It was the best day since leaving Gardens; the first day that Catania had seen the Trappers truly happy since the Cree came down. Their lost loved ones were beginning to let them go. . . . She sat with Jack, Torrey, and Garden May—the girl staring dreaming at the fire, the men playing pick-up sticks. Jack had lost the first two games; Catania supposed he'd done that as a gift to Torrey.

She sat with them, watching the rack of ribs roasting in its fire, to see it didn't burn—and thought that in such a warm-country season, where water often didn't freeze at night, and only morning frost lay on the grasses . . . thought perhaps with good hunting, and Garden girls for the men to share till love made choices, that there would be no more trouble, and they would find a new Range, and be happy.

It was thinking so restful that she dozed until the meat was done.

But that night she dreamed she sat in the Running-dog bus, with its travelers whose destinations waited forever. She sat with the eyeless withered child in her lap, holding the frozen toy bear. The bear whispered a secret into the child's ear, and the blind child turned up her shriveled face and whispered to Catania.

It was a secret she didn't wish to hear.

* * *

They went due east for many days into country as open as the sky, once passing big grassy bumps and lumps beside a slow river. Micah Olsen dug into a bump to look for good metal, but found only a piece of low wall made of spoiled gray stone with sticks of rusted iron stuck into it. The sticks broke when he gripped them, and were no good for anything.

They travvied on, living off antelope meat—now with wild spring onions—and also the meat of a brown and white cattle-cow startled out of shallow brush. They had more than they could eat, and kept the nanny as a pet though she was troublesome to milk, and only the Garden girls and Dummy cared to drink it.

The Trappers stayed happy, traveling and hunting. At night, the women gathered around Susan Monroe and her baby, playing with Small-Sam, warming themselves at him as if he were a fire, while the men tended dogs, sharpened broadheads, and told stories of the Range. Now, no one asked them not to tell those stories.

None of the men came to Catania for Sunday fucking after prayers, since Jack stood in their way—and all the Garden girls but May and Ruth Bissel would do it.

So those many traveling days were easy days, and everything happened as it should, except the healing of Jack's eyes. His eyes were red, and the left eye, after it had been rinsed, would make pus in its corner again.—If not for that, Catania would have been happy for those days to last forever.

But though pleased with open country, the Trappers were tired of feeding greedy grass fires and guarding them from spreading— so they were happy to come to a deep flowing spring shaded by hardwood trees. And though it was early in the day for camping, they stayed.

These trees' branches were easy to break away, and the Garden girls used their axes to chop them into firewood, so there could be a big camp fire, steady, and easy to control. Though soon after the fire was made and burning, Jack and Newton came back to camp from a no-game hunt, and pulled wood away to make it smaller, so it showed less smoke.

Spring water tasted better than the melt they'd taken from Slow-River-by-the-Bumps, so the Trappers emptied their water-skins and refilled them. There were little fish in the spring, and Dummy took off his buckskins, jumped in, and tried to catch them. But they were too small, too quick to be caught—and though Dummy promised not to pee in there, no one believed him, and Ben Olsen made him get out.

That evening, the women, searching along the spring for onions, found tiny blue berries all shriveled from winter. There were enough for everyone to have a mouthful. Dummy, and May and the other Garden girls, had their berries with the nanny's milk and claimed that was very good.

That night was only a quarter-moon night, so the stars were bright as on the Range but more of them, since no mountains' shoulders stood in their way. In this open country, there was no end to stars. Catania lay with Jack, tangled under furs too warm, his arm heavy across her breast, and looked at the stars to count them.

Though one copybook had described them as perfect burning of the tiniest things, and as far away as the farthest possible away, it seemed to Catania they must be more than that to be so beautiful. Old Doctor Monroe had said the sun was a star, which might be true, since it seemed friendly, and tried to help against Cold-times. . . . She lay a long while watching the stars, until they sent her to sleep.

* * *

Jack jolted against her, was being shaken—and Catania woke to dawn's first light.

"What?" she said.

Newton, crouched naked beside them in frost and drifting mist, said, "*Something*, Jack."

Jack sat up, and Newton put his hands on the ground, pressed down hard, and closed his eyes.

Catania, who had thought she was dreaming, watched Jack do the same. Then both men were quiet, their eyes closed.

"Spotted cattle?" Jack said. "Running?"

"No." Newton took his hands from the ground. "Riding horses."

Jack stood and shouted "Up!—Up!" The Trappers woke, rolled out of their bedding and reached for bows and lances before thinking of bows and lances.

"Riding horses!" Jack said, stringing his bow. "I've never seen them."

"I have," Newton said, and called out, "Get back into the trees! People are coming on riding horses, and coming faster than friendly!"

Dogs were barking in their lines—at the sounds, or the smell of strange animals coming.

The Garden girls were up with their axes and trotting alongside as the Trappers backed to the little grove of trees. There was a rapid drumming, like partridges courting, but loud, and becoming louder.

Susan, holding the baby in his blanket, ran calling "Jennifer!" and an arrow came whistling out of soft gray light and struck the back of her head. The point came out her mouth so she bit it as she fell dying, and the baby fell with her.

Catania ran with her lance where Helen Weber was helping Jennifer, who was limping along on her bad leg. There was a rush, a rush and hammering on the ground. Catania turned with her lance and saw a man coming at her through the air, riding high on a black animal's back. She saw the animal's nostrils and eye. It had no antlers. The horse-rider was a small, flat-faced man with big shoulders in a thick jacket. He swung away from her lance-head—then swung back all in an instant, and hit at Catania with a very long knife. Its blade was an arm long, and shone as it came down.

She thought it must be a sword-knife from the copybooks, and fell fast to avoid it.

Then she was up and the small man was gone, but three others coming. Arrows were sneezing through the air.

Two of the three men ran their riding-horses at Jennifer and Helen Weber. Helen lanced the first horse—it yelled and swerved away—but the other man leaned down to hit Jennifer with his sword-knife as Catania was running to them. He hit Jennifer once, and blood came down her face. She drew her knife to strike at him, but she limped and was too slow. He made his riding-horse dance away, then came back and hit her with the sword-knife again, with the point of it. Catania saw that go in, knew Jennifer was killed—and a terrible rage came into her at this end to traveling peace. She couldn't wait to reach this rider, was too impatient to run to him, so she threw as hard as she could throw. Her lance sailed over and slid into his back.

He screamed, reached behind him to feel what had happened—and the lance shaft wagged as his riding-horse went this way and that. Helen Weber ran to him, put her lance in his throat to stop his noise, and was killed as she killed, when two arrows and then one more struck, snatched at her, and turned her almost around before she fell.

Catania saw three horse-riders sitting on their animals beyond the camp, shooting with short, deep-curved bows—shooting fast. They had killed Helen.

Taking her bow off her back, Catania slid an arrow from her quiver and nocked it as the three horse-riders suddenly made their animals come running. They were shooting as they came. It was clever, how they shot while riding.

"The trees!" Jack said. He had come to stand beside her. Naked, he thrust his lance in the ground, then drew his bow as a horseman went riding by. He shot—missed, and seemed startled to have missed—then dropped his bow and took up his lance as he ran at that rider.

Arrows were stitching the morning air like sewing needles, the horse-peoples' fletched white, the Trappers' fletched in family colors. Jack ran shifting between them, very fast. The rider saw him coming and rode to meet him, leaning over his animal's neck so his sword-knife was pointed at Jack. He was smiling.

They'd almost come together when Jack suddenly changed stride and ducked under the horse's head to its other side. The horse-rider whipped his blade up and over, but not in time. The lance took him in the belly, and Catania saw Jack brace himself and heave the man up off his animal and into the air on the lance-head, screaming, smiling no longer.

Jack held him there a moment like a banner, while arrows hummed past, then threw him away.

Two more horse-men, though riding fast and shooting from the edge of camp, were caught by Trapper arrows. And Catania shot a horse beside the spring. The rider leaped away as the animal went down, and Millie Auerbach stepped from the trees and shot him through the heart. It seemed to Catania these horse-people were surprised to be fighting other archers, and didn't like it.

But they liked it well enough that five, then one more, came riding into camp like wind in a storm, sweeping through very fast, and shooting as Trappers came out of the trees shooting at them.

Two of those men were hit hard, one after another, and fell from their animals quilled with Trapper arrows.

Newton and Chapman Olsen ran out naked with their lances. Chapman threw, hit a rider so he swayed and jounced on his horse. The animal turned, confused—and Jack was there, stuck his lance up into that man and killed him.

Newton dodged a rider's arrow—a difficult thing for so big a man to do—and lanced that shooter's horse as Chapman, standing beside him, was struck in the back by another horse-man's arrow. As he staggered, a rider wearing a wide red-leather belt rode past and hit him in the neck with a sword-knife, so his blood sprayed out and he fell dying.

Carl Auerbach lanced the horse-man whose horse had been killed, and Joan Richardson ran out from the trees—stopped running to shoot—and put an arrow into that red-belted man, so he turned and tugged at it. Joan drew and shot him again, through the lungs, and he rode his horse away slowly, his head thrown back, making bad sounds of trying to breathe.

Only two more horse-riders came into the camp, coming very fast, calling to each other and shooting. Ben Weber hit one in the throat. Catania shot at the other, missed, then ducked aside as his arrow whined past her ear. As she nocked another arrow, she saw a group of horse-men sitting on their animals at a distance, out of bow-shot. They were watching the fight. One was holding a slender pole with animal tails hanging off it.

A man cried out behind her, and she turned and saw one of the riders—this one a very big man—stumbling, staggering along, bleeding from his mouth. Two Garden girls were hurrying after him with blood on their axes.

Now, only one horse-man was left in the camp, and he rode across it shooting, until a Trapper arrow caught his horse, and it screamed and fell. As it went down, the rider kicked free, rolled on the ground, and got to his feet with a sword-knife in his hand. Catania saw he was dressed brightly, in yellow and red and blue— and supposed all the horse-people had been dressed brightly, though she hadn't noticed it before.

Naked men rushed past Catania, Jack and Newton running at the rider with the sword-knife. He cut at them quickly, left and right, so the steel glittered. But—Jack on one side, Newton on the other—they stepped in, out, then in again together and took him in their hands.

Then the horse-man was like a weasel caught between a wolf and a bear; they gripped and grappled him, twisted his right arm out of its shoulder joint, then bent him back and back. The man screamed a word and Catania heard his spine break like a branch.

. . . There were no sounds after that but from hurt riding-horses, and Susan's baby crying. None of the horses had antlers— they were exactly as the copybooks had said.

We have had a bad battle at Sad Spring, with people who had no reason to come and fight us. We would have shared meat with them, would have let them have spring water if they'd asked, but they were unfriendly people—good archers, flat-faced with tilted eyes. I believe Mary once asked me if we had seen such riding men.

This battle was the end of peaceful traveling, and I do not expect peaceful traveling again, so I am trying to remember each of those good days, and that way keep them.

Susan is dead. Chapman Olsen is dead, and Joan Richardson's son, Del. Helen Weber was killed, and Jennifer Weber, and Bailey Auerbach back in the trees; they were both limping, and too slow. Sweet Lucy Edwards is dead . . . and one of the Garden girls, Francine Kemp. Del liked Francine, so perhaps they are together now.

Paul Auerbach was hurt, and Rod Sorbane. Small-Sam was not hurt—and after trying and trying him for a hungry day, he finally took the nanny's teat. The nanny hated it, and looked so offended I laughed for a while, and then I cried. The baby means very much to me—as if he is all our lost Range, all our lost people.

We killed thirteen horse-riders, and sent another away dying, with two barbed broadheads in him.

Newton has not spoken since Lucy was killed . . . and I am worried that Joan Richardson is going mad.

FROM THE JOURNAL OF DOCTOR CATANIA OLSEN

The Trappers traveled east, traveling sadly from Sad Spring. Those who spoke about the fight agreed that it had been one thing to read about horse-riding in copybooks, another thing to see it done—and done by good archers.

Tattooed Newton spoke to no one, hadn't spoken since Lucy was wrapped in hide like the other dead, and tied to rest in a tree at Sad Spring.

Joan Richardson spoke, but only in anger—and was always armed, so the others left her alone.

It was quiet traveling, with no sign of more horse-people. They had come and gone as the antelope rain had come and gone.

Even without rain, the Trappers had water. And it was fortunate the skins had been filled before the fight, since during it Torrey had wounded a rider in the trees, and Garden May had followed that man down to the spring and butchered him in the water with her ax.

... The evening of the third day of quiet traveling, they camped as high as the open country allowed, and set watchers to guard their back-trail. Then they dug pits and started small fires that made little smoke, so no one would know where they were except by following their travvy drags, and so come to their arrows expected.

Catania sat by a fire with Jack resting his head on her lap, being patient as she washed his eyes clean of pus. She washed them gently with water boiled in a trade-kettle, then washed them with more water, adding a pinch of salt to burn away tiny germ badness.

Jack lay still as if this did not hurt him. He hadn't changed since Sad Spring, but everyone else had changed. It seemed to Catania that the Trapper men and women, more so than the Garden girls, were smaller, harder, tighter in upon themselves than they had been. Their faces had become older, harsher faces.... They had been in one fight too many. As she had been in one fight too many, and was likely even uglier now than before.

Newton had still not spoken. Lucy had kept Wandering Newton a Trapper—now, he was once again as if a stranger, and silent.

Jack blinked saltwater from his eyes and started to sit up, but Catania held him for another rinse to wash the salt away. And as she did so, gently, a slow and dreadful cold rose in her, and she saw Mary again, humming a song with no words while searching . . . searching through her little boxes for what she wished to put into her cup of vodka. Vodka she never drank, only held, until she threw it into Jack's eyes.

She'd said, "Forgive me, Catania."

"But I have nothing to forgive you for."

"Say it. Say that you forgive me. . . ."

Catania looked down, and now saw clearly what she had not permitted herself to see before. Jack's left eye was clouded, red as coals—and the other coming to be the same.

Still good enough, though, to see her face.

"Trade-honey," he said, "—don't be afraid. I've known for many days." He got up, took his lance and walked away.

Then Catania felt as Joan Richardson felt with her son dead—as Newton felt, with his Lucy killed and tied in a tree. And as a piece of them had died, so a piece of her died while she sat there, though Jack Monroe was not yet blind.

* * *

They traveled another day, then quiet-camped and told stories. The Garden girls, who had no stories except from copybooks, or about garden-growing or what this or that Lady had done, loved to hear about mountains and the Wall and Old Man Glacier. About white bears, brown bears, wolves, and snow-tigers. It seemed to them the Range had been a wonderful place.

There had been stone mountains west of Gardens, the girls said, but trees had covered them into high green hills.

That evening, Jack knotted a strip of brown woven cloth around his head to cover his worst eye, the left, and wouldn't let Catania tend him any more. When she tried, he pushed her hand away, spilled the boiled water.

They lay that night side by side in silence, though he let her take his hand and hold it until moonset. In the morning, though, Jack went apart, and Catania saw he intended not to be close to her anymore. She supposed he thought that would be a kindness.

They broke camp, and travvied out into the warmest morning they'd known ever, the warmest even the Garden girls had known, so the Trappers wore only their trousers and moccasin-boots.

At midday, a line they'd been watching across the eastern horizon slowly became darker. As the sun tilted west, this line moved toward them, broke into tiny pieces . . . then became banners and many men riding through the grass.

The dogs began to yelp and whine.

There was no spring, no grove of trees for cover. Nothing but the grass and openness.

"Circle," Jack said, and although two Garden girls began to weep, the Trapper women didn't. They hauled their travvied sleds into a low barricade, and staked their teams to a single circling line around it, so as to be able to cut the dogs quickly free when the time came. . . . Then they settled into this slight fortress with their longbows strung, arrows nocked, and lances standing ready beside them. The Garden girls sat together at the center, some still weeping. All, except Garden May, held their axes across their knees. She cradled the baby in her lap.

Catania went to stand beside Jack, though he said nothing to her. She had a favorite arrow, the last of favorites—its shaft special Salesman ash, turned, warmed, then soaked and dried again, perfectly straight and heavier than a hunting arrow's. It was a war arrow, its head small, bright as jewelry, and too sharp to test for sharpness. It was a pleasure to put to the string.

"I can see to hit horses," Jack said, without turning to her. "You kill the men."

Then Catania felt the pleasure of a third wisdom's coming to her—deeper knowledge than the Running-dog bus, deeper than

Mary's nasty flying—and she understood how a good death's moment may balance the longest life.

The line of horse-riders came on. Some carried long staffs, with big woven-cloth banners ruffling in breezes blowing over the open country. The banners were white, with a round blue flower painted in the middle. There were many horse-riders, more than a hundred. More than two-hundred.

"Different!" Newton called out. "Different . . ."

And they *were* different from the ones at Sad Spring. These were bigger men, and, it seemed to Catania, riding bigger horses. They wore odd leather hats with the brims turned up in front—pinned up; she saw little metal sparkles as they came. More metal shone and twinkled on their shirts. Their arms were bare.

The riders were carrying long lances; a few had bows in cases by their riding-seats. They all had long straight sword-knives hanging at their sides.

Suddenly, a mountain-ram's horn—or more likely something of metal—made a long, bright, hard sound, and the horse-men stopped all together a distant bow-shot away.

"Map-Texas cavalry," Newton said—then said it louder, so everyone could hear. "Map-Texas cavalry! I've seen them at Market."

Catania saw the word 'cavalry' come from copybooks and stand before her.

The Trappers and Garden girls waited and were silent, as the many horse-riders waited and were silent, so only wind made sounds in the high grasses, stirred and rumpled the cavalry banners.

After a while, two men came riding nearer. They rode without guiding their horses, with their hands held out and open to show they carried no weapons.

"Don't kill them," Newton said.

The men rode near enough to be shot. Then they stopped their horses, and each swung a leg over the low riding-seat he sat in, and slid down to the ground. It was a surprising thing for the Trappers to see that the animals then stood still and began to eat grass. They didn't wander as dogs would have; didn't lie down, either.

The two men walked closer, then stopped. One—a short wide person wearing a big hat—called out: *"Speak book-English?"*

"Yes, we do," Jack called to him. "Now, you go your way, and we'll go ours."

The man smiled at Jack. He was close enough that smiling could be seen. "We'll talk a little, first," he said. "Come out and speak with us."

"Newton?" Jack said.

"I know these people," Newton said. "—Know about them, anyway. We have nothing to lose by talking."

"All right," Jack said. He lowered his bow, stepped out past a staked team, and he and Newton walked off into the grass.

Then Jack turned and called, "Catania." She slid her heavy arrow into her quiver, and went after them.

"We'll kill those two big-hats," Torrey said as she went, "—if they act a trick."

The two horse-riders were waiting. . . . Catania saw that the short wide man was even wider than he'd looked from a distance, and seemed very strong. He wore trousers, boots, and a long leather shirt with no sleeves and many little iron rings sewn on it. He had a fighter's face, heavy and weatherworn, with pleasant and unpleasant mixed together in it. He reminded Catania of Sam Monroe.

The man standing beside him also wore a big leather hat and an iron-ring shirt, but was thinner and younger. He looked like someone who thought more than he fought. Both riders—cavalry-men—were unarmed. They'd left their long sword-knives hanging on their riding-seats.

"Who the hell are you people?" The wide man said. He had eyes with no color but the black pupils in them. "Where do you come from?"

"Who the hell are *you* people?" Jack said. "Where do *you* come from?"

The thoughtful-man made an impatient little click with his tongue, but the fighting-man smiled. "Fair enough," he said, "I suppose courtesy's in order. I'm Colonel—you know what a colonel is?"

"We are book people," Catania said, and was interested to meet a colonel—another copybook thing come alive. She was interested, and being interested, supposed it was not her time to die, after all.

"I see." The fighting-man looked at her. "Of course, Lady. Well, I'm Colonel Maitlan of the Texas Arm; this is Minister Robinett . . . and those people," he turned his head to the cavalry-men, "—are mine. We are fighting Kipchak Russians, come over the northern strait and down the west ocean coast."

"I'm Jack Monroe," Jack said. "We fought some of those, probably, five days ago."

"Well," the Colonel said. "*Did* you now. . . ."

"He said so." Newton, standing back a little, gave them a bad look.

Both riders looked more closely at Newton then—and the Colonel said, "Jesus Christ!" Minister Robinett said, "Sir, we didn't realize."

"Nothing *to* realize," Newton said, and seemed angry with them. "These people want to be left alone."

"Well, we won't trouble them," the Colonel said. "We respect Middle Kingdom, and have ambassadors there, and they send ambassadors to us."

"I understand," Newton said, but still seemed angry.

"Well . . . well, so you people fought the Kipchaks. It must have been a scouting party—and I suppose they thought you were scouting for us." The Colonel bent, picked a stem of winter grass, and chewed on it. "Those sons-of-bitches have come to lower Texas all the way from Map-California. How many did you kill?"

"Thirteen," Jack said. "And one riding dying."

"Proper!" said Minister Robinett. "Oh, very *proper*! And do your people depend on Lord Jesus?"

"Yes," Catania said, "—but not day to day." The Colonel laughed as if she'd said something funny, but Minister Robinett didn't laugh.

The Colonel and Minister Robinett sat on their heels in the grass as if they were the Trappers' friends, and the Colonel asked where they'd come from, and why.

"I'm not being rude, sir," he said to Newton. Then he looked at Jack, and said again, "I'm not being rude. I'm asking to be aware of unpleasantness."

It made good sense to Catania, so she told him about fighting and running from the Cree. But she didn't tell him about Gardens.

"My," the Colonel said, "—if it isn't one thing, it's another," and looked proud to have recalled such an apt Warm-time phrase.

"Very nice, Harvey," said Minister Robinett.

"—And you're going . . . where? I'm not being rude."

"Map-Arkansas," Jack said.

"But that's all Middle Kingdom, now." The Colonel looked at Newton.

"It wasn't," Newton said.

"Yes," said Minister Robinett, "—but now it is. There was a fair agreement."

No one said anything for a while. They squatted or knelt on one knee in the grass, the sun warm on their shoulders. Then one of the cavalry-men called out to the others, and all the men got down from their riding-horses at the same time. They stood staring at the Trappers and dog-teams, and the Garden girls.

Newton stood up. "Jack," he said, "—come and talk with me." And he walked away.

Catania stayed with the two cavalry-men, and asked where their women and children were, and whether their women rode horses and were cavalry-people.

"My wife is dead," the Colonel said, and said nothing else.

"Our women stay and hold our farms and stock," said Minister Robinett. "They wind crank-crossbows like Boxcar-men, and shoot them very well—but they don't ride with us and fight. They stay safe in our homes, and care for the children."

"What lucky women!" Catania said, and supposed it must be true, since they had no reason to lie to her.

. . . When Jack and Newton came back, Jack said to the cavalrymen, "We've decided our people aren't going to Map-Arkansas."

"That's probably best." The Colonel threw his chew-straw away, and he and Minister Robinett stood up. "Middle Kingdom is for Middle Kingdom subjects only."

"Yes," Newton said.

Then they all stood without saying anything for a while. It was so quiet, Catania could hear the wind and little spring insects in the grass, could hear the riding-horses grazing.

"We have some tobacco," the Colonel said, "—if you'd care for it."

When no one said they'd care for it, Minister Robinett said, "There's going to be fighting all over this country out here. We have five thousand more horsemen coming to join us. There are a number of these Kipchak Russians, and they're quick movers. . . ."

"Perhaps you people could go north," the Colonel said. "No fighting past the Handle up there—winter will be back soon enough, and then you could use those sleds your dogs are dragging."

Newton and Jack said nothing.

"Could we make a home?" Catania said. "Are there mountains?"

"No, Lady," the Colonel said. "It's rough country, but fairly flat. Grass tundra. Good for sleds in winter, though, and very good for horses in spring and summer."

"I'll tell you what," said Minister Robinett. "We had to put some of our cattle herds up there when these Kipchaks came over from Map-California. And I'd say if your people—what do you have, about thirty of you? If you'd agree to watch our cattle through the winter, keep wolves and bears, panthers and cow thieves off—if you'd move the stock where winter grass will grow and keep them out of piled-up drifts—then that would be a favor."

"If the Selected Men say yes," the Colonel said.

"They'll say yes," said Minister Robinett. "It makes good sense, and spares the herd guard to come down to fight."

"And if these people go north to watch your cattle," Newton said, "—what do they get in return?"

The Colonel glanced at Catania in a friendly way, then reached out and put his hand on Minister Robinett's shoulder. "Well, Charlie, will you and the Selected say, 'a home'?"

"Yes," said Minister-Charlie Robinett, "—I'll say that, and on my honor." He made a little bow to Newton, then a little bow to Jack. "Sirs, for that service—say for three years watching the northern herd—these people will be Map-Texas people as much as any of us, and our country will be their country."

"And you will give our people horses," Jack said. "And teach them, through this spring and summer, how to ride."

The Colonel stood thinking—making the mouth of whistling, without whistling. Then he said, "Be more useful, at that. And we have the remounts to spare. . . . Yes. We'll send horses with you, and two men to take you up to the herds and teach you riding."

"Then I agree," Jack said, "—if our people agree."

"And if they say bargain-yes," Newton said to Minister-Charlie Robinett, "—be sure you hold to it."

"We will," the Colonel said.

* * *

It was not until Catania was sitting on a travvy listening to the Trappers argue, their shouts and quarrels, that she realized Jack would not be going north to watch Map-Texas cattle.

Our people, he'd said, and *Them.* Not *My people.* Not *Us.*

Jack was not going north. And Newton would not be going north, either. Lucy was dead, and the cavalry-men had known something about him that spoiled his being a Trapper.

Joan Richardson was shouting. "Monroe, you have led us rot-ten! Are there more of us than there were, or less? *Where is my son?*" She ground her teeth so the sound could be heard by everyone. "I won't follow you to sit and look at cattle all the day and night."

Jack answered her as if she'd been polite. "I don't think you'll find herding easy. I think you'll find it hard to do. These Texas people are making a bargain; they are not giving us a gift."

"No gift at all," Joan said, "—to go north with bad-luck you!"

"No," Jack said, "—not with me. I go differently." Then he walked away as he always walked away, so it was settled.

No one said anything as he went, though Catania, if she had not been holding the baby, would have stood to call Joan a bottom-hole, dead son or not.

"—And what about you, Spotted-face?" Joan said to Newton. "Are you afraid to go and look at cows and make them walk here and there? Is that more than you can do?"

Newton smiled at her as he always smiled at her, as if he knew a secret—and Joan spit, but only near his moccasin-boots.

"I'm not going north, either," Newton said. "But what these Texas people offer you is a good offer, and not a lie."

Then the others said nothing, not even Joan. Though Jack and Tattooed Newton were men it was more comfortable to hear tales about, than to live with—still, the Trappers had leaned on them since the Cree came down.

"I'll be going with Jack," Catania said, and thought how Mary One-eye would have despised her for it, and believed her weak in duty to go with a man only because she loved him, and he was going blind.

"But then we'll have no doctor," Rod Sorbane said, and Catania saw bleak faces.

"You will have a doctor," she said. "A learning doctor, but probably a better doctor than I have been."

"No," said Garden May.

"Yes," Catania said. "And by that quick 'No' before I called your name, you proved yourself."

"I won't do it."

"You *will* do it. You will put down your ax, and go to Torrey's travvy for my medicine books, and begin to read them. You will learn to make some happiness out of sickness-sorrow, and ease the Sunday anger of lonely men."

"I won't."

"Be quiet," Catania said. "Do as you're told. And we will see if your mother was right or wrong about you."

Garden May, who had been so rough and jolly, grew red in the face, then began to weep. She struck her ax into the ground as if the ground had offended her.

Catania stood, and settled Small-Sam in his blanket poozy on her hip. "I have been a selfish doctor," she said. "Now, you will have a better one."

She walked away—not to follow Jack, just then, but to follow herself as she had been, to take a last look at that Catania, who had been a Trapper and a Doctor, and now was only a woman with a scarred face.

What she had been was gone, as what the Trappers had been would soon be gone. They were too few, now. They would go north, and guard the cavalry herds, and they and their dogs would grow older, then old, and their children and their children's children would ride horses wherever they went, and be Map-Texans. . . . The last of the dogs, white-muzzled, would long since have died, lying like a hug-pet at the hearth. The long sleds would hang in their smoke-sheds for a life or two, then be broken and thrown away, and there would be no Trappers, anymore. . . .

Jack came to Torrey, and sat on the travvy beside him. "I won't be going north—Newton won't be going either—so you'll be the leader now."

"No, you come with us. Stay with us, Jack."

Jack shook his head. "I won't be going with you. But you'll do very well," he smiled, "—though not at pick-up sticks, unless you find another sick-eyed man to play against."

Torrey didn't smile. "I'm not the leader."

"You will be. Now, listen, Torrey—are we friends?"

"Yes."

"Then be a friend, and lead them. You would have to anyway; I have only a little looking-time left."

"No." Torrey sat with his head bowed, then wiped tears with the back of his hand. ". . . All right. All right, I'll do it."

"Good friend," Jack said. "Now listen, May will be the doctor, and you will have to share her."

"Yes, I know that."

"I wouldn't share Catania, and it made bad feelings. Now, there are too few of you for bad feelings."

"I understand," Torrey said.

"Then also understand that there are men and women you can't be sure of killing in a fight—as I could have, even Newton."

"Don't tell him so," Torrey smiled.

"No," Jack said. "Even if it were still true, I would never tell him so—as there will be many truths *you* cannot tell people, anymore. And you'll have to expect them to do what you wish them to do—and expect so surely, that they'll do it."

"Not easy," Torrey said.

"No, not easy, and will never become easy. Don't suppose they'll like it; don't suppose they'll like you as they used to. Lean on yourself, and May, and no one else."

"Good advice," Torrey said, and sighed.

"Good advice I've learned late," Jack said. "And keep watch on the cavalry-men. The others can set distrust down—but you, never."

"I understand," Torrey said, and stood. "We had fair trapping, didn't we? That time on the mountain. . . ."

"Fair trapping," Jack stood with him. "And a brave wolf."

"Take my travvy and team with you."

"No," Jack said. "You'll need them in the north."

"At least take Three-balls. He'll fight for you, and give you warnings."

"He's more likely to bite my hand off," Jack said.

But Torrey didn't smile, only shook his head and looked sad, though Jack put an arm around him, and hugged him as if they were brothers.

. . . . It was sun to middle-sky, and very warm, when the Trappers harnessed their teams to travvy, prepared to travel north. Jack, Catania, and Newton, carrying their packs and weapons, had come to them to say goodbye.—Now that they were parting forever, Trappers who had never been friendly to Jack and Newton became friendly, spoke kindly, and hugged them.

Dummy Olsen brought small spring beetles, black and green, as parting gifts—though from what he said, it was plain he thought they were parting only until next morning.

The women came to Catania—all except Joan Richardson—and asked her last questions about body-things that concerned them. They made soft sounds at the sleeping baby, stroking and kissing him until he woke blinking in the bright sunlight. Catania saw they wanted to take Small-Sam with them, but none asked her to let them do it. They saw *no* in her eyes.

When the Trappers were ready to travel, the Colonel and Minister-Charlie went to their riding-horses. The metal horn made its high hard sound, and the cavalry-men climbed onto their animals. The harsh horn called again, and all the riders, except two, turned their horses west and rode away in ranks together.

The Colonel and Minister-Charlie raised their hands in goodbye as they went past. And the two Map-Texas cavalry-men left behind, came riding over to the Trappers. Each had a long woven line tied to his riding seat, and twelve horses trailing, tied along that line.

One of the cavalry-men was very big; the other not so big.

The big man had heavy shoulders under his iron-ring shirt, blue eyes, and a long wind-burned face. There was a red birth-stain, shaped like a small hardwood leaf, at his left temple. "Who's runnin' you people?" he said.

Torrey walked up to him. "We run ourselves."

"Run yourselves poorly," the big man said, and the other horse-rider laughed. "Now, we're ordered to go north with you an' these horses, an' try an' teach you somethin' better than steppin' in dog-shit." He smiled, leaned from his riding seat, and reached down to hold-and-shake Torrey's hand. "Patterson," he said.

Torrey reached up and took the big man's hand. "Torrey Monroe."

Patterson gripped Torrey's hand, and didn't let it go. Muscles stood out down the man's long bare arm.

Torrey tried to take his hand away, then tried again, holding his face still against hurting. The big man held him a little longer, then let him go, and sat back in his riding-seat, smiling.

Jack had been walking along the travvies, saying goodbye. When he'd said goodbye to Martha Sorbane and Myles Weber, he walked over to the big cavalry-man's horse. "Jack Monroe," he said, looking up with his left eye bandaged, his right eye rimmed red. "I won't be going with you. Have lucky traveling." He held out his hand.

"Not going with us?" Patterson said. "Oh, dear." The smaller rider laughed as the big man leaned down to take Jack's hand, smiling. The muscles came up on his long arm.

For a little while, Patterson kept smiling. Then he stopped, and his face grew grim. "Let go," he said. But Jack still held his hand, looking up in a friendly way. The leaf-mark at the big man's temple turned deeper red. "*Let go my hand*," he said—and there was a little snapping sound, like a twig breaking. Then Jack let him go.

Trappers with lances had come to stand near them.

"Torrey," Jack said, "—people with strung bows should travel beside these two. If they draw weapons or try to ride away, kill them, take the animals, and teach yourselves horse-riding."

"We will," Torrey said.

The two cavalry-men said nothing. Patterson sat on his riding-seat holding his hurt hand with his other hand, to comfort it.

As the Trappers travvied out—the two riders and their led horses with them—Catania settled the baby on her hip, loosed the nanny's line to let it graze, and stood with Jack and Newton, watching them go.

. . . The riders on their tall horses could still be seen for what they were, long after the dog-teams and Trappers were only movement through high grass, and gleaming lance-heads. And though their harness-bells were gone, taken for silence in war, still they seemed to sound faintly.

"Farewell," Newton said.

Catania had read that word many times, but had never heard it used.

The baby makes do with goat's milk—but because of it, I'm washing many crapkins whenever we find water. What strange creatures women are, to find pleasure in washing crap-cloths....

I dream of Trappers now, more often than of the Running-dog Bus and Flying Mary. Sleeping, I see their faces more clearly, and know them better, than I saw or knew them on the Range. In only this way, losing has been gaining.

Garden May took my medicines and medicine books, and might as well, since none of them helped Jack. He cannot see with his left eye, and sees less and less with his right. Now, too late, I think I know what was in Mary's vodka. I believe it was fine powder seeds from a forest mushroom.—How like her to have used what I'd first challenged her to use against us. I'd forgotten that she did not forget.

If it was fine powder seeds that settled, and grew to spoil Jack's eyes, then only right-away rinsing might have helped him, and I did not do it.

...We three and the baby have gone the rest of the goodbye-day, then another, and now camp to sleep and let the nanny graze.

FROM THE JOURNAL OF DOCTOR CATANIA OLSEN

18

Jack had tried to sleep apart from her the first night traveling, also the second night. But both times, Catania took the baby and her bedding, lay down beside him, and he'd let her stay.

Under only fox fur, with the baby sleeping between them, Catania closed her eyes against starlight and moonlight to better imagine this was the way she would always lie—with Jack and Small-Sam—until the baby was grown to a boy and became restless for furs of his own.

Jack had traveled the day in front, as always, carrying his pack, his bow and quiver, his lance balanced in his hand. He'd trotted only a little more slowly than before, his head cocked for better seeing with his right eye. Newton had stayed back, as Catania had stayed back, and let Jack lead them over this country's slow rises and falls, its brown, rustling, deep winter grass, its soft feathers of spring green appearing.

Catania lay with her eyes closed, and knew how bad a person she must be; how selfish not to mind entirely that Jack was going blind and could never leave her. These were thoughts so terrible, it seemed to her that Jesus, if he heard them in the mountains, would certainly come down to punish her. But what woman would not wish, in dark secret, to have Jack Monroe for her own, with a beautiful baby sleeping between them?

Turning on her side, Catania wept quietly as she could for her lost Doctor's-honor.

. . . She woke at moonset. Jack was up out of the furs, standing with his lance in his hand. Newton, across the fire pit, stood naked, listening. His knife-blade shone in starlight.

There was no wind, but Catania heard something like soft wind combing in the grass to the west, the way they'd come.

Jack walked back-trail, and was gone in shadows. Newton stayed in camp, silent, while Catania armed herself.

There was a sudden thrashing of struggle out in the dark, then the sound of a blow struck. Catania and Newton ran that way through the grass, and were met by Jack, all silver and shadow, coming out carrying someone in his arms. He walked to the fire pit, eased the person to the ground beside it, and said, "Only her."

Catania struck flint and steel to start the fire burning. And the three of them, Jack's head cocked like a hunting dog's, watched as the firelight bloomed and showed them Joan Richardson lying asleep, blood at the side of her mouth.

She slept a little while longer, then woke, said, "Someone hit me," and seemed to go back to sleep again.

"She drew her knife," Jack said.

After a while, Joan opened her eyes and lay whispering to herself. When Catania knelt to her, Joan made a sound and shoved her away. Then she looked up, saw Newton, and held her arms out to him like a child.

Newton stood watching her, but didn't move.

"Do what you should do," Catania said to him—still surprised at Joan's coming, despite what she and other women had long suspected. "Newton . . . Lucy's gone. And this woman has waited for you long enough."

Newton stood and said nothing for a little while. Then he said, "Floating *Jesus*. . . ." and bent to pick Joan up. She gripped him and clung to him as he carried her past the fire to furs and set her down. She wouldn't let go . . . whispered and whispered to him.

"Jack," Catania said, "—did something happen to the others?"

"I don't think so. I think she just came following Newton."

Catania could see he was trying not to laugh. "It's not funny."

"I know," Jack said. But he started to laugh, and had to put his hand over his mouth to be quiet.

"It's not *funny*."

"Then what is it?" Jack said, and went on acting in a very childish way.

. . . In the morning, except for always being beside Newton, touching him, smiling at him—though he didn't touch her, or smile—Joan became Joan again. "Any fool," she said, "—could have followed the trail you people made through this old grass.

And nanny-goat shit left on the trail, too. You're careless travelers."

"The others are all right?" Catania said.

"They're all right," Joan said, and from the way she said it, Catania saw she had set the Trappers aside.

. . . Late in the day, Jack trotting ahead, parting the tall grass before him with his lance, they came to steeper rises. And from the highest of these, all of them but Jack could see stands of trees to the east.

"At last," Joan said. "We will be out of this trail-telling grass, that makes such poor fires."

They camped in early evening—and had made their last grass fire—when several animals came past, rooting and grunting out of sight of the camp. Jack, Newton, and Joan had picked up lances to follow, when one animal, perhaps curious, came back and stuck its head out through grass-stalks to look at them.

At first, Catania thought it was a very ugly dog—then she saw it wasn't. "It's a copybook *pig*!"

The others shouted and began to chase, while Catania stayed with the baby. She had a strange fear they might lose the camp in such high grass, lose the baby there and never find him again. So she stayed while the others hunted.

The little copybook pig—or something very like a copybook pig—was a fast runner. Catania could hear grunting and shouting going away as fast as sled dogs could travel. The sounds curved one distant way, then another, then circled half around the camp. When Catania stood tall and jumped a little, she could sometimes see Jack and the others running far away, before they were lost in the grass again down some slight slope.

. . . Near dark, when the three came back, Catania heard them laughing and knew they brought meat. The little copybook pig had been too curious.

"Peccary," Newton said, while sliced meat was cooking over twists of grass. "Not an actual pig, but almost. Actual pigs are the best animal-meat eating of all."

" 'Actual,' " Joan said. "Newton knows more Warm-time

words than anyone. . . ." And she smiled at him as she'd been smiling at him, though he didn't smile back.

Late that night, almost morning, Catania heard angry whispers across the fire, then someone was hit with an open hand. There was struggling . . . then silence.

Soon, there was softer, slower struggling, and Joan said, "Oh . . . thank you. Oh, *thank* you." Then Catania heard the sounds of fucking, and covered her ears to give them privacy. . . . Though when they were done, she heard Joan say, "My dear, I know I can never become her."

After that night, they were five friendly travelers, walking now up through low hills and hardwood. Joan argued less, and only once asked where they were going.—It was a question that hadn't occurred to Catania. She supposed she hadn't cared.

When Joan asked, Jack had answered, "Going to choose. Maybe Map-Mexico, very south—"

"I can't go down to those provinces," Newton said. "My people aren't welcome there." They were hunting in trees between two hills, all but Jack with arrows to their bowstrings, for deer. His bow rode on his shoulder as it had for many days, unstrung.

"All right," Jack said. "Then we might go very east, to Map-Tennessee. Would be long traveling, but there're supposed to be mountains. Soft mountains." He cocked his head to see Newton better. "But we have to go through Middle Kingdom to get there, and over the river."

"Jack, we can get through Kingdom," Newton said, and seemed annoyed. "There are always travelers going through."

They found no deer that day—but Joan shot one the next, a small buck in velvet. And for six days after, eating peccary-pig and venison, they went deeper into the hills and seasonable trees, so they camped with fine hardwood fires. The last of winter's snow still lay in hollows where the sun couldn't reach, but the air stayed summer warm. . . . They had the good dried meat to eat, and birds' eggs, and spring onions come up with the new grass. Small-Sam made faces on the nanny's teat, at the taste of wild onions from her grazing.

On the seventh day, Newton found bear-shit in the morning. "Oh, good new meat," Joan said. Jack came and they handled the scat, breaking it in their fingers.

"Fresh by half a day," Joan stood and wiped her hands on her hide trousers. "Maybe fresher."

"That's cub crap," Catania said. "—Small-Sam has made me familiar."

"Yearling cub," Newton said.

"Still, the mother will be near." Jack lifted his head, as if to smell the mother bear. It was something he did more and more. "Out of their winter den, and hungry."

"Bear meat!" Joan tossed her lance and caught it.

"They'll be moving," Jack said. "Eating spring greens already, down in this warm country." He shrugged off his pack, setting his bow and quiver beside it. "Let's climb the hill . . . watch for them." He walked away upslope, his lance-head dipping to touch ahead from time to time, moving brush aside that might have tripped him.

Joan and Newton dropped their packs and started up after him. Catania put her pack down, made sure the baby was tucked deep into his blanket-poozy on her hip, then tied the nanny to a barebranch bush, and followed.

It was easy climbing up through spring grass and sapling trees. The trees already showed green buds and tiny leaves along their branches. But it seemed to Catania a fragile green and temporary, beside memories of spruce, fir, and hemlock on the Range, whose green—dark as evening—had never failed . . . whose perfume had drifted over snow and steamed from carved tea-mugs when friends gathered.

The memories struck her like a blow, so she paused to catch her breath before she climbed again. The people and places of the past seemed too much to have lost, unfairness unbearable compared to this strange horse-ride-or-walk country with its brittle trees hiding their foliage from winters. Warm country—though probably it would not have seemed warm to the Warm-time people . . . people only inconvenienced by Lady Weather, until the cold came and killed them.

At the crest—bare, broken gray rock—they looked out over hollows and the nearest hills.

"They'll be on slopes," Jack said. "Where the sun is striking. . . ." He turned his head as if he were looking with them, as if he could see clearly out over the country. The wind was from the north, cool through the sunshine, and was pushing clouds along so their shadows drifted over the hills.

The baby woke, making the high humming that came before his crying. Catania reached down and put the tip of her finger to his mouth. "Shhhh. . . . No noise, hunting." Small-Sam hummed a while, regardless; she felt the soft vibration at her finger. And it was then, on this hill in warm country, that a page of love never copied, never read by her before, turned over. The baby had done nothing to earn it, but it was given, nevertheless. And what had been only Catania and much of Jack Monroe, was shoved over for room, and that small space taken.

They saw nothing for a while. Then Newton said, "Next hill over." He pointed with his lance—and a small brown bear, dark as tree-bark, was suddenly easy to see and surprisingly close. It was rooting in bushes across a two bow-shot hollow.

Jack looked as they were looking. "Hillside . . . ?"

"Yes," Joan said. "Halfway up. A yearling cub."

"Mother'll be around the hill," Newton nocked an arrow to his bowstring. "Maybe feeding a little higher."

"We can climb and kill the cub before she comes," Joan said.

Jack started down the hill toward the hollow, going down fast into brush and through it.

"He's making noise!" Joan hissed after him, "Go *slower*."

"Jack. . . ." Catania called, softly. But he paid no attention, and the three of them went after him, going quietly as they could.

It was steep down to the hollow's hardwoods, and once, when she couldn't see him, Catania heard Jack's lance shaft tap against a tree-trunk.

"He's going too fast." Joan came sliding, jumping down the slope past Catania, who was being careful because of the baby. "He's going to scare the bear away!"

Catania fell behind . . . and when she came out of brush into the hollow's stand of trees, the others were already through them and climbing the next hillside.

When she caught up with Joan and Newton, they were standing in knee-high grass, watching Jack above them.

"Stupid," Joan murmured. "He's going to scare that cub to running." She looked at Catania. "If he can't see to hunt anymore, then he *shouldn't* hunt, and cost us meat."

Catania saw Jack on the hillside above them, almost a bowshot away. He was going slowly now, carefully, to get closer to the young bear—moving a little . . . then not. Stalking in a sort of swaying way, as if the wind was responsible for how he went.

Catania stepped to the side, and then could see the bear above him. The cub had stopped feeding, and was up on its hind legs in the grass, listening, questing for a scent.

"Upwind, at least," Newton said.

Catania thought Jack would wait for the cub to begin feeding again. But he didn't. He climbed closer. She could see them both very clearly. A cloud had shadowed the hillside, and now was gone, so Jack and the bear cub were in bright sunlight, with only a long lance-throw over gently blowing grass between them.

"He should have let Newton go up," Joan said, "—or me. He's not going to hit anything. . . ."

Suddenly Jack stood and started running, his lance ready. And Catania saw the bear-cub, startled, jump up and begin to run away across the slope. It was bawling like a hoarse and frightened child, running, with Jack after it.

"Mountain Jesus!" Joan said. "A Fool-do, a *Fool*-do. It'll call the mother!" She and Newton, and Catania after them, went up the hillside. The cub was gone, crying out of sight around the hill's shoulder. Jack was following.

"Why did he do that?" Catania said. As she watched, the cub came suddenly back—but was no cub.

"The mother." Newton started climbing the slope ahead of them, going fast, looking for a shot. Then they heard him say, "*Shit*...." He stood still alongside a rock outcropping, and lowered his bow.

As Catania caught up, Newton took hold of her arm. She tried to pull away, but he held her. "No," he said, and held her hard.

Above them, the mother bear was coming across the hillside, running fast as the riding-horses had run. She was making deep grunting sounds, coming through the grass.

"Jack!" Catania twisted in Newton's grip.

Joan came up beside her, said, "Oh, dear...." and held her other arm.

"*Jack*...!" Catania screamed and began to fight them, trying to reach her knife.

"Hold her!" Newton said. They held her, and the baby cried at the struggle.

High on the hill, Jack stood leaning on his lance as if impatient with waiting. He heard Catania call his name. The bear, he saw only as something dark and swift and growing. He felt the ground faintly tremble. Jack braced the butt of his lance into the hillside, footed it with his boot, then swung down behind the outstretched shaft so there was only the bright point, low, for her to run upon. He had forgotten, for a moment, why he was there.

Recalling, he stood and let the lance fall into the grass. A woman was screaming. Jack supposed someone was watching, as he and Sam had watched their father die.

He took a breath of sunny day to last forever, and drew his knife as the bear came to him. Old Mother would have to pay at least a little....

* * *

"Ohhh...ohhh." Catania was crying out because of something bad she couldn't remember. Joan, helping to carry her, was weeping—a very strange thing.

Catania wondered for a moment if a disease had come and killed the baby; something too bad to remember had certainly happened. But when Newton took her up in his arms, she saw Joan was carrying Small-Sam—then knew that Jack wasn't with them, and was dead.

"The bear," she said, when she woke in camp to night and firelight.

"Gone," Joan said, sitting by her, "—and the cub. We didn't think Jack would have wanted them killed for doing what he wished to be done. The mother bear went limping, though."

"Jack. . . ." Catania said.

"In a tall tree," Newton said from across the fire. "Wrapped warm in pelts. He has his weapons with him."

"Prayers . . . ?"

"The 'Yea, though I walk,' " Newton said.

"I don't want to go see him." Catania began quiet crying. "I don't want to see him. It makes him too dead."

"Here," Joan said, and she lifted the baby from her lap, and gave him to Catania. "See? You still have a man."

* * *

For many days, as they went east, then south, Catania cared only for the baby. She leaned her heart against Small-Sam as if he were grown and strong. She wrapped herself around him like a summer vine and cared for him only, and not herself or her memories of anyone, even Jack—though for several nights, she dreamed of Jack standing on the hillside, waiting for the bear. In each succeeding dream, the bear had come closer to him.

Those mornings, she woke frightened, anxious about the baby, and wasn't satisfied until she had him out of his blanket, and examined him all over for fear of disease, or a bite by the nasty insects they saw more and more as the air warmed and grew wet.

There was game in the deep woods as they traveled through such warmth that they sweated in their buckskins, and went wearing only trousers and boots. They saw an actual pig in the forest, huge, dark-haired, and tusked, but that was late in an evening, so they couldn't hunt it down.

The morning after that no-hunt, they came to a wide way covered in crushed white pieces that Newton said were shells from water things. The sunshine was very bright, and the wind smelled slightly like blood. "Salt air," Newton said, "—from the Gulf Entire."

Very soon, they met other people on that path. Not mountain hunters, not Garden men and women, not the small horse-riders or Texas cavalry either. These were people Catania had never seen before, never read about. Some of these travelers were tall, some short, and all with very different faces, not like Gardens' men and women, who'd looked to be close families. And they wore odd cloth clothes: robes, or tight trousers and shirts, or what must be copybook skirts and dresses—all of them in different colors.

Nearly the first of those strange people—two old men and two old women, barefoot in red-striped shirts and trousers—had turned to stare at Newton, and one had made a bow. Then those four had turned and gone back the way they'd come, but faster.

Newton had said, "Christ on a crutch." Startling words, and certainly very old.

As they walked along, he asked Catania for one of the lengths of white Gardens cloth she cut Small-Sam's crapkins from. He took the long piece, draped it around his neck like a winter scarf, then drew a fold up across his face so only his eyes showed.

"Why do you do that?" Joan said.

"For a good reason," Newton said, and said no more. But the women noticed that once his face was covered, no one looked at him or bowed. A few rude strange people, passing by, did sometimes stare at the women's bare breasts as if they'd never seen breasts before.

There were too many strangers on the white-shell path, and they became too many more. Most walked, but some rode horses or smaller, long-ear, not-quite-horses. Twice, people came by on four-wheel horse-wagons that worked very well on the path. Catania could see that these were the wheels-only, not the wheels-gear. They were perfect for paths—though, of course, not snow—and must have been very useful in Warm-times.

It was all interesting, but there were so many strange people and their clothes and animals and made-things, that it became unsettling, and Catania had to close her eyes sometimes as they went along, for privacy.

"Do we have to go the same way all these rude people do?" Joan said. "Look at them! Those over there are fat as babies. Disgusting—if they had to fight, they'd fall over."

"Be quiet," Newton said, and sounded like a man expecting trouble, though Catania couldn't imagine most of these strangers troubling anyone. Most of these odd people talked nonsense as they went, like children. And looked soft as children.

"Burned men!" Joan said once, as four dark people rode past on little long-ears.

"Not burned," Newton said. "Black men, whose people came from Globe-Africa. Many Kingdom officers are black."

" 'Globe Africa . . .' " Hearing that, Catania became interested again in the strangers that came traveling, so she didn't feel so uneasy having them come and go. She asked Newton questions about them, since he appeared to know, but he gave her short answers, and seemed a slightly different man with his face hidden, all but his eyes.

Catania supposed Newton didn't want his tattoos to be seen—and have more old people bowing, or cavalry-men calling him 'Sir.' It was his life before becoming a Trapper, that he was covering with Small-Sam's crap cloth.

Joan didn't like any of the people coming by them, so she went and traveled off the path a while. Catania saw her from time to time, among the odd trees and brush that grew there. Flower buds, each bright red with a yellow heart, were breaking open in the bushes and vines, and there were little purple blossoms. Many nasty insects, most very small, came flying in the path, and touched Catania's face . . . seemed to drink sweat from her skin.

After more traveling, and at the sun's best height, Joan came running from odd woods and said to them, "Come look, come look!"

The woods were even stranger to be in than to see from the path. The dirt was soft dark-yellow sand, and there were bushes with tall pale-green leaves pointed as needles, and low-growing thorns that snagged and stuck. The nanny didn't try to graze them. . . . There were fat, curving, tall gray trees with no branches except at their tops—and those were strange branches, like wide green hands with many thin green fingers. The air smelled very much like fresh blood.

"Look!" Joan stood on a soft edge of sand, and pointed out into the air.

The salt-blood wind was coming to them over the edge, and Catania went to see. She was startled to be so high on a bank—then stood astonished at water forever.

It lay out and out from them, and no far border could be seen. Green and blue—not ice gray, though she saw some winter ice still floating in it—it was a bigger water than any melt lake below the Wall. So much bigger, there was no comparison. It wrinkled as the wind blew over it, and little white birds went gliding above.

One of these came flying down the edge of the bank, and as it passed, Catania saw it was a sizable bird after all, the color of steel, rather than snow, and its wings were bent at an angle.

"The Gulf Entire," Newton said, took off the cloth scarf, and wiped sweat from his face. Then he pointed with his lance to the right. "That way, west along the Gulf . . . then far south to the northern provinces of Empire Mexico."

He swung his lance to the left. "This way, east to Middle Kingdom—beginning at Market, very soon—and much farther, Kingdom River."

"Jack said Map-Tennessee." The nanny, bored, butted Catania's leg gently.

"Farther and farther east," Newton said, and leaned on his lance. The Gulf's wind stirred his short dark hair. "—Then north again." He looked better, more Newton, without the cloth across his face.

"That's traveling and traveling," Joan said. "Is there hunting all the way?"

"A Warm-time year of traveling," Newton said, "—into winter and through it."

"Hunting?"

"Yes—but carefully in Middle Kingdom, and with permission."

"I ask no permission," Joan said.

"*Permission*," Newton said. "Because all game is the King's."

"But that's a very bad thing." Catania pushed the nanny away. The nanny liked her.

". . . Yes," Newton said. "I believe it is."

They stood on the soft edge of sand, and looked out. There was no end to the Gulf and no edge to it except below, where the green and blue water came to the land on a wide wash of yellow-white sand. It eased Catania's eyes to see so far from a high place, restful as looking at mountains.

"See it?" Newton said.

Joan and Catania both said, "What?" Then almost together, "It's a bird. A big bird on the water. . . ."

"No," Newton smiled at them. "A sailing boat."

"*Pequod!*" Catania was very excited to see the same sort of thing, even though this bird-looking boat was too small to go and hunt great whales.

"Amazing," Joan said, as they watched it. She rarely said 'amazing.' Catania couldn't remember the last time Joan had said it.

They stood on the soft edge and watched the boat go past so far out on the water, driven by the wind.

"Sails. . . ." Catania wondered if all boats were as beautiful.

"It trades at little ports," Newton said. "Places along the Gulf."

They stood watching until the trade-boat was almost lost, then lost completely, in sun-sparkling on the water.

"Light strikes the wrinkles," Joan said, ". . . the waves."

"That's right." Newton tied the scarf across his face again, then walked away back into the odd woods. And though they could have watched the Gulf Entire much longer, Joan and Catania took up their lances and followed him, the nanny very lively, making little jumps.

* * *

Late the next morning, their seventeenth day in warm-wet country—and traveling alongside even more and more kinds of strangers—they heard faint sounds that slowly became a distant rich music of many drums and flutes, but also things that sounded as the Texas cavalry horn had sounded. And there were other, softer noises, like wild geese calling all together.

"How beautiful!" Catania said. She and Joan stopped walking to listen better. "What makes such beautiful music?"

"A band," Newton said. "A band at Market."

"A band of who?" Joan said, and when Newton laughed behind his cloth, she hit him lightly on the arm with her lance shaft. "We're not fools."

"No," he said, "—you're not. Those are music-makers playing many different instruments together. Not only drums and flutes, like Gardens'. These are a band—but for music, not hunting or war."

Catania and Joan stood still a little longer, listening, the nanny restless on her lead. "It is like Mountain Jesus speaking," Catania said. "Many voices in one voice."

"That's so," Joan said, and she and Catania walked on with the goat, listening.

"Wait." Newton stepped off the path and walked away into the woods, apparently to pee.

A man came calling down the way—a little man with bare crooked legs—who walked hunched under the weight of a small fat wooden keg as he wove through the crowd.

"*Guggle-oh!*" the little man called. He wore a long green shirt that came to his thighs, and a cord belt with a metal cup dangling from it. "*I have Guggle-oh!*"

" 'Guggle-oh' what?" Catania said to him, as he came by.

"Barley-whisk," the little man said. He mumbled and was hard to understand.

"Selling drinks of it?"

The little man nodded.

"Not vodka?" Joan said.

The little man shook his head.

"Strong drink?" Catania said. "Strong?" and made a muscle in her arm, patted it.

"Yes," the little man said, smiling at her. He had no teeth at all, and that was why he mumbled.

"Two drinks," Joan said, and the little man nodded, swung the keg off his back, pulled a small stopper out—then waited.

"Oh." Catania shifted the baby's poozy, and searched in her possibles-sack. She took out one fine steel arrowhead and offered it, though it seemed too much to give, and would leave her with only nine. "For two drinks." She held up two fingers.

The little man took it, stroked the steel, tested the broadhead's edge with his thumb—then nodded, tipped his keg, and poured the metal cup full.

The drink was brown, not clear.

Joan took the cup—had to bend a little, since it was tethered—and drank all the brown drink in five long swallows.

Then she stood and blew her cheeks in and out. There were tears in her eyes.

"Good?"

"Different," Joan said, and cleared her throat. "But good. It tastes of things. . . ."

The little man filled the cup again, and Catania stooped and drank all the brown drink down. It tasted only hot at first, like good vodka. Then it tasted of several things; there was a sweetness to it. ". . . Different," Catania said.

Newton came out of the woods, lacing his buckskin trousers.

"Do you want a brown drink?" Joan said.

"No." Newton motioned the Salesman away, and the little man stoppered his keg, slung it on his back, and walked off, calling "Guggle-oh."

It seemed funny to Catania and Joan, so as they walked along, they occasionally said "Guggle-oh" to each other for the fun of it.

Soon, there was such a crowd of strangers traveling, that persons sometimes touched them. Joan would curse and shove them away with her lance shaft, and Catania had to do the same, or be jostled holding the baby. But no stranger touched Newton without saying they were sorry to have done it. Unfair, Catania thought, and only because he was a man, and so large—and of his face, only his bear's eyes were showing.

In a little while, they and the goat came with many others under a large sign of wooden letters that was hung across the wide path from tall poles at each side of the way. The large sign read: M-A-R-K-E-T.

"No trouble, now." Newton said. "This is Kingdom's Gulf Gate for trade. No trouble is permitted here.—Joan?"

"I hear you. I don't make trouble. Why not 'Catania'?"

"All right, then—both of you. . . . We go quietly through this Warm-time measured mile. Then we'll be left alone to travel, if we leave others alone."

"I don't make trouble . . ." Joan said—then turned to a man walking near her. "Is it that you've never seen a tit? Then you can stare at this nanny's!"

The man she spoke to, very tall and wearing a long brown robe, looked away and said nothing. He was barefoot, his face was shaved, and his hair was tied up in brown cloth ribbons.

"Joan, I mean it," Newton said.

"I don't have to bear this strange thing's fuck-look!"

Catania stepped between Joan and the brown-ribbon man. "There's no trouble," she said, "—but some of these men stare at our breasts in a rude way, even though there are naked people walking." And there were. There had been families of naked people walking on the path a while ago. The men had had hair yellow as the Gulf sand, and little pieces of wood had been stuck through their lower lips. They'd carried body shields made of cattle-hide with the hair on—the first shields Catania had ever seen—and short stabbing spears.

"Assags," Newton had called the spears, and said they were very nice weapons, as long as you had a shield, too. Border Roamers, he'd called those people. Said they didn't read, and were fewer than they had been.

The music of one band, then others, came whistling, singing, crashing in metal and drums as they walked into Market. Joan and Catania—prompted by their swallows of brown barley-whisk—danced a little to it as they went along, Catania dancing gently so as not to trouble the baby. They danced in circles, tangling the nanny's line, so that tripping and leaping, she seemed to dance with them.

"There's another one," Joan said, meaning a man staring at their breasts.

"Then let's trade for cool shirts." Catania hauled the goat in and settled her.

There were many cloth lean-tos—striped red-and-white, green-and-white, and black-and-white—set up on both sides of the path. At each stand, different things were being offered: leather work—harness, belts, sheaths, and possibles sacks; little boxes of bright jewelry stones; jointed toys for children that danced at the ends of strings; shining rings and bracelets; made-boots and strap sandals. There were clay jugs, painted with flowers looking almost real—and at another stand, metal pots and kettles in every size.

More things, and more people, than Catania had seen, even in Gardens.

There were smells of food—some wonderful, and some not wonderful—and smoke from stands with iron grills and griddles drifted in the air amid the noise of strangers talking and trade-arguing in shade beneath striped cloth.

Newton led them off the wide path to a narrower way, where there were only cloth-trade stands. The first had blankets, and none of those as fine as Gardens'. But the next two traded women's clothes, and at the second, Joan and Catania found almost-white shirts—claimed by the Salesman to be loomed of Empire cotton—loose enough not to hinder drawing a bow.

Joan chose a shirt with yellow flowers sewn at the neck, to set off her braid of long red hair. Catania's flower trim was sewn in little red blossoms and green grass, so she would have forever spring at her throat.

They each traded an arrowhead for their shirt, though reluctant to part with it. The Salesman, who had green ribbons woven through his beard, admired the fine steel broadheads—tested their edges with his thumb, and cut it slightly.

"This Market is costly," Joan said.

Then Joan and Catania paraded their new shirts, both still slightly dizzy from guggle-oh, and turned this way and that to show them off while Newton stood impatient. Then, Joan said, "Food."

"All right," Newton said, "—but we'll eat walking. I want to get through here, and gone."

And as they'd been lucky with shirts, so they were lucky with food—and hadn't gone a stone's throw down another path through strangers, before there was a lean-to stand of cloth striped blue-and-gold that could barely be seen for cooking smoke. When they went to it, they found thin, oiled wooden sticks, each with several pieces of fat mutton stuck on it, grilling over coals. The mutton smelled almost as though from mountain sheep, but not quite.

"What do we trade?" Catania looked in her possibles and took out another arrowhead. She thought Joan was right—Market was costly.

The man turning the oiled sticks with quick fingers was handsome and looked strong. He had only a mustache, no beard. "Two of those good pieces of steel, Lady," he said, "—for three shish, heavy with meat." And when Catania paused to consider, added, "Also a North Map-Mexico apple to divide among you."

"One arrowhead." Newton stood leaning on his lance.

"Not quite enough," the mustached man said. "Almost, but not quite. Now, the fox-fur tied to the tall lady's pack. . . ."

"Take it," Joan said, "—if you can wear it in air so warm."

"For the fur," Newton said, "—six shish that *we* pick, and an apple for each."

"Not fair," the cook said. "Absolutely not fair. . . . But, I'll trade out of kindness."

So, eating fat-dripping mutton certainly less fine than mountain sheep's—Newton lifting his face-cloth to chew it—and keeping their apples for later, they went down the Market ways through noise and talk and music.

"A pleasure," Catania said, and found she was enjoying strangers, as long as there were stand-foods and stand-things and band music to enjoy as well. She wished they could go see one of the music bands, their odd instruments. She missed her harp.

"Steel," Joan said, stopping at a black-and-white striped lean-to. There was a woman, very tall and very big, selling there. She was large as two women, and wore tight yellow clothes. "Steel. . . ." Joan looked at knives ranked side by side on a polished board, picked up a heavy curved blade, and handled it.

"Five-hundred times folded," the big woman said. She had a girl's voice, and eyes bright as a squirrel's. "Forged, folded, then hammered out to fold again."

"Joan, we need to keep on," Newton said.

"This is a fighting lady," the woman said to him, and smiled. "—I can see it. Should she not have fine steel?"

"When we have time," Newton said, "—and silver to trade for it."

Joan put the curved blade down. "Your husband is a fine smith."

"I have no husband." The big woman held out hands larger than Newton's, calloused, and scarred by burns at the forge.

"Joan, we need to go," Newton said, and walked away so Catania, then Joan, had to follow or lose him.

A man was chanting "Best . . . best . . . *best*." They saw him standing on a plank platform beyond the lean-to stands. He was calling to many Market-strangers gathered before him. There were naked people standing in a line on the platform, each with an iron collar on.

"He's trading *people*," Joan said.

"Slaves." Catania stood staring.

"Yes," Newton said. "We need to keep moving."

"If a person is such a dog he can be traded," Joan said, "—then he is dog enough to trade."

"The children are not dogs." Catania pointed with her lance. "There are children there."

Newton walked them away from their argument, and past a wonder. A man was eating fire from a burning stick, stuffing the flames down his mouth, then drawing them out still blazing and with no harm done.

—And right after, an even greater wonder. A man and woman drew bright thick golden water, thick as honey, out of a small furious furnace, twirling the stuff on a long pipe-rod. Then they blew into the pipe's end so the hot honey-water slowly grew into round clear hot ice, that cooled and cooled until, when it was struck free, it had become a trade-glass bottle, shimmering and beautiful.

"That is how it is done!" Catania stared until Newton took her arm and tugged at her to come along.

"We're going too fast," Joan said to him. "You're being unkind to hurry us."

"It's necessary."

"It is not necessary," Joan said, following him with a sullen face.

Still, she was no help when Catania wanted to stop at a big wooden bench, round as a wheel-gear, that circled an iron post. Four men were trotting, pushing at its edges so it spun around and around. People were giving these men little pieces of metal in trade for a seat on the spinning bench, and riding it, whirling, laughing.

"Oh, what a wonderful thing!" Catania reached into her possibles for an arrowhead to trade for a ride, but again Newton said,

"No time. We need to get through this place and out of it." So she put her arrowhead away, and followed with the nanny, looking back as she went.

"Anyway," Joan said, "—it would likely have upset the baby."

"You could have held Small-Sam for me, Joan." The nanny suddenly leaped ahead, pulling so Catania almost stumbled. Something made a hard clicking sound behind them.

Catania turned—and jumped back, holding the baby's poozy to her hip.

Joan turned too, and said, "Mountain *Jesus!*"

There were two things just behind them—big, bigger than riding-horses. They had no pelt; their skins were mottled gray, and running sweat that smelled like men's. They looked fat at first, and seemed to squat on long forearms and short hinds, with no hooves, but huge flat hands and feet.

Their heads—large as the heads of snow-tigers—looked like foolish men's, with white hair cut short, round empty blue eyes, and wide, lolling tongues. One stared down at Catania and the nanny-goat, licked its lips, then made the quick hard clicking noise again with its teeth.

"*Bad things!*" Catania stepped back for room to lower her lance, and Joan did the same beside her.

Newton stepped in front of them. "I said, '*No trouble!*' Now, put those lances up, and both of you come walk beside me."

A woman called, "Stand out of our way, savages!" She was sitting on the tooth-clicking creature's broad slanting gray back. "Or don't you understand book-English." She was a pretty woman, in boots, a dark-blue robe, and a wide-brim blue hat. Her long dark hair fell free.

"*Savages?*" Joan said.

"Those are made man-things!" Catania called to the riding woman. "We heard of those, and it's true. You're riding things made in women's bellies!"

"Be quiet!" Newton said, and took Catania's arm and Joan's, to keep them still. Market people were watching.

"At least they can speak." The man riding the other thing gave them an enemy look. He also wore blue—a long coat and wide-brim hat. "*Get-on!*" he said, hitting his riding-thing with a short whip. It grunted and came pacing so fast that Newton had to pull Joan and Catania aside as it went by. The woman, riding after him, said, "*Four* goats. . . ." and smiled.

Catania shook her lance after the blue-hats, and shouted, "You are the animals—look what you've made!"

" 'Goats?' " Joan said, and perhaps made angrier by barley-whisk, jerked her arm from Newton's grip and stepped away. "Stay!" she called to the blue-hat people. "I have a courtesy-lesson for you!"

The woman rider turned on the back of her thing, and drew a sword-knife from a long sheath beside her—a curved sword-knife, and slender. The man had turned also, but hadn't drawn a weapon.

"Shittinwoods!" the blue-hat woman said, and laughed at them.

"Wait for me, nasty laugher," Joan called. "I'll put steel into your mouth, where pee-dicks usually go!" And she dropped her pack, and ran at them.

Catania let go the nanny's lead and raised her lance—then remembered the baby on her hip as Newton ran to catch Joan. He ran fast, reached out, gripped the collar of her new shirt and yanked her back. Joan fought him, and while struggling, threw her lance—and would have hit the woman's riding-thing but it spun and ducked away, showing its teeth, so the lance hummed past and slid into the dirt.

Then the woman with the sword-knife called, "I'll see you two bitches burning!" The man said something to her, and she straightened her big hat—it had tilted on her head when her riding-thing turned so quickly.

"Let me *go*." Joan tried to kick Newton where it would hurt, but he shook her, cuffed her to furious silence—then glanced at Catania and said, "No more from you, either."

Newton looked so funny with his crap-cloth scarf, and trying to deal with two angry women at once, that Catania grew calmer and turned her lance butt-down to lean on, though she'd marked the blue-hat woman and wouldn't have missed the throw, barley whisk or not.

Some of the strangers around them were shouting, calling out so loudly it troubled her hearing, though no one had been killed, or even cut.

Though Newton still held her, Joan yelled at the riding woman, "Come here! Come *here!*" But the woman only shook her head, smiling, so Catania wished she *had* thrown her lance. Then the woman wouldn't be smiling and sitting on a nasty thing.

Something odd sounded through the people's shouting—a regular thudding, like padded sticks beaten together—and all the people around them moved back, and back. Many walked away.

"*Perfect*," Newton said, but not as if meaning perfect, and Catania turned and saw that men were coming—but walking like one man, stepping all together in heavy boots, left foot then right, which made the thudding sound. She thought this was almost certainly Warm-time marching. The men wore leather shirts and heavy leather skirts, with strips of blued steel fastened to them. And each wore a round metal hat with a brim all around.

These men had short straight sword-knives at their belts, and carried crossbows bigger than the ones the Garden Gold-bracelets had used. There were bent metal handles on the sides of these weapons. . . . It was strange to watch ten, twelve men walking as one. Stranger even than the first-pulp mill's duty-dance. Catania thought it possible they were copybook soldiers.

"Do we fight?" Joan said. But Newton just looked at her, so Catania supposed not.

"All chases circle back," Newton said, and sounded tired.

"Troublemakers in Market!" the blue-hat woman called, and the man climbed down from his riding-thing, and came over to meet the probably-soldiers.

"You turd," Joan said to the blue-hat man, but he paid no attention.

"Kingdom-guest," a probable-soldier said to the blue-hat, and stepped away from the other marchers, "—if you and your lady wife have been troubled in Market, we'll deal with it."

This man had a grim face that had been cut and its bones broken. He seemed to Catania a serious person and a fighter. Certainly a soldier, though looking odd in his round metal hat. He had a dark dot tattooed on each cheek.

"We have been troubled," the blue-hat man said, "—and threatened by these two shittinwoods women, who have no notion of conduct. One threw a lance." He said this, but didn't draw a weapon, so Catania saw he was relying on the soldier to fight for him. "I'll be fair, however, and say the man here did not offend us."

"These people," Catania said, "—they are riding very bad things!"

"Women," the soldier said, and sounded like any man saying, 'Women.'

"But still troubling," the blue-hat woman called, "—women or not." She sheathed her curved sword-knife. "I'm a woman, and I've been troubled in Market, and Boston will not be happy to hear it!"

"You kiss my butt!" Catania called to her. "And tell Boston he can kiss my butt, too."

"You see," the blue-hat woman said, "—how we've been troubled by these ignorants?" Like a dog taking drift from its master's mood, the gray thing she sat on hunched its high shoulders, turned its head, frowning, and stuck out its thick pale tongue like an angry child.

"If you don't become quiet," the soldier said to Catania, "—if both you tribeswomen don't become quiet, you'll find yourselves chained in a fire."

"You won't live to see it, Broken-face." Joan put her hand on her knife.

Newton shoved her back. "Shut your mouth." Then he said to the soldier, "Let it pass."

"No," the blue-hat man said to the soldier, "—do *not* let it pass, Two-dot, or we'll report you upriver."

"These are only women," Newton said, "—and strangers here, and have a baby with them. No one has been injured—"

"That one threw a lance!" Blue-hat said.

"It slipped from her fingers."

The soldier shook his head. "I cannot let it pass." And though that was all he said, and Catania saw him make no motion, suddenly all eleven men behind him drew their short sword-knives, so the blades hissed free together.

"Floating fucking *Jesus*. . . ." Newton reached up to loose his face cloth, pulled it free, and threw it on the ground.

"Oh . . . Oh, may I beg your pardon?" the blue-hat man said to Newton. "Because indeed I do, sir. Indeed, I beg your pardon."

The soldier knelt on one knee. And though he'd said nothing and made no motion, his men all did the same.

"Get up," Newton said to him, but the soldier didn't. "Get *up*," Newton said. Then the man got up, and his men with him, and sheathed their short sword-knives.

"Is my beg-pardon accepted?" the blue-hat said.

"Louis, what is it?" the woman called over, and the blue-hat called back, "Be still!" Then said, "My wife. . . ."

"What do you want me to do?" the soldier said to Newton.

"Go away," Newton said. And to the blue-hat, Louis, "You go away, too."

The soldier did as he'd been told. He fitted himself back into the others, said four words, and they all turned together, then went away as they'd come, like one person walking.

Louis Blue-hat had gone back to the woman, who was looking questions. "Just be quiet," he said to her, climbed onto his riding-thing, and kicked its ribs so it hunched itself and swung away, showing huge gray buttocks. Its testicles were gone. The back legs were like a man's, but made massive, bent, and thick with muscle. Louis rode away, and his wife rode after him.

"What a surprising thing!" Catania said. "I thought we would have to fight."

"Newton," Joan said, "—who are you to them, that you sent them away and they went?"

"Foolishness," Newton said. "Old foolishness. Because of my family, I have dice-eight dots across my face. For Boxcars, these are important things." He picked up his pack. "But Boxcar things have never been important to me. Joan, go and get your lance. And no more trouble—you understand?"

While Joan, silent, went to get her lance, Catania said, "Have things changed, now?" The nanny had come back to her, trailing its lead.

"Yes," Newton said. And he seemed a different, weary Newton. "Yes, they've changed. Better we had stayed and become Map-Texans, but I thought I could travel through."

When Joan came back with her lance, she said, "Newton, if you hadn't held me, I would have hit her. It's your blame."

"I accept it," Newton said, smiling though he seemed so troubled—and Catania saw he found Joan amusing, was fond of her in that way. "Now we have to get out of Market fast as we can without running." He picked up his scarf from the ground, and drew the cloth across his face again.

"Why not run?" Catania said.

"If we run," Newton said, "—we'll be chased for thieves." But even so, he started walking so fast, striding through all the strange Market people, that Joan and Catania had to trot a little to keep up. They hurried down several turning paths, passing striped lean-to stands on either side all along the way—the Salesmen calling after them to buy this or that—until Newton led down a steep sand-bank, and out along the edge of the Gulf.

Here, there were no trade goods, but only people camping to spend another day in Market. They were cooking their own food in little fires on the sand. Their children played in the blue-green water, running in, screaming at the chill, then running out.

Newton trotted along the beach, and Catania's catching-up hurry disturbed the baby. The nanny, tired, had to be tugged along.

"Give me that." Joan took the goat's lead.

Catania saw a marching-soldier standing up on the bank. He'd taken off his iron hat, and stood between two trade-stands, watching them.

"I think we have to go faster." Catania lifted the baby off her hip and held him in her arms. "I think we have to run."

Then they did run, Small-Sam crying, annoyed by the jouncing, and the nanny bucking at the end of her lead. Although many Market people saw them running along the Gulf's sandy edge, no one shouted that they were thieves, or chased them.

Soon, there was only faint music to hear from musical bands. Fewer lean-tos stood along the high bank, and fewer people were camping down by the water. They were coming to the end of Market.

"We're almost out," Newton said. "Bigger than it used to be. . . ."

There was shouting above them.

"I see the place-sign," Joan said, and Catania saw it a bow-shot away and higher on the shore. It was the same as the first Market sign had been—square letters made out of heavy sticks to spell the word, and fastened high between two tall poles—though MARKET looked odd, read from the back.

A wall built of very big stones came down the bank and far into the water. Newton led them up alongside that wall, the tired nanny making *naaa-naaa* sounds.

At the top of the bank—the leaving-Market sign only a little way away—there was a silent crowd of Market people. Soldiers were shouting, pushing them back from the wide white-shell pathway that ran under the sign, then away to the east.

Newton slowed to walking, so Joan and Catania did the same. They walked to the path while the crowd watched them, but made no noise. The soldiers had stopped shouting, stopped shoving people.

Newton stepped up onto the white path, then stopped and stood still, so Joan and Catania did the same.

Everyone was watching them. Catania supposed the blue-hats had persuaded the soldiers that she and Joan should be burned after all. Her heart seemed to freeze in her chest at the thought of the baby burning, or lost and left without her. She looked, and saw that Joan thought the same. Joan's face was white; her knuckles were white on her lance shaft.

An old man was standing under the Market sign. He was hairless, very thin, and naked except for brown short pants. The old man stared at them for a moment, then began dancing a slow dance.

He sang as he danced, a whining little song about sunshine. He raised one bony knee high, then put it down and raised the other, then did the same again, but quickly. He made stroking motions in the air with his hands.

Catania saw four people standing behind the dancing man. One was a gray-haired woman in a long dress, paneled green and blue. The other three were soldiers, who wore little gold and silver pieces on what must be chest armor, made of blue-tinted steel.

Catania saw more of the ordinary marching-soldiers, many more, standing in rows across the pathway east.

"What do we do?" Joan said to Newton.

Newton said nothing for a little while. Then he took the cloth from his face, put down his pack, and stood leaning on his lance. "We wait for Gerald Kaufman to finish dancing."

The old man—Gerald—smiled at Newton when he said this, as if they were friends, and kept dancing. Catania thought it very limber and pleasant to watch, though he never jumped off the ground or pretended to shoot game. Old-Gerald had no hair on him at all. Even his armpits had been plucked. Since he'd smiled in such a pleasant way, and was known to Newton, it seemed to Catania that there was no intent of burning.

Old-Gerald finished his dance and his song of My-Only-Sunshine at the same time, by doing three quick little hops and making a yelping noise with each hop. It was interesting to see an old person so lively.

Then, his dancing done, he came up to Newton and hugged him. "His second son," he said. "Where in Floating Jesus's name have you been for four years?"

"His *third* son, and not needed here," Newton said. "I've been. . . . elsewhere."

"Second son, now," the old man said, and stood back from Newton to look him up and down. "Your brother Michael was killed in Map-Arkansas, coming to a fair agreement. Your brother Adrian is north, persuading file-tooth tribesmen on the Ohio. Now, you are Newton Second-son—and bound by duty to your father, and Kingdom's people."

Then, Catania saw in Newton's face a loss great as his loss of Lucy. He looked like an injured boy, though armed, and grown so large. "And if, even so, I choose to pass you by, Gerald, and go on my way?"

"My dear, dear Prince, ask us for anything else but your leaving, and we would die so you might have it."

"An exaggeration."

"But not *much* of an exaggeration." The old man laughed, and the gray-haired woman and the soldiers all laughed just afterward.

* * *

"Would it be a good life for Small-Sam with your people? Would he be happy?"

They stood in bright morning sunshine, on the polished yellow-wood floor of a boat—certainly, Catania thought, a 'deck,' as in *Or the White Whale*. The deck moved as the water under it moved, and shifted beneath her feet.

"Would he be happy?" Newton said. "Perhaps."

Catania's question was the same one she'd asked in the wonderful tent and pavilion Old-Gerald had provided the night before.

Her same question, then. And Newton's same answer, as the three of them sat on orange-striped cushions, eating roast actual-pig, drinking warm dark cereal-beer, and listening to the musics of a soft band of three stringed instruments, with only a small finger drum and a shake-patty Newton called a tambourine.

Old-Gerald had seen they were given all those things, and thick carpets with stories woven into them, and also a small enameled stove of red coals glowing against the evening's chill. . . . Soldiers had stood armed outside, standing still as if they'd died and were shrouded in their last-look ice.

Tattooed Newton had been called a prince by all the Kingdom people—and each time they spoke to him, and called him Second-son, and Prince, he seemed to Catania to grow sadder, more silent, and separate from the Newton he had been on the Range.

In the beautiful tent—so much more spacious than any house had been on the Range or in Gardens, Catania had asked questions about Middle Kingdom for Small-Sam's sake. Newton had an-swered, but never said truly welcoming words for the baby. Never said why he had left, those years ago, to travel to the mountains and become a Trapper.

Joan, impatient, had put a pork bone down hard on her painted plate. "Here is everything we want, Catania. Everything is being offered to us, to our Newton. What fucking thing is wrong with you?"

"Joan, these people tell even *themselves* what to do. They are order-givers and order-takers. And it seems—from what Newton will not say—that some of the orders are bad."

"Catania. . . ." Joan had picked up her bone, torn a piece of meat from it, then put it back on her plate and wiped her mouth with her sleeve. "Catania, we are not in the free mountains, and can never be again. Now, there will always be orders."

"You are not the Joan I knew, to say that."

"No, now I'm a sensible-Joan—but you are not changed!" Joan had reached for the pork bone as if it was a weapon. "You are the same stupid Catania and not to be trusted with the baby."

"Try to take him from me," Catania had said.

Then Newton, sounding like a prince, had said, "Be quiet, both of you. I've heard enough from you, today." Then, more softly, he'd said, "I've heard enough from everyone. . . ."

Now, standing in bright morning light off the shore of the Gulf Entire, Catania knew the boat was a goodbye-boat. Still, she asked once more. "Couldn't be a good life with your people, for the baby?"

"Perhaps a good enough life," Newton said, and Catania saw he was no longer even partly the Trapper she had known. A more complicated Newton had come to rest behind his eyes, as if a twin had taken his place amid the crowds of Market.

"Small-Sam would be happy, Catania." Joan certainly looked pleased to be on the boat, and going east to Kingdom River with Newton. She looked happier than she had since her son, Del, was killed. "Newton," Joan said, touching his arm, "—is a better-than-chief here, so we will all make the baby happy."

Catania stood, considering. Small-Sam slept in his poozy at her hip. She swayed slightly as the deck swayed. This goodbye-boat was painted blood red, and floated out on the Gulf, though tethered to a wooden water-dock. It was a big boat—a 'barge,' Old-Gerald the Market Governor had said. There were five musicians sitting in the front of it, and twelve of the soldiers standing together. Lines of shirtless men were sitting along each side, holding long paddle-oars to make it go. These men wore iron collars, and were harnessed with chains.

"I can tell you're still thinking stupid," Joan said. "Of course you and the baby must come with us. Where else would you go?"

"Jack said we might go south . . ."

Joan made an impatient face. "Jack is dead."

Catania turned to look along the boat again. A metal fire-pit was set in sand at the center of the deck, with coals burning dull red under a long steel grill. A thin man in a soft white shirt and trousers sat on one side with long-bladed knives and forked instruments on a folded red cloth. There were little bottles also, some of oil, some with leaves in them, cut fine.

A naked boy, very fat, lay on the other side of the pit, crying. His arms and legs were tied tight. All his hair had been shaved away, and he'd been rubbed with oil so his skin shone.

Catania and Joan had asked about the tied boy when they'd walked down to the barge-boat from the night's fine pavilion.

They'd asked, and Newton had said, "It can't be helped," and gave them a warning look. Gave Catania, particularly, a warning look.

Then he'd said, "It's a welcome. But an unusual thing, now."

The naked fat boy was crying; there was snot down his face. He tried to say something, but couldn't catch his breath. The man in white clothes reached over and hit him with a long wooden spoon.

Catania wished to take that man and cut his throat on his own grill. "Tell me, Newton, in honor—were you happy here?"

"No," Newton said, and looked out over the water, instead of into her eyes.

"Would Jack have been happy here?"

". . . No."

"Then Small-Sam cannot stay."

"Foolish Catania!" Joan said. "Why would you leave us and be alone? You've never been alone—it might make you die."

"I'll have the baby."

"Yes, and you'll have the goat. That is still being alone." Joan was getting angry. "Suppose we took the baby from you after all, for your being such a dummy?"

"I won't do that," Newton said.

"I could do it," Joan said.

"I don't think so." Catania shifted her grip on her lance, and thought how difficult it would be to fight Joan Richardson on this boat, and not have the baby hurt as she did it.

Newton stepped between them, and the soldiers on the boat put their hands on their sword-knives' handles.

"Very well, Selfish!" Joan said. "Selfish Catania. Take the baby so he dies on some dark road because you were so greedy to have him—"

Newton reached quickly, took hold of Catania's lance shaft and held it. "Trade-honey. . . ." he said, though only her father and Jack had ever called her that. "Trade-honey, you would not be happy in Kingdom—and Small-Sam would not be happy with you unhappy. So take him, and go on your way."

Catania turned and went up the narrow plank bridge to the water-dock—went up quickly in case Newton changed his mind and sent the soldiers to take the baby. She wanted to run, but had to stop on the dock to untie the goat . . . and found she couldn't go away without goodbyes.

She called down to them. "We haven't said goodbye!"

Newton smiled up at her. "Goodbye, Doctor. You made Jack Monroe happy as he could be made. All honor to you."

Joan said nothing. Then she set her lance aside and came up the plank walkway. "Oh, foolish Catania," she said, and there were tears in her eyes. "Will you forgive foolish Joan, and remember our Trapper times?"

"Always. . . ." Catania said.

Joan hugged her, and bent to kiss the baby. Then she went back down to the barge-boat.

"Catania," Newton called up to her, "—if anyone, south, asks why they should do you a kindness, tell them it would please Kingdom's Second-son, who in time will return all favors—and all offenses."

"I will," Catania said, and stood watching as the rowers, spoken to, lifted their paddle-oars, then dipped them together. And steadily, steadily, the boat swam away into sunrise water, far out on the sun's own path, and the musicians began to play.

It was surprising how clearly the music sounded.

Small-Sam and I journey alone. We go Warm-time weeks south, with nanny-goat and memories.

The memories sometimes crowd us on the road, when I travel dreaming—and Trappers walk with us or go sledding by on snow invisible, racing, laughing, their harness bells ringing so the baby wakes and cries.

I woke once in a field, and by starlight thought I saw a wolf standing over the baby's blanket by me. But when I drew my knife, I woke truly, and saw it was Three-balls— there, then fading away—come in his dream to my dream, to visit.

When Jack walks beside me, always in bright sunlight, I know it, and keep my eyes on the path so as not to see him.

FROM THE JOURNAL OF DOCTOR CATANIA OLSEN

19

Doctor Serrano had been up all night at Wrightsons. Their son had stepped on a rusty horse-nail in the stable, and Serrano had cut that small injury wide open and cleaned it with cactus brandy, then let it bleed, then cleaned it with brandy again and left it open and lightly bandaged. In time, the Wrightson's son—a brave well-behaved boy—would either die breaking his bones in convulsions, or he would not.

The trip to Wrightsons, the medical work, and the trip back home, had taken the whole night from dark to dawn. It was therefore no pleasure to have maid-Peggy come wake him so early, saying, "Doctor, there is a barbarian at your door."

"When not?" Doctor Serrano said, and climbed out of bed feeling old. He put on his robe, and went down the hall to see who was troubling him.

He opened his door, at first saw no one, stepped out onto the stoop and saw a small brown nanny-goat. Then he saw the goat-herd sitting in sunlight against the wall of his house. The barbarian stood up—a man, he thought at first—then saw it was a woman. She had an infant slung in a striped blanket at her hip.

The doctor examined this specimen—a Northerner, obviously a cold-country tribeswoman, very tall, scarred ugly (fortunate that injury had missed the trigeminal nerve), and dirty as her goat. As he examined her, the specimen seemed to examine him.

"*Doctor*?" she said. She spoke ugly book-English of course, like most in these northern provinces, descendants of those Greenos the cold had driven down so long ago. The Beautiful Language, lost here, was now only spoken far to the south, past the mountains.

"Yes, I'm a physician," Serrano said, and sighed. It was difficult to imagine what might be unhealthy in such a female brute. She was armed, of course. There was a lance, and bow and quiver, leaning against the house wall beside a backpack.

Then she made a gesture so familiar, so simple, so trusting that

Emmanuel Serrano found himself, as always, wearied by it, and inescapably touched. The tall creature, her eyes pale and chill as the ice she'd been born to, lifted her baby from its blanket and held it out to him to be cured.

The morning was cold in nearly the last of eight-week summer, too cold to examine the infant by his front door—an examination providing entertainment, as well, for any mule driver come down the street.

Maid-Peggy would simply have to deal with any fleas. . . .

Doctor Serrano held his front door open, and gestured the woman into his house. She glanced at her weapons and pack, then came without them.

The goat trotted after her. "No," Serrano said, "—not the goat."

Putting the baby back in its carry-blanket, the woman led the goat back out and tied it to the front gate. Then she came back, stepped inside, and walked slowly down his hallway, apparently astonished by a floor of warm tile, and pictures along the walls. An engraving, particularly, stopped her and she stared at it.

El Cid in battle with the Moors.

"Fighting isn't like that," the creature said.

"Oh?" This was going to take the whole morning; there would be no getting back to bed.

"They are too . . . composed."

So. Height, a scar, and—it seemed—a brain and Warm-time vocabulary. "I suppose," Serrano said, "—the picture isn't quite realistic."

The woman suddenly turned to him with the most extraordinary expression of rage and terror—and a knife, a long knife was out, and she leaped this way and that in the hall, all the while clutching the baby to her. Her movements reminded Serrano, in the midst of his shock and startlement, of a sort of insanely violent series of spasms.

"That," the scarred woman said—now standing still, thank God, "—that is like fighting."

"I see . . ." said Doctor Serrano.

In good morning light, the baby lay on the examining table in the back room. Looking up, he observed Serrano with much the same steady attention as his scar-faced mother—or perhaps not his mother, considering the milking goat.

"Are you the child's mother?"

"Before, no. Now, yes." She was standing near, watching what he was doing with the baby.

"I'm being certain his eyes can follow my finger," Serrano said, to allay any misapprehension; the long knife and leaping-about not forgotten.

"I know," the woman said.

... Then "I'm tapping his belly, listening for any odd sound of distension—of swelling."

"I know," the woman said.

"... And now, I'm examining his mouth and gums, to observe any lesions, and the commencement of teething."

"I know."

Doctor Serrano, really quite tired, had heard enough 'I knows.' "Listen—whatever your name is—you *don't* know. That's why I'm a doctor and you are not!"

"I am a doctor," the scarred woman said. "And scientific. I don't shake bones or talk to any spirit but Mountain Jesus."

"Ah ... Really? Well, then, you have no need of me, *Doctor*."

"I don't know warm-country diseases. I thought it might be just-beginning pops."

"What might be?"

"This." The scarred woman leaned over the baby and pointed to the scattered rash along his plump thighs. She gently turned him over. "And here." Same slight rash on the child's bottom.

"Apparently, *Doctor*," said Serrano, "—you have never seen heat rash on a child."

"A rash from being warm?"

"Too warm, yes. He needs to be out of his blanket and get some sun the next week or so, before the cold comes down."

The scarred woman struck her forehead quite hard. "And it

was in my books! But I'd never seen it, actually." Serrano saw tears of distress come into her eyes.

"Well . . . I didn't mean to be rude. It occurs here in the south—not, to be sure, a problem for long. But in the eight summer weeks, we do see it sometimes."

"Entirely not serious?"

"Oh, entirely not serious, and certainly isn't the pox."

"Pops?"

"*Pox*."

"Pox. . . ."

Serrano went down the hall, found maid-Peggy's sack of cornstarch in the pantry, then came back. The scarred woman was bent over the baby, murmuring to it.

"Excuse me." Serrano took a palmful of cornstarch, and lightly powdered the baby with it. "Keeps him a little dryer. . . . Do you know what commences this sort of irritation?"

"The books said something the skin dislikes—a plant juice, perhaps. Or a food his gut dislikes—eggs, or kinds of fish. Or a place where so-tiny bacteria like to grow."

"Yes. . . . Well, Doctor, this is a so-tiny bacteria problem, but not a serious one. Dryness, cleanliness, and fresh air are the medicines for it. You can have some of this cornstarch to take with you."

"He has no other warm-country sickness?"

"None," Serrano said. "There is nothing wrong with this baby, except an apparent diet solely of goat's milk. He's almost ready to begin solid food—but soft solid food, mashes and so forth. Vegetables, and very finely ground meat. And not too much, at first."

"I knew that; I knew it was nearing the time to do that."

"In another few weeks."

"You have given me such fine information," the scarred woman said, and wiped her eyes on the wide sleeve of a flowered shirt, once white, now sweat-stained and grimy. "What can I trade you in return?"

"I suppose," Serrano said, "—that payment of money is out of the question? Any small gold piece or silver piece, even a small piece of copper?"

"I had many little gold pieces," the woman said. "Dancing Old-Gerald gave me a small bag of them as Newton's friend, and all the food I could carry. . . . Some of the little pieces I paid to a person with a two-horse wagon, to bring me south for several whiles. And I gave the rest to another man who told me he would get a fine warm-country doctor to come look at Small-Sam. But he never came back, though I waited. I was afraid it was the beginning of pops—pox."

"Well . . . never mind. What's your name?"

"Catania Olsen."

"Never mind, Catania Olsen. We doctors often go unpaid."

"True," the woman said. "Often I haven't been paid for service." She picked up the baby, cradled him, and made kissing sounds against his cheek. "But I can do something for you in trade. Is there someone, a bad person, that I could fight for you, since you're old? I'm a woman, and not a great fighter, but I am competent."

"I'm sure you are. I'm sure you're a very competent fighter, Doctor . . . Olsen, but I don't need one. What I need is my breakfast, which, I suppose, you and your child can share with me, as Christians after all. And then, you can go on your way."

"But what can I do for you, in trade?"

"Nothing. Not necessary."

"It is necessary. Don't you have work to be done?"

"Doctor, I have only breakfast to be eaten, and perhaps a nap to be enjoyed."

"Work," the woman said, and seemed ready to stand in the back room for a week or two, waiting.

"Oh, God. . . . Let's see. Well, if you want to, you can clean out my garden shed. You could do that. I have men coming to tear it down, and it has to be cleaned out first."

"Agreed."

"Agreed? Good. Just put the tools and so forth, put everything aside neatly. I'll show you, after breakfast."

Maid-Peggy, serving in the dining room, strongly disapproved; Serrano supposed she had fleas in mind, though she dallied with the child a little. The baby behaved quite well, took some of last evening's broth, burped soundly, and shit.

"Tell me, Doctor Olsen, where you studied your medicine."

"With Doctor Monroe," the woman said, and took her last bite of ham. She had eaten fastidiously enough, though with her long knife, and her fingers. "I was his apprentice."

"I see. And what did that doctor suggest, if, for example, a patient's skin and the whites of his eyes became yellow?"

"He suggested crab-cancer or lump cancer, but more likely troubled liver, gallbladder, or the duct." The eggs seemed to have gone down well, and the ham. The coffee, however, appeared to puzzle her, as well it might, since it was cheapest Empire-grown and nearly undrinkable.

"And if it proved to be the gallbladder? Sensitivity, occasional lancinating pain?"

The woman set down her coffee mug—a decisive downing. "Then, no fat meat at all, not even a little. No trade-salt or trade-pepper. Rest, boiled water, spruce tea."

"And if the condition worsened?"

"Wash hands, blade, and site with vodka, then cut through skin, and eighth and ninth rib, under the right arm. Twist hand through a smallest possible incision into the upper abdominal. Feel under hepar-liver for swollen hot goose-egg-to-fist-sized vesica-gallbladder, and cut it free quickly as possible. Sew the severing by touch alone, then clean and close up and clean again. Bind ribs firmly, but allow free breathing."

"Bind ribs . . . yes. And have you done such surgery, Doctor Olsen?"

"No, thank Lady Weather."

"I have done it three times, though a little differently than you describe—but fundamentally the same. I saved one patient out of the three. I think the other two died from the pain I caused them."

"Doctor Monroe did one of those, when I was little. Bertram Sorbane lived, but he stayed a little yellow."

"My one that lived, stayed a little yellow, too."

* * *

Doctor Serrano was wakened from his *siesta*. He'd been dreaming of his son—Miguel smiling, saying something droll—when he woke to sunny afternoon, loud hammering, and the sounds of splintering wood.

He groaned, got up, put on his robe and went to see what was happening. The noise was coming from the back of the house.

Standing out on the steps in brilliant sunshine, he saw his guest in violent action amid the wreckage of the garden shed.

The baby, naked on his blanket, was watching as Doctor Catania Olsen—having emptied the shed and stacked that material in good order by the back fence—was proceeding with the dismantling of the structure.

She was a formidable sight. Naked to the waist, her small breasts seemed the only soft things about her. The rest of the torso was long, very lean, and muscled nearly like a man's. Scarred, as well, by what must have been fighting wounds, though none of those was as grim as the puckered scar down her right cheek.

Hers was a body capable of great sustained effort—that effort now being directed against the garden shed, or what remained of it. . . . She was using the ax with ferociously directed swift swinging blows, so the shed's structure was broken and smashed apart.

Doctor Serrano considered for a moment what the males of her tribe must have been capable of. "I have . . . I have men coming to do that."

She apparently didn't hear him amid the thuds and crashes. *"Doctor Olsen—I have men coming to do that!"*

She paused—the ax paused at least—and she stood restless with interrupted motion. "I trade for treatment," she said.

Serrano saw that her light-brown hair, fallen loose from the thick braid she'd kept it in, was slightly streaked with gray, though she was still a young woman. A sign of the hard lives led in the north—with two-week summers, not eight. . . . He noticed she'd brought her weapons to the backyard with her.

"You've done enough."

"No." She stood with the ax in her hands, looking south, out over the meadows behind the house. "Mountains," she said.

"Yes, the *Sierra*." Serrano glanced with her at that distant great *cordillera*, southern peaks gleaming with forever-snow. "Yes," he said, "—mountains."

"Are there people there?"

"I believe so," Serrano said. "Shepherds, bandits, tribal savages. . . . Now, you've done enough work for me."

"Not enough."

"If you do more, I will have to pay you." Ah. . . . Serrano saw the notion strike her.

"Pay me what?" That spare, iron torso was running sweat, but she'd not been breathing hard at all.

"You're a doctor with, it seems, no medicines, no instruments," Serrano said. "For completing this destruction, and stacking the ruins neatly, I will make up a medical-carry, also with some instruments I can spare, and give it to you."

And as soon as he'd said it, thought himself an old fool. Then thought again, as he saw her face.

. . . The doctor gone back into his house, Catania set to finishing her work. Soon, there were only blocks of some gray made-rock left. The shed-house had been built on them. These seemed too weighty to knock loose with the butt of the ax, so she searched the small yard for its largest stone . . . and found one, almost black and a little smaller than a person's head.

She straddled a row of the made-rock, and swinging the heavy stone down hard with both hands, beat at the gray blocks until they began to crack, then break. Working slowly down the rows, hammering, she broke all the blocks into small jagged pieces, then dug out what remained with her hands. . . . When she was finished, there was only a square of four shallow ditches where the shed-house had been—and nothing left to do but gather the wood and broken rubble, and set it carefully along the stick fence.

Catania was stacking things neatly, when she heard a large bird's wings, like an eagle's wings, flapping almost above her. But when she looked up, the late-day sun almost in her eyes—she saw it was a man.

It was a small round-faced man dressed in a long dark-blue cloth coat that flapped and flapped as he flew. He wore a wide-brimmed blue hat—the same as the thing-riders had worn at Market—and sailed slowly through the air above her, just within bow-shot. He was making the same straining face Garden Mary had made, but was sitting up straight, with his legs crossed . . . and flying higher, flying faster.

"*Jack*," Catania said, as if Jack might come to her, and her breath left with his name. . . . The flying man glanced down, saw her, and gave her a bad look.

Catania turned and ran across the yard for her bow. She strung it fast, then set an arrow to the string for her shot. The flying-man was already past the roof-corner of another house, out over the meadows.

Catania bent her bow, wishing so much it was Jack or Torrey shooting as she let the arrow go. It was a good shaft and streaked straight out. If the flying-man had paused only a little in the air, it would have reached him. But he was sailing away, and though the arrow tried, and Catania prayed it on, he was going too high and too quickly, so the shaft fell hungry.

"*Holy Mother!*" the old doctor said, and Catania turned and saw him standing at his back door. "What did you *do*?"

"I missed him," Catania said. "I'm sorry."

"Never, never, *never*," the old man said, his face pale. "Never attempt against one of those people! They are the Empire's friends, for one thing!"

"If it was rude, I'm sorry."

"Much worse than rude," the old man said. "If you'd hit him—forbid it, Saints—much worse than rudeness would have happened!"

"I apologize. . . ."

"Why did you do it—shoot at him?"

"I know that bad-wisdom flying," Catania said. "They helped kill tribesmen, north on the ice . . . and two of them wanted to burn me and Joan Richardson alive. Doctor, they twist babies in their mothers and make monsters of them—I've seen it!"

"I know," Serrano said. "I know. . . ." He put his finger to his mouth so she wouldn't say more.

Catania spoke more quietly. "He gave me an enemy look, so my bow called me to come get it and kill him."

"Please Mother Mercy no one saw you." The old man looked so troubled that Catania said, "The shed-house is gone," to comfort him.

". . . Yes, I see that it is. Now come inside, *please*. You'll have the evening meal, but then you should be on your way in case someone saw what you did."

"I have to go find my arrow," Catania said.

"Dear God," the old man said. "No good deed goes unpunished." Certainly a Warm-time phrase.

Catania went out into the meadow to find her arrow—picked its yellow-edged fletching out of green summer grass—then came back to the house. She led the nanny to Small-Sam for suckling. He took the milk . . . was patted to burp and burp, then fell asleep.

The evening meal that maid-Peggy brought them was made of vegetables and flat baked grain-dough, and a sauce so hot that Catania drank two mugs of southern wine, her first wine—though she'd read of it many times—and found it much milder than vodka, and cool in her mouth.

After dinner, there was a treat. Crystal powder was sprinkled on it, sweet as honey, but with no taste but sweetness. Catania thought it was probably copybook sugar, made from cane grown down where summers were even longer.

The treat under the powder was much stranger and more valuable. It was the color of shit, but each bite had more tastes than one bite should have. . . . Then all the tastes gathered together to become a single wonderful one that stayed in her mouth for a while.

"Chocolate," the old doctor said, and smiled at her, so Catania supposed he'd forgiven her worse-than-rudeness in shooting at the flying-man.

While she finished her powdered piece of chocolate, Doctor Serrano advised the best way for her and Small-Sam to travel from his house. ". . . Down across the meadows, and away from the village to the path west, a narrow path. Then west on that path for many days to the Royal Road." He called, "*Peggy . . . I think another piece of the chocolate.*—So, west to the Royal Road, then along that to towns and cities, all offering reasonably safe and comfortable living for a woman and child, since the Empire's soldiers police them."

. . . When she'd finished her second piece of chocolate, and said a thank-you to this country's Jesus for creating it, Catania followed Doctor Serrano down the passage to his examining room, carrying Small-Sam asleep in his blanket.

The old man showed what he'd put in a big strong-cloth carry for her.

There was dried mutton, and dried apple—and little cloth sacks of medicine, each with advice written on a small piece of fine paper, and tied to its closure with twisted string. There were many of these little sacks, and also curved needles, gut-thread, and fourteen instruments.

There were three lancet-knives—large to small; six wonderful little vessel clips; a scoop spoon; fine bone-saw and coarse bone-saw; a long probe and a short probe. Best of all, a long-handled *very* slender pliers, for taking out small things that were deep. . . . All made of fine steel.

"Can you spare these?"

"I can spare them, Doctor," the old man said. "They're old-fashioned, but of good quality. Remember, use any harsh-liquor rinse, and scrub. Clean medicine is best medicine."

He sounded just as Doctor Monroe had sounded so long ago. Catania, considering that southern people might not kiss faces, took his hand, kissed that, and thanked him for kindness.

"No, no," the old man said, taking his hand away. Then he said, "Here . . ." took a thick copybook off a shelf against the wall, and gave it to her. "I can spare this, too. . . . Know it by heart."

The copybook was titled *Elements of Medical Practice,* and had been written by Jacob Stein, MD. There were drawings in it.

"This is an endless-gratitude gift," Catania said, leafing through it.

"Nonsense. Only a professional courtesy."

Catania lifted her backpack, shrugged it on, then put the copybook with her medicals in the carry, and set its wide strap on her left shoulder. She stooped to pick the baby up in his poozy, and slung it on her hip.

So weighted, she went out the door and carefully down the back steps. She took her lance from where it leaned against the house, then fitted her bow and quiver over her right shoulder.

"Goodbye," Catania said, untied the nanny at the fence, and led her through the garden gate.

"Farewell, Doctor," the old man said. It was the second time Catania had heard that Warm-time word for parting.

There was only a while to the last of light. She walked down into the meadow, the goat capering on its lead so its shadow— and hers, with her burdens and slim shaft of lance—were printed out on the field beside them.

It was a relief to be under the sky again—sweeter, after accustomed long traveling, than the kindest stranger's roof. Even finer than chocolate.

Catania settled the pack and carry, settled her bow and quiver on her shoulder, settled the baby on her hip . . . and accepting heaviness that held her hard to the ground, walked through tall grasses, green in slanting sunlight. She swung her lance as a staff.

Doctor Serrano's way had been the path beyond the village meadows, that ran west and west to the Royal Road, then to crowded places where Small-Sam might grow to be a man in heat-rash warmth and safety.

But staying south was to go as Jack had wanted, as he'd called out at Long Ledge when they fled away. 'South . . . south. . . .'

The mountains—the *Sierra*—rose in a distant wall before her, peaks glittering with ice, their snows shining in sunset colors. Shepherds, bandits, savages lived there, breeding hard sons in cold country . . . and perhaps in need of a doctor.

More than twenty years later, Middle Kingdom thrives.
A new enemy sweeps east from the Map-Pacific Coast.
And Sam Monroe has grown to be a man.

Kingdom River

Available from Forge Books
in May 2003

Clean, her hair done, seventeen-year-old Martha was scrubbing homespun small-clothes—just discovered dirty beneath her father's bed—in the tub on the dog-trot, when she glimpsed metal shining through the trees. She took her hands off the rippled board, shook hot water and lye suds from her fingers, and watched that shining become soldiers marching up along the river road.

There was a short double-file of men, East-bank soldiers armored throat to belly with green-enameled strips of steel across their chests . . . light steel strips down their thighs, sewn to the front of thick leather trousers. An officer was marching in front, and so much be a lieutenant. Lieutenants marched with their men, and never rode.

As Martha watched, the lieutenant and his men reached the cabin path—then turned neatly, and marched up it. They were coming to her father's house, something soldiers had never done before. These were crossbowmen—heavy windlass bows and quarrel bundles strapped to their packs, short swords and daggers at their belts. Long green-dyed woolen cloaks, rolled tight, were carried over their left shoulders.

"*Daddy!*" She thought surely William Bovey had died after all, and they were coming to take her to hang.

More than three Warm-time weeks before, Big William Bovey and two other large men had come out to the cabin, angry over a deal for a four-horse wagon-team, and begun to beat Edward Jackson with sticks and their fists. Martha had run into the farry-shed, taken up a medium hammer, and come out and brained William Bovey. Then she'd beaten his friends so bones were broken, and they'd run.

Bovey, a corner of his brain tucked back in, had been asleep ever since at his aunt's house up in Stoneville. It was the opinion of Randall-doctor that he would never wake up.

"No death done," the Magistrate had said.

And that had been that. Until now.

"Run!" her father said—too late, as the old man was usually too late.

Martha stood waiting, drying her hands on her apron, and wished for her mother.

The lieutenant was young, but not handsome, a freckled carrot-top in green-steel strap armor. His face was shaved clean, like all soldiers'. He swung up the path to the door-yard, and his men marched behind him—twelve of them and all in step, their steel and leather creaking, till he put up his left hand to halt them.

"Well, Honey-sweet, you're certainly big enough." Though slender, the lieutenant had a deep voice. His breath steamed slightly in the morning air.

"What do you want here?" Martha wished her father would say something.

The lieutenant smiled, and looked handsomer when he did. He had one dot tattooed on his left cheek, two on his right. A big man behind the lieutenant—a sergeant, he seemed to be—was smiling in a friendly way. The sergeant was bigger than Martha, as a man should be.

"Get what things you can carry," the lieutenant said, not in an unpleasant way. "You're coming with us."

"Is William Bovey dead?"

"I don't know any William Bovey. I do know that you are ordered to come with us. So, get your whatevers; put your shoes one—if you have shoes—and do it fairly quickly."

"No," Martha said. The big sergeant frowned at her and shook his head.

"Ralph, be still," the lieutenant said, though he couldn't have seen what his sergeant was doing. "Now listen, even though it may cost my men some injuries," his soldiers smiled, "I will have you subdued, bound, and carried with us as baggage, if necessary. Don't make it necessary."

"But . . . *why?*"

"Orders."

Her father still said nothing, just stood in the doorway silent as a stick. Suddenly, Martha felt she wished to go with the soldiers. It was a strange feeling, as if she had eaten something spoiled.

She turned to Edward Jackson, and said, "You're not my father, anymore." Then she went into the cabin to get her best linen dress, her sheepskin cloak, her private possibles (a bone comb, clean underwearers and stocking folded in a leather sack) and her shoes—one patched at the toe.

They walked south—the soldiers marched, she walked— through the rest of the day. Martha had started out beside the lieutenant, but he'd gestured her behind him with his thumb, so she'd stepped back to walk beside the sergeant, Ralph, the one who'd frowned and shook his head at her. He was even taller than she was, and wider.

It had always seemed to Martha, when she'd seen them in parade at Stoneville, that soldiers marched slowly. But now, going with them, she found that they moved along in a surprising way. It was a steady never-stopping going, nothing like a stroll or amble, that are up time and Warm-time miles until her legs ached and she began to stumble.

Ralph-sergeant took her left arm, then, to steady her. He smelled of sweat, and of leather and oiled steel.

* * *

The second day, in the afternoon, they reached Landing. Landing was the farthest from her home Martha had ever been. The Yazoo river came to Kingdom River there, and her father had brought horses down for the fair, one time, and she'd some with him.

Martha and the soldiers marched past loads of stacked lumber, sheep-hides, sides of beef, pig, and goat . . . sacks of coal from Map-West Virginia, crates of warm-frame cabbages, onions, cucumbers, broccoli, cauliflower . . . barrels of pickles, brine-kraut, smoked and salted river char.

The soldiers marched past men shouting and flicking their slim blacksnakes at Sweat-slaves trotting pokes of last potatoes up the ramps of two big pole-boats painted dark blue. A herd of spotted cattle was being run down to a black barge, forty or fifth of the animals, driven by rust-colored dogs and three men with long sticks to prod them.

There was a wonder floating at the end of the dock—a galley beautiful as the circus boat that once came down from Cairo. But this one was painted all red as fresh blood, not striped green and yellow, and there was no music coming from it. A long red banner hung from the mast, stirring a little in the breeze.

The galley had one bank of oars, just above where the iron skate-beam fitting ran—and a red sail, though that was bundled tight to a second mast slanting low over the deck, reaching almost from the front of the boat to the back.

The lieutenant marched his men and Martha right up a ramp and onto the red galley. Everything there was the same bright red, or brass this's-and-that's so bright in the sunshine they hurt her eyes. A line of men sat low on rowing benches along each side. They were naked, with steel collars on their necks, and none of them looked up.

"You're late!" a soldier called, standing on a high place at the back of the boat. He wore a short sword on a wide gold-worked belt. A long green wool cloak, fastened in gold at his throat, billowed slightly in the river wind. His chest was armored in green-enameled steel, but with pieces of gold handling from short green ribbons there.

He was much older than the lieutenant, and had an unpleasant face, made more unpleasant because his lower lip had been hurt, part of it cut away so his teeth showed there. He had five blue dots tattooed on each cheek. . . . Martha had never seen a Ten-dot man before. Never seen more than a Six-dot, and that was only once at the Ice-boat races.

Bad-lip pointed at Martha. "This is the object of the exercise?"

"Yes, sir," said the lieutenant.

"You, Big-girl—sit up here out of the way, and rest. We have cranberry juice; would you like some of that?"

"Yes, thank you." Martha came and sat on a little step below where he was standing. The Bad-lip Lord leaned down and gripped her shoulder. "Some muscle there, he said. Then, "Captain! South, to Island—at the courier beat!"

"At your orders, milord." A black man in a long brown cloak was standing back by a sailor at the wheel. "*Loose! Loose and haul!*"

Barefoot sailors Martha hadn't noticed were running here and there untying ropes. The whole boat swung out into the river, dipping, rolling slightly. And, so suddenly that she jumped a little, a deep drum went *boom boom*. Then *boom boom* again, and the rowers' long oars came out, flashed first dry then wet as they struck the water all together, and the boat started away like a frightened horse. They were surging hissing over the water, gray birds flying with them, circling the long crimson banner that unfurled, coiled, and weaved in the wind. Martha could hear it snapping, rumpling.

A boy in white pants and white jacket came running to her, knelt down, and held out a blown glass cup—glass so clear she could see the juice in it perfectly, juice the same blood-red as the boat.

Martha thought of asking the boy why she was going where she was going, then decided not.

She had heard that Kingdom's rowers were whipped—and this was certainly a Queen's boat—but no soldier whipped the red boat's rowers. Still, they worked their oars like farming horses in summer furrows. She could feel the boat's *heave* . . . and *heave* at each stroke they pulled together. The red sail was still furled . . . the wind blowing cold upriver, into their faces.

The juice in the beautiful glass was sweet and bitter at once. Martha's never tasted it before, and didn't know if she was supposed to finish it all, or only sip, and leave the rest. She looked up to see if the Bad-lip Lord was watching, and he was.

"It's for you, Ordinary. Drink it."

So she did. The juice grew sweeter with each swallow, and she hoped it was a River-omen of sweeter things to come.

* * *

The sun's egg had just sunk west to touch the water when the brown-cloak Captain said, "Passing Vicksburg bluff." Martha looked over and could just see a line of green and perhaps a fortress, east, high along the bank.

Soon after, the Captain said, "Island." And Martha saw, downstream, and far, far out into the current, what seemed a great walled town rising from the river, its stone gray and gold in evening light.

Amazed, she clapped her hands. It was a place Martha'd heard of all her life, but had never thought to see. She swayed where she sat, then swayed again as the rowers' steady beat shifted, and the blood-red boat swung farther from the shore. They were going out and out where the great town grew from white water.

Soon she could see the town was made of walls and towers, all built on hills of heaped boulders, each larger than a house. Everything was heaved up and up out of the river, so the cold current foamed white and struck in waves against the stone.

Closer, they swept on. Martha, looking ahead through the boat's rigging, saw Ralph-sergeant near the bow, talking . . . laughing with another soldier—and beyond them, a great tower of gray stone standing out into the river.

The boat swung out to pass the tower's base where the river's current curled against it like goat's cream. Chunk-ice in the current bobbed and struck and granite. Beyond, there was a great stone gateway, wise as a meadow and arched over high in the air with what seemed a spider's web of iron . . . the span of an iron bridge, where Martha saw tiny soldiers looking over. Harsher wind blew through the gateway, and a river current seethed flowing into it. They turned with that tide—the red boat leaning, pitching—and ran on into the harbor, oars lifting then falling to splash in foam . . . that became quieter water.

They were in a made pond-lake, oars now barely stroking, with walls rising high around them like the eastern mountains Martha had heard of, where Boston's creatures hunted. She saw a row of long gray wharves with boats and great ships tied to them, and Sweat-slaves working, loading and unloading. Even in this deep harbor, the current swirled, complaining. There were slow whirl-pools, and the river's icy wind gusted here and there, trapped by stone.

A file of Marines stood in order on a far dock as the red boat rowed slowly in. The Captain said something to his wheelmen, and Martha felt the board slowly turning toward those men. She had gotten used to that lifting sliding motion, and thought she might become a barge-woman, being so at ease riding a wet-water ship.

They drifted in, the oars folding up and back like a bird's wings . . . and the red boat struck fat canvas cushions at the stone dockside with a squeak and three thumps. The sailors heaved out heavy lines; three wharfers caught them and cleated them in.

"Up." The Bad-lip Lord gestured Martha after him, as he gang-plank was sliding out and down.

She had no time to smile goodbye to Ralph-sergeant—needed to nearly run down to the dock, her possibles-sack flapping at her hip, to keep up with the Bad-lip Lord. The file of Marines, who had struck their two-color breastplates with armored fists to greet him, now followed, marching very fast. The harbor and docks were quickly left behind. Their bootsteps echoed off stone walls, stone steps, echoed down passages under overhangs masoned from great blocks of granite. Many passages, many turnings, left and right and left again. In shadowed places, Martha saw, through narrow slits, a flash of steel in lantern light.

* * *

Thus Martha came to Island, and her life was changed forever.